Azazeel

'*Azazeel* takes fifth-century quarrels in the Coptic church as the ground for an ambitious investigation into good and evil, faith and doubt.' Boyd Tonkin, *Independent*

'In Jonathan Wright's supple translation there are memorable passages… [the novel's] strength lies in its ingenuous narrator and the resonant play of ideas' Maya Jaggi, *Guardian*

'A believably human and universal tale… the writing is unflashy and sincere, neatly matching the monasticism at the book's heart' *Observer*

'An utterly absorbing read. The vividly observed historical and geographical setting provides fascinating proof of how East and West were already clashing within Christianity more than 1,500 years ago.' *Spectator*

'An astonishing feat of imaginative fiction… *Azazeel* might be the most compelling and inventive novel published this year. A triumph.' *Irish Examiner*

Every man has his devil, even me,
but God helped me against him
and he turned Muslim.

A saying of the Prophet Muhammad,
cited by Bukhari

Translator's Introduction

This book, which by my last will and testament, should be published only after my death, contains as faithful a translation as possible of a collection of parchment manuscripts discovered ten years ago in the archaeological ruins which abound to the northwest of the Syrian city of Aleppo. These are the ruins which stretch for two miles along the sides of the old road linking Aleppo and Antioch, ancient cities with origins dating back to prehistoric times. This paved road is thought to be the last stage along the famous Silk Road, which in distant times started in the farthest reaches of Asia and ran its course to the Mediterranean coast. These manuscripts, with their writings in old Syriac or Aramaic, have survived in exceptionally good condition, although they were written in the first half of the fifth century of the Christian era, or, to be precise, 1,555 years before our time.

The late Venerable Father William Cazary, who supervised the archaeological excavations there and who died tragically and unexpectedly in the middle of May 1997, thought it likely that the secret of the survival of these manuscripts lay in the quality of the parchment, on which the words were written in black ink of the best quality available in that remote period, as well as the fact that they were stored in the tightly sealed wooden box in which the Egyptian-born monk Hypa deposited them, preserving a record of a remarkable career, an unintended history of the events of his troubled life and the vicissitudes of the turbulent age in which he lived.

Father Cazary thought that the wooden box, which was embellished with

1

delicate copper ornamentation, had not been opened throughout the intervening centuries, which suggests that he, may God forgive him, did not examine the contents of the box carefully, perhaps because he was wary of unrolling the parchments before they received chemical treatment, for fear they would crumble between his fingers. So he did not notice in the margins of the manuscripts the occasional notes and comments written in Arabic in fine Naskhi script in about the fifth century of the Hijra era. It seems to me that these were written by an Arab monk who belonged to the Church of Edessa, which adopted Nestorianism as its dogma and whose followers are known to this day as Nestorians. This unknown monk did not want to reveal his name. (I have included some of his significant notes and comments in the margins of my translation, while others I have omitted because of their dangerous nature. The last thing this anonymous monk wrote, on the back of the last parchment, was: 'I will rebury this treasure, because it is not yet time for it to appear.')

I spent seven years translating this text from Syriac to Arabic, but I then regretted my work on this story of Hypa the monk and I was reluctant to have it published in my lifetime, especially as I was already feeble from old age anyway and my time was drawing to a close. The whole story consists of thirty parchment scrolls, written on both sides in a thick Syriac script in the old tradition of writing Syriac which specialists know as Estrangela, the oldest and classical form of the alphabet. I have tried hard to find any information about the original author, the Egyptian monk Hypa, beyond the facts that he relates about himself in his story, but I have found no trace of him in any of the old historical sources. Modern references are devoid of any mention of him, as though he never existed, or rather he exists only through this autobiography which we possess. I have, however, confirmed the authenticity of all the ecclesiastical characters and the accuracy of all the historical events which he mentions in this extraordinary document, which he wrote in an elegant hand without excessive indulgence in the flourishes encouraged by old Syriac writing in Estrangela, a naturally decorative style.

The clarity of the script has enabled me in most instances to read the text with ease, so I have translated it into Arabic without worrying that the original might be defective or garbled, as is the case with most writings which have survived from this early period. I must not omit here to thank the venerable scholar, the abbot of the Syrian monastery in Cyprus, for the important observations he made on my translation and for corrections to some old ecclesiastical expressions with which I was not familiar.

I am not confident that this translation of mine has succeeded in matching the Syriac text in beauty or splendour. Not only was Syriac exceptional from this early date for the abundance of its literature and the sophistication of its writing styles, but Hypa's language and diction are a model of clarity and eloquence. Many long nights I spent pondering his incisive and expressive phrasing and the succession of creative images which he conjures, all of which confirm his poetic talent, his linguistic sensitivity and his mastery of the secrets of the Syriac language in which he wrote.

I have numbered the chapters of this story in line with the sequence of the scrolls, which naturally vary in size, and I have given the scrolls titles of my own devising to make it easier for the reader of this translation, which marks the first publication of this text. For the same reason I have used in my translation the modern names for the cities which Hypa the monk mentions in his story. So when he talks about the city of Panopolis in the heart of Upper Egypt, I have translated the name from the Greek to Akhmim, the name by which it is known today. The Syrian town of Germanikeia I have rendered by the modern name of Marash, and the Scetis Desert by Wadi Natroun, the name by which it is now known, and so on for the other towns and places which appear in the original text, unless the old names of these places have acquired a significance which the new names might not convey, such as Nicaea, which now lies within Turkey. Although it is now known by the Turkish name Iznik, I have preferred to call it by its old name because of its special importance as the site of church councils. For it was in this city in the year AD 325 that the First Ecumenical Council took place and the Egyptian priest Arius was condemned as a heretic, excommunicated and exiled. As for places which occur in the story and which are not well known, I have included both their old and new names, to prevent confusion.

After the Coptic months and years which the writer mentions I have put

3

the equivalent months and years according to the Christian calendar used today. In a few instances I have added essential observations in brief and some of the Arabic comments which I found in the margins. I then appended to the story some photographs relevant to the events it relates.

Alexandria, 4 April 2004

Starting to Write

Mercy, my Lord. Mercy and forgiveness, our Father in Heaven. Have mercy on me and forgive me, for as you know I am weak. My merciful Lord, my hands tremble in fear and dread. My heart and soul tremble at the vicissitudes and turmoil of this age. Yours alone is the glory, my merciful Lord. You know that I obtained these scrolls many years ago, on the shores of the Dead Sea, to write on them my poems and my orations to You in my times of seclusion, that Your name may be glorified among those on earth, as it is in heaven. I had intended to record on them my supplications, which bring me nearer to You and which may after me become prayers recited by monks and godly hermits in all times and all places. Yet when the time came to make this record, I was about to write such things which had never before come to my mind and which could have led me to the ways of woe and evil. My Lord, do You hear me? I am Your faithful servant, the perplexed, Hypa the monk, Hypa the physician, Hypa the stranger as people call me in my land of exile. And You alone, my Lord, know my true name, You and those in my first country, which witnessed my birth. Would that I had never been born, or that I had perished in my childhood without sin, to be assured of Your forgiveness and Your mercy.

Have mercy on me, O merciful one, for I am fearful of what I am about, but I am under duress, for You know in Your farthest heavens how I am beset by the entreaties of my enemy and Yours, the accursed Azazeel, who does not cease demanding that I record all that I have witnessed in my life.

And what worth does my life have anyway, that I should record what I have witnessed in it? So save me, O my merciful Lord, from his insinuations and from my own iniquity. My Lord, I still await from You Your signs, which have not come. I have bided my time for Your forgiveness, but so far I have not doubted. If You wish, O You of sublime might and glory, to provide me with a sign, then I accept Your command and obey. If You leave me to myself, then I am lost, for my spirit has been put to the rack, buffeted between the temptations of the accursed Azazeel and the torments of my longings after the departure of Martha, who helped to overthrow the inner regimen of my life.

I will kneel to You tonight, O Lord, and pray, then sleep, for You have created me prone to dreams for some secret reason. I will sleep a sleep full of dreams, and in my sleep send me from the bounty of Your grace a sign to light my way, inasmuch as in my waking hours Your glad tidings have remained beyond my reach. If by your sign, my Lord, you bid me refrain from writing, then I shall refrain. But if You leave me to myself, then I shall write. For, my Lord, I am but a feather tossed upon the wind, snatched up by a feeble hand intent on dipping the quill in the inkwell to record everything that has befallen me, and everything that has happened and will happen with the Rebel of Rebels, Azazeel, to Your frail servant, and to Martha. Mercy, mercy, mercy.

✝

In the name of God on high,[1] I hereby start to write my life as it has been and as it is, describing what happens around me and the terrors that burn within me. I begin my chronicle (and I do not know how or when it will end) on the night of the 27th day of the month of Thout (September) in the year 147 of the Martyrs, that is the year 431 of the birth of Jesus the Messiah, the inauspicious year in which the Venerable Bishop Nestorius was

---

1. In this part of the manuscript, there is a noticeable trembling in the writing of the words.

excommunicated and deposed, and in which the foundations of the Faith were shaken. I may recount the transgressions and torments that came to pass between me and the beautiful Martha, and the doings of Azazeel, the insidious and accursed. I will also narrate some of my dealings with the abbot of this monastery in which I live, and where I have not found peace of mind. In the course of my story I will tell of events I have lived through since leaving my original country near the town of Aswan in southern Egypt on the banks of the Nile. The people of my village believed the Nile flows from between the fingers of their god as the water falls from the sky. In my childhood I believed the same myth, until I learnt what I learnt in Naga Hammadi, Akhmim and later in Alexandria, and realized that the Nile is a river like other rivers and that all other things, like everything elsewhere, differ only to the extent that we make them different by shrouding them in delusion, conjecture and dogma.

Where should I begin my narrative? The beginnings are intertwined, teeming in my head. Perhaps, as my old teacher Syrianus used to say, beginnings are merely delusions we believe in, for the beginning and the ending exist only along a straight line, and there are no straight lines except in our imagination or on the scraps of paper where we trace our delusions. In life and in all creation, however, everything is circular, returning to where it began, interwoven with whatever is connected. There is in reality no beginning and no ending, only an unbroken succession. In the universe the connections never break, the weft never unravels, and the branching never ceases, nor the filling and the emptying. Any one thing is successively connected, its circle expanding to mesh with something else, and from the two of them a new circle branches off, meshing in turn with other circles. Life is full when the circle is complete, and drains away when we end in death, to return to whence we began. How confused I am, what is this I am writing? All the circles turn in my head and only moments of sleep bring them to a stop. Then my dreams start to turn, and in those dreams, as when I am awake, the memories teem and wrench within me. The memories are like overlapping eddies, circle after circle. If I yield to them and put them in writing, then where should I begin?

I will begin with the present, from this very moment, from my sitting here in my room, which is no more than two yards long and two yards wide. There are Egyptian tombs that are larger. Its walls are of the stone with which people build in these parts. They bring it from nearby quarries. The stone was white but today it has lost its colour.

My room has a feeble wooden door which does not shut tight. It opens to the outside where there is the long corridor passing by the rooms of the other monks. There is nothing here around me but a wooden board on which I sleep, covered with three layers of wool and linen, the soft bedding and the blanket, although I am accustomed to sleep seated, in the manner of Egyptian monks.

In the left corner, facing the door, stands a small low table with an ink-stand on top and the old lamp with its pathetic wick and its dancing flame. Under the table are blank pieces of white parchment and pieces of pale parchment from which the writing has been washed off. Next to the table is a bag containing scraps of dry bread, a jar of water, a bottle of oil for the lamp and some folded books. Above them I have hung on the wall a picture of the Virgin Mary, in relief on wood, because it gives me comfort to look at the face of the Virgin, the Mother.

In the corner of the room alongside the door there sits a wooden trunk decorated with copper engraving, which a rich man from Tyre gave me full of dates after I treated his chronic diarrhoea and took no fee for my services, reviving the tradition of the eminent physician Hippocrates, who taught mankind medicine inasmuch as he dared to write it down in books. I wonder if it was Azazeel who prompted him to write.

If I finish tonight what I am starting, I will put what I have written in this trunk, along with the proscribed gospels and other forbidden books, and bury it under the loose marble slab at the monastery gate. I will fill up around it and cover the slab in soil. I will have left something of myself here, before I finally depart, when I end the forty days of seclusion which I begin today as I start this writing, about which I have said nothing to anyone.

My room lies on the upper floor of the building and is one of twenty-four similar rooms where the monks of this monastery live. Some of the rooms are locked up, some are storerooms for grain and one is for prayer. The ground floor of this building contains the monastery kitchen, the refectory and the large reception room. Twenty-two monks live in the monastery, as well as twenty novices who serve the place until they take their vows as monks. The large monastery church has a temporary priest who is not a monk but was originally the priest of the small church which stands among the houses scattered at the foot of the monastery hill. He has been serving the monastery church since the old monastic priest passed away some years ago, pending the ordination of another priest from among the monks. The ordination would take place in the Antioch church, to which this monastery is subordinate. The ordinary priests have wives in whose arms they sleep, while we monks sleep alone and on most nights we sleep seated, or do not sleep at all because we are busy with prayers and singing long hymns of praise.

The abbot lives in a separate room, which has at the corners four old Roman columns which used to stand in the large courtyard in front of the large monastery church. When they joined up the columns with thin walls, the columns became the corners of the large room. Next to his room is the small church where we usually pray. The big church has two doors, one on the monastery side and the other overlooking the hill outside the wall, as though it were two churches, one for the monks on most days and the other for the faithful and the parishioners who come on Sundays and holy days to attend mass. Those who come later do not find space inside and have to squeeze in outside the dilapidated wall, around the outer door.

My room is the little circle of my tangible world, surrounded by a bigger circle which is this monastery, which I have loved from the first day I came inside years ago, where I have stayed ever since and where I was blessed with the peace of mind which I had long sought before coming here, until the events that I will relate took place.

I came to the monastery from Jerusalem, Salem, Yerushalayim, Urusalim, Ilya, al-Quds, the House of the Lord. Many names has this holy city borne, this city surrounded by wilderness on all sides. I lived there several years before I came here, fulfilling the will of the Lord and following the guidance and advice of Nestorius, although he, God help him today, had first invited me to go with him to Antioch and live there till the end of my life. Then something came up and instead he urged me to come here. In his own hand he wrote me a letter of recommendation to the abbot, and destiny led me into events which I have witnessed or suffered, events which I would never have expected. Under my rough pillow I still keep the letter Nestorius sent with me to the abbot. The abbot gave it back to me when I asked him for it, a year after I came here from Jerusalem. Jerusalem, how far away you seem now, how my days there seem like a dream that shone in the firmament of my dull life and then went out.

Why has everything gone dark? The light of faith which used to shine inside me, the peace of mind which kept me company in my loneliness, like a candle in the night, my serenity within the walls of this gentle room, even the daylight sun, I see them today extinguished and abandoned.

Will these cares depart my soul? Will joyful news come to me after that which came to us from Ephesus, where the priests and bishops beleaguered the blessed Bishop Nestorius and toiled until they brought him down? Time has brought me down, care and anxiety have overcome me. What will become of deposed Bishop Nestorius, whom I knew in the days when he was a priest? We met in Jerusalem when he came on pilgrimage with the delegation from Antioch, four years before he was consecrated Bishop of Constantinople. We met at a time which now seems distant, after long years have passed, and in the meantime the places, the cities have come to seem remote, impossibly remote.

Were we really in Jerusalem?

The House of the Lord

I well remember how in the middle of the day I entered Jerusalem from the dilapidated part of its high walls, the part which in former times included the great gate known as the Zion Gate, and set down my travelling stick there, after long wanderings among the villages of Judaea and Samaria.

I entered Jerusalem at about the age of thirty, my body and soul exhausted by travel on earth and in the heavens and by roaming through the pages of books. I entered it with unsteady steps, close to collapse, in the dog days of Abib (July), and at the door to the great church I fell in a swoon. Some of the pilgrims carried me inside for the priest of the Church of the Resurrection to attend to me. He laughed when I told him I was a physician and a monk, and when I recovered from my fainting fit he joked with me, saying, 'I knew you were a monk from the cap on your head, but from your fainting I could not tell you were a physician!' Then he asked me my name and I told him it was Hypa.

'Have you come on pilgrimage, or do you intend to reside amongst us, holy monk?'

'On pilgrimage first, then let the will of the Lord be done.'

I spent days in Jerusalem as a pilgrim after three years touring the Holy Places, in line with the advice of St Chariton the Monk, who worshipped incessantly in a desolate cave near the Dead Sea. When he bade me farewell, Chariton said, 'My son, do not enter Jerusalem as soon as you reach the land of Palestine. Enter only when your heart is ready for pilgrimage and your spirit is prepared, because pilgrimage is just a journey of preparation, and travel is just a revelation of the sacred element hidden in the essence of the spirit.'

On my wanderings I had passed by the places where the disciples of Jesus the Messiah once lived and where the Apostles began their mission. I spent months following in the footsteps of Jesus, as described in the Gospels and other books, starting with the town of Cana near Nazareth, where the Messiah performed the first of his miracles, when he changed water into wine for the wedding guests to drink, as it says in the Gospels. In Nazareth I found no vestige of his presence and no building left to speak of his time. I was puzzled, and I went out of my way to the other villages mentioned in the Torah, the Gospels, the canonical holy books and the non-canonical books which we have recently come to call the Apocrypha. On my journeys many doubts plagued me and I suffered terrors in my sleep, until three years of wandering had passed and that clear night came when I saw Jesus the Messiah in a vivid dream. His light filled the heavens, and in Aramaic he said to me, 'If you are seeking me, you who are perplexed and astray, set aside your self, and leave the dead, and come up to see me in Jerusalem, that you might live.' Jesus was addressing me in my visions, from up on his Cross, and there was no one around me in the wilderness.

At dawn, the day after this annunciation, I set off straight towards Jerusalem. My heart rejoiced along the way, as I asked the Lord to purge me of the effects of drowning in seas of doubt, to bring tranquillity to my soul through his bounteous grace and to bestow upon my heart sound faith and the light of certitude.

From the environs of Sidon, where the annunciation came to me, except for two hours in the dead of night when I tried to sleep under a tree, I did not stop until I reached Jerusalem, where I intended to settle for the rest of my life. But under the tree successive visions kept me awake: the Saviour suffering on the Cross of Redemption, the lamentation of the Holy Virgin Mother, the cries of John the Baptist in the wilderness, and what happened to me when I was in Alexandria. I could not sleep that night.

I entered Jerusalem from the Samaria road in the heat of the day, and I was gripped by those feelings of alienation that overwhelm me in large cities. The heat was fierce and the tumult great. On my way to the Church of the Resurrection I passed by markets and many houses, monks and merchants and people of every kind – Arabs, Syriacs, Greeks, Persians and those of other nations whose languages I could not make out when they spoke amongst themselves. I had forgotten the tumult of big cities during my long wandering through the villages of Palestine, and I fled from the crowd to the walls of the church and its big open door. I had hardly arrived when I was overcome by my hunger and exhaustion and from assiduously glorifying the Lord. My bag, laden with books and papyrus scrolls, weighed heavy on me, and then I fainted that faint for which the priest of the church treated me.

I spent days among the monks as a pilgrim and they were kind to me, although they often asked me about the lands I had passed through and the hardships, and about the saints I had met or the martyrs whose tombs I had visited. They were insistent in asking about Alexandria and I answered them to the extent that the time, place and circumstance demanded, enough to satisfy the curiosity of the monks and priests who were asking.

In my first days in Jerusalem, I thought about the secret of pilgrimage and asked myself what drove me out of my native country and brought me to this holy spot. Could I not have touched the essence of holiness in my soul while secluded in the desert close to my homeland? If a place can reveal what is inside us, and travel can bring that to light from the depths of our being, is it not possible that humility, chastity, the monastic life, and constant prayer and glorification of the Lord can bring to light divine grace and the saintliness that is latent within us? Where then lies the aura of places? Is the aura a secret inside us that pervades places when we reach them after travelling with impatient zeal? The awe I felt when I reached the walls of the Church of the Resurrection, did it arise from my sense of the imposing building, or was it from the meaning implicit in the event of the resurrection itself? Did Jesus really rise from the dead? As God, how could he die at the hands of men? Is man able to kill and torment God, and nail him to a cross?

'Would you like to stay in the church with us, or will you live in the city to treat the sick among the people of the Lord and those who come here as pilgrims?' The kindly priest asked the question several days after I arrived, and I left the choice to him. No one chooses, but rather it is the will of Heaven, which permeates things and words until it mysteriously reaches us. I said that to him and he smiled in satisfaction.

Then God's will was done and the priest of the Church of the Resurrection gave voice to it: 'You can live in the room which the monk from Edessa built, close to the courtyard of the church. I mean that room which is on the right as you go out through the main gateway. You can stay there, and be with us and with the people at the same time. The room has been closed since the monk went to his resting place two years ago, God have mercy on him. He was a saint. I'll ask the courtyard servant to clean it out for you and you can stay there from tomorrow.'

I realized then that they were wary of me, and not yet comfortable with this Egyptian monk who had descended on them without a letter of recommendation and without any explanation. If I had stayed inside the church, they would have accepted me among the monks only after years of observation. If I had stayed in the city, the tumult would have killed me. The place suggested was right, halfway between the city and the church, neither here nor there, like me: betwixt and between.

I spent my first night in the Edessan's room, as they called it, happy that I was staying in a place where the Lord was worshipped faithfully for twenty years in succession. I saw that as a good sign and a refuge for my troubled soul. Here right by me was the Church of the Resurrection, to which I had been called, and from my only window I could see the groups of believers and lay people who came to the church on pilgrimage and on visits throughout the year.

The monks and priests who serve the Church of the Resurrection are good and simple, and most of them warmed to me when they learnt that I practise medicine and the art of healing. They were not interested that I was a poet. The servitors of the church, the deacons and the young priests were friendly towards me and often dropped in, seeking treatment. As for the old priests and the senior monks, I would go to them inside the church when they summoned me.

Most of the diseases among the people in Jerusalem arose from the arid climate and the lack of diversity in their diet. Most of the time, their staples were olive oil, coarse bread made from unsifted brown flour, goat's cheese and meagre fruits. The people of Jerusalem have a rough life. The weather is mild most days in summer, but bitterly cold at night and in winter.

When I had settled in somewhat, months after moving in, and my doubts had abated with so many believers around me, I started to compose hymns in Syriac, drawing inspiration from the heavenly spirit which glorified the place and filled it with awe. Here is part of a long hymn I composed during that time:

> *This is where the light of Heaven appeared,*
> *Banished the dark from the face of the Earth and*
> *   gave souls comfort against affliction.*
> *This is where the Sun of Hearts rose,*
> *With the radiance of the Saviour, shining with*
> *   compassion on the Cross of Redemption.*
> *What is the Cross?*
> *It is the upright pole of sanctity, intersected by the*
> *   crossbeam of mercy.*
> *Let us open our arms to the horizon of mercy and*
> *   stand upright, facing sanctity.*
> *Let us be a Cross that bears its cross,*
> *And follows Jesus.*

The days passed quietly in Jerusalem, mild and monotonous until after the winter of the year 140 of the era of the Martyrs, or year 424 from the birth of Christ, and the city was preparing for Holy Week and Easter. I began to see more caravans of Arab merchants arriving in the square in front of the church. The goods became more colourful on the shelves of the city's stalls, which had previously been bare. People were elated, and my heart had tremors whenever Holy Week approached. Before dawn I kept having dreams telling me that some great event was about to happen, but I would drive these thoughts away. Shortly before the holiday more and more sick visitors came to see me, many of them suffering from the ailments of travel, especially the old among them. I treated them with humectants and medicines which doctors call cordials, changing the patients' habitual diet only when necessary to help them recover their strength.

Of all the big processions which passed by me on their way to visit the church, one from the cities of Antioch and Mopsuestia was especially imposing – dozens of priests, monks and deacons walking reverently in their solemn ecclesiastical garments, led by a man carrying an elegant cross decorated on the edges with gold leaf. Walking gravely seven paces behind him came Bishop Theodore of Mopsuestia,[2] the scholar and commentator, and behind them a large gathering of believers and lay people, chanting in unison: 'Hosanna to the son of David, Hosanna in the Highest. Blessed is he who comes in the name of the Lord.'

I was watching them in wonder from the window of my room, and I saw the cortège passing through the large door into the church, like a throng of angels which had come down to Earth from Heaven. There were more than twenty priests and close to a hundred deacons, while the retainers walking behind them were too many to count. Bishop Theodore looked tired but cheerful. I decided to make my way through the cortège and I went right up to him. I kissed his hand and he kissed my head, as he did with a man of Kurdish features dressed in the Damascene style. Heavens knows what was in my heart, and in his mysterious heavenly ways the Lord brought about a meeting between me and the bishop two days later in a way I had not expected. The next day in the afternoon a priest from Antioch and two deacons came to me and asked me to go with them to the bishop's quarters

2. At this point someone has written in Arabic in the margin of the parchment: 'A strange thing happened to me two days ago: I saw His Holiness Bishop Theodore the Interpreter in a dream, blessing this journey of mine to Jerusalem and calling on me to stay there for the rest of my life. The bishop is one of the most revered patriarchs of the Church and in our monasteries we still read his commentaries on the Gospels and the Acts of the Apostles. It is written in the original Greek and as far as we know has not been translated into the language of the Arabs among whom we now live and whose language we speak.'

in the east of the city to check his health, or so they said. I asked them politely, but in surprise, how it was that their delegation did not have a physician. The priest said that the physician of their church was with them, then added gently and calmly, 'But Nestorius the priest wants further reassurance on the health of the venerable Bishop Theodore.'

That was the first time I had heard the name Nestorius and that would be the first day I saw him. I set off with them after filling my bag with herbs which invigorate and strengthen the heart and seeds which settle the stomach. I closed the door of my room firmly and we walked together, with the priest from Antioch ahead of us. We walked for about half an hour, enough to bring beads of sweat to our faces under the midday sun. I was wearing the cassock of a Jerusalem monk, which the goodly priest had given me a month earlier as a sign that I was accepted among them. At the door a priest from Mopsuestia received us and gave us cold water, for which I thanked the Lord. When I entered the bishop's quarters I suddenly felt that something momentous was about to happen. We followed a long corridor and from a door on the right at the far end came a calm and solemn voice: 'Blessed physician and venerable father, His Holiness Bishop Theodore is talking to some guests. Would you like to go in now or would you rather wait here until they come out?'

It was the priest from Mopsuestia, and I asked his leave to go in and listen, if that was possible. He nodded solemnly in agreement and gently opened the door for me. The room was spacious and shady, roofed with palm fronds and airy. In the centre lay matting sprinkled with water perfumed with essence of basil, and on rows of benches on the four sides sat goodly men, monks, priests and deacons, about forty people in all, and their features indicated that most of them were people from the north. They had faultless pale complexions and their beards were bright white or blond, so much so that I was embarrassed that I was so brown and sallow and that my unkempt beard did not suggest that I was a skilful physician.

In those days I did not care to trim my beard, as I have done recently. I sat in the place closest to the door, and in the centre of the opposite side Bishop Theodore was sitting on an antique wooden chair with armrests. He did not notice when I came in quietly and sat down on the bench opposite his chair at a distance. His words captivated me and I paid full attention to their subtlety, which I have often recalled. The clarity of his diction penetrated easily my heart and mind. I remember today much of what he said and when I returned to my room in the evening I wrote it down. Speaking in Greek, he said:

'On this holy ground where we are honoured to come as pilgrims, dear friends, the new age of Man began. Jesus Christ marks the divide between two ages and he initiates the new era of mankind. The first age began with Adam, and the second began with Jesus Christ. Each of the two ages has its nature and rules, known to our merciful God from eternity. The Heavenly Father created Adam in His image, that he might be immortal. But Adam was seduced by Satan's temptation and disobeyed the Holy Lord and ate from the forbidden tree in the hope that he would become a god. The accursed Azazeel deceived him with his whispering. Adam sinned and was punished with expulsion from Paradise, judged by the holiness of the Lord God.

'But because the Lord in His mercy loves mankind and originally created him without sin, He did not want to leave him stained with his first sin till the end of eternity. Mercy prevailed over the Lord and He sent His only son Jesus Christ in perfect human form to redeem mankind, save the world from the sin of Adam and through His sacrifice open a new age for humanity. After the Messiah, He sent the Apostles to guide us and give us the Gospels. What does gospel mean? As St John Chrysostom says, it means news of joy, because the Gospel brings glad tidings of reprieve from punishment and forgiveness of sins. It brings absolution, consecration and a heavenly legacy which puts Azazeel to shame, and it graces us with abundant hope.'

The voice of Bishop Theodore rang throughout the spacious hall and a sense of humility settled on those seated. All eyes were fixed on the bishop, as were mine. I wished then that I had started my theological studies under him and had drawn water at the well of his eloquence, which so impressed one's heart and mind and rescued one's spirit from anxiety and doubt. My mind wandered for a moment, then I listened again to more from the Bishop of Mopsuestia, that fine town in the heart of Anatolia. His voice, now gentle, again filled the council room:

'Dear friends, look at the sermons of Jesus Christ and rejoice in the words of cheer which St Matthew the Apostle has preserved in his Gospel. He tells us in every time and every place: "Blessed are the meek, for they shall inherit the earth. Blessed are those who mourn, for they shall be comforted." Before Christ, was there ever such good news as this? Or such a sign of exultation? Know that Christ came for our sake, and we must live for His sake. His incarnation, suffering, dying and resurrection from the dead are a victory over Satan, and atonement for the sins of the first man, who was deceived and sinned. Our faith in Christ is the way out of the age of sin towards the prospect of salvation which the will of the Lord has granted us. And so, dear friends, be Christians and call on your people to have faith, that they may be, and you with them, truly the children of God in the new age of mankind. Cross the bridge which spans the sufferings of Jesus, that you may be as perfect as your perfect Heavenly Father. The sign that you have crossed that bridge is baptism. Baptism is a rebirth, a resurrection of the spirit from the death of the body, a way to grace and union with Christ. Baptism is salvation and a new creation, so know in your hearts the secret of baptism.'

When the bishop spoke the word 'baptism' I gave a slight shiver, which no one noticed but a bright-faced priest of about forty years sitting to the right of the bishop. I found out later that he was the reason I was summoned – a famous priest of Antioch originally from the town of Germanicia or Marash with the ecclesiastical name of Nestorius, one of the most loyal disciples of Bishop Theodore and one of the greatest admirers of his interpretations of the Gospels.

As the sun set, the bishop of Mopsuestia showed signs of fatigue. His tone slackened and his voice fell quiet as he wrapped up his speech to his audience, who seemed overcome with spiritual rapture, as though his talk had raised them to the highest heavens. The last thing he said to them was this: 'We were but dead and Adam had destined us to annihilation by committing the sin of rebelling against his creator, and Satan remained immortal, but when the Lord appeared to us in Christ, by the grace of God a chance arose for us to escape annihilation and death through repentance and approaching the prospect of salvation through the door of baptism.'

A monk of Arab features, advanced in years, mumbled as if he wanted to say something. When Bishop Theodore looked at him encouragingly, the priest asked him about a sensitive subject. How, he said, did we inherit from Adam the sin of rebelling against God? What was our fault, we his descendants, who did not commit this sin? The bishop answered him with a smile. 'We commit many other sins, no less grave than rebellion and eating from the forbidden tree, although we are the sons of Jesus, not because we inherited from Adam his sin, but rather because we inherited from him the disposition and readiness to sin. This is a long subject, holy father, and we can discuss it at length in a future session.'

Nestorius stood up, signalling that the lesson was over, and everyone prepared to leave. They blocked my view of Bishop Theodore as they approached to receive his blessing by kissing his hand. I stood up and I saw Nestorius lean down to take the bishop's hand and guide him through the throng to his room. As he passed in front of me, he looked towards me with serene affection, as though he had known me a long time. His look disturbed me.

Before they summoned me I spent a long hour in the spacious hall with some of the monks and priests. In the meantime they brought me a plate covered with a Damascene napkin with decorated borders, holding the fine fruits which grow on the trees of the north. Bishop Theodore was not suffering from a specific disease but his seventy-four years, coupled with the rigour of the pilgrimage journey, had exhausted him. I realized that two days earlier when he passed in front of me at his awesome appearance at the head of the procession, but I did not want to hurry in telling him what I knew of his condition. Instead I approached him, showing the appropriate solicitude and reverence. I took his hand gently and kissed it, then began to take his pulse. It was rather weak. I took from my bag some herbs which invigorate the pulse and stimulate the flow of blood from the heart. I asked that they be boiled on a low fire, then left to cool, and he should drink them warm.

Nestorius gestured to one of the deacons standing at the door, and the deacon rushed off to do what I requested. We stayed silent a moment as Bishop Theodore looked towards me, and I looked towards my feet. When the servant came in carrying the cup, Nestorius took a drink from it before offering it to the bishop.

'How do you find the taste, dear Nestorius?'

'Good, your Grace the Bishop. It is sweet and aromatic and will cure you, God willing.'

The bishop cheered up and signs of relief appeared on his face. He sat up straight and began to sip from the cup. 'God bless you, Nestorius, God bless you, Father physician. What is your name?'

'Hypa, your Grace the Bishop.'

'Strange, Egyptian, when did you adopt this non-Egyptian name?'

'When I left Alexandria, father.'

'And where had you been before?'

With great courtesy Nestorius interrupted the conversation and asked the bishop to lie down a little to rest. The bishop answered him with a sweet smile, teasing him affectionately. 'Leave aside your paternal feelings, Nestorius, because my father died long ago and I am on my way to join him. Let me speak to this physician monk for I am pleased to see him. The innocent surprise in his eyes reminds me of the surprise I used to see in the eyes of my brother in spirit, John Chrysostom, when we were young.'

Nestorius shook his head in submission and prepared to leave the meeting. In a low and gentle voice, he said, 'As you wish, your Grace. I will see you, Hypa, in the big room after you finish your conversation.'

'No, Nestorius, sit with us, and you, Hypa, tell me where you were born and when you went to Alexandria.'

Nestorius gestured to the three deacons and the servants at the door, and they all left. Our conversation continued until the servant of the lodge came in carrying dinner on an old wooden table. He put it to the right of the bishop's bed. Theodore sat up straight and invited us to gather around the food. He joked to Nestorius, saying in Syriac, 'These morsels may be the last supper for me.'

'May the merciful Lord prolong your life for us, father, for we shall always need you.'

I ate with them shyly and the food was wholesome and delicious, and when I praised the taste, the priest Nestorius said to me in jest, 'This is blessed food, cooked in psalms on a low fire of hymns.' We smiled at his humour and the bishop turned again towards me, encouraging me to continue what I had been telling him. I had already spoken of my birth in the village south of Aswan and my studies in Naga Hammadi and Akhmim. Of course I did not tell him the misfortunes that befell me on the bank of Elephantine Island or the horrors that took place in front of my eyes in Alexandria, or my flight from that city the day of the great terror.

The bishop was interested and listened to me politely. He was smiling and I did not want to dispel his smile by speaking of misfortunes or recounting the vicissitudes of life. He chewed a piece of food which Nestorius offered to him, soaked in olive oil and mountain marjoram, and asked me, 'Have you studied logic, my child?'

'Yes, your Grace, I studied it in Akhmim from a non-Christian man who came from around Assiut. He was proficient in the old philosophies, and erudite.'

'That's logical, my child, for from those parts came the most important philosopher. Do you know who I mean, Hypa?'

I hesitated a moment and then, in deference to the status of the bishop, I said, 'No, your Grace, I don't know.'

'Tell him, Nestorius.'

'Your Grace, you mean Plotinus.'

'Yes, Father Nestorius, yes.'

Nestorius smiled and from the corner of his eye he gave me a look that meant he realized I had refrained from answering out of politeness towards the bishop. I looked at my toes in embarrassment. Bishop Theodore did not notice any of this. He was looking up around the room and seemed to be talking to himself or confiding with his old colleague John Chrysostom. 'I often think of Plotinus, and of Egypt. I think many elements of our religion come from there, and not from here. Monasticism, love of martyrdom, the

22

sign of the cross, the word "Evangel", even the Holy Trinity, which is an idea that first appeared clearly with Plotinus, for in his book, *The Enneads*, he says…'

I don't know why but I suddenly jumped in, and without a thought interrupted the bishop's meditations. 'No, father, Plotinus's trinity is philosophical: with him it's the One, the First Mind and the World Soul. The trinity in our religion is heavenly and divine: the Father, the Son and the Holy Ghost. There's a big difference between the two.'

'Gently, monk, you should not interrupt his Grace the Bishop in that way.'

Nestorius's decisive words brought to a stop my sudden and senseless outburst. My embarrassment was unrelieved by the sympathy of Bishop Theodore, who looked at me with great affection, with his same smile, though now rather faint and tired.

The bishop put his right hand on my left shoulder, blessed me with a prayer and made the sign of the cross on my brow with his finger. Then he crawled towards his cushion and there was nothing for me to do but leave. I apologized to the bishop in a stammer and wished the ground would swallow me up, to spare me my embarrassment.

'Never mind, Nestorius. Youth is a blazing torch. At your age we too were on fire. Dear Nestorius, accompany the good monk out and be good to him, for I do love him.'

'Don't worry, father. I'll walk with him as far as his room, at the gate to the Church of the Resurrection. I am going there for the night prayers and to attend mass.'

'God bless you, Nestorius.'

When we left the lodge, two deacons walked behind us, along with a thin man of about forty who I think was one of the servants of the Antioch diocese. They walked close behind us and we walked without talking, with Nestorius praying under his breath and me in embarrassed silence.

Halfway he opened the conversation with a question. 'Hypa, have you read Plotinus's *Enneads*?'

I answered cautiously: 'Yes, father, and I studied it for several months in Naga Hammadi, and I have a copy which is more than a hundred years old.'

'Good, I would like to read it.'

His answer reassured me and I set aside some of my caution. I wanted our conversation to continue, so I told him the book was in my room. Then I added hesitantly, 'I also have another book you might want to see, might want... It's Arius's book entitled *Thalia*.'

'*Thalia!* We read that poem long ago in Antioch, and I thought our copy was the only one to escape being burned. Anyway, let me see your copy. Is it complete?'

'Yes, father, and written in Coptic on papyrus.'

'In Coptic! Amazing. How many languages do you read, Hypa?'

'Four, father. Greek, Hebrew, Coptic and Aramaic. And my favourite is Aramaic, because that is the language Jesus the Messiah spoke.'

'We no longer call it Aramaic, but Syriac, to distinguish the blessed Christian era of the language from the earlier pagan and Hebrew era.'

'I agree with you, father, I agree completely, because languages do not speak for themselves. People speak them. And if they change, the language changes, and Jesus the Messiah changed the language as He changed its people. He made it a holy language.'

'True, Hypa, true, my child.'

What he said put me at my ease and I set aside more of my caution. I wanted our conversation to last till night ended. Our walk had brought us from the narrow lanes to the wide avenues, and as the large square opened in front of us the big church loomed, with its lofty domes, like a dream wrapped in the star-studded blackness of that clear spring night.

When we could make out my room from afar, after a moment of silence Nestorius said, 'God preserve you, Hypa. Talking of Jesus the Messiah, do you have a copy of the Gospel of Thomas?'

'Yes, father, and I also have a copy of the Gospel of the Egyptians, and the Gospel of Judas, and the Book of Secrets. I like to collect books.'

Nestorius smiled and told me I kept all the forbidden books. I said the authorized books were available in the church and everywhere. His smile broadened. After we said the night prayer in the Church of the Resurrection, I took the opportunity to invite him back to my room. He liked the idea and agreed. I was glad that he agreed, but I did not know that this meeting, which lasted till the brink of dawn, would change my life and that afterwards I would move from Jerusalem to the north, where I am settled today in this isolated monastery, far from my native country, impossibly far.

✝

We came back from the big church to my room, anticipating a friendly meeting. That night I felt a deep tranquillity in the company of Nestorius. I opened the door, lit the slender lamp hanging in the right-hand corner and gave my important guest a welcome. When I opened the only window, a cool breeze from the clear sky wafted in, and an air of friendliness filled the room.

Nestorius looked long at the picture of the Virgin hanging over the bed and said nothing. After a while he looked around the room and said, 'Your room is clean and tidy, Hypa. That shows your personality. Where are the books you told me about?'

'Under the bed you're sitting on, father.'

'Call me by my name, Hypa, for we are all brothers. We are all feeble sheep in the fold of the Lord.'

'No, you are more like the shepherd, father, God preserve you with His eternal and everlasting care.'

He laughed an agreeable, luminous laugh as he stood up to let me fold back the Damascene camel-hair kelim, the decorated kelim which right now is spread beneath me. In fact it's been my only carpet ever since. I lifted the slats of the bed, exposing the books and papyrus scrolls. When I lifted the last slat and all my hidden treasure appeared, Nestorius leant out of my window and called the three retainers. When they were close, he told them to go back to the lodge.

'It looks as if I'll stay the night with you, Hypa.'

'I would be delighted, blessed father. I'll sleep on this bench.'

'I don't think either of us will sleep tonight.'

All the while that Nestorius was carefully examining my treasures I kept turning to his radiant face, as I prepared for the two of us a warm drink of aromatic mountain mint and a plate of dates and dried figs. His figure showed dignity and genuine goodness. His wide eyes were of a colour which blended green and honey, full of curiosity and intelligence. His white face was slightly flushed and his neat beard was pleasantly blond, with some grey hair which added to his radiance. His manner had a divine serenity which many monks lack, both young and old.

I put his cup of mint down near to him, turned up the lamp and sat on the bench opposite the bed which doubled as a hiding place. I contemplated his radiant smile and saw him as a sublime example of what a man of religion should be.

'Cicero's speeches! You cunning Egyptian monk. You like rhetoric, as we do. What's this large volume? *The City of God*,' he said, shaking his head in surprise.

'Yes, reverend father, it is Bishop Augustine's book. These are the first and second parts of it, because he has not yet completed the book.'

'I know, Hypa, I know, but I'm surprised it has reached you here.'

'Reverend father, the pilgrims bring with them all things new and old, and they give me books sometimes, and sometimes I buy books from them, but this book is not quite new, because the first part is dated the year 413 of the birth of our Saviour Christ, and that is more than ten years ago.'

He asked me if I knew how to tell when the book was written, and out of deference I said no. I asked him to do me the honour of telling me. He turned towards me, his smile yet more radiant with divine grace. He told me of events of which I knew but had never connected. In summary, he said, 'Augustine is a holy man and no previous African bishop has been the like of him. Perhaps no one of such virtue and high-mindedness ever lived in the city of Hippo. But he joined the service of the Lord late, after spending most of his life as a soldier and fighting many wars. In the year 410 of the Glorious Nativity, the war took place in which Rome famously fell to the Goths, even if they did not destroy the city as was expected of them. Rome, as you know, is the capital of the universe and the city of the world. If the world falls, the heavens rise! In exchange for the fall of the city of man, the glory will be to the city of God. After deep thought in the three years which followed the temporary fall of Rome, he wanted to declare that it was fallen for ever. He declares in the title of his book that the city of God will never fall, unlike the city of man which is of necessity ephemeral. He also wanted to absolve Christianity of the ignorant accusation that it caused the terrible fall of Rome.'

Then he asked me about the rest of my hidden treasure, and I took out the bag in which I keep Egyptian texts. He began to ask me the titles of the books and Coptic papyrus scrolls, and sometimes I would answer him before he even asked me. After looking long at the Coptic translation of the *Maymar of the Holy Family's Journey*, written by Bishop Theophilus the Alexandrian, Nestorius looked distressed and suddenly was lost in thought for I know not what reason. To bring him out of his reverie, I said, '*The Maymar of the Holy Journey* is well known in Egypt. Have you seen the Greek original, father?'

'I have seen it, but Hypa, I wonder at the audacity of that bishop. How can he tell stories about the Blessed Virgin Mary, and describe her and cite her words, based only on his claim that he saw her in a dream? Ha, we don't need that. What is this old Coptic scroll and what are these fine images drawn on it?'

Silently I thanked the Lord for steering the conversation away from the subject of Bishop Theophilus and his book, because I grew anxious, and I still do, whenever I hear mention of the bishops of Alexandria. Hurriedly I answered Nestorius's last question. 'Nothing, father, it's the Book of Going Forth by Day, which tells of the Day of Judgement and how the dead should testify for themselves in the presence of God, according to the ancient Egyptian belief, and those are pictures of the old gods, very old gods.'

'Extraordinary pictures, and who is this man holding the potter's wheel?'

'They call him Khnum, father, the god Khnum. The ancients believed he formed mankind from clay, then Amun blew into the clay to give man life. An ancient belief, father, an ancient belief.'

'Khnum, strange name. Does it remind you of anything, Hypa?'

'Yes, it does remind me of things, but how did you know, reverend father?'

'From your troubled heart. In fact I can see you are about to cry.'

+

Telling secrets has never been my practice, nor has trusting anyone. But that night I went and told Nestorius about the temple of the god Khnum which receives the flow of the Nile at the southern tip of Elephantine Island in southern Egypt, near Aswan. I told him about the archaic aura of reverence and sanctity which diffused for centuries through the temple and its compound. I told him about my father and how he used to take fish every other day to the sad priests who had lived entrenched within the temple for years, under siege, grieving that their religion was dying out with the spread of belief in Christ. My father would take me in his boat whenever he visited the temple, to offer the priests half of the fish his nets had caught over the past two days. We would go to the temple secretly at dawn.

I could not help but weep when I described to him the terror of that dreadful dawn, when I was nine years old. The ordinary Christians had lain in wait for us at the southern quay, close to the gate of the temple. They were hiding behind the rocks before the boat docked, then they rushed towards us like spectres fleeing from the bowels of hell. Before we had a chance to recover from the shock of seeing them, they were upon us from their hiding place nearby. They pulled my father from his boat and dragged him across the rocks to stab him to death with rusty knives they had hidden beneath their ragged clothes. I snarled, cowering in the corner of the boat to defend myself. But my father was defenceless, and as they stabbed him he cried out for help to the god he believed in. The priests of Khnum took fright at the sounds which broke the silence and lined up on the temple wall, watching what was happening below them in dread and confusion. They raised their arms in imprecation to their gods and cried out for help. They did not realize that the gods they worshipped had died long ago and no one would hear their fearful prayer.

'Poor thing, and did the mob come close to you that day?'

'I wish they had killed me so I could be at rest for ever. No, father, they did not come so close. They looked at me like wolves that have had their fill, then came to the boat, grabbed the basket of fish and threw it at the temple gate, which was firmly closed. They carried my father's mangled body and threw it on top of the basket. His blood and flesh, and the fish, mingled with the dust of the earth which was no longer holy. Then the thrill of victory and vengeance took possession of them and they shouted out and raised high their arms, stained with my father's blood. Holding the rusty bloodied knives in their hands, they began to gesture at the terrified priests on the wall. They cheered and exulted, as they sang the famous hymn: 'Glory be to Jesus Christ, death to the enemies of the Lord, glory be to…'

I began to sob and Nestorius stood up and put his arm around me. I was cowering just as I did the first time, the time when he sat next to me, patted me on the head and made the sign of the cross several times on my brow. He kept repeating, 'Calm down, my child.' Then he said, 'My child, our life is full of pain and sin. Those ignorant people wanted salvation on the old basis of oppression for oppression, and persecution for persecution, and you were the victim. I know your pain was great and I feel it. May the merciful Lord bestow on us His compassion. Arise, my child, and let us pray together the prayer of mercy.'

'What use will prayer be, father? He who died is dead and will not return.'

'Prayer will avail, my child, it will avail.'

I heard Nestorius's voice tremble. When he raised his bowed head from his chest, I saw that tears were running into his beard and that his eyes were inflamed and red from grief. Pain filled the lines of his face, reflected on his brow in the form of a deep sorrow.

'Have I grieved you, father?'

'No, my child, don't worry. Arise and let's pray.'

By the meekness of the Virgin we prayed, and we prayed long until dawn came to paint the black of the sky a deep blue. As we sat in silence right after praying, I could hear from afar the crowing of cocks and the twittering of the birds which sleep on the branches of the trees in the courtyard of the church. Nestorius broke our silence by inviting me to go outside with him and walk around the church wall. 'May we receive,' he said, 'some of the mercies of the Lord at this blessed dawn.'

✝

Between the first break of daylight and the time when the morning sun had spread across the ground around us, we walked twice around the large space within the walls of the church. Then we went to the opposite side, where the houses are clustered together as if for safety. The morning sun is troubling to those who have stayed up all night – as I have long seen and felt – and I still suffer from it on most days. In rhythm with our leisurely step Nestorius told me some of his childhood memories from the town of Marash, some of the events of his youth in Antioch, stories about him and his master Theodore of Mopsuestia and other things that had happened to him in the course of his life. On that Jerusalem day that inadvertently brought us together, Nestorius was forty-one years old. Of course I will not say now what he told me about himself that day, because it would not be right to write that down, and I know that he told me what he told me only to cheer me up, trusting me with secrets that had nothing to do with me and which I could not possibly disclose here.

After we had finished our second turn around the walls and were heading towards the houses, I saw from afar people beginning to stir about their usual daily business. I noticed three deacons of Antioch waiting for us at the door to my locked room, looking around anxiously. When we reached them, Nestorius said goodbye to me and went off with them towards their lodge. But first, with a smile laden with the burdens of our long night, he said, 'You may join us today at lunchtime, and if you cannot, I will meet you in the church courtyard at the ninth hour of the day,' meaning in the afternoon when we say the last of the daytime prayers.

I went back to my room so completely exhausted that I almost fell asleep at the door. When I was inside I collapsed on my bed, and slept a deep sleep with no dreams. At noon the clamour of visitors at the door of the church awoke me and I stood up, my body heavy and my soul drained. With unsteady steps I made my way towards the jar of water, took a listless drink, then washed my face with drops of water which I poured into the palms of my hands. When I half-opened my window, the light poured in and filled the corners of my soul with its sudden radiance. I was reorganizing the treasures hidden under my bed when a gentle knocking on the door disturbed the calm, and I heard a call I had grown accustomed to in those times: 'Father, physician monk.'

It was an Arab man dressed like a merchant, come to report to me that he had a cataract in his left eye two years earlier and now he was losing the sight in his right eye, because the water in his eyes was not staying together in one spot so that it could be drawn off through a thin tube. I gave him a powder and told him to use it as a poultice and come back in two months. In two months! I wonder, did the man come back two months later and find me gone?

That day the Arab man asked me how much he should pay and I told him the usual, 'The Lord will reward me, but if you want you can give something as a donation to the church.' The man thanked me and tried to kiss my hand, then left. When I closed the door behind him, I reverted to my inner world full of the worries of a lonely man and the sudden flashes of light which would come upon me without warning. I finished off sorting out my books and scrolls and arranged them under my bed as they were. When I had organized the meagre belongings in my room, I went out in the early after-noon into the courtyard of the church.

The weather was not hot but I took shelter in the shady corner. In my usual place on the right side of the courtyard, beyond the big door, I leant the back of my head against the leafy tree which was my favourite there. I felt as weary as a traveller back from a long journey. I closed my eyes and began to fantasize that the tree and I had become one. I felt my soul slip out of my ribcage and infiltrate the trunk of the tree, then plunge deep into the roots of it and push on up into the high branches. My being swayed with its leaves, and when some of them fell from the branches a part of me fell with them. At the time I remembered the fragments of Pythagoras I had read in Akhmim, where he says that in a momentary flash he remembered many of his previous lives, including one life in which his spirit was a tree. I wanted to become a tree like this one forever, a tree that gave abundant shade but did not fruit, so that no one would throw stones at it, but that people would love for its shade. This is a dry country and the aridity is severe, and if I became this tree I would take pity on those seeking my shade, and my shade would be a solace I would give them without recompense. I would be a refuge for the weary, not a temptation to those seeking fruit. That day I prayed with the fervour of someone who is far from home, and far from himself, and I called on the Lord within me. 'My merciful Lord, take me to You now, and save me from my ephemeral body. Have I not lodged my soul in this beloved tree and come closer to perfection, for every midday I take pity on the pilgrims who visit this sacred spot, pilgrims purged of sin through your light. In winter I will wait for Your love of the world to fall as rain, and every morning breathe in the dewdrops which the cold of the night brings to me, and nothing will divert me from singing the praises of Your heavenly glory. Trees are purer than mankind, and love God more. If I became this tree, I would spread my shade over the wretched.'

'Are you asleep, Hypa?'

I came to my senses, and was delighted when the priest Nestorius took me by surprise and sat next to me. I sat up straight and shook my head to say that I was not sleeping. In Syriac, not the Greek which was his customary language, he asked me kindly, with intent to jest, 'In which sea of thoughts were you drowning, good Egyptian?'

'Father, strange thoughts sometimes assail me. I was wishing I could become this tree in the shade of which we are sitting.'

'Where do these ideas come from, my child?'

'From deep inside me, and from the distant past. Pythagoras used to say…'

'Pythagoras! That's part of the old pagan culture, Hypa.'

It troubled me that I was always so impetuous in his presence, but he relieved my embarrassment with a kindly gesture, touching my cap with his holy fingertips and starting to recite a psalm under his breath. He closed his eyes as he made the sign of the cross on my head, which was covered with a cap decorated with crosses. In a whisper, as though he were addressing the angels of heaven, he said, 'You are blessed, Hypa, with the light of the Lord,' and I calmed down.

'Father, do you think that paganism is all evil?' I asked.

'God does not create evil or do evil, and evil does not please him,' he replied. 'God is all goodness and love, but people went astray in olden times when they imagined that reason was enough to know the truth, without salvation coming to them from heaven.'

'I'm sorry, reverend father, but Pythagoras was a good soul, although he lived in pagan times.'

'That may be, because the time before the coming of Christ's glad tidings was also a time of God, and God's sunlight shines on both the good and the evil, and who knows, maybe God in his omnipotence wanted to prepare mankind for the coming of the Saviour's gospel through flashes of enlightenment which paved the way for Christ, and the closer the time approached the more frequently the signs of his coming appeared, until there came the great sign, John the Baptist, the voice crying in the wilderness.'

I liked what he said, and saw in it a plausible answer to a problem which had long troubled me, by which I mean the mysterious connection between Jesus the Messiah and his cousin John the Baptist. How was it feasible that John the Baptist, as a human, could baptize God, or the Son of God, or the image of God, or the messenger of God, according to the various theories about him? I asked Nestorius, 'Master, do you believe that Jesus is God, or is He the messenger of God?'

'The Messiah, Hypa, was born of man, and humans do not give birth to gods. How can we say that the Virgin gave birth to a god and how can we worship a child a few months old, just because the Magi bowed down and worshipped him? The Messiah is a divine miracle, a man through whom God appeared to us. God became incarnate in Him to make of Him a harbinger of salvation and a sign of the new age of mankind, as Bishop Theodore explained to us yesterday at that meeting where I saw you for the first time. By the way, why were you upset when the bishop referred to the mystery of baptism?'

'You are observant, father.'

'That is not an answer.'

Nestorius made that last remark in jest, as though he wanted to put an end to the formality between us and encourage me to speak. That's why I had no problem divulging to him one of my biggest secrets, and I was pleased that my secret did not surprise him. I told him words to the effect that I had doubts about whether I was baptized, because my mother assured me she had me baptized when I was an infant, but my father denied it, and I don't remember that I went to church in my early childhood, so I find myself more inclined to believe my father. At the time I did not want to tell Nestorius I had baptized myself, after I left Alexandria. I said, 'It seems, father, that I was not baptized as a child.' I expected that my words would surprise him, but instead he surprised me, saying in a soft voice, 'It's not your fault. You must have been baptized, or you will be baptized, God willing. But how did you become a monk when you had doubts about your baptism?'

'For years I attended the big church in Akhmim, and my teacher the Akhmim priest deemed me suitable for the monastic life, and he initiated me when I begged him to. I had not told him of my doubt about my baptism because I had forgotten the events of my childhood, or had chosen to forget them.'

'No matter, Hypa, many besides you are baptized late, and some of them have become bishops with the passage of time. Ambrose, the Bishop of Milan and Nectarius, the Bishop of Constantinople, were baptized only on the day they were consecrated as bishops. The Emperor Constantine himself was baptized only on his deathbed, and he was called the Beloved of God, the Defender of the Faith and the Ally of Jesus.'

I noticed that he mentioned the Christian titles of the Emperor Constantine in a tone that combined derision and sadness, and I wanted to hear from him more than he had disclosed. Proud of what I knew and keen to understand more, I said that the emperor performed for Christianity momentous services which have lasted till our time, for in his age the people of our religion were a powerless minority, no more than one tenth of the population of the Empire, and now they have become the majority in the Empire, both east and west, only one hundred years after the ecumenical council at which this emperor presided. I added, 'I mean, father, the Council of Nicaea at which Arius was excommunicated for saying the Messiah is

34

human rather than divine and that God is One, unaccompanied and undiluted in his divinity.'

'You are truly devious, Hypa. What do you want to know from me, you clever physician, you monk who doubts his own baptism?'

I realized from his joking that he was not upset at what I said and would be happy to talk frankly about the mystery of this matter, which our clerics do not like to tackle. I was impatient to know what he thought of the controversial Arius, whom the church of Alexandria hates more than it hates Satan himself. At first Nestorius tried to divert me from my intention by asking if I was content living in Jerusalem. But I begged for a clear answer on what he really thought of Arius and his ideas. 'Tell me the truth as you see it, reverend father,' I implored him, 'for you are shrewd of vision, god-fearing, pure in heart and judicious in reason, and my interest in knowing of this matter is great and keeps me awake at night.'

'Fine, let's get up and walk over to the lodge, because I'd like to check up on Bishop Theodore. I'll tell you about Arius and his heresy while we're on our way.'

We did not take the direct route to the lodge, but went out of the church gate and walked to the right alongside the high wall, then crossed the open space that stretches from the end of the church wall to the beginning of where the houses are clustered, on the eastern side of the city wall. This route was quieter and more pleasant, and further from the tumult. We were walking at a steady pace, stopping sometimes when Nestorius was busy clarifying a subtle point, and so we arrived after an hour or more. On the way he told me things I hesitate to write down now, especially in these dark and gloomy days.

✝

Sleep is a divine gift without which the world would go raving mad. Everything in the universe sleeps, wakes up and sleeps again, except our sins and our memories, which have never slept and will never subside. Today I awoke from a sleep full of dreams so strong they seemed like reality, or perhaps it is my reality that has collapsed and faded until it has turned into dreams? I have started to feel the breath of death close by me, almost brushing me. Will I perhaps die in my sleep or in the church at prayer time? I think that my fear of the end, and not Azazeel's insistence, is what drives me to write. Or perhaps I want my voice to reach beyond whatever comes to an end with my death. Last month the oldest monk in this monastery died and was buried there. He died on the threshold of the Lord, free of all sin. How will I die, and where?

✟

Writing raises within us storms we have stifled, digs our memories out of their hiding places and brings to mind the most atrocious of happenings. In distant, receding periods of my life my faith has consoled me and filled me with joy. But today gloom surrounds me on every side and tempests rage within me, strong enough to cut me adrift from all creation. What will be the fate of Nestorius after all that has happened to him? Where, I wonder, will I go after I complete this chronicle? Will I again see my beloved Martha who has gone? I thought she had left me in peace, but after she was gone I felt the sting of anxiety and the tremor of desire. I wish I had stopped her going to Aleppo and saved her from the danger of singing at night among the drunken merchants and the villainous Arabs, and saved myself from what I am suffering now. Since she left I have never forgotten her tearful eyes, and my worry for her has not abated.

'You are the reason, Hypa, you are the reason, because she begged you to save her from that, and to save yourself, but you did not dare.'

'Azazeel!'

'Yes, Hypa, the Azazeel who comes to you from within yourself.'

Thus is the trinity of my torment completed – my worry about the fate of Nestorius, my curiosity about the fate of Martha, and Azazeel's sudden appearances. How long must I bear this torment, and when will I be free of this triple affliction? O God, save me, for I...

'Hypa, don't be silly and carry on with what you were writing.'

'And what was I writing?'

'What Nestorius told you at the eastern wall of Jerusalem. Fear nothing, for writing will not make matters worse and I don't think anyone will read what you write for years, so write tonight, that you may be truly yourself. Who knows, poor man, maybe after your forty days of seclusion news will come that Nestorius turned defeat into victory. Perhaps you will see Martha again in her lovely Damascene dress and take her with you when you depart, as expected. Perhaps you will find joy with her for the rest of your life and the anguish in your heart will abate.'

Azazeel has strong arguments and he usually wins me over. Or is it that I have emboldened him by tugging him towards myself, as he claims, with my constant hesitation and my chronic worrying? In any case, there is no cause for concern. The morning is nigh, and there is nothing dangerous in what I am going to write now. This piece of parchment is almost full and only this small space remains clear of ink. In it I shall write a summary of what I heard that day from Nestorius. I will write it in my own words, in Syriac, so that it is binding on me, not an argument against him.

The reverend Nestorius said to me in Jerusalem that day, in his elegant Greek accent, 'The truth is, Hypa, that it is all a fraud. Satan was the driving force behind everything that happened a hundred years ago at the Council of Nicaea. By Satan I mean the devil in the form of temporal power, which goes to people's heads. Then they challenge the authority of the Lord and tear each other to pieces; then they lose heart and are scattered to the wind. Their passions overwhelm them and they act foolishly and violate the spirit of the faith in seeking to obtain the vanities of the transient world. What happened in Nicaea, Hypa, was null and void through and through. Emperor Constantine was in such a hurry to declare his sovereign authority over all Christians that he would not wait until his new city Constantinople was complete before calling the ecumenical council, so he held the council in nearby Nicaea.

'A year earlier the emperor had been busy with a single purpose – to assert his authority through war on his former military comrades, and when the wars ended in their defeat, he wanted to gain spiritual authority over his subjects, so he called the heads of all the churches to the ecumenical council, ran the sessions and interfered in the theological debate. Then he dictated the resolutions to the bishops and priests who attended, though I don't believe he ever read a single book of Christian theology. In fact he didn't understand Greek, the language in which the theological debate raged between the bishops in Nicaea, and basically he wasn't interested in the theological dispute between Arius the priest and the bishop of Alexandria of his time, Alexander. That's clear from the emperor's letters to them, in which he describes their disagreement over the nature of Jesus Christ as trivial, vulgar, foolish and crass. He tells them they should keep their opinions to themselves and not bother people with them. The letter is famous and there are copies of it in the diocese.

'Then the emperor took sides with Bishop Alexander to secure Egypt's wheat and the annual grape harvest. He excommunicated Arius, banned his teachings and declared him a heretic to please the majority of his subjects and make himself the champion of Christianity. Emperor Constantine let the wisdom of Arius go to waste in the past, just as his wisdom goes to waste today at the hands of the ignorant people who claim to be his followers and who adopt him as a way to heresy and to undermine the faith. The Arians who now fill the land around us do injustice to Arius, just as Emperor Constantine did a hundred years ago, when he sanctioned his assassination in broad daylight.'

'Just as the emperor, father, ordered the burning of his books and all the Gospels which people had, except the four famous ones. But what do you mean, father, by the wisdom of Arius?'

At the time we were walking under the canopy of a large shady tree, at the end of the church wall, in the quiet spot overlooking the city wall. Our conversation had removed the walls between us, and Nestorius stood there in a moment of meditation. Then he turned towards me as though he were about to throw a heavy stone at me, and he was surprised later that I had not been surprised at what he said. I will never forget his face as he gently began to speak. 'I understand, Hypa, the significance of your studying theology in Alexandria and I know everything they taught you there, and everything they told you about Arius and his opinions, which they consider heresy. But I see the matter from another point of view, the Antioch point of view if you wish to describe it as such. I find that Arius was a man full of love, honesty and spiritual power. The events of his life, his asceticism and self-denial, all confirm that. As for what he said, I see it as merely an attempt to purge our religion from the beliefs of the ancient Egyptians about their gods, because your ancestors also believed in a holy trinity, made up of Isis, her son Horus and her husband Osiris, by whom she conceived without intercourse. Are we reviving the old religion? No, and it is not right to say of God that He is the third of three. God, Hypa, is One, unaccompanied in His divinity. Arius wanted our religion to worship God alone. But he sang a song which was unfamiliar in his time, recognizing the mystery of God's manifestation in Christ but not admitting Christ's divinity, recognizing Jesus the son of Mary, a gift to mankind, but not recognizing any divinity other than the one God.'

'But in that, father, he did not go beyond the belief of the ancient Egyptians, who finally concluded that God is one and superior to everything that is holy. Arius, nonetheless, did break with the consensus among the people of his time, and he said what he said, and the fires of heaven singed him.'

'The fires of Alexandria singed him, Hypa, and when the emperor recalled him from his long exile in the land of the Goths, to reconcile him under duress with the bishop of Alexandria, to ensure peace and tranquillity and gratify the great city, he was assassinated with poison.'

'He died from poison!' I cried that out, then I checked myself and looked around me. The only people passing nearby were two women wearing black, with veils of the kind worn by Jewish women. The women looked towards us when I shouted and one of them scowled, while the other smiled. Nestorius took no offence at my sudden outburst, and answered me softly and gravely. 'That's what I think most probable, because the day before he was expected to meet the emperor and the bishop of Alexandria, Arius and some others were out walking at noontime, when suddenly he had stomach pains, right out of the blue, and he turned aside to answer the call of nature. Much blood and pieces of his stomach and intestines spilled out of him, and he died a shocking death because he fell into the mess he had excreted. That was on a Saturday afternoon in the year 336.'

'And what happened after that, father?'

'Nothing. Bishop Alexander was delighted and went into seclusion to pray. Emperor Constantine was relieved at the death of Arius, whose followers and friends disowned him. All the bishops condemned him and renounced his opinions in a statement they submitted to the emperor.'

'The man was a lost cause.'

'And his opinions almost disappeared with him, especially after the bishops gathered in Antioch five years after his death, for the Council of the Dedication,[3] and drafted a statement in which they said with outrageous effrontery, "We have never been followers of Arius. How could we, as bishops, follow the words of a priest?" That's how Alexandria triumphed. Talking of Alexandria, Hypa, were you there when the philosopher Hypatia was killed?'

His question hit me in the gut like a fiery liquid, dispelling the gentle evening breezes which had started to blow. His unexpected question threw me back to a past which I had thought was forgotten. I was stunned, remembering suddenly the terrible event which drove me out of Alexandria to wander through the land of the Lord. At the time I kept my feelings under control but despite myself I could not hold back a few tears at the memory of Hypatia and her screams when she cried out for help. Nestorius sensed my distress and showed divine compassion. When he turned me gently towards him and gave my left shoulder a friendly shake with his right hand, I felt the urge to weep, but my shyness prevented me.

'Take it easy, Hypa. You're exhausted. We have spoken much today, and your company has delighted me. Here's our lodge nearby, so go back to your good and holy room to rest the night, and tomorrow I will await you in the early morning at the church door. We will pray and then have breakfast

3. The council which took place in Antioch in 341 on the occasion of the opening of the Golden Church.

40

together and you can tell me, if you want, what happened in Alexandria on that day. I'll see you tomorrow, God willing.'

I realized that day that Nestorius was indeed a priest with spiritual power, and a monk who deserved reverence. I saw in him my father who was snatched from me, my lost father, although Nestorius did not resemble him in appearance and was not old enough to be the father of someone my age, other than in the ecclesiastical sense of the word. On that day long ago, in the torrent of my confusion, I forgot to tell him that I wanted to see Bishop Theodore to check up on his health and to receive his blessing. I withdrew from this bewildering situation with a mumbled farewell. 'I'll be there in the morning, at the time of the third prayer. I'll wait for you, father, and I'll tell you everything if you will honour me with another visit to my humble room. I'll tell you what happened because I was there that day and I witnessed it from close by.'

I hurried back to take refuge in my loneliness. On my way back I prayed to the Lord that I would not find any patients awaiting me at my door, and my prayer was answered. I shut the door and did not light the lamp. I knelt on the ground in the darkness and said my prayers devoutly, hoping that I would calm down. But that night I tossed and turned without a moment's sleep, as happens whenever I remember Alexandria. My bed was like a bed of nails and as the dark night progressed I mingled copious tears with fervent prayers. 'Oh God, help me through Thy mysterious loving kindness, for my endless sufferings are unbearable. Save me through Thy grace, Father in heaven, hallowed be Thy name, from the agony of the memories that teem within me. Grant me, God, a new birth through which I may live without memory, or have mercy and take me unto Thyself, far from this world.'

That night I prayed mightily that His mercy might descend on me from heaven, but the Lord did not answer my prayers, and my Alexandrian memories swept me away like the waves of the sea.

The Capital of Salt and Cruelty

I well remember how, in my youth which is gone and never will return, I left Akhmim bound for Alexandria, inspired by great hopes. It was exactly midday and in the church they were preparing for the prayers of the sixth hour, which take place precisely at noon. I headed under the full sun to the east bank of the Nile, to the place where the sail boats tie up. It was a short distance but the quay was empty and the sun was fierce. In the afternoon sky blazed the July (Abib) sun, which knows no mercy. The ancients in their golden age believed that the sun was the manifestation of the power of the god Ra, who was the chief of their gods…their gods which have vanished, the memory of them dead along with those who invoked them.

At the quay I found shade under the solitary tree. It was as slender as me and its leaves hung down over the edge of a miserable canal that took its water from the Nile during the time of the summer flood. From my bag I took out the small icon from which I am never parted, an image of the Holy Virgin Mary, and I began to meditate on the details of her tranquil face. Should not the Lord have given me a mother as immaculate as the Virgin? I was about to drift off into a reverie, when I noticed the approach of a young man of about twenty years, followed by a monkey. The two of them came with leaps and bounds, as though animated by a single spirit. The young man looked towards me with a smile before embarking on the mission for which he had come, by which I mean climbing the tall palm tree nearby, which was loaded with dry dates no one had gathered in the winter. Some of the dates had fallen but others remained in place.

'These dates are full of sugar and taste delicious,' the young man told me, as though he knew me well, or perhaps because he wanted to tell me why he had come, as if he were asking my permission to climb the tree, which was not mine anyway. Or perhaps he was asking for a blessing because he thought well of me, or of the monk's habit I was wearing. He pointed upwards to the top of the tree, with his arm outstretched. The monkey went ahead and the two of them climbed the palm tree without great effort, as though they were walking along the ground. The monkey reached the top first and began to jump for joy from frond to frond and cluster to cluster of dates. The young man watched the monkey warily for a while, until he was sure that the top of the tree was free of snakes and scorpions, then continued to climb into the crown and began to shake the hanging clusters. After several minutes of a shower of dates they came down even faster than they went up. The young man picked out those dates which worms had not damaged and put hand-fuls of them into the fold of his pale jellaba. He came and threw some of the dates into my lap without saying a word. The man had a strange smile. He did not wait for me to give him a word of thanks or bless him with a prayer, but took his monkey on his shoulder and disappeared into the fields. At the time I thought God had sent this young man as a good omen, or that he was one of the angels of heaven who fill the earth and hurry from person to person without anyone knowing they are there. But I did not ask myself at the time how an angel could bring along a monkey.

Later in the day a boat tied up on its way to Lycopolis (Assiut), a town on the banks of the Nile two days to the north of Akhmim. The boat people were in a hurry and they approached me, asking if I wanted to sail with them, and I saw this as a sign from God inviting me to visit Assiut's holy site, the shrine on the mountain known as Qusqam, where the Virgin Mary stayed with the infant Jesus the Messiah when she brought him to Egypt to escape the oppression of the Romans. The boat owners soon set sail and the wind was favourable for sailing, and I reached Assiut at noon the fol-lowing day.

The city is very large and most of the inhabitants are Christian, with some pagans, but in general pleasant people. Their houses are spacious and attached to each other. At the time I thought it the biggest city in the world, but I had not yet been to Alexandria, or Jerusalem or Antioch. From Assiut I headed west to the place where at one time the holy family took refuge in the desolate mountains. I did not find much there but I did not regret visiting the place.

I climbed up to a place hidden away in the mountains and found a wretched church surrounded by some dilapidated buildings which I doubted went back to the time of the Holy Virgin. Some hermits were there, living a life of poverty in which I did not sense as much spirituality as I had hoped and expected. I felt melancholic and after two days I went back to Assiut with a group of other visitors, about a dozen of them. Halfway back, I was approached by an elegantly dressed man who, in spite of the heat, was wearing a cloak of fine black wool with a decorative border of shiny black silk. His appearance and his sly demeanour struck me as strange. He did not have a cross hanging around his long neck. When our eyes met he smiled and looked even slyer, and his eyes shone with intelligence. I was wary of him and slowed my pace. He walked slower too until he came level with me and prepared to speak. Despite myself I looked at him. His face was covered in white leprous spots which stood out the more for his brown complexion. In Greek, which people rarely use in that country, he said straight out: 'How did the Virgin come here in flight with her infant son, years after the death of the ruler they claim killed the Jewish children? And why did she go back to the dry yellow country after coming to Egypt's green valley?' He said this quietly and in a mischievous tone, then turned aside from the group's route back to Assiut, taking a path to the northeast, and slipped off into the fields through the scattered thickets of reeds until he disappeared from sight. Why am I telling you all these details?

I spent several confused weeks among the monasteries and churches of Assiut, then left the city for Alexandria on a river boat owned by some poor merchants originally from Heliopolis. They were good people but they never stopped taking strong drink and, when they were drunk, singing loud comic songs. When I embarked with them I was wearing the cassock of an Egyptian monk, which is now compulsory for all monks. Out of deference to my cassock, after agreeing to let me travel with them, the boat people refused to let me pay the fare. One of them, a Christian of course, said, 'For us, father, it's enough that you bring your blessings to our boat.' It was the first time any of them had called me 'father'.

For the days of the journey they mostly ate cheese, onions and salt fish, which I had never eaten, following the advice of my uncle who brought me up after my father's death. On the river trip I vowed to fast and for the whole eight days of the journey I had only dried dates and water, seasoned with my prayers. The day we reached the furthest point they wanted to travel down the Nile, the owner of the boat asked me where I was heading next, and when I told him he gave me some advice. 'Don't go into Alexandria in your monk's cassock because in that troubled town you don't know who you're going to meet first.' And he gave me some of his clothes.

In a sudden flash I realized that he spoke the truth and that our Father in Heaven wanted to convey this message to me through the voice of this man. With a heart full of affection and gratitude I wished them good fortune, then made my way northwest through green fields stretching as far as the eye could see. The flatness of the land and the broad vistas frightened me. There are no hills in the Nile Delta to restrict the view, just open plain, endless cropland and kindly people whose womenfolk go out with them to the fields. Near the town of Damanhour I found a group of peasants heading to Alexandria on their donkeys. I went along with them, dressed in a gown of the kind we wear in the south of the valley, where gowns are fuller at the sleeves and in the chest. I carefully folded up my monk's cassock and the distinctive cap we wear and put them at the bottom of my bag, under the books, with the old wooden cross between them.

In the group bound for Alexandria there were ten men, seven mules, three sheep and two women, one of them old. Their guide was a pompous man who never stopped making suggestive remarks, including the obscenities which pagans use. In a whisper he asked me why I was going to Alexandria and he laughed when I told him I was going in search of learning.

'In Alexandria there are nicer things than learning,' he said.

I did not ask him to explain but he volunteered to elaborate. He moved his head close to my ear, until I could smell the unpleasant smell of onion on his breath, and whispered, 'Alexandria is a city of whores and gold! Are you planning to stay there, southerner?'

'That depends on the will of the Lord.'

'Which lord would that be, cousin? In Alexandria there are many lords. The important thing is to have a relative there or you will suffer greatly,' he said.

'That depends on the will of the Lord whose glory is in heaven.'

'Ah, so you're Christian. So you have half the city, congratulations to you people of the tormented and crucified god.' He chuckled. 'You have half the world and there's nothing for me, the eloquent peasant, now that my old gods have grown old… Strange world!'

The midday heat grew fiercer as we walked hour after hour, and the pompous and loathsome guide never stopped talking. I asked a man who looked friendly and he told me in the Coptic dialect of the Delta that it was only two hours' walk to Alexandria. The closer we came the more the green receded and more and more patches of rock and sandy ground appeared, separating the fields one from another. The advance of brown around us troubled me, for brown is the colour of death, sterility, and the temples of the dying gods. Never before had I seen this dull brown spread across the face of the earth until it reached right to the horizon. The shouting of the guide, the eloquent peasant, compounded my unease as he hurried us on to our destination. 'If we reach the gates after sunset, you'll have only yourselves to blame!' he said.

I tried to calm him down gently but to no avail. I explained to him that the old woman who was with them was ill and it would be hard for her to travel faster than we were already going, but he was not convinced. The cropland had completely faded away around us as we progressed, and the colour brown prevailed, the colour of autumn and of sin. As the sun prepared to set, a green blob loomed in front of us and at first I thought it was the city of Alexandria and I let slip my conjecture. The pompous guide ridiculed me and shouted at me in derision. 'Alexandria green! Ha! No one colour can dominate the city of every colour.'

After an hour of walking I realized that the green blob was the swamps and woods which ring the city on the southern side, close to the shallow lakes and the canal which comes from the Canopic branch of the Nile. I also realized that we would have to trace a long circle to enter the city from the western side, through a gate they call the Moon Gate. The brown now came back, to cover the earth again after a light redness had tinged it at sunset. After an hour's walking the city of Alexandria appeared to us from afar like a dream. The eloquent peasant dug his heels into his donkey's belly and headed off. 'I'll catch the gates before sunset, so I can spend the night inside the city!' he shouted with disdain.

The priest of the big church in Akhmim had told me that Alexandria, from the time it was founded and for a long time after, did not allow Egyptians like us to stay the night inside the city. The situation changed with the passage of time and after our faith spread the city became open to all. I still remember the priest's face and the way he shook his head that day as he said, speaking in the Sa'idi dialect of Coptic: 'The day will come when we will not let pagans or Jews stay the night, neither in Alexandria nor in all the big cities. One day they will all live outside the walls and all the cities will be for the people of the Lord.'

I also knew that outside the walls of Alexandria there were poor people who had been living in wretched houses for decades, but when I arrived I was amazed at the number of tents which sheltered the descendants of those who were expelled every night and the profusion of miserable houses which the Egyptian peasants had built west of the city wall. When we arrived the travelling party dispersed around me without anyone saying a word and I found myself lost among hundreds of poor people, the sheep of the Lord, clamouring around the pots where their evening meal was cooking. Around their humble dwellings children were shouting out at the sight of their exhausted fathers coming home after a hard day's work. Surly guards were looking around among the throng, and there were monks with long beards, strikingly unkempt and smiling at no one.

The owner of the big tent, which rested on pillars of cheap brick, shouted at me, demanding that I pay for a night's lodging, and I quickly complied. Staying the night at the walls of Alexandria is expensive for strangers. In our country no one charges when they take in guests. If I had kept on my monk's cassock, I could have stayed in the clean church which I had just passed and from which I heard the loud voice of a man preaching in Greek. Of course, at the time, I did not think of changing my clothes. That would have aroused suspicion and could have caused me problems. I said to myself, 'Never mind. I'll go into the city as I once was – a poor man from the south of the valley, whose father fished from the Nile, keeping away from the crocodiles and the hippopotamuses. I am like the people who throng around me and my best protection is to mix in with the flock of the Lord and take refuge among them.'

I withdrew to a corner of the large tent, exhausted, and felt around in my bag for the letter I had brought from the Akhmim priest who had taken my monastic vows. The letter was addressed to the priest Yoannes the Libyan, who lived in the big church known as the Church of the Wheat Seed and also as the Church of St Mark, to place it under the patronage of St Mark the Apostle and the Evangelist, who preached the gospel in the city and was killed by its rulers. When I felt the letter of recommendation with the tips of my fingers, it reassured me a little.

I intended to spend days wandering around the city before going to the church, to see first everything I wanted to see and then to present myself to them and see what they wanted me to see. I thought I would learn much in Alexandria, as many had assured me, and this idea comforted me. I groped around inside my bag, brought out a handful of dry dates and started to chew them slowly, mindful that the Lord in His grace has granted us the pleasure of feeling sated after hunger.

A man nearby, shabby in appearance but with friendly eyes, smiled at me. I offered him some of the dates and he took them. Then he stuck his hand into his bag and brought out a piece of cheese to offer me. I declined but did not tell him I was fasting. He asked me where I came from and without thinking I said Naga Hammadi. His face lit up and he said, 'I'm originally from Ansina (Samalout). I was born there but I've lived here many years.'

The man shuffled towards me and began to tell me about his hometown, which lies in the heart of southern Egypt to the east of the Nile. He said he grew up in a village near a mountain called Bird Mountain, because birds come and land there every year and fill the air around. Then they suddenly leave after one of the birds sacrifices itself by putting its head in a hole at the foot of the mountain, and something unknown inside the hole wraps itself around the bird's head and does not let go until the bird's body has dried up and its feathers have fallen out. That is a sign for the rest of the birds to dive into the Nile and fly away at night, only to come back next year at the same time and repeat the cycle.

The man whispered to me that in his hometown there are many 'changelings', by which he meant old statues, including a strange statue of a man copulating with a woman. At the top of the mountain there is a church where monks live, called the Church of the Palm because when Jesus the Messiah passed by there during the Holy Family's journey to Egypt he left the impression of the palm of his hand on a stone which turned soft for him, as a miracle and as a lesson for those who came after. 'He also left the stick with which he brushed the flies off his sheep and goats,' he added. I said to the man, whose name I no longer remember, 'But Jesus the Messiah came to Egypt only as an infant.'

'What are you talking about, cousin?' he said. 'Jesus the Messiah lived his whole life and died in Egypt.'

I realized that the man knew nothing, or perhaps he knew something I did not know, or perhaps the two of us dreamt up what we thought we knew. I had no desire to continue talking with him so I told him I would like to go to sleep, then I covered my head with an old piece of cloth which the owner of the tent had given me and tried to sleep seated, as is my custom on dark nights, and most of my nights are dark.

Before sleep overtook me I started thinking about Bird Mountain and the church at the top of the mountain. I should have passed by this town on my way so I could see the wonders that are there. We miss many things along the way. Egypt's towns are full of wonders and miracles because they are full of believers. That night I could not sleep for the succession of sights I had passed on my journey and through my whole life: the young man and the monkey who climbed the palm tree before my eyes as though rushing to reach the dates; the church as small as a room where I spent the night on the banks of the Nile in Assiut, to which I was taken by a deacon who came from a town called Qous; sailing down the river on the boat of the poor merchants, and their ceaseless clamour; the tearful eyes of the deacon from Qous as he bade me farewell after the three nights I spent in the room attached to the little church which he served; my mother's startled appearance when I told her I knew she had betrayed my father to her relatives, the ignorant Christians, and I ran away from her and she could not catch up with me and after that day I never saw her again; the time I wept when I found out she had married one of those relatives who killed my father; the image of our house from which I fled; abandoning my mother after I ran away and she remarried; the day I threw myself into the arms of my uncle who came looking for me and whom I saw in the guise of the Saviour; going to the big school in Naga Hammadi when I was ten years old; my uncle's wife, a woman of Nubian origin, and the smell of the delicious food she cooked for us at dusk.

I had almost fallen asleep, but I woke up when a stout priest with a stentorian voice came into the tent. He did not even wait till he reached the centre of the large tent, but began shouting out his sermon as soon as he came in on us: 'I bless you, children of God, in the name of Jesus Christ, God the Lord, the Saviour,' he said. 'I grant you heavenly blessings, flock of the Lord, come close to Jesus Christ, as He is close to you. The Lord loves you, so love Him. Pray to Him before you sleep and when you awake. Sleep in the arms of His mercy. Love is the spirit of God, so love your brothers and your children, and love your enemies.'

Nearby a peasant of malign appearance whispered to those around him, with the sarcasm of a lost sheep, 'And does his master Cyril love his brothers the Jews?' Those around him stifled their laughter, and one of them said, 'Of course, he loves them so much he kills them and throws them outside the city walls.' The priest with the stentorian voice did not turn towards them. Perhaps he did not hear them, or heard only the words he had memorized and repeated to them each night. He wrapped up his noisy sermon, which had wrenched me away from my secret memories, with these words: 'Children of God, the house of the Lord is open to you. Come to church on Sunday morning and obtain his blessing. Turn to your Lord, so He will turn to you. Join the apostles, the saints and the martyrs.'

After spewing this mouthful at us the priest left haughtily, as though he had preached the Sermon on the Mount, followed by the fat and silent soldier who had come in behind him. The people in the tent responded with murmurs and suppressed laughter, then busied themselves with idle chat as they passed around pieces of coarse bread, salty cheese and salted fish. The smell of onion filled the tent. I stretched out in my spot near the tent door, where the smell was less intense, and succumbed to a flood of dreams.

I had many visions that night, none of them reassuring. I slept restlessly until awoken at dawn by the clamour of those sleeping around me. I mean their loud snoring, as well as the noise of those around the tent – the crying of an infant, the shouts of a man selling curdled milk and the chirping of the sparrows. I wished I could go back to sleep because I had a long day before me and did not know when it would start or end. In front of me lay an awesome world, concealed from me behind the gate of the great city. But I could not go back to sleep, so I made do with closing my eyes until the light had covered the ground and God's sun shone on the righteous and the wicked, as it is written.

I left the tent to look for some water to wipe my face, but could not find any. The people were busy with the start of another hard day in their lives. At their usual early hour they headed to the city gate. I was amazed to find that the city gate was not closed at night. In fact it was never closed, and the bottom part of each door was buried in sand which had turned to rock and salty rust, showing that it had not been opened for many years. So why did these people sleep outside the gate?

The river of poor people streaming towards the gate swept me along. They were walking with heavy steps, not rushing. I walked along with them, succumbing to the current in this river of poor people as it submitted to the will of the Lord. The faces of those going in were sallow, their clothes old but clean, and they exuded a mysterious euphoria that belied their appearance. In a flash I realized that all of them, Christians and pagans, were the children of the Lord.

The guards were at the gates, carefully examining those going in. They did not stop anyone, even if their alert posture suggested they were about to do so. The city wall was high, higher than any wall I had ever seen. Other guards stood on top, looking lazily towards us. The gate in the wall was wide enough to take many at a time. In the open gate there was a smaller door, wide enough for one person. The rust on the edges of it showed that it too had not been opened for many years. I do not recall seeing a single smile the day I passed through the Moon Gate.

Alexandria is amazing, vast in extent. Its streets easily absorbed the river of people coming in, as though they were ants walking along a crack in a great rock. The streets were paved with small grey stones and there were pavements on the sides of most streets. That was when I understood the meaning of the word 'pavement', which the priest from Damietta, my teacher in Naga Hammadi, used to use in his speech. The streets are clean, as though the city were a newlywed who washes every night and wakes up cheerful. The labourers wash it every night and sleep outside the walls. On that early morning I did not see many of the city's inhabitants. In my first country, they would say the Alexandrians are not like us, they like to stay up late and do not get up early.

The magnificence of the Alexandria houses and churches did not surprise me, because in Egypt I had seen old temples which were much more splendid than these buildings, but what did surprise me around the city was the tidiness and the elegance – the roads, the walls, the house fronts, the windows, the little gardens at the entrances, the balconies edged with flowers and decorative plants. The whole city was carefully constructed and elegant, although this ubiquitous beauty did not make me feel that Alexandria was the city of God Almighty, as they call it. I thought it more like the city of Man.

'Hey southerner, this is the way to the stadium. Are you going there? Or to the Egyptians' quarter?'

'No, uncle,' I said. 'I'm going to the sea.'

'The sea is everywhere. Go back where you came from, then head left, cross the Canopian Way and keep walking north. Keep the Boucalia church on your left and walk till you find the sea. In fact the sea will find you.'

I thanked the volunteer guide, the guard of a house, and went off as he described. And why didn't he leave me to wander around as I wanted and as the Lord wanted for me, so that I could see things that I did not expect? The Boucalia church which he mentioned I would see some months after that. It is said the remains of St Mark the Apostle are preserved in it. As for that day, on my way I crossed a small stone bridge over a freshwater canal which flows from the south of the city to the north and then debouches into the sea. I did not follow the course of the canal but preferred to walk east along the Canopian Way, the large street which cuts the city in two halves. The northern half is where the rich live, while the poor live in the south, though the poor of Alexandria are richer than the rich in my native country.

When the sun had ascended to its zenith, life crept into the side streets. The number of people was greater than I had surmised. I passed one group of churchmen going north, surrounded by workmen carrying pickaxes and reciting after them: 'In the name of Jesus the true God, we will demolish the houses of the idols and build a new house for the Lord.' The three phrases rhymed in Greek, with a rhythm different from the Syriac text, but Alexandrians do not speak Syriac.

I hurried away from them until the large church appeared on the left. I did not go their way but walked east with the Canopian Way, which was wide and elegant and extended all the way from the Moon Gate, where I entered, to the Sun Gate in the east of the city. Behind it stretched the houses of the Jews which I passed the day I left Alexandria three years later.

The Canopian Way is a world in itself, fully paved and with elegant houses on both sides. Into it flow other smaller streets which run south and north. Everything around me that day was amazing, except for that wretched statue which stands in the middle of the road. I found out a few weeks later that it was a statue of a god they call Serapis, and the former bishop of Alexandria,

Theophilus, had preserved it from the Serapaeum temple after he brought the temple down on the heads of the pagans who had sought refuge inside. The bishop had set up the wretched statue in the middle of the road to intimidate the pagans by reminding them of the fate of their god, and to immortalize his triumph over them by humiliating their god forever. The great temple was destroyed in the year I was born, I mean the year 117 of the Martyrs, or the year 391 of the glorious birth. For thirteen years the statue stood as an effective witness to the abject state of an extinct paganism. It was moving to see it, covered in the droppings of sea birds and surrounded with rubbish on all sides. It seemed to be laughing, its feet planted in the paving stones of the street, with no plinth on which to stand.

I did not look too closely at the statue, so as not to attract the attention of the Christians and pagans passing around me. Nobody should notice me, neither these nor those, nor even the Jews who endured the hatred of both groups in the city. The pagans hate them for their avarice and the Christians detest them for betraying the Saviour and handing him over to the Romans to be crucified. I wonder, was he really crucified?

In a square halfway along the long street, my train of thought and the rhythm of my pace were broken by the voice of a crier shouting out in Greek from the seat of his mule. 'Governor Orestes invites scholars and students to a lecture by the Savante of the Ages on Sunday morning at the Great Theatre.' I was surprised when I established that he really was saying the Savante of the Ages. Could a woman scholar gain such prestige? At first I doubted I had understood the phrase correctly, although the different female and male forms of the words in Greek leave no room for ambiguity. Then I doubted the sanity of the crier, although he looked serious to me, and being serious, so I was taught in Akhmim, is the opposite of insanity.

My doubts drove me to abandon my caution. I caught up with the crier and asked his young servant, who looked at me in astonishment and did not answer me. The crier had stopped the mule by squeezing his legs against her belly and he reached into his bag to take out a long-necked white earthenware bottle from which he drank a mouthful. I took the chance to ask him, 'Uncle, where will the lecture be?'

'What are lectures to you, peasant? Or perhaps you're after the sweets the governor gives out there?'

'I don't eat sweets,' I said. 'I only want to know who this Savante of the Ages is.'

'A peasant who doesn't eat sweets, speaks good Greek and doesn't know Hypatia. That, by Serapis, is amazing,' he said.

The crier left me, moved on scornfully and started to shout out the same phrase again: 'Governor Orestes invites scholars and students...' He disappeared down a side street, leaving me puzzled as I thought about the woman who might be the Savante of the Ages.

After this intellectual detour I reverted to the objective from which I had been distracted, that is to reach the sea. I kept walking east along the Canopian Way until I met a large street heading north. I had passed the place which the volunteer guide, the house guard, had described to me, but I hurried on in the hope that I would reach my destination, or make a second attempt. The further north I walked, the more I felt the sea. Little by little, the surface in the side streets grew more sandy and the houses were more scattered. The stone of the walls was eroded and pale, and I later learnt that this was an effect of the sea air close by.

The sea had a strong smell and as the sound of the waves started to caress my ears a strange feeling enveloped me. When the sea appeared between the houses, I quickened my pace until I reached the wide sandy area which extended beyond the houses. One of the houses was as big as a palace, the last of the houses with handsome walls. At the big gate an elderly guard was sitting, an emaciated sheep lying at his feet. I walked past them without noticing them, and the guard too did not look towards me. It was the sheep that looked.

When I saw the sea, enclosed by the sandy spit which jutted into it, I walked along until I came close to a rocky patch in the middle of the spit, then followed a sandy path which wound between the rocks. The Alexandria rocks are rough and ragged, with sharp edges. They are not like the smooth oval rocks which the Nile brings rolling down from heaven and which come to rest on its banks in my native country. That day the sea seemed to have no banks, although it had looked small to us in the maps in the geography book. I walked away from the rocks until I reached a wide sandy area and the sea surrounded me on three sides. Close to where the foam of the waves melted away I threw down my bag, which had grown heavier and heavier the longer I carried it. I stepped forward eagerly until the seawater touched my feet. The vastness of the sea frightened me and I almost fainted in terror at how far away the water stretched. I extended my arms as though I were about to take off and filled my lungs with the wind blowing across the waves. I was enchanted by the sensation of the sea around my ankles and the gentle tumbling of the waves as they broke at my feet.

The sea. It is the great water from which existence begins. Beyond this sea lie other lands, and beyond those a greater sea which surrounds the world. I can remember now that moment twenty years ago. I can almost feel the spray touch my face and the awe that stopped me in my tracks on the shoreline, where I stood stiff as an ancient statue.

The smell of the sea was unfamiliar and the water salty. I longed to plunge into this vast ocean, as I used to swim in the Nile in the days of my childhood. I knew from books there were no crocodiles in this sea, nor hippopotamuses, and no iguanas live on the banks of it, but I was wary of the dangers which this great sea might be hiding.

I looked in all directions and saw no one in the distance. I dipped my hands into the sea and rinsed my face in the salty water, and my anxiety abated. I stepped forward hesitantly until the water reached my knees. I felt another sensation which I had not known before: there is no mud or ooze at the bottom of the sea, just the expanse of sand with the waves above, rolling in one after another. The waves were buffeting me and stimulating senses which I had forgotten. I closed my eyes, yielding to the slapping of the waves, which was gentle and exciting. One wave almost knocked me over and I laughed out loud in a way I had not heard myself laugh for many years, and would not hear for many years to come. I hurried back to the shoreline, put my bag next to a rock protruding from the sand, threw my wretched gown on top of it and rushed into the water. My God, my heart beat in ecstasy at that moment.

Swimming in the sea is easy. The water lifts you up and the current does not pull you as the Nile would do in the days of my childhood. The water of the Nile is fresh and the bottom is muddy, but this sea is salty and you can see right to the sandy bed. I was standing with the water up to my chest and touching my shoulders, yet I could still see my feet, the sand and the pieces of rock resting on the bottom. If you go into the Nile you disturb the mud at the bottom and the water gets murky, and the murk could hide crocodiles. But the sea has no dangers to threaten swimmers and spoil the pleasure of returning for a while to the primal water from which the world began.

Because the surface of the water buoyed me up without great effort on my part, I was able to look around at the sky and the horizon around me. Towards the west I saw big ships far off, and to the east seagulls were flying along the beach. The seagulls were plentiful and it was wonderful to see them fly. I wonder if these are the birds that every year visit the Bird Mountain which the man in the tent told me about.

On the surface of the water I was full of glee. On the glistening surface of the water tremors of inner warmth dispelled the chill within me and stilled the trembling in my limbs. When the sea lifted me up, I felt like a baby emerging from an enormous womb. Strange sensations assailed me. I had an urge to touch and be touched and I felt the tingle of desire. Although I had never in my life known a woman, and had never intended to do so, yet at that moment I thought of that pleasure and it came to my mind that the sea is a playful woman who gives pleasure to men who swim in her, without making them answerable for any sin. The sea is a mercy from God to the deprived, glory be to You, most merciful of the merciful.

I abandoned myself to the clear water, lying on my back on the surface and stretching my arms out wide. I used to do that in my youth on the surface of the Nile, then I came to do it in my room when I was alone, and it gave a sense of serenity. I would lie outstretched on the ground, spread my arms and float into heavens of my imagining. But when I did that in the sea of Alexandria, it was different. The seawater buoyed me more than the Nile water did. I was lighter and the sunlight sparkled where my floating body met the surface of the waves. The light bounced off my naked body, as the rays crisscrossed over my brown skin and bathed it in a strange radiance. It was the first time I had thought my body beautiful and my brownness pleasing. Unlike the river, the sea reveals the wonders of divine creation in the universe and in our bodies.

On the surface of the water I recalled with delight how I would lie on the hill on which stands the house where I was born, where the doves would land around me. When the sun had declined from the high point of the sky towards the horizon, I became aware of pangs of hunger. The beach seemed a long way off and near my clothes I noticed someone waving to me with their arms. I felt a sudden alarm and apprehension. My arms and legs sprang into action to take me back quickly to my clothes. But after moments which seemed an age I realized that I was not making progress towards the beach. I began to swim faster but I moved no closer to my goal. Suddenly I was exhausted and my right arm almost froze rigid. I let my body float to have a rest for a while but I panicked when I realized the water was pulling me out to the open sea. I resumed swimming, exhausted, but the pull of the sea was stronger than the constant strokes of my panicked arms. That's when I understood that the sea is treacherous.

The person standing on the beach gave up waving at me and disappeared from sight when the waves rose between us. I was completely exhausted and the sea was relentless. When I was sure I was drowning I shouted out despite myself. Then I suppressed my desire to shout to save what strength I had left for the swim back. The pain in my left arm was excruciating but I kept paddling with it. To myself I chanted, 'Jesus Christ, stay with me now and I will vow all my life to You.' I swam faster and faster, and suffered greatly for the predicament I had brought upon myself. After a long struggle to overcome the current dragging me out, I found that my strokes were pulling me towards the beach. I was gasping for air but delighted to survive. When I reached the point near the beach where the waves break and die away my foot touched the ground and I thanked the Lord with a troubled heart.

I stumbled towards my bag and when I found no one else on the sandy beach I thought for a moment the person who waved at me, warning me of the danger of drowning, was not human, but rather an angel sent by God from heaven to save me from wandering into danger. I said to myself that our Father in heaven is merciful to us and the secrets of his creation never end, and that after this I would never go close to the sea again.

A gentle laugh rang out from the direction of the nearby rocks and I stood up from where I was lying on my back. I looked towards the sound in alarm and saw a white woman in Alexandrian dress, with bare breasts and arms. The woman staggered forward, as though she too had just survived drowning in some capricious sea.

'You're a proficient swimmer, and lucky too,' she said.

'Who are you, my lady?'

'My lady!' She laughed. 'I'm Octavia, the servant of the Sicilian gentleman, the silk merchant,' she said.

I looked at her askance, as though I were dreaming or had died drowning and come back to life in another age. I looked around me: the seagulls were still flying and the houses in the distance were still in their place, as they had been. A cold breeze brushed me and I came to my senses. What had brought to this place this servant who did not look like other servants? I could think of no answer, so I asked her in a stammer and she replied without hesitation.

'Poseidon sent me, the god of the sea who saved you. I am one of his mermaids.'

She laughed again. 'Please, don't joke with me.'

'Don't scowl, southerner. I will tell you everything.'

She said her name was Octavia and she came to this place most days when her master was away on business and had taken all his other servants with him, and the only person left with her in the house was the guard sitting at the gate. She liked to come here, so she said, to tell her cares to the sea, because it kept secrets. Looking towards the waves, she told me people did not frequent this beach because it was so rocky and the currents so dangerous near the coast.

'Ah, now I know what happened to me. But how did you know I was a southerner.'

'From your accent. I also know you are hungry now, from being in the sea so long. Come and have something to eat.'

At the time I did not know how to answer her. I was dying of hunger, and embarrassment. She kindly spared me my blushes, addressing me with a mixture of firmness and coquettishness of a kind I had never experienced.

'Bring your bag and come,' she said.

She walked towards a large crevice between the rocks and I stood where I was, paralysed and enchanted, watching from nearby the flirtatious way she walked. She was in her forties, or her thirties, I don't know. Her body tended a little towards the plump side, and very much towards the soft, and she swayed as she walked, like a trail of incense smoke. I wonder if that day she planned to seduce me, or perhaps that is the way women are in Alexandria.

I shall stop writing now, for the memories are teeming inside me. My head and my hand are heavy. I shall make do with what I have recorded tonight and resume writing in the morning, if I wake up. Anyway this piece of parchment is full up and tomorrow I will need a new piece on which to record another endless whirl of memories.

Octavia's Enticements (1)

I have long loved the things which take place only inside me. It comforts me to weave events in my imagination and live the details of them for a moment in time and then bring them to an end when I choose. This has been my way of protecting myself from temptation to sin, and staying safe. But what happened on the rocky sandy beach in eastern Alexandria was different. It was real, and it troubled me for a long time to come.

The air turned cold when I stepped out of the sea after surviving the treacherous currents, and I was alone with the woman called Octavia. I was not in charge of events. She organized everything because, as she told me on the third day, she was expecting the fulfilment of a prophecy which an old woman priest at the demolished temple had foretold for her. I will tell the story of what happened between us.

When Octavia left me with my clothes and walked flirtatiously towards the rocky crevice, I stood paralysed, with my eyes fixed on her. Before her firm and shapely buttocks disappeared between the rocks she looked towards me with a look that made my head turn, and pointed with her left hand to below my stomach. 'Are you going to stay standing like that forever,' she said. 'Put on your gown to hide the state you are in and follow me quickly.'

I panicked when I noticed that my little devil was erect under my pants, which were soaked in salty water. I quickly turned towards my bag and grabbed my gown from on top of it, and threw it on. I picked up my bag and walked to the stony cave nearby into which she had vanished before my astounded eyes. I wanted to apologize to her for everything and thank her, then ask leave of her and walk away, dragging my failure and my indecency behind me like a tail.

I stood in front of her, embarrassed, at the entrance to the small rocky cave where she was sitting in the middle. She was taking things out of a small box of the type that peasants make for their masters out of strips of palm branch. From where I was, and from the way she was sitting, I could see the firmness of her breasts. Before that I had seen the breasts of women suckling their babies but what I saw that day was different. God made the breasts of women for them to suckle, so for what other reason did he create these breasts?

Octavia was busy with what she was doing. She spread a large cloth on the ground and carefully put at the four corners pieces of the marine flint which was scattered around the surface of the cave. Then she started to arrange the food on the cloth: boiled eggs, loaves of white bread, white cheese, another cheese that was even whiter, water or wine in a white earthenware bottle. Everything on the big white cloth was white, and her diaphanous dress was white too. Her ample breasts, white. Her skin, everything, white. I was quite astonished.

'Sit here,' she said.

I sat down submissively, bewitched. I yielded to her and she induced in me a pleasant torpor. She did what no one had ever done to me before, even in my childhood, or has done since. She began to put food in my mouth and smiled at me until I swallowed each piece, then put in the next. I resisted at first, but then I began to enjoy it and I ate from her hand happily, like an infant at the breast.

I was so full I thought I could never be hungry again. When I closed my lips tight to decline the last morsel, she brought it back to my mouth until I opened it. Her right hand reached out gently for the bottle, and with charming tenderness she stretched out her left hand towards my left shoulder and pulled me down gently towards her breasts.

I was shocked and I shouted at her in alarm, 'What are you doing?'

'I'll give you a drink of the sweetest Alexandrian wine, my way,' she said.

Her way was that I rest my right cheek on her left breast, until half my face was flat against the softness of her ample breasts. I resisted her a little and then gave in. Close to her I did not sense any danger of sin, but rather I felt that I was diving into her and forgetting everything else. When she put her left arm around my shoulders I felt she had enfolded me for ever and that my separate existence had ebbed away until it vanished in her warm embrace. With her right palm she started to bring the bottle to my lips and tease my mouth with the mouth of the bottle. Then she poured into me sips of her heavenly wine. I had never tasted the equal of this wine and since those days of mine with Octavia I have not tasted any wine at all. When I had drunk my fill, I shut my eyes. I felt a drowsiness permeate my senses, taking me up to seventh heaven. I did not open my eyes until I heard her say, 'Drink some more. Wine is good for you, my love.'

'"Your love", how can you say that?'

'Don't ask, and don't argue with mermaids. Shut your eyes so you feel me more,' she said.

The sun was preparing to set, and the silence around us was total, except for the sound of the waves. I shut my eyes in spite of myself and could not resist her overwhelming Alexandrian presence. It seemed to me that she was right, and when I shut my eyes on her breasts, I did feel her more, and when she ran her right hand gently across my neck, I went into a trance. She began to caress my shoulder blades and run her fingertips over my hard bony chest. I felt her left hand kneading my flesh and the aromatic breath of her sighs brushed my face. Her right hand found its way into my pants, which were still soaked with salty water and semen that had leaked out. Her hand was plunging down, invading my terrain, and I surrendered completely, from the tips of my toes to the parts of me that were huddled in her embrace. When the palm of her hand touched my right knee and she pulled me force-fully towards her, I lost control completely. I was Adam when he was about to leave the Garden of Eden because he was about to enter Paradise and eat again from the tree. Driven by this forbidden lust, replete with magical allure, I was about to take her right then and there.

'Easy, my love. Your body is wet with seawater. Your body, my love, is firm as a tree in autumn. How I love how that tree is firm!'

At that time I was not myself. I felt as though the firmament above had stopped turning and the Nile far away had ceased to flow, and there were no humans left on the face of the earth and the angels had vanished from heaven. I ejaculated inadvertently, and she laughed. I wanted to wrap my arms around her but she resisted. Coquettishly she pushed my hand off her shoulder, then pulled it towards her mouth and kissed the tips of my fingers. She prolonged the kiss, and when I felt her tongue touch the fingertips, I came close to fainting.

'The sun has set, my love. It will turn cold. Come to the house. It's nearby and no one is there but the goodly doorman.'

I sat up straight, and she nimbly gathered off the ground everything she had unloaded from her basket – the white cloth, the empty wine bottle, and the silver bracelets she had taken off while she was putting food in my mouth. When she stood up like a spreading holm oak, and I like a stiff palm, she explained to me in a whisper (though there was no need to whisper, since we were alone) that I should follow close behind her and she would lure the house guard away from the gate.

I walked not too far behind her and saw her say something to the elderly guard. Then the man disappeared from sight behind the silent houses, followed by his emaciated sheep, which had looked towards me in the same way as dogs look. I stepped forward towards the big house and she was waiting for me with a smile at the gate. The guard's room was attached to the outer wall and behind the wall there was a large garden and then in the centre an elegant two-storey building raised on sturdy pillars. She quietly shut behind us the gate of the neat garden, full of colourful bushes and flowers which in the light of the sunset took on a pink hue that enhanced their splendour. I looked around, wondering to myself: 'Could Paradise be more beautiful than this place?'

It was like a wonderful dream from which I did not want to awake. Octavia opened the house door with a brass key which she took out of the light palmwood box and gestured to me to enter. Kingdom of heaven!

In a whisper I said to her, 'What's all this luxury?'

She smiled and took my arm to her bosom. She clutched my hand with one of hers and with the other she picked up a lamp which gave light without smoke. On our way from the vast hall to the upper floor I saw beauty all around me. As Octavia walked along with her lamp my eyes would fall upon a niche of decorative marble or an extraordinary statue of one of the pagans' false gods, or fine silk coverings skilfully embroidered. The stairway linking the two floors was all of white marble and each step was carved with a different design, with decorative touches using coloured marble inlaid into the white. Each step had its own motifs, different from those of the other steps. How much money and time, effort, artistry and craftsmanship went into making this stairway! Even the remains of the amazing temples spread along the Nile valley, which the long-living ancients built over many years,[4] do not show such precision or craftsmanship. I asked myself at the time, 'Will our religion give to future generations beauty such as that which the pagan times have offered us?' This question continues to nag me after all these years and remains without an answer. Oh Octavia, oh the memory of your enticements, and your time which is passed.

She lit another wick. Its light, and her light, shone out at the head of the stairway. I looked behind me and on the floor of the hall below I noticed an image drawn in mosaic tiles. That night I could not make out the details but in the morning I discovered it was the picture of a dog. I was surprised and Octavia explained to me what was behind it: 'This sad dog, depicted in a large circle out of small pieces of marble, with a spilt bowl of milk next to it, was a dog that belonged to the Sicilian master, who wanted to immortalize his faithful dog when the animal was dying of some disease. So he commissioned skilful artists to depict it on the hall on the ground floor in front of the staircase, so he would see it every day when he came down the stairs from the upper floor.'

On the upper floor of the house there was the bedroom and when I saw

4. It was widely believed in early times that the ancient Egyptians lived long lives, and so were able to build pyramids and enormous temples. The Jews and early Christians saw confirmation of that in the references in the Old Testament to people living hundreds of years and some of them close to 1,000 years. The truth is that the average lifespan in ancient Egypt was only about thirty-six years. (Translator's Note)

it, I asked Octavia: 'If this is the merchant's bedroom, then what would a king's bedroom be like?' She answered to the effect that her master was obscenely rich and I could spend the night in his bed if I wished. Naturally I declined.

At the time my mind was preoccupied with this Sicilian merchant, about whom I learnt from her that he was not fully Sicilian and that it was his father who moved from Sicily to Alexandria in his youth with his family. At first I thought he must be deranged, even if he was rich and loved the arts and was loyal to his dead dog. He was a strange case, this man, commemorating his wife, who had died years before his dead dog, with only a single statue in his vast bedroom, while he immortalized his sad-looking dog with this extraordinary mosaic. The next day Octavia told me that the owner of the house wept for months when he walked over the dog depicted on the floor. He wept for months for a dog! I puzzled at the strangeness of this new world and then I remembered my native country, where the dogs are pitiful, along with the people.

I spent three nights in succession with Octavia on the roof of the house, and no one else was aware of us. I decided nothing. From the first night on, it was she who took me from the upper floor of the house to the place where she lived in the rooms above. She took me up to the heights with confident steps. After the big staircase, we climbed another small stairway, which took us to her spacious and charming room, carefully constructed on the roof of the house. Around it the roof was paved with marble tiles, surrounded by an elegant wall. Around the edge of the roof stood short columns in the shape of graceful naked women, carrying between them a long marble table carved to depict various fruits. In the equally spaced gaps between the naked statues the sea was visible, and the sky floating above the sea. I wanted to move closer to the wall to see the magnificent view from there, but Octavia warned me that if I did so I might be spotted by the guard, who was unaware of my presence.

When we went into her room, Octavia lit a metal lantern which beamed its light around the room, and with an unexpected kiss she lit a flame inside me too. Until then I had known the word 'kiss' without understanding what it meant. She hugged me and told me softly that she could smell on me the scent of the sea she loved. Then she asked me to wait a moment and tottered over to the wall. She called the guard and told him something I could not make out, then came back smiling and reassured, to take me into the bathroom next to her room. It was a small room with a marble tub in the middle, similar to the grey granite sarcophaguses common in the caves in my native country, except that this tub was of white marble, had short legs and was carved on the sides with pictures of wrestlers.

With a laugh she pushed me towards the marble tub. I stepped towards it timorously. With her hands she lifted my gown and I did not stop her, then she sat me naked in the middle of the tub and started to pour the sweet water around my trembling body. I yielded to her, enchanted by everything around me. She poured an aromatic oil into the tub from a bottle on a nearby shelf, then took some water in her cupped hands and began to scrub my hair. She left me to finish off washing and when I had finished I stepped out of the marble tub, taking care not to slip, but heedless of falling submissively into the chasm which I was approaching. I put on the short loose gown which Octavia had given me when I went in.

When I came out I found her in another dress, not the white one she had been wearing. In the moonlight the new dress seemed even whiter and more revealing. At the bathroom door she clung to me, embraced me at length with a love untainted by lust. She sighed and my chest touched the warmth of her bosom. Then she let go of me to spread a carpet on the marble surface of the roof, a carpet neither eastern nor western, unlike any carpet I have seen before or after. It was more highly decorated than other carpets, and larger, softer to the touch and with finer colours. Its embroidered edges were the limits of our world throughout the night, until the rays of the morning sun dislodged us from it.

Octavia brought from her room everything we might need – a jug of water, a silver bowl of fruit, two pillows and a blanket of soft coloured wool. Her fragrance enveloped me when she sat close by me, whispering how important it was that we should lower our voices so that the guard would not hear us, the guard on duty with his sheep outside the wall. Then she stretched out comfortably on her back, smiling at the faraway moon. I almost overcame my usual hesitation and stretched out my hand to touch her breasts, but she asked me to be patient and brought the bowl of fruits closer to me. The fruits were of a kind unfamiliar to me and I had never tasted anything so delicious. She asked me in a whisper about the fruit in my country. 'Limes, doum fruit and dates,' I answered with a subdued laugh.

I moved closer to her without touching. She lay on her back again and had me stretch out next to her. The stars were like the stars in my home country, and the heavens like the heavens that were there, but the Earth was different, and I was different.

With her soft fingers she started to play with the tips of my fingers, and when I looked towards her I saw a tear run down from the corner of her eye. Before it reached her ear I wiped the tear away with the fingers of my left hand, and asked her, 'Why are you crying now?'

'That's a long story,' she answered tersely. Then she wiped the rest of her tears from her eyes and leant over towards me. She was resting her head on her left arm and pinning me down with her right arm draped across my chest. She wanted, as she said, to look at me at length because she had waited a long time for me. I did not understand what she meant and when I asked, she said, 'I'll tell you everything tomorrow morning. But for now let me see you shine like a dream by the light of the moon.'

'I don't understand a thing. What do you want of me?' I asked.

'It's not important that you understand now. What matters is that you feel! Tell me, my love, how old are you?'

'Twenty-three or twenty-four,' I said.

'I thought we were the same age. So I'm five years older than you, but anyway you are taller than me and more beautiful. Come to me.'

With the palm of her right hand, which was lying on my chest, she turned my face towards her, leant towards me and gave me a silken kiss. She was fulfilling her wish, without allowing me to fulfil mine. I was thoroughly aroused and her seductive charms had lit a fire within me. I suppressed my desire for her until it subsided, and I decided to stay calm because I felt a certain anxiety creep up on me. She asked me if I thought her beautiful, and impetuously I said she was the most beautiful of women.

'And have you known many women?'

'No, you are the first woman to touch me. I mean, you are the most beautiful woman I have ever seen in my life. Believe me.'

'I'll never ever believe you. Come on, tell me about the women in your faraway southern country.'

'They are tough like me, and sad. You are very different, prettier and gentler. You are an exception among women.'

'Ah, you are so eloquent,' she said.

Her phrase encouraged me and I sat up straight a little to face her and tell her with pride that I knew by heart the poetry of Homer and Pindar, and that I had read all the works of Aeschylus and Sophocles.

'You are well educated. Have you come to Alexandria looking for work?' she asked.

'No, I've come to finish my medical studies,' I answered.

The word 'medical' had a magical effect on her. She raised her eyebrows and her face beamed with a smile that showed her sparkling teeth. The light of the moon enhanced their whiteness and their sparkle. She bent her face – in fact her whole body – towards me and pushed me flat on my back again, throwing herself at me passionately. Until then I had thought that when a man is alone with a woman he mounts her, but what happened then is that she mounted me. I cannot write down the rest of what happened between us on that first night, our night. It was full of the forbidden pleasures which brought Adam out of Paradise. I wonder, did God expel Adam from Paradise because he disobeyed His order, or because, when he discovered secretly Eve's femininity, he understand his own masculinity and how he was different from God, although God had created him in His image.

In the morning the sun disturbed us and forced us into her room. In the room I learnt from her that she was the widow of a poor man who used to work with her in this fine house. She objected strongly to my calling her house a palace. Sadly and gently she said: 'You haven't seen the palaces there were in the Brucheum.' She meant the royal quarter of Alexandria. My imagination ran riot thinking how they might be, these palaces which I had not seen, and would never see. At the time I was sitting on her bed and she was on top of me again. She again asked me how old I was, and when I said twenty-three she quickly replied that even if she was five years older than me what mattered was not the age difference between us. She said with passion that women who love men younger than them make them the happiest of men and that she would make me the happiest of the happiest.

Stupidly, with intent to tease her, I said that Cleopatra, when she fell in love with Mark Antony, did not make him a happy man. She turned him into a man who killed himself, defeated, disowned by his family and friends, and divorced from his wife who was the mother of his children. Looking deep into her startled eyes, I said, 'His wife was called Octavia, like you, and she was the sister of the ruler of Rome, Octavian, his old friend whom he turned against, and they became enemies after they had been like brothers.'

She interrupted me, her cheeks flushed in anger. 'Enough of those old stories and believe what I say. I will make you the happiest man in the world,' she said.

'How? I mean why?'

'You are full of questions. I'm going to leave you for a moment now. Stay here and I'll tell you everything when I come back.'

She left me drowning in confusion, thinking that things had taken a strange turn. One day earlier the current had almost swept me out to the treacherous sea and now this delightful woman was taking me I knew not where. Somehow I fell asleep; then I woke up when she came back carrying food, which I could tell by the smell.

'Octavia, I don't eat fish,' I said.

'Fine, we'll eat anything else. I'll give the fish to the guard, and I'll bring some cheese and grapes for us.'

I did not answer, and she did not await an answer. She stood up hurriedly and came back after a while, wearing a serious expression which she had not had the day before. As on the first occasion she started to put the food in my mouth with her hand. I was not hungry and she ate only a couple of mouthfuls. She took away the plates from between us and sat down affectionately next to me, smiling at my surprise and anticipation. Then she began to tell me the story.

I still remember how she sat and her gestures as she spoke. In fact I still remember her words to the letter.

'After my husband died I wanted to devote myself to the gods and serve one of the temples still remaining in the city. The Sicilian master did not agree. He loves me as his daughter. It's he who taught me to read, when I was ten years old.'

'And why did he stop you serving in the temple?'

'He said that the gods no longer need anyone to serve them, but people to weep for them. He gave me advice, saying, "Mourn a while, my daughter, for mourning is human, and with time your sadness will diminish, as with all things human, and one day you will find another husband."'

I learnt that this Sicilian master of hers did not believe in any particular religion, but in the truth of all religions and all gods, as long as they help refine mankind. She put her head on my shoulder and whispered that her master always asserted that God appears to man in a different form in different times and places, and that this is the nature of divinity.

'A strange opinion,' I said.

'That's nothing to do with us right now. Let me finish.'

Her face took on a wholly serious guise, but she remained beautiful none the less. She leant back against the wall next to the bed and began to tell me how the days passed sadly after her husband was gone, especially as the Sicilian master, whose presence used to fill the house, left a few days later on his annual trading trip, which took him away for months. The Sicilian master made two trips a year, one short trip to Antioch which lasted a month, and a long one which lasted three or four months. The long one took him to the Western Pentapolis, the five Libyan cities, whence he would sail north and dock a week in Constantinople, then sail to Pergamon and dock in Cyprus and Sicily before returning to Alexandria. He was in his sixties and owned three large ships. He had no family or descendants, and every time he left she would hear him say that this might be his last trip and if he died at sea then he gave her this house, on condition that she did not dismiss the guard. He had deposited some money for her in a secret place in the house which no one but she could reach. She said she always hoped he would come back from his trips and did not hope to own the house or the hidden money. She believed in the ancient gods, especially Poseidon the god of the sea, and she spoke about him with great reverence.

The afternoon shadows had lengthened, so she rose to light the lamp and then came back to nestle in my embrace and continue her tale. 'When the followers of the Christian bishop they called Theophilus destroyed all that remained of the great temple which stood at the western end of Pharos island, where the harbour is, the remaining priests of the temple fled and scattered across the land. An old priestess from there took refuge in our house because she knew I revered the god Poseidon and always prayed to him to protect the ships of my Sicilian master. The priestess stayed with me, here on the roof of the house, for the final weeks of her life. She spent most of her time at this wall, looking out to sea. A few days before she died, she called me to her room and, as she lay on her death bed, in a voice as true as an oracle, she told me: "Octavia, do not be sad, Poseidon will send you from the sea a man for you to love and who will love you. He will wipe away your tears and fill your days with joy, and he will come to you after two signs."'

When Octavia asked what the two signs might be, the priestess told her that they would be two signs in the course of time: two days, two weeks, two months, two years. The priestess died and the days passed slowly for Octavia until two full years had passed and she began to doubt the prophecy. When she saw me drowning, then survive the drowning, and come out naked but for my wet undergarments and my unknown fate, she was convinced of the truth of the prophecy. She smiled at the memory, as though a mysterious joy had suddenly swept over her, and she added, 'For the last two years I thought my man would be a sailor coming off a ship but then I found you coming to me carried on the wings and the waves of the great god.'

'Is that why you called me "my love" as soon as you saw me?'

'Yes, because I fell in love with you two full years before I saw you, and maybe even before that,' she said.

At the time I did not know how to answer her. I pulled her close, wrapping my left arm around her lazily. She rested in my embrace, then fell asleep like an infant, leaving me to a storm of thoughts and fancies. I wondered,

'What shall I do with this white woman who is sleeping against my chest and whose naked legs give me such strange ideas or, should I say, drive me wild? Should I give up what I have set my mind on for years and stay in her bed for the rest of my life? Is her ample love a substitute for my great dream – to excel in medicine and theology? When her husband died I was an adolescent in Naga Hammadi, thinking of marrying a Nubian girl in the same way as my uncle, whose house I was living in. The Nubian people marry their daughters only to their own menfolk, except on rare occasions. My father's father came to their country from the centre of the Nile valley, lived among them and died among them after becoming one of them. My father and uncle were born there. My uncle married one of their women, while my father chose a wife from the villages of the Delta and she later became my mother.

At the age of eighteen I was excited to see the mating of the birds and the farm animals and my uncle brought up the question of marrying me to a girl from the Nubian people, since he was popular among them, and he could have arranged it for me if he had been enthusiastic. But for some reason, which escaped me at the time, he advised me to keep studying medicine and theology. My uncle was a good Christian and very ill. It was he who enrolled me in the church in Naga Hammadi and in the school and church in Akhmim. He must be dead by now. I wonder if he wanted me to become a monk to make me forget what my father's killers did. They killed my father and one of the thugs married my mother. How can the memories be erased? My mother… how could she consent to marry one of the killers? My father was a good man, and I never saw him reproach her and he never beat her. He used to take me out to throw his nets in the Nile from the oval rocks which are thought to be sacred heavenly eggs which descended with the waters of the Nile to protect those who stand on them from crocodiles, which are also sacred. I used to delight in the fish trapped in his nets, and he delighted in my delight. Why did they insist on killing him in that way? Jesus the Messiah, I can feel the pain in the heart of the Virgin and her grief for you. I feel the depths of her torment the day they knocked the nails into your hands and feet splayed on the Cross, and I am splayed like you on the cross of memories, and overcome by the agony of loss.

'My love, are you crying? I have saddened you with my story.'

'No, Octavia. Stay sleeping. I am weeping at the misery and despair of this world.'

'Never mind, my love. Please don't cry. Come to the arms of Octavia who loves you.'

We embraced and drifted off to sleep in each other's arms. Sleep is a heavenly mercy for all creatures. But that night I did not sleep at all and woke up early to find her moving gracefully around the room, happily coming and going. When I opened my eyes, she threw herself nimbly towards me and stretched out on her stomach next to me. Her face was beaming with a beauty which reached from the middle of her bed to the ends of the universe.

I noticed that my brown skin had taken on a slight ruddiness, and my body was now the colour of a copper vessel, and at first I thought the reason for that was the obscene things we had done together. But Octavia, rocking with laughter, told me the secret behind that was the sun the day before, combined with the salty sea air. Then I understood why the whiteness of her body was tinged with red. I lay next to her, comfortable in my nakedness, and that was the second time I felt that my body was beautiful, the second time and the last of my whole life.

She flirted with me and kissed me on the mouth, then invited me to a bath she said was full of hot water and aromatic herbs which are brought from the countries of the east. As she got out of bed, she told me she was going to take my clothes from my bag to wash them, and I screamed out as though scalded, 'No! Don't do that.' I added in panic, 'I don't like anyone to wash my clothes. I've done that for myself for years.'

'But my love, Octavia wasn't with you all those years.'

'Please, don't contradict what I say.'

She did not contradict me. She wrapped her arms around me, a hug big enough for me and all my memories, with all the secret agonies and the few moments of happiness. In fact her hug was big enough for the whole world. She whispered in my ear that I was not used to her yet and that our time to come would see to that. Her breath was warm on my chest and her lips were hot on my neck, kindling my desire for her.

When she undressed me again in the bathroom next to her room I detected in her eyes a look of desire. I too was desirous of her, and confused. I felt the water and found it warm and so inviting that I was happy to sit at length in the marble tub with the four carved legs. I rested my arms on the sides and stretched out my legs in the water. She started to massage my shoulders gently yet with passion. I closed my eyes and tried to distract myself and to calm down by thinking about anything from my past, but the memories eluded me as though Octavia's touch had erased everything I had ever seen before I met her.

Gently she had me lean forward so she could massage my back, and I followed the guidance of her hands. The panic that hit me when she had almost emptied out my bag had now subsided. The monk's cassock and the wooden cross would have shocked her, but I had stopped her at the decisive moment. Dark thoughts and questions churned in my mind: how long would this disturbing state last, this transient happiness, this delusion? I am not deceptive by nature and I had never lied in my life. So why had I been misleading her, and going astray with her, since the moment I saw her? The Lord could see me, and see her, and He would not forgive me for what I was doing. He would not spare me His punishment unless I repented and He showed mercy. If He wished, He could pardon me. If He wanted, He could torment me in punishment for my sin. He had tormented me before without me committing any sin. Or perhaps all that was the penalty for this. What about Octavia's sins? Would the Lord punish her for them or let them pass because she was pagan and did not believe in Him? Did He punish only believers, I wondered? I think that in the end He will forgive everyone because He is compassionate.

I suddenly decided to stand up and put on my original gown. I would ask her to come and visit the cave between the rocks, and in the place where I saw her for the first time I would tell her everything about myself, and everything would end where it began, and I would go back to the purpose for which I had come – medicine and theology. Then I would go back one day to our village and open up my father's house, which had been closed for years, and live there a monastic life treating the sick. At my hands, miracles would take place to confirm the existence of the Lord, and the people there would forget what had happened to my father and my mother. I would choose for myself an ecclesiastical name that I liked and was comfortable with, and I would…

'What are you thinking about, my love? Are you thinking about me when I'm with you?'

'I want to get out of this big bathtub and visit the rocky cave by the sea,' I said.

'We'll go later. Come, my love, and I'll dry your body.'

The questions kept churning in my mind. Why was this woman pampering me? How could she give me such effusive love, enough to drown the world, although she did not know me, and I knew nothing of her other than what she had told me? She must have hidden things from me and these things she had hidden must be terrible. Anyway, she is a pagan woman and believes in the foolish myths about the Greek gods, the gods who trick each other, wage war on mankind, marry often and betray their wives. What sick imagination produced the gods of Greece? And what is stranger still is that there are people who believe in them – such as Octavia, who believes that the sea god Poseidon sent me to her. But the sea has no god and nobody sent me, yet how can I know for sure that she is wrong and I am right? The Old Testament, which we believe in, is also full of deceptions, wars and betrayals, and the Gospel of the Egyptians, which we read although it's banned, contains material which contradicts the four orthodox Gospels. Are the two of them fantasies? Or does it mean that God is secretly present behind all religious beliefs?

'Put on this clean gown, my love, so you don't get cold. I'll wash the seawater out of your own gown.'

I awoke from my musings and firmly refused to put on the Sicilian master's clean gown which she offered me. I would feel ill at ease if I wore a flowing silk garment. Only women wear silk, but the men of Alexandria have strange ways of dressing and affectations unfamiliar to us Egyptians.

I quickly picked up my gown and threw it on my naked body, embarrassed at the way she was watching. I beat her to the door of the bathroom and as I shielded my eyes with my hands from the glare of the midday sun she hugged me from behind and began to rub the palms of her hands across my chest, resting her head on my back. I stood there motionless and she stood there purring with pleasure. After a long moment of silence, I turned to face her and told her sullenly that she still did not know my name and had not even shown any interest in asking me what it was.

'My love, I know the name which I have given you and which no one else will share: Theodhoros Poseidonios.'

Octavia took me by surprise with her boldness and her headstrong temerity. Did she think herself a god, giving people names? It's true she had chosen for me a distinctive name, which in Greek meant 'divine gift from Poseidon', but I reacted angrily, and she then acted playful. If I didn't like that name, she said, she would give me another name instead – Theophrastos, which literally means 'divine speech'.

'Octavia, stop your madness, because that's not my name either. These are all Greek names, but I have an Egyptian name.'

'Forget about Egypt and Greece now. You are the one who proves that the god speaks the truth, so your name from now on is Theophrastos, or Theodhoros Poseidonios. Choose one of the two and tell me so I know what to call you. Come now and let me show you the house.'

At the time I did not know how to answer her. But she did not give me a moment to hesitate. She took me by the hand and left the bathroom, saving me from my own confusion. A part of me wanted her, and loved her intelligence, her cheerfulness and the smell of her body. Yes, Octavia was clever, honest and desirable, but she had brought me to perdition and I had done the same to her, twice. Ah, who can put an end to the storm of my sorrow? I am going to stop writing now and rest a little. I'll resume writing if I wake up.

✝

What does Azazeel want from me, and why is he pushing me to record the past, and the present? He must have some evil purpose, in line with his nature. He has already tricked me and tempted me into writing about the sins and obscene things I did with Octavia. Now my soul is defiled and befouled.

'Was your soul immaculate, Hypa, before you began to write?'

'Azazeel, you've come!'

'Hypa, I've told you many times that I don't come and go. It's you who conjures me when you want to, because I come from within you and through you. I spring up when you want me to shape your dream, or spread the carpet of your imagination or stir up for you memories you have buried. I am the bearer of your burdens, your delusions and your misfortunes. I am the one you cannot do without, and nor can anyone else. I am the one who…'

'Have you started chanting a hymn to glorify your own satanic self?'

'Sorry, I'll keep quiet.'

'What do you want now?' I asked.

'I want you to write, Hypa. Write as though you're confessing, and carry on with your story, all of it. Say what happened to you two as you went down the stairs.'

✝

Confession is a wonderful rite, purging us of all our sins and laving our souls with the water of the divine mercy which pervades the universe. I will confess to these scrolls, concealing no secrets, in the hope that then I will find salvation.

The stairway between the roof of the house and the upper floor had ten steps, equal in number to the heavenly intelligences between God and the world, according to the sad philosopher Plotinus. On the top step Octavia held me tight, took my lower lip between her lips and began to run her tongue along the line of it until I almost passed out from the tremor of pleasure. She beamed and told me that this was the first of ten kisses she was going to lavish on me. As I descended to the next step down, she slipped her left hand through the opening in my gown, squeezed under my right arm and pressed me hard against the wall. She was one step above me, and bent her head down towards my arm and nibbled my earlobe, like an infant sucking a nipple playfully. When she breathed into my ear, I shivered inside. At the next kiss I reeled and almost tumbled down the stairs. So I sat down, in a daze, and let her do what she wanted with me. She pulled off her clothes and I pulled off mine, full of desire. The other kisses I cannot mention.

By the end of the stairway we had fused together, as though we were the primal substance from which the universe began. One moment she was under me, then on top, like a wild cat ravishing its prey and in turn being ravished. When our passion abated, we arose exhausted and picked up our clothes. She took me by the hand to show me the house by the light of the day, which now filled the place. Octavia was affectionate, bold and reckless. I walked behind her, chased by my thoughts and by all the possibilities: I might fall in love with her and grow accustomed to her voluptuous outbursts, but I would never succumb to her. I might stay with her for only a few days and then go about what I came to Alexandria to do, and not let myself become attached to her. I would not choose for myself a pagan name derived from Greek. Whatever happened, I would not allow an Alexandrian widow I had known two days to deprive me of my name and my language, however beautiful she was and however impulsive her pagan lust. I would not allow Octavia to sweep me away. I was very young at the time. I wonder, if I had deferred to her, would our grievous fate have been different? Who knows? It's no use wishing now, what's done is done. What we did has passed and never will return.

We looked down from the upper floor, on the picture of the sad dog, and I asked her, 'Why did they call you Octavia?'

'My father married twice and had many children, and I was the eighth of his ten sons and daughters,' she said.

'Then I will call you Timahshmoune, which means eighth in Egyptian, like Octavia.'

She smiled sweetly and serenely and did not comment on what I said. She took me into a large room with a floor and walls of fine white marble and in the centre a bath twice as large as the one next to her room, and with more carving. She told me her master had brought this extraordinary bath from

Rome. The bath was truly amazing, as was everything in this room and the other rooms. But suddenly a mysterious sadness came over me, welling up from inside, and distracted me from my surroundings, and I was no longer interested in these mundane and ephemeral vanities.

As she took me around the whole house, I walked with her, but my mind was elsewhere and wary. I felt that she was tempting me, trying to make staying with her seem more attractive, and I resisted by saying to myself, 'How could I consent to be a servant in the home of a Sicilian merchant, and husband to a pagan servant woman who is five years my senior and always taking me by surprise with her irrepressible sexual desires? Who knows, maybe her master sleeps with her! If not, who else taught her all this debauchery she has shown me? Her master must be a real libertine who follows his desires, fills his house with loose women, spends his nights in Alexandria in their arms and has Octavia join them.' At that moment I felt a powerful hatred for this man and intense anger towards this woman, who had almost made me fall in love with her and forget all my hopes.

'This, my love, is the library,' she said.

Her words, and her gentle touch on my shoulder, broke my train of thought. When we went into the room, I was in awe at the number of books arranged on shelves the length of the wall and the scrolls set in holes in the walls. I had always loved books. I wanted to be alone and I almost wept for no reason, maybe because of my constant frustration. I asked if I could stay a while with the books and my request pleased her. She kissed me on the cheek and said she would go to prepare lunch.

Octavia left me puzzled in the midst of the vast room. I looked around the walls, which were full of cavities for storing papyruses and shelves for arranging books. In those days I could read in Greek and Egyptian but I had not yet mastered Hebrew or Aramaic. In the library I found books in other languages, such as the upstart language Latin, and eastern languages the likes of which I had not seen before. How many languages did he read, this libertine merchant who did not believe in any god? Or perhaps he bought the books to show off, as most rich and stupid people do. No, it didn't look as if he were showing off, because on his elegant desk in the corner of the room I found books strewn around and two folded volumes on papyrus, with comments in Greek written in a fine hand. When I leafed through the volumes on his desk and on the shelves, I found marginal notes and commentaries all written in the same hand and signed with his name. So it was he who read Greek and the other languages. As far as I could tell from his intelligent comments, most of his reading was in history and literature. The man had several old copies of Aesop's fables and the poems of Heraclitus, the philosopher. He also had a theological epistle by Origen. I began to turn the pages of the books and open out the folded scrolls, and on the edges I could see more comments and marginal notes.

'My love, the food is ready, come on.'

'I'll stay another hour. I'm not hungry now,' I said.

'Come on, the food will go cold. Don't vex me as the Sicilian master does. It's obvious you like books just as he does.'

'Could you bring the food here?' I asked.

'No, that wouldn't do. We'll eat in my room. The books won't fly away. Come on, leave that book, because I'm very hungry and I miss you so much.'

She took the book from my hand and put it back in its place on the shelf. She opened the thick leather cover and said with a chuckle, 'Aristotle, do you want to make us miss our delicious hot lunch, for the sake of this man?'

What she said startled me, and the way she made fun of the great philosopher. 'What's that you're saying?' I said in anger. 'Aristotle is the teacher of the ancient world and the first person to give mankind the principles of thought and the science of logic.'

'Ha, so before him mankind didn't know logic and the principles of thought? Anyway, I don't like him because in his books he says many foolish things, and claims that women and slaves share the same nature, different from the nature of free men. Retarded!'

'Octavia, that's no way to talk. But I see you are familiar with the learning of the ancients.'

'Ha, I know some things and the Sicilian master likes to read me ancient texts. He's interested in teaching me. A neighbour of ours, a rich Christian, saw him one day reading to me in the garden of the house and said, "The Sicilian is giving the snake poison to drink." Our new neighbour is also retarded, like your old friend.'

I didn't know how to answer her, and she gave me no time to think. She pulled me gently by the hand out of the room and at the door she gave me a long hug. Octavia never stopped. 'This kiss is an appetizer,' she joked.

We sprawled on the floor of her room and while she put food in my mouth in the usual way, she said the Sicilian master would like me, because he liked learning and scholars. She said he was friends with the governor of the city and had many acquaintances. He would help me to study medicine and she would surround me with her love until I became the most famous physician in Alexandria, in fact the most famous physician in the world. To my surprise, she added: 'My love, you will be more famous than Galen and Hippocrates, and all the followers of the god Asclepius.'

'Octavia, you do know a lot,' I said.

'All I want to know is you. Tell me, are you happy with me? No, don't answer now. Be patient and you'll see. The Sicilian master will be back in a month and I'll tell him everything about us and he'll welcome you amongst us.'

The Sicilian master! I felt hatred towards him, a deep hatred, mixed with a certain reverence and foolish envy after I had seen his comments and annotations. Bewildered, I let slip my thoughts: 'Does the Sicilian master sleep with you?'

My question shocked her and tears suddenly welled up in her eyes. Her face went red in sadness and in anger. I had not meant to say that exactly, but rather to ask what kind of relationship they had and did the man flirt with her when he was at home, especially as she was a single widow with strong desires, or rather whether he asked her to warm his bed on winter nights and relieve his loneliness when he missed his dog. I meant, did he, as her master, have a right to sleep with her?

Octavia bowed her head and looked at the edge of the carpet without saying a word. When I tried to placate her by giving her a hug, she slipped away and burst into tears. I regretted offending her and thought of standing up straight away in front of her and leaving, to end everything between us in a single move. When I suddenly arose she seemed to understand what I intended and she grabbed the hem of my gown. I stopped and she, still bowing her head, pulled me to the ground. I sat down, my eyes pinned on the half-open door.

A long silence reigned between us. It was she who broke it, saying in a trembling voice, after wiping her cheeks, that she did not understand anything I was saying, because the Sicilian master was just like a father to her, in fact more like a grandfather than a father. It was he who had brought her up after her mother and father died. He was a man who took pity on the afflicted and, so she said, every year donated half of his earnings from trade to the poor of Alexandria.

'I apologize, Octavia. But you are very beautiful, I mean...'

'Enough, don't apologize, and I'll forgive you because you don't yet know the man you accuse,' she said.

Octavia's Enticements (2)

L ife is unfair. It carries us along and distracts us, then it takes us by surprise and changes us, until we end up quite unlike what we once were. Was it I who was in Alexandria twenty years ago? How can life now hold me to account for the mistakes and sins I committed in those days? How can the Lord on the Day of Judgement take us back and hold us responsible for what we did ages ago, as though we lived one life without changing in the course of it? It did not take me long to realize that I had misjudged Octavia and her Sicilian master, but by then it was too late, and the dead had died and the living were as dead.

Octavia remained silent that night, other than for a few words. Her silence troubled me, until I began to feel drowsy and I fell asleep on her bed. The last thing I was aware of before I slept was the sad way she looked at me as she pulled the cover over me. She woke me early in the morning by moving about, and I was reassured to find her smiling and sitting on the ground next to the bed. In front of her lay the breakfast she had prepared for us, spread on the ground. In the morning I again apologized for what I had said the previous night but she put a stop to my mumbling with a touch of her fingertips on my mouth, and a tear which glistened in the depths of her eyes. She changed the subject by asking me about my native country and my early life. I answered as best I could without saying anything important, but she hung on every word I said.

'Come and I'll show you something,' she said.

She pulled me by some invisible leash, and we went downstairs to the big bedroom with the Sicilian master's bed in it. I had seen the room before from the door but this time we went in. Octavia opened the window and the door to the large balcony which looked out over the beach and the sea nearby. Light flooded the place. I did not go out on the balcony in case the guard or some passer-by saw me, although I would have liked to sit a little on the sturdy wooden bench, contemplating from this unusual angle the merging of the sea and sky.

'That's the Sicilian master,' she said.

Octavia pointed to a wooden coffin leaning upright in the right-hand corner of the room, on the side opposite the balcony. The coffin was finely painted with the image of a grey-haired man in Greek dress of the type worn by rich people. There was an inscrutable sadness in his eyes, and an intelligence. The image was drawn in the style common among the rich in Memphis and Alexandria, who had their faces depicted on their coffins and were then mummified and buried in them when they died. Mummification is a traditional pagan custom. The ancient Egyptians used to preserve their bodies after death in granite sarcophaguses on which they had images of the old gods carved. Then, in more recent times, the sarcophaguses were made of wood and they started to paint a picture of the dead person on the lid. When I looked at the picture of the Sicilian I realized that Octavia meant to show me that he was advanced in years and had the sedate appearance of a philosopher. As if to reinforce the impression left by the picture of the man, she added, 'He lives an ascetic life, keeps his coffin in his bedroom and always thinks about death. On most days when he is in Alexandria, he sits on this balcony of his and looks out to sea, or reads books.'

'Why does he look so sad?' I asked.

'Because he's lonely. He's also a poet. Would you like to see his poems?'

I agreed. She took me to the large library, took from the drawer of the desk some papers with poems written in Greek in the same hand I had seen in the margins of the books. Without me asking, Octavia left me in the library, but first she gave me a quick hug and repeated in my ear in a whisper, 'I love you.' I stayed silent. After a long kiss at the base of my neck she left the poems in my hands and told me she would go and make us a delicious lunch. She came several times to look over me with a smile, and I was happy among the books.

The Sicilian master's poems were like his picture – gentle and sad. Most of them were ironic meditations on life and the sea, in the style of the ancient poets and the modern philosophers. I liked some of his lines of poetry, and on one of the occasions when Octavia dropped by I asked her to bring me some paper so I could copy them out. She gave me a long scroll of papyrus and two pieces of skilfully tanned goatskin parchment. I did not copy the Greek poems in the normal way, because of their excessively pagan nature, but instead I wrote the words vertically, from bottom to top, in separate columns, so that if the lines were read horizontally or in any way other than my way, they would look like just individual words with no meaning, and individual words are harmless and bring no sin. The sin comes about only when the words are framed in sentences.

In the same manner I copied out some of the commentaries the Sicilian master had written in the margins of the Greek translation of the Old Testament – I mean the translation known as the Septuagint – and his commentaries on some of the Gospels. His commentaries would begin with the phrase, 'How could anyone believe that...' and then he would provide a summary of the verses, and comment on them saying that it was logically impossible to accept such ideas. As far as I could see, the man did not understand that religion has nothing to do with reason and that faith is faith only if it defies reason and logic, or else it is thought and philosophy. But none the less I pitied this bewildered man at the time, just as today I pity myself for my own excessive perplexity.

At noon the room filled with the smell of delicious cooking. I closed the door, opened the window carefully and continued rummaging through books and copying out commentaries. The papyrus scroll was not yet full when Octavia came in with her usual good cheer to invite me to eat. I asked for a little more time, but she insisted. She was wearing a thin blue dress open at the front and the arms. Her thick brown hair ran riot around her smiling face. Octavia was a beautiful woman.

I rose with her, leaving the books, the inkstand and the scroll on the floor, in the hope of coming back after lunch, but I never did come back. Even the scroll I abandoned there.

✛

I was in a good mood when we went to her room. The food was in bowls spread on the floor. It wasn't the food that pleased me, but rather the way Octavia took care of me. After my father died I was not accustomed to having anyone give me the affectionate attention that she lavished on me. Despite her entreaties I could not eat much, although the food was delicious. My desire for her was stronger than my appetite for food, and she detected my desire from the long looks I gave her and she did not resist when I moved towards her and pulled her close. I suddenly felt that I loved her and that perhaps she was worth staying with for the rest of my life. I said to myself, 'Why not? I'll study medicine and practise in this big city. I will not renounce my religion, but I will give up the monastic life. My country far away has nothing to entice me to go back. Octavia will be my home and the refuge of my soul. Why not? I have never seen a more beautiful woman, nor one gentler or kinder. Even as a pagan, is she not purer in heart than most of the Christian women I have known? I mean, those I have seen from afar. But who can be sure she won't betray me one day as my mother betrayed my father? If I were to anger her one day for some reason, she could turn against me as women always turn against their husbands, for women are fickle by nature.'

Tenderly, as she lay in my arms, I asked her if she would keep on loving me whatever happened. Her answer still rings inside me and echoes in my heart. 'Whatever happens, my love. I'll spend my whole life at your side, looking after you, my one hope. I waited for you long and dreamed about you often, and I'll never find anyone better than you.'

'Then let the Lord's will be done,' I said.

'My love, don't speak that way like the Christian people. I hate them.'

'Why, Octavia?'

'Because they are like locusts. They eat everything that is ripe in the city, and make life gloomy and cruel.'

She was about to expound at length with disparaging remarks about those of our religion, so I changed the subject by asking her about this Savante of the Ages whom the crier was talking about in the main street.

She sat up straight and her face shone again. 'He means Hypatia, the daughter of the scholar Theon, the Pythagorean professor,' she said. 'She's a famous woman, beautiful and intelligent, and she visits us here with the friends of the Sicilian master at those soirées which go on for hours. She always calls me "my dear sister Octavia".'

'In what fields does she give the lectures the crier is inviting people to?' I asked.

'In mathematics and philosophy, but not in medicine. Don't imagine that I will let you get close to her, or else you might fall in love with her and abandon me – although she is much older than you,' she said.

'Don't joke, because I really do want to find out more about her.'

That day she told me much about Hypatia, the woman known as the Savante of the Ages. She spoke about her with pleasure in the telling and in a way that stimulated my interest in seeing her. Octavia said Hypatia taught at the theatre in the city centre. Her father Theon used to teach in the great temple, the Serapeion, which once stood proudly in the Egyptian quarter in the south of the city. But the Christians destroyed it and brought it down on the heads of those inside in the days of Theophilus. She meant the bishop. When I asked her what days Hypatia taught on, she looked at me from the corner of her eye, with an oblique look that mingled jealousy and a desire to pick a quarrel, and she did not answer. When I insisted, she said Hypatia lectured on Sundays because it was quiet in the mornings when the Christians went to the Church of the Wheat Seed to hear the sermon of their current leader, who had succeeded his uncle Theophilus at the head of that church which had turned the world dark! I was startled at what she said and her outspokenness frightened me.

'Do you mean Bishop Cyril?' I asked.

'May the gods bring his dark days to a hasty end,' she said. 'He has made the city as gloomy as a ruin since the time he took charge. But you're strange! You know Cyril but you don't know Hypatia.'

'Octavia, I don't know anything here. Before I saw you, all I'd seen of your city was the stretch I walked from the Moon Gate to the beach where I almost drowned in front of your eyes.'

I will never forget her sudden happiness, as she shouted in glee, 'True, my love, my heart, true. Now I'm happy and certain that the god sent you to me, truly and honestly.'

'Now we're back to superstitions.'

'My love, you are the most beautiful superstition I've known, and I'll continue to believe in it for the rest of my life.'

The curtains of the evening had fallen and I felt that I was quite adrift in Octavia's orbit, drowning completely in the torrential river that she was. She encircled me on all sides, as the Great Sea surrounds the whole world. I said to myself, 'I'll make up my mind tonight. I'll think carefully, then decide tomorrow at dawn what will become of us.' That was what I intended, but I did not know what would happen, unaware of what fate would bring.

Octavia invited me to her bed. The world had fallen still around us and inside us. She told me she wanted to take a light snooze. I had no desire to sleep so I asked her if I could go back to the library. She answered in a friendly manner, full of ambiguity and redolent of vice, 'If you stay with me, I'll teach you things you won't find in books.'

I tried to be serious in the hope that she would comply with my request, but her high spirits overwhelmed me and I found I had no choice but to submit as she pulled me towards the bed. That day I really did experience with her what no one could find in any book, because Octavia had talents unheard of by those who write books. We lay there naked until night encroached on us and the cold began to bite. She pulled the blanket over us, wrapped her arms around me and prepared for sleep.

Then suddenly she stood up, her lively mind taken with a whimsy. 'My love, come with me and I'll show you the wine cellar,' she said.

'I want to sleep.'

'Sleep! If you're tired at the beginning of the night, how will you be at the end of it? Come with me, I'll fetch you from the cellar the best wine in the world.'

Octavia never stopped.

SCROLL SIX

The Decisive Point

I remember well that to reach the cellar we went down the stairway leading to the roof, and then the big staircase linking the two floors, and then another stairway behind the wooden door at the end of the large hall with the image of the sad dog on the floor. The last stairway was made of stone and the steps grew wider the more we descended towards the cellar.

The air in the cellar was damp and cold, and the smell was strong. The floor was stone and on top of the flagstones, thick oak planks had been laid. I had not realized that cellars could be so wide, because the houses and temples in my first country did not have cellars, and I had thought that a cellar was a low passageway under big houses and palaces, like a corridor, and that it was necessarily narrow and confined. But with Octavia, by the light of her metal lantern, I saw a whole storey with high walls, supported underground on rows of strong marble pillars, with each row connected by a brick wall. There were three shelves on either side of each wall, and on each shelf so many jars it would be hard to count them.

'We have enough wine to last a thousand years,' she said proudly. 'Come this way, where there's the vintage wine from grapes pressed in the best years.'

'Why do you lay down all this wine? Does the owner of the house think he's going to live forever?' I asked.

'Take it easy, my love. His father had much wine made for him, and he has brought some kinds of wine from Greece and Cyprus, because they used to have many guests here and hold large banquets. I've seen that ever since I was a little girl.'

She took me to a corridor that ran between the lines of jars and at the end of it she reached behind the jar next to the wall and took out a bottle of clear green glass. She took two steps back until her bottom was against me and, rubbing her bottom against my groin, she said, 'This is excellent wine, just right for our little party!' She turned her face towards me with a smile and continued to gyrate against me. 'I saved it here for us months ago, because I liked the taste,' she added.

I forgot myself at the time, and I was annoyed that it was always she who took the initiative. This time I felt the urge to do so myself, to make her feel that I was strong. I was young and rash. I turned her by the shoulders until her face was towards the wall and then I pushed her forward, my hands on the sides of her back. She moved forward obediently. I blew at the flame of the lantern and it went out, and darkness enveloped us. Her front was against the damp wall and my chest was against her warm back. In the darkness I fondled her body and found it completely submissive. She put her hands against the wall and bent her head forward a little. I lifted my gown off and took down my undergarments. Then I lifted her dress off. She had nothing underneath for me to take down, and we were completely naked. She made much noise as she moaned, and asked me to split her in two. O my God, it is most improper, all this that I remember and that I relate after the passage of these long years.

We staggered up to her room from the cellar, and that night we fell asleep sitting on the cushions scattered around the floor, without a taste from the bottle of wine. The next day I woke up early and Octavia was asleep beside me like an indecent dream. Quietly I went down to the library, with my bag in my hand for fear she might look inside it when she woke up. I quietly opened the window and the place filled with light. I sprawled on the floor, resuming my session among the books. I finished off my copying from the margins of the holy books, I mean the Sicilian master's commentaries on the verses which caught his attention. While I was putting the copy of the Old Testament back in its place on the shelf my eye fell on a large volume, and on the inner cover I found a title describing its contents: *Epistles and Fragments of the Ancient Philosophers of Alexandria.*

I already knew many of these texts because the authors were well known, but some of the epistles and fragments were completely new to me and I had not heard of the authors in our schools in Akhmim. I took the big volume back to my place on the floor and began to read writings which surprised me, especially fragments attributed to an old philosopher I had not heard of, by the name of Hegesias the Death-Persuader or advocate of suicide, according to the introduction to his fragments. I was about to embark on choosing some of these fragments for copying onto my scroll when Octavia arrived in alarm, her face quite yellow. The tresses of her ample brown hair covered her shoulders and her creamy breasts were heaving as she panted.

'You're here! I thought you... Why did you take your bag with you?' she said.

'What's the panic? I saw here older and more accurate copies of some books I have in my bag, and I wanted to correct my copies,' I said.

'My love, I beg you, don't frighten me again by leaving me suddenly. I almost died of worry for you. Come, let's go back to our room, come on, my love.'

She threw herself in my arms, like a child whose father has returned after a long journey. At the time I did not feel her nakedness so much as I felt her anguish. I took her in my arms with paternal affection, with none of that lust which swept us off our feet the night before, and she was comforted. As I inhaled the scent of her hair, I was close to certain that she loved me more than my mother loved me. Did my mother hate me, as she hated my father? And did she later love her wicked husband?

I could feel Octavia's tears running down my bare chest, washing away the pains of my boyhood. I held her closer and ran my hands along her shoulders and down her bare arm, and she calmed down. Should I have trusted

Octavia in those days more than I did? Who knows, and what use is it now? Anyway, we take a serious risk if we feel safe, just as we take a major risk if we believe in something.

'Never leave me, my one love,' she said. She wiped away her tears with her hands and forced a smile to her lips. She was looking at me with frenzied passion, her tearful honey eyes full of love and awe. When her smile softened, and her eyes recovered from the flood of tears, she took me to the roof of the house without us saying anything, as though for the moment we were content with the messages that passed from eye to eye.

She made me stop outside her room until she came back wearing the white dress I had seen her in the first time we met, carrying in her hand the Sicilian master's gown with the embroidered hems, the gown I had previously refused to wear. Her eyes were begging me and she took off my gown. I put on the other one in silence, or rather she put it on me. I would have liked to stand a while at the wall which surrounded the roof but she warned me gently again and took me affectionately into her room. She opened the window and the room filled with the light that flooded the roof.

She sat on the edge of her bed, stretching her arms towards me like a bountiful mistress, tender, generous and cheerful. But at the time my thoughts recurred. 'Who can say that these traits will last forever? Nothing lasts forever. What if she betrays me? For women are by nature false. She may lose her temper with me one day for some reason and denounce me to the men of the church and expose my secret to them. She would say that I seduced her or that I was a monk and debauched her. The church of Alexandria by all reports is strong and decisive. Most of its men are cruel, and what might they do to me? Will I meet here the same fate as my father?'

'What's the matter, my love? You seem distracted. Take this apple.'

'An apple! I don't like them, because that's the fruit that led to Adam leaving Paradise.'

'What's this nonsense?' said Octavia. 'Who told you this superstition, my little child?'

Confused and without thinking, I said sharply, 'It's written in the commentaries on the Old Testament.'

'Ha, the Old Testament. That's a wonderful book, always mocking the ancient Egyptians and making allegations about their women. My master used to read it to me, and he would smile and shake his head in amazement.'

I was furious at what she said, and it angered me that she was showing contempt for the Old Testament of the Lord, which we have believed in for hundreds of years and which the Jews believed in before us. I was furious despite the many doubts I had about the material in the Pentateuch. But whatever the case, no one should show contempt for the beliefs of others, or else all beliefs would seem hollow or be treated with scorn, and no religion would hold good for anyone.

I said to myself that maybe the time had come for some frank talking between us, so I said firmly, 'Octavia, you shouldn't make fun of people's beliefs.'

'Don't get angry like that, my love. From now on I'll never make fun of anyone's belief, as long as it upsets you. So don't make me angry, and take this apple from my hand,' she said.

I took the apple reluctantly. Octavia lifted my hand with the apple to my mouth, while I thought about the Book of Genesis. I bit off a small piece of the apple, and had an overpowering sense that I was Adam, who was tempted by his wife and deceived by the accursed Azazeel. Adam then passed on the original sin of disobedience, the first sin. The well-known verses of the Old Testament, which no one other than us can believe, stuck in my head. Some questions nagged me: why did the Lord tell Adam to stay away from the trees of knowledge and of eternal life? Why was the Lord angry when Adam ate from the tree of knowledge? According to the Book of Genesis, he said to himself, 'The man has now become like one of us; knowing good and evil. He must not be allowed to reach out his hand and take also from the tree of life and eat, and live forever.' So the Lord God banished him from the Garden of Eden to work the ground from which he had been taken. After he drove the man out, he placed on the east side of the Garden of Eden cherubim and a flaming sword flashing back and forth to guard the way to the tree of life... Why in the first place did God want man to remain ignorant? Was the knowledge that Adam obtained a prelude to him obtaining eternal life? Who are those about whom the Lord said that Adam had become one of them? If Adam and Eve had remained ignorant, would they have lived forever in the Garden of Eden? Is it right that immortality should go along with ignorance and disregard for nature? What exactly did they find out when they ate from the tree? Was it what I have discovered with Octavia over the past few days, what she has dragged me into without any planning or intention on my part? Am I perhaps repeating Adam's deed, and will I anger the Lord so that he orders another expulsion? Whence and whither will he expel me, when I have been an outcast for years, without a place or a purpose?

I was tormented by the thoughts induced by this pagan mistress who had me sitting on her bed. But was Octavia the mistress or the slave of her desires? With this apple of hers did she perhaps mean to take us back to sin, and thus to the start of a new creation? She had taken me out into a sea of sins, and how was I going to save myself from drowning? And now she wanted me to spend my life with her. How so, when she did not know true faith, and did not know that I was from the people of faith?

'What are you thinking about, my love?'

'About marriage. I mean your late husband. Was he ill?'

'No, he was twenty years older than me. He was very fat and weak, but he wasn't ill. He died in the western temple.'

A sadness came over her as she told the story of what had happened to her husband, on the day she described as inauspicious. Her pagan husband had always asked her Sicilian master to bring him incense from his travels, for him to deliver to the temples and come back happy in the evening. She used to worry about him, but he would make light of her anxiety. He did not think that temples had become dangerous places and he used to repeat within her hearing empty meaningless phrases such as 'Our god Serapis is the god of the world, and we have to show our respect for him in spite of all the Christians, including Emperor Theodosius himself.'

I understood from what she said that her late husband was a little foolish and misguided. She melted my heart as she sat there, sadly telling her story. Her hair framed her face as though she was a flower about to wilt. I should have embraced her at that moment and told her that I would be the best of husbands to her. But I said to myself, 'Anyway she didn't love her first husband, and she says she loves me, so perhaps the Lord took away her husband to give her a better one.' My mind was vacant, I was in a stupor. She was continuing her story, telling me that her husband went out one morning to put some incense in the small temple which stood to the east of the harbour, and he was surrounded there, meaning that Christians surrounded him. She sobbed as she spoke. 'He was killed by the criminals and the monks who led them, as they destroyed the temple.'

'What are you saying? Monks don't kill people,' I said.

'The monks in Alexandria do. In the name of their wonderful Lord, and with the blessings of Bishop Theophilus the fanatic, and his successor Cyril, who is even more fanatical.'

'Please, Octavia.'

'Good, enough of such talk now. But why do you seem so hurt, my love, and so biased in their favour? They pursue us everywhere, expel their brothers the Jews, bring down temples on top of those inside and call us filthy pagans. They are spreading around us like locusts, and filling the country like a curse cast on the world.'

'Please.'

'What are they to you? Why are your eyes so red and why are you about to cry?'

'Because I… '

'Because you what?'

'I…'

'You what?'

'I'm a Christian monk.'

✝

A long moment of shocked silence passed. Octavia bowed her head, then looked towards me. Her face was flushed with anger, and her eyes inflamed with a furious sadness. Suddenly she sprang to her feet and stood like one of those massive ancient statues, full of pagan vigour and ancestral bitterness. She stretched her right arm towards the door and shouted at me in a fearsome voice, like the rumbling of Alexandria thunder or the howling of a raging pagan wind, 'Out of my house, you wretch. Out, you villain.'

The Missing Parchment

I threw down the silk gown in the middle of the room and grabbed my own gown from near the door. I put it on as I hurried down the stairs. I felt as though I were falling into a void and my soul had been wrenched from my body. I stepped on the picture of the sad dog on my way to the door of the mansion. Before I opened it, from above and behind me, there came the sound of Octavia's wailing and steady groaning. As I rushed out of the door and crossed the garden to the half-open gate, I could just about hear her. The glare of the sun on the stretch of sand hurt my eyes and the hot sand hurt my bare feet.

I turned my face towards the sea, indifferent to the look of surprise from the guard when he saw me suddenly coming out of the garden gate. I did not glance at him and I did not look back when his sheep walked a few paces behind me. I had never felt so humiliated in my life. I was insulted and outraged to the utmost extent.

Did all this really take place, twenty years ago? How is it that I feel it is still happening now? Poor Octavia. If only you had been a little more patient with me. If only I had known what fate had in store for me? Or... now... my hands are trembling. Dear Octavia, I can write no longer.[5]

---

5. This is all that is written on the seventh parchment. Between the lines there are many erasures and overlapping circles. In the margins in an unsteady hand the monk Hypa drew in the space surrounding the words many crosses of various sizes. (Translator's Note)

Alone Among the Rocks

A ny memory is necessarily painful, even if it is a memory of happy moments, because it hurts for having passed. I would like to go out right now to the edge of the monastery wall and shout towards the north where Nestorius is in trouble, and to the south where Martha has disappeared. If I shout out with all the pain inside me, will some-one hear my voice arrive, or will death come? Or will the permanent loss and the sorrows torment us?

What should I do about these worries, when I am the prisoner of my fear, cooped up with my memories? Should I tear up the parchments and knock over my inkwell? Or rend my garments, as John the Baptist did, and cry in the wilderness? Or roam the faraway regions of the past and resume writing, to finish what I started, then depart this place, never to return?

Oh Octavia, you paragon. I vividly remember how, when she cruelly threw me out of her paradise, my steps led me from the seas of sand around her house to the cave among the rocks.

My steps led me there without any forethought on my part, or perhaps I wanted to ask God's forgiveness and await His mercy, in the place where I disobeyed Him for the first time. As soon as I entered the cave, I cowered in a remote corner and pressed my right shoulder and my knees against the damp wall, hoping to protect myself from the echo of my breakdown. I was a total wreck. After a moment of complete shock, I suddenly sobbed with tears of remorse. This is where Octavia knelt and took the white food out of her basket. And this is where I stood captivated by the beauty of her breasts, and here my face touched her body and her light shone over me for the first time. Here was the moment which has passed, the moment which engulfed me and threw me into a bottomless pit.

I had around me only the void and the sound of the sea. I pulled up my heavy bag, which was twice my weight, and threw my head on it, a head full of nothingness. The emptiness in me was painful, as was my loneliness. I fell into a trance, just like Jesus's disciples on the evening of the Last Supper, when He told them that He was soon to leave them and go to His Father in heaven.

I was startled out of my slumber several times, and woke up to distressing dreams. The last time was at sunset on the second day. I wanted to go back to sleep, back to unconsciousness. The floor and walls of the cave recoiled from me, and I wanted to doze off and not wake up. But I did awake and I could not sleep again until the following dawn. I had many hallucinations and fears haunted me. I was afraid of myself and of the days to come, of being alone among the rocks, and of the possibility that the cave was the lair of monsters. At the time I was not yet certain that Alexandria did not have hyenas or roaming wolves, and that giant lizards did not emerge from the sea, or crocodiles like those which come out of the Nile in the evening. There is nothing more dangerous than monstrous creatures moving around at night and roaming at dawn.

After some fretting I realized that the rustling sound I could hear was the scuttling of the sea crabs which spent the night in the fissures of the rock. The light of the moon illuminated the entrance to the cave where the sands were interspersed with scattered lumps of rock. Except for the spot lit by the moonlight I could not see anything distinct around me or in front of me. I decided to turn my back to the entrance, turn my face to the wall, and lose myself in righteous prayer and fervent supplications, in the hope that the Lord would have mercy on me and forgive me for what Octavia and I had done. When I prayed for mercy for her, my eyes flooded with tears again.

While I was absorbed with my prayers, it occurred to me to stay in the cave for the rest of my life, devoted wholly to worship, and to abandon medicine. Everything I had desired, I would renounce, and I would become, if my motives were sincere, a saint. I also had hopes inappropriate for a monk. 'As the days pass, people will find out that I live here, and they will come to share in my spiritual power, and I will set the most impressive example of asceticism. Each day I will eat only one date, and when I grow thirsty, I will put the date stones in my mouth and move them around, and that will quench my thirst, as we used to do in the village when we were young. If the thirst persists, I will wet my lips with seawater and return to seclusion in the cave. It is said that the people of Alexandria do not respect outsiders, but they will welcome me when they see my piety, my godliness and my devotion to worship. The blessings of heaven will descend on my cave, and miracles will take place at my hands. Octavia may come among the throng to visit me one day, when she has seen the light. She will see me surrounded by the radiance of sainthood. I will not trouble myself with any of the vanities of this world, but only with praise of the Lord and observing the true nature of existence manifested inside me. I will burnish my soul until it becomes like a mirror, and I will transcend the cares of this world.'

These thoughts comforted me and relieved my anguish. But with the light of the morning, hunger began to bite, distorting my thoughts and my naive hopes. I took a date out of my bag and chewed it slowly. It aggravated my thirst and even moving the date stones around in my mouth did no good. So I went out of the cave, alert as a cornered fox. As I went down to the sea I found no one around as far as my eyes could see. Everything but the air was still. I wetted my hands and put the water to my lips and tongue. The saltiness inflamed my thirst. I went back to the cave, dragging my feet, and huddled in the corner like a sorry cat licking a deep wound which there was no hope of healing. I realized that sleep was my only refuge. I tried to make myself drowsy and after long suffering I slept a deep sleep.

I came out of my unconsciousness at noon to the sound of the seabirds, and to my hunger and thirst. I had never known hunger and thirst of such intensity. I put another date in my mouth, and slowly began to suck the juice. After a while I emerged from among the rocks and started to look around me. There was no one but me. Octavia was not standing in the spot where I saw her on the day when the current took me.

I realized then that I do not like the sea. The Nile is more beautiful and gentler. The Nile draws life to its banks, while the sea drives from its shores everything that grows green. Nothing borders it but rocks. Alexandria is a city of sea and rock, a city of salt and cruelty. My solitude was tearing me apart, and the effects of feeling like a stranger were wearing me down. In the early afternoon a powerful idea came to my mind. I thought it would prove my repentance, and bring me closer to the state of sanctity which I had invalidated. It would single me out from all my contemporaries, and I would be distinguished among them, and no one else would be able to do the same: I would castrate myself.

I decided to go out immediately and look among the sand for a hair from a horse's tail, wash it well in the seawater, take it back to the cave, and tie my testicles with the hair. I would bear the pain for days until my testicles fell off and I could relax for ever. After that I would not fall for the enticements of women. I would become like the angels. The gospel calls on us to do that but we have not responded because we are weak. The verses are clear in the Gospel of the Apostle Matthew: 'For some are eunuchs because they were born that way; others were made that way by men; and others have renounced marriage because of the kingdom of heaven. The one who can accept this should accept it.' I would accept it voluntarily, content to sacrifice myself on the altar of chastity. I would do that, God willing, in the morning.

But gently, Origen had done many years ago what I intended to do the next day. Some considered him a saint, while others thought he had done wrong. The bishop of Alexandria in his time – Demetrius, known as the vine-tender – condemned his deed and described it as an abomination. He was angry with Origen and dismissed him as head of the theological school, even expelling him from the church hierarchy. So how would they view my deed when, if I went ahead with it, I could not possibly replace what I would lose and neither could I possibly join a monastic order? In other words, there was no way to resist selfish desires and the lusts of the flesh. They would excommunicate me and throw me out of the church, wrapped in shame and accompanied by resounding curses. My idea was hopeless. I will never think of castrating myself again.

Shortly before sunset I was apprehensive about spending another night in the cave, so I went out to the beach and walked westwards. In spite of myself I looked several times towards Octavia's house and also fell on my face several times too. The sun was about to set, its redness enhanced by the blue of the sea on my right, while on my left I came across more and more houses the further I walked towards the centre of the city. The houses also had more floors and grew increasingly grand and palatial. A little further I noticed some guards by the sea but I did not approach them. I realized that I was about to reach the site of the royal quarter, which was no longer royal now that most of the palaces were haunted and a refuge for dogs. I avoided going west and headed south to wander among the houses, on the chance of finding there some warmth for my tremulous heart, and water or food. In the distance I saw a church with a big cross on top and I headed towards it, touching with my fingertips the valuable letter of recommendation buried in my bag.

At the door of the church there was a crowd of Christians talking in whispers. There was goodness in their faces and around their necks hung crosses of dyed wood and carved ox bone. They did not look at me and I did not hesitate. I went straight up to them and addressed them. 'Good evening, my brothers. I am a stranger from the south, and I bear a letter for the monk Yoannes the Libyan.'

They did not know him and took little interest in me. One of them advised me to ask after him in the Caesarion church and told me how to reach it. I left them and headed in the direction suggested. Out of shyness I had refrained from telling them I was very hungry and thirsty. At one of the junctions I asked a doorman to give me a drink of water and he did so. He asked me where I was going and seemed angry when I told him. I can still remember the suspicious look he gave me when he found out I was looking for a monk who lives in a church. I mumbled him a thanks and passed on. After a while I came across the ruins of an old dilapidated house, and I sat for a moment to rest my feet, leaning my back against the crumbling wall.

The night weighed heavily on the sky and the stars looked as if they were struggling to relieve the darkness. Alexandria's houses take no notice of the dark. The windows are ablaze with lights and nightfall does not stop people moving about, for they love to stay up late, and I think they do not sleep much, either at night or by day. They are fatter than the people in my native country and they have whiter and fresher complexions. Good wine makes the complexion radiant and improves its colour.

I did not rest long at the abandoned house, though I did think of going in and spending the night there, but changed my mind. Twice along the way I asked for the Caesarion church before I reached it. It overlooked what they call the eastern harbour, because a larger harbour lies to the west. This Caesarion church was big, with high walls covered in scratches and damaged. I later discovered that it had been a temple, then became a church, and later reverted to a temple for pagans.

At the door to the church I was accosted by a man wearing a tight ecclesiastical cassock close to bursting from his vast body. He had a strange appearance: the body of a wrestler dressed in the cassock of a priest. His eyes were intense and his face had the cruelty of an executioner rather than the humility of a priest. Because my clothes disposed him to despise me, he looked at me with contempt, folding his arms across his chest. With an anxious tongue I asked him if this was the Caesarion church, and he nodded his head, pursed his lips and looked as if he were about to bite me on the shoulder. Softly I asked after the priest Yoannes and he shook his head violently as if to say he did not know him and did not want any more of my questions. I moved away from him hurriedly until I reached the junction between the street coming from the sea and the big Canopian Way. I then should have crossed the Canopian Way, headed right towards the southern quarter of the city, known as the Egyptians' quarter, and slipped in among them. But I was walking aimlessly, unaware of the layout of the city or how its quarters were arranged.

I thought of leaving the city to spend the night outside the walls, to return in the morning as though I were entering for the first time, undoing everything that had happened over the last few days. I headed towards the walls with a resolve to leave, but on my way I passed by the large garden surrounding the Great Theatre. When I went in and found it empty and a good place for people like me to sleep, I abandoned my resolve to leave the city and huddled up under a large tree from which hung branches coiled like the braided hair of girls. Sleeping here was safer than sleeping in the rocky cave, and warmer, so I lay down hungry to the grassy smell which diffused from the ground. Many times that smell came back to me later, in places where there was no grass.

That night my sleep was full of dreams and my dreams were full of Octavia, Octavia the gentle and cruel, Octavia who cried and laughed, the sleepy, the cheerful, the righteous, the pagan, Octavia the angry. At dawn I opened my eyes and realized that it was Sunday, the day of the lecture. I said to myself, 'It wouldn't matter if I stayed another day in the city wearing my southern clothes. I'll see Hypatia, then leave the city to spend the night among the wretched peasants. Tomorrow I'll come back here in my monk's cassock and go straight to the great Church of St Mark, where I will find the people I really belong to.'

The Sister of Jesus

I remember well how I crept like a thief towards the door to the Great Theatre and how embarrassed I felt at my ragged clothes among the elegant people, although the monastic life teaches us not to care whether clothes are ragged or not. The guards at the door showed me the way to the lecture and I went in with the others. It was a large hall set on the western side of the theatre, not part of it but surrounded by the same garden. The audience for the lecture was large, and included women. It was the first and only time I attended a lesson given by a woman. Everything in Alexandria is strange and different.

All those coming in for the lecture were speaking Greek and all had studied philosophy. That much was clear from their mutterings and subdued discussions. Before the lecture started their talk was full of the names of ancient philosophers, but they did not mention any of the saints or martyrs, as though they were living in another world. At first I thought I was going to hear a very pagan lecture, but then I discovered that mathematics has nothing to do with paganism or faith.

At the entrance to the hall stood a sun-clock and the shadow of the dial was almost touching the pointer indicating ten o'clock in the morning. People had come early. I stayed among them an hour, absorbed in myself, while they were busy with their quiet chatting and discreet laughter. They had clean clothes and their faces showed signs of ephemeral worldly affluence. I sat close to the door, at the end of the third row of wooden benches.

In my discomfort and from the feeling that I was out of place in the audience, I sat as rigid and brittle as a piece of old wood.

Moments before Hypatia appeared, a man sitting on my right in the second row looked towards me and greeted me with a smile. I returned the greeting with a timid smile, because a smile is the only answer to a smile. The fat man was about to start a conversation, had not the trumpets sounded to herald the arrival of the governor of the city, Orestes, who sat in the middle of the row. His retinue spread out to the sides and the first row filled up. Hypatia came into the vast hall and everyone stood up for her, including the men. They stood up so suddenly that I did not see her enter. When they had applauded her and sat down again, I watched her walk up the two steps to the podium. She stood like a dream before the audience, who settled down on the benches. She prepared to speak and everyone fell silent, as silent as the statues in the long Avenue of Rams in Thebes.

Before Hypatia uttered a word my heart began to flutter and race, so much so I feared that those around me would hear my troubled heartbeat. Hypatia was a dignified and beautiful woman, very beautiful in fact, perhaps the most beautiful woman in creation. She was about forty years old, and her nose and mouth, her voice and hair and eyes, were all perfect. Everything about her was magnificent. And when she spoke she was even more sublime. Several months later I learnt that she had been interested in learning since childhood at the hands of her father, the famous mathematician Theon, and that she had helped him while still an adolescent with the commentaries which he wrote on the works of Claudius Ptolemaeus, author of the *Geographia* and the Great Treatise[6] on astronomy.

Hypatia. When I write her name now, I can almost see her in front of me, standing on the platform in the large hall like a celestial being who had descended to earth from the mind of gods to bring them a divine message of compassion. Hypatia had what I had always imagined to be the appearance

6. In the margin of the parchment it says in Arabic: 'He means the Almagest, which remains the standard work on astronomy up to present times. I have seen an old Greek copy of it, and several Arabic translations with copious annotations, in our church in Edessa.'

of Jesus the Messiah, combining grace with majesty. Her limpid eyes were slightly blue and grey. Her forehead was broad and radiated a heavenly light. Her flowing gown and her bearing had a dignity to match the aura which surrounds deities. From what luminous element was this woman created? She was different from other women, and if it was the god Khnum who shapes men's bodies, then from what fine clay did he shape her, and with what heavenly essence did he mould her? Oh my God, I am blaspheming.

✝

Once she had mounted the platform, Hypatia was silent for no more than a few seconds. Then she raised her eyes towards her silent audience and started to speak. 'Friends, a few days ago I received from the island of Rhodes letters containing many observations and comments on what I have said in my lectures explaining the eminent Diophantos's book on calculating unknown numerical values. In view of the extremely specialist nature of the subject, I shall postpone a discussion of it until after this lecture, lest I bore those among you who are not mathematicians, although I believe the philosophy which most of you want us to talk about today can be solidly based on mathematics. You know, my brothers and sisters, that Plato the Great wrote on the door of his school in Athens, the Academy, the words: "Only he who has studied mathematics enters here." Nevertheless I will speak first about philosophy, then read my lecture in a separate session to discuss the mathematical questions which arise in the book of the eminent Diophantos the Alexandrian, for those of you who wish to follow the subject with me.'

I was following her avidly with my eyes. She had looked towards me twice during her speech, and her eyes frightened me. I had studied philosophy for years in Akhmim, but I had never heard anyone say such things. She was explaining to us in elevated Greek how the human mind can discern the order inherent in the universe, and through thought reach to the essence of things and thus identify their accidental and variable qualities. Phrases from basic philosophy tripped off her tongue, phrases which I had long heard from others, but when she spoke them it was as though she was opening my mind and instilling them inside. Even when she talked about the well-known theories of the Pythagoreans, such as their saying, 'The world is number and harmony', from the depth of her expression and the succinct way she expressed it I realized that all beings emanate from the rhythms of a single system, and I understood from what she said things I had never understood from other philosophy teachers.

Before the end of the lecture the idea occurred to me to be a disciple of Hypatia for the rest of my life, or a servant who walks behind her. I thought that if I went back to Octavia and apologized to her for deceiving her for a whole three days she might forgive me. I would argue that I was afraid to lose her and decided to stay silent because I had done wrong. And Octavia would forgive me, and kiss me again, and I would live with her and forget the illusions which drove me and took my steps I know not where. I would come to know the Sicilian master when he came back from his journey, and know Hypatia from close by and study medicine until I excelled in it, and maybe find a cure for the disease we call Aa.[7] My thoughts wandered and I was too distracted to follow the rest of the lecture.

Then I listened to the end of the teacher's lecture, and what she said still sticks in my mind. 'My friends, even if understanding is in fact an intellectual process, it is also a spiritual process, because the truths we arrive at through logic and mathematics, unless we feel them with our souls, will remain raw facts, and we will fall short of grasping how magnificent it is that we perceive them. Two hours have passed that I have been talking to you and I know that I have gone on too long and tired you. So accept my apologies and my appreciation that you attended today. I'll come back to this hall in half an hour to talk about the mathematics of Diophantos. Those who choose to honour me by taking part are welcome, provided they are students of mathematics, lest they hate it and hate me with it.'

The audience smiled and some of them laughed, and all prepared to go out behind her. I stayed planted at my place like the stones of the Pyramids,

---

7. The Aa mentioned twice in this parchment is probably the ancient Egyptian name for the disease which we now know as bilharzias. (Translator's Note)

like the oval rocks on the banks of the Nile in my old country. Hypatia would come back in half an hour, and where else could I go?

The rows had almost emptied out, except for some disciples who stayed gathering together their papers and moving to the front-row seats with their books. The governor, his retinue and the public were hovering around Hypatia at the table, a table weighed down with varieties of sweet pastries. So that's what the loudmouth crier meant, the day I came into Alexandria. I don't like sweet things and I did not eat any with them on that day, even though I was so ravenous with hunger that I almost fainted. Out of modesty I made do with two dates which were in my bag, and refrained from standing in my tattered clothes among the elegant people who were eating.

After a long half-hour, the voices coming from behind the door went quiet, and the governor and most of the public left. Hypatia came back, surrounded by a small group of scholars and students of various ages. She mounted the platform, as she had done the first time, and the hall fell quiet as it had done before. There were no more than twenty people and I was still in my place on the third row when she pointed at me and said, 'You can come to the front row, if you like.'

'No, my lady, I'm comfortable here, but thank you for your kindness.'

'Thank you for your kindness! Strange words, brother stranger.'

'I'm from the south, reverend lady.'

'Welcome to our city.'

I did not understand most of what Hypatia said in her second lecture. I was merely staring at her, regretful that in my youth I had avoided studying mathematics. When she spoke I was full of enthusiasm and I made a resolution to do something which in fact I never did. 'I'll study mathematics with medicine and theology. I'll study the principles of geometry and arithmetic first, then specialize in them and excel.' In those days I was like a dry leaf tossed by the wind, and I think I'm still like that!

After the lecture the audience hovered around her again. I don't know how I found the courage, but I approached Hypatia fearlessly, and without her asking me anything I told her I had come to Alexandria to study medicine and I planned to stay in the city five years to absorb the learning, then go home and treat the sick in my home country. I added in my outburst that throughout my stay in Alexandria I would eagerly attend all her scientific sessions, even the mathematical ones. Throughout she smiled and took an interest in what I was saying, emboldening me to speak at length, though my only motive was to keep looking at her. When I stopped speaking, she spoke. 'So I'll see you here next Sunday, good southern friend.'

'My lady, do you not give lessons in medicine?'

'No, my friend, I'm very sorry.'

As she answered my sudden question, her smile was enough to dispel my loneliness, my hunger and my sense that I was a stranger. She pointed at one of those standing around her, five middle-aged men and a thin woman, and said, 'This good colleague of mine, Synesios the Cyrene, also wanted to study medicine at the start, but ended up studying philosophy.' She looked at him out of the corner of her eye. 'And now he wants to renounce philosophy, and believe in its antithesis!'

The man by the name of Synesios gave a pleasant laugh and tossed his head back a little. He put his right hand on my left shoulder affectionately and said, 'Don't believe the savante, my brother, for she twice strayed from the truth in what she said; firstly when she described me as a colleague, when I am merely her disciple and she my teacher, and secondly in that, if I follow the way of the church, that does not mean that I will renounce philosophy and believe in its antithesis.' Everyone laughed at what he said, except me, and they prepared to leave the hall. I never saw the man called Synesios the Cyrene again after that day but I heard later that he became a great man of the church in the Western Pentapolis known as Libya, in fact the bishop of one of the five cities, I think the city of Tolmeita, also known as Barca.

They all went out and I tarried a while, my legs heavy. I had no idea of my purpose after this lesson, which I would have liked to last forever. Before disappearing behind the door, Hypatia smiled and looked towards me as though she were impressing my features on her memory for the next occasion when she saw me, the occasion which I wish had never come. Hypatia left like a delightful dream which gladdened a sad man's heart for a moment, then faded forever.

At the theatre door I stood lost in thought as she mounted her two-horse carriage. The train of her embroidered robe was the last I saw of her, and the last beautiful thing I saw for days to come. When her carriage disappeared from sight, I was back to my loneliness and anxiety. I had nowhere to go. For a moment I stood helpless, everything jumbled up inside me. With heavy steps I turned towards the big garden, and when the sun rose high in the sky I went back to the tree under which I had slept the night before. Under it and around it many people were taking cover from the midday sun, and among them was something I never expected to see: a group of my school colleagues from Naga Hammadi, all of them in ecclesiastical garments.

As soon as they saw me they gathered around me, delighted at my surprise arrival, though it was in fact they who took me by surprise. They asked me what brought me here and I said I was lost. They asked me about my church clothes and I said they were torn and dirty and I was keeping them in my bag until I could mend and wash them, and to save myself from ridicule by the pagans. They asked me where I was going and I said I had a letter for the priest Yoannes the Libyan. They knew him and led me to him, and so for the first time I entered the great Church of St Mark in Alexandria, the Church of the Wheat Seed, surrounded by eight monks.

When Yoannes had finished reading the letter of recommendation which had been in my bag, he lifted his face and asked me quietly and concisely after the health and circumstances of his friend who recommended me. I reassured him and did not tell him I knew that they both rejected the ideas and the violent acts of the previous bishop, Theophilus, and that they had written each other letters about that, although in their youth they were his disciples and believed he was fighting against the paganism which had long struggled against Christianity. When they found him prolonging his war indefinitely, they shunned and avoided him. I also did not tell him that his friend had sent me to Alexandria after the bishop's death in the hope that the situation would calm down. I did not hint at any of this, even remotely. I just mentioned some of the stories he had told about them when they were monks at St Antony's monastery and when they were neighbours to St Shenouda the Archimandrite, the head of the solitaries in Akhmim. His face showed signs of relief and when I finished he invited me to rest from my long journey, and he called on his servant to show me the way.

The servant first took me to the vast refectory and ate some hot food with me. Then he took me to a guest wing with many very small rooms, and told me that in a few days I would move from these temporary quarters to a monk's room. Two days passed as I swam in the seas of the church, which have no shores. The church had dozens of priests and monks, and hundreds of visitors and people came all day long to pray, seek blessings or confess. The church never slept; it was a beehive always glorifying the kingdom of God. Even in the depths of night, when they lit the prodigious and extraordinary lantern which hung in the church, it seemed to me that this place was the world where I truly belonged, and I told myself often in those days that I was not part of this ephemeral world. The Lord had chosen me for some mysterious purpose known to him, so let the Lord's will be done.

I ended up staying in a small room inside the church, surrounded by other rooms occupied by many like me, servants of the Lord. Most of them were monks from the Western Pentapolis and Upper Egypt, and some were priests who had come on short missions from faraway places, such as Abyssinia, where they speak that strange language. In the early days no one paid me any attention, except a visiting monk originally from a small village near the Muharraq Monastery, which I had passed by on my way to Alexandria. The remote monastery was built years ago by the late Bishop Theophilus in the Qusqam Mountain overlooking Lycopolis (Assiut). The monk was staying in the next room, waiting to leave with the Abyssinians, to live in their land and never come back. I no longer remember his name, perhaps Bishoy, but I am not certain now. 'Bishoy' in the Egyptian language means 'elevated' but this monk was short. I was drawn by his dignity, goodness and the fact that he was a stranger. At the time he was about thirty years old and spoke the Sa'idi dialect of Egyptian like me. We used to chat between the prayers and the masses, and on our way to the refectory. After a few days we became brothers in the fold of the Lord. When I told him on Saturday that I planned to go out the next day to go to Hypatia's lecture, he shouted at me,: 'That's quite wrong.' He told me in alarm that if this act was committed, it could never be forgiven, and he advised me never to mention her name again. 'It would be a mortal sin. Would you miss the Sunday sermon by Pope Cyril, the great bishop, to go and see a harpy! That sin would never be pardoned if you committed it. As for me, you have nothing to fear. I'll consider it a bad joke, and will never mention it to anyone.'

I had a sleepless night, torn by every conflicting thought. Should I forget that I had seen Hypatia and devote myself to my purpose in coming, then go back to my native country safe and sound? Or should I leave the church forever? Should I go out tomorrow morning and never come back? At least I am not a prisoner between these walls. What's the point in staying? Jesus the Messiah began his great mission among the people, not between walls amidst monks and priests. There was real life around him, yet why should we die before death comes? But I am safe in the church, after I was homeless, and the men of the faith are my real family, since I have no earthly family except my uncle who is weakened by the Aa disease and who I doubt will still be alive when I return. Who would I go back to if I returned to my home country? And which is my home country? Is it the village of my uncle who's waiting to die? Is it my father's village, where no one will know me? Or the village where my mother settled? My mother who slept every night in the arms of a man with sin on his hands. I hate him and I hate her, and the hatred will kill me. But I should love my enemies and do good to those who have done me ill, to be truly Christian, and truly loving. I have seen real love only in a pagan woman, who met me by chance on the beach and took me into her paradise for three nights together and four unforgettable days. If I went back to Octavia, would she accept me or would she again call me vile and despicable? That was the first time anyone had insulted me and I will try to make sure it's the last. No one will dare insult me as long as I am a monk in the great church, and perhaps I will rise in the clerical hierarchy until I become bishop of one of the big cities. But what do I want with a bishopric? Will it compensate me for my dream of excelling in medicine, and my hope of curing Aa? Will I follow my earthly ambitions, after promising my ailing uncle that I was giving my life to Jesus the Saviour? That would not be right of me, and that way I would lose my reason for living. What if tomorrow I offered to live in Hypatia's house to serve her and learn from her? She would agree and she would help me study medicine in the Museion or scientific academy and I would be a distinguished doctor within only two years, because I had studied medicine extensively in Akhmim. Of all its many branches the only one I lacked was anatomy, and the doctors of the Museion had been dissecting for hundreds of years and knew all the secrets of medicine. That's what I told myself that night, though I had not yet discovered that the Museion had closed down years earlier.

That night my brain kept churning with conflicting ideas. My heart ached and my spirit was broken. I thought, 'If I leave the church, and leave it when they know who I am, they will see me as an apostate and they will persecute me as they persecuted those who renounced Christianity in the days of Emperor Julian.' Christianity was now the official religion of the whole empire and I would not survive denunciation by the fearsome group called the Lovers of the Passion. Because of them I would meet the same fate as my father, and they would rejoice as my mother rejoiced. But I was burning with desire to see Hypatia the next day. I would discuss philosophical matters with her and I would rise in her estimation, though she in any case esteems everyone. She is true to the meaning of her Greek name Hypatia: sublime. She was only ten or fifteen years older than me, and that's not a big difference. Let her adopt me as a son or a younger brother, or maybe the day will come when she will fall in love with me, and we would be like the couples Octavia spoke of when she said that women who love younger men make them the happiest of the happy. But there is no happiness or joy in this world.

I awoke from my reverie to the sound of the bells for Bishop Cyril's sermon, and I went out with all the others as they left their rooms. I was squeezed between hundreds of people going into the church. The nave was full and there was no longer any way to leave or to move from the spot where I was stuck among the monks, priests, deacons, gospel readers, initiates great and small, former wrestlers who had become believers, members of the Lovers of the Passion group, sons of penitents who had rejoined the church, bewildered followers of the Tall Brothers, and groups of monks from the

Wadi Natroun monasteries. I was surrounded on all sides by the army of the Lord. Their chant, which made the nave quake and the walls tremble, foretold that great news and momentous events were nigh. When the chant reached its climax and their voices were close to cracking, Bishop Cyril appeared above us in his pulpit.

The bishop's awesome aspect stunned and amazed me. It was the first time I had seen him, and after that for the next two years I would see him every Sunday morning without exception. I also saw him the day of the private meeting, which I will relate if the occasion arises to speak of it. When I saw the bishop for the first time I was astonished, because he looked down on us from a pulpit with walls covered in gilt. That was just one level, and above it there was an enormous wooden cross holding a statue of Jesus made of coloured plaster. From the forehead, hands and feet of the crucified Christ flowed blood coloured bright red.

I looked at the ragged piece of cloth on the statue of Jesus, then at the bishop's embroidered robe. Jesus's clothes were old rags, torn at the chest and most of the limbs, while the bishop's clothes were embellished with gold thread all over, so that his face was hardly visible. Jesus's hands were free of the baubles of our world, while the bishop held what I think was a sceptre made of pure gold, judging from how brightly it shone. On his head Jesus had his crown of thorns, while the bishop had on his head the bright gold crown of a bishop. Jesus seemed resigned as he assented to sacrifice himself on the cross of redemption. Cyril seemed intent on imposing his will on the heavens and the earth.

The bishop looked at his people and his flock, and gazed around at the crowd which had pressed into the nave of the church. He raised his golden sceptre and they fell silent. Then he spoke, saying, 'Sons of Christ, in the name of the living God I bless this day of yours, and all your days. I start my sermon with the truth which Paul the Apostle speaks in his second epistle to Timothy when he says to him, and to every Christian in every time and every place: "Endure hardship with us like a good soldier of Christ Jesus. No one serving as a soldier gets involved in civilian affairs – he wants to please his commanding officer. Similarly, if anyone competes as an athlete, he does not receive the victor's crown unless he competes according to the rules.'"

I thought for a moment that the bishop meant me by what he said and that this was one of his mysterious miracles. He raised his voice until it reverberated against the walls of the solemn church. 'Let me start with this. Let me remind you that we live in a time of sedition, thus we are in the midst of a holy war. The light of Christ has spread so that it today almost covers the earth and dispels the darkness which lasted so long. But the forces of darkness are still nestling here and there, looking down on God's earth in the guise of sedition and of heresies which burrow into people's hearts. We will not cease fighting them as long as we live. We have dedicated ourselves to our Lord Jesus Christ. Let us be the soldiers of the truth, content only with the wreath of heavenly triumph. Let us be loyal to the religion of the Saviour, that we may join the martyrs and the saints who passed through the world to obtain heavenly glory and eternal life.'

I noticed many eyes full of tears and many faces almost bursting with enthusiasm. All eyes were pinned on Bishop Cyril, who had full command of their emotions. His Greek phrases were powerful and eloquent, as though he spoke with the tongue of the apostles and with the heart of the early fathers. My mind wandered and I gazed into the far distance. Then he caught my attention again, saying, 'As for those who call themselves the Tall Brothers, we will not review their case, which has been decided, and we will not engage in a new heretical dispute to examine the soundness of the beliefs of their master Origen, after Pope Theophilus, the bishop of this great city, condemned him, thirteen years before he proceeded to the higher kingdom. I will not repeat to them the resolutions of the Holy Synod of the church of Alexandria, which condemned Origen in the year 135 of the Martyrs, that is the year 399 of the incarnation of Christ. I will not repeat to you the resolutions of the subsequent synods which affirmed the condemnation, deposition and excommunication of Origen, for there were many synods held in Jerusalem, Cyprus and Rome. I will not repeat to you the resolutions passed by the eminent fathers at those synods, because they are well known and widely circulated. Those who are literate may read them, and those who do not read may go to the church library and ask one of the fathers to read them to you. But I say today that I will not allow any review of the beliefs of a philosopher who died a century and a half ago, a philosopher who worked on theology and went astray and committed heresy, a philosopher whose ordination as a priest was invalid. Let his followers, the Tall Brothers,[8] hold their tongues and behave humbly, as Jesus Christ behaved humbly. They should cease touring the towns, tall and giddy with doubts, and cease stirring up trouble and heretical notions which threaten the true faith, the true faith which we have devoted our lives to defend, as righteous soldiers of Jesus Christ.'

Suddenly one of the people standing shouted out, in a voice so raucous that he almost wrenched his throat from the shouting. 'Blessed are you from heaven, Pope. Blessed are your words in the name of the living God!' He began to repeat the same phrase, until the others behind him started repeating it too. The enthusiasm almost unhinged the minds of the congregation, and their chants to Bishop Cyril shook the walls of the church. The bishop made the sign of the cross in the air and raised his sceptre for the crowd twice, and their enthusiasm exploded insanely. Some of them fainted and fell among the throng, some of their bodies began to convulse with the chanting, and some of them closed their tearful eyes. The bishop, or pope as they call him in Alexandria, turned and disappeared behind the door to the pulpit amidst a group of senior priests holding crosses bigger than any I had ever seen.

The days in the Church of St Mark passed monotonously, except for the noisy Sundays. Little by little I submitted to the will of God. Yoannes the priest took care of me from afar and always recommended that I avoid

8. In the margin of the parchment, someone has written in Arabic: 'This refers to four monks who were brothers and were followers of Origen, whom they considered a saint. The four brother monks were tall in stature, hence their name the Tall Brothers. After Alexandria expelled them, they travelled from town to town, proselytizing for their sect, and they gathered followers who glorified and sanctified Origen.'

mixing with the Alexandrian monks, especially those who called themselves the Lovers of the Passion. There was among them a monk advanced in years whom they greatly feared and some months later I discovered why I stayed clear of his cruel gaze. The old monk was originally from Upper Egypt but none the less he did not like those who came to Alexandria from there. He came across me one day in the nave of the church, when I had been there about a year. He summoned me with a wave of the stick with which he supported his seventy years. When I approached him, he whispered, 'Go back to your country quickly. Alexandria is not the place for you!' His voice was most like the hissing of a viper and his tone was as sharp as a scorpion's sting. I did not understand his intent and when I told Yoannes the priest about it, he advised me to stay away from the old monk. Some days later the servant in the guest wing, after looking around carefully, told me a hidden secret. 'That old monk is a Lover of the Passion and one of the heroes of the church. In his youth he was part of the group which assassinated the bishop of Alexandria, George of Capadoccia, and cut him up with cleavers in the streets of the eastern quarter.' The servant added in a whisper, after looking round again, 'That was forty-eight years ago, in the year 77 of the Martyrs,' meaning the year 361 of the Nativity.

I asked him, 'Why did they do that to the bishop of the city?'

'Because he was imposed on us by Rome, and he was a renegade sympathetic to the views of the accursed Arius.'

In the tedious years I spent in Alexandria I attended classes in medicine and theology regularly, and I was known among the people of the church as someone who prayed often and spoke little. They had a good opinion of my righteousness and piety. As the days and months passed I forgot what had happened to me in my first days in the city and no longer heard news of Hypatia or anyone else until those critical days in the year 415 of the Glorious Nativity when murmurs reached the men of the church that the dispute between Pope Cyril and Orestes, the governor of Alexandria, had flared up. Reports spread that a group of church people had blocked the path of Governor Orestes and thrown stones at him, although he was originally a Christian and in his youth had been baptized in Antioch by John Chrysostom, and although Christ at the start of his mission forbade the Jews from stoning the harlot, on the famous occasion when he said: 'He that is without sin among you, let him first cast a stone at her.'

But at the time this dispute between the bishop and the governor did not interest me in the least, and I was distracted from it by my daily concerns, my prayers and my tedious studies. I had no desire to listen to rumours or follow the news, until the name Hypatia started to come up in most gatherings when people talked. I thought I had forgotten her completely but whenever I heard her name I found myself troubled, and my heart raced at the memory of her.

I hankered to find out what was happening beyond the walls of the church, and I started to follow the stories and the latest developments. I started by asking Yoannes the priest, who rebuked me and told me to attend only to my purpose in coming to Alexandria. A few days later I repeated my question delicately and he advised me to stay away from the subject and to take an interest only in what I was in the church to achieve. I asked others and from them I did not obtain any news that was reassuring. But from the gossiping of the servants who came back and forth between the city and the church, I established that the bishop's hatred for Hypatia had reached a peak. They said that Governor Orestes had thrown a Christian man out of his council, and the pope was angered. They said the governor opposed the pope's desire to expel the Jews completely from Alexandria, after Bishop Theophilus had expelled them to the Jewish quarter on the eastern side of the city, beyond the walls. They said the governor was supposed to be an ally to the people of our faith, but the devil Hypatia was pushing him in the other direction. They said she operated by magic and made astronomical instruments for astrologers and charlatans. They said many things, none of them reassuring.

The days that passed were charged with tension until that inauspicious Sunday came, inauspicious in every sense of the word. On the morning of that day, Pope Cyril went off to his pulpit to give his weekly sermon to the crowds, but his looks were downcast. He did not view his audience with his usual pleasure at seeing them. He bowed his head for a long while, then rested his golden sceptre on the balustrade of the pulpit and lifted his arms to heaven until his wide sleeves fell back and his thin arms were visible. His fingers were splayed in the air like the tines of a fork, and in a thunderous roar he started to read the prayer recorded in the Gospel according to St Matthew: 'Our Father which art in heaven, hallowed be Thy name, Thy kingdom come, Thy will be done on earth as it is in heaven.'

The bishop began to repeat the prayer and the people started sobbing as they repeated the prayer after him. Then his voice turned fiery. 'Children of God, friends of the living Jesus. This city of yours is the city of the Almighty Lord. Mark the Apostle settled here, on its soil lived fathers of the church, the blood of martyrs flowed here and in it the foundations of our faith were built. We have purged it of the Jews, who have been expelled. God helped us to expel them and cleanse our city of them, but the remnants of the filthy pagans are still raising strife in the land. They spread iniquity and heresy around us, and intrude insolently on the secrets of the church. They ridicule what they do not understand and talk in jest about serious matters, slandering your true faith. They want to rebuild the great house of idols which was brought down on top of them years ago. They want to revive their abandoned school, which used to instil darkness in the minds of men. They want to bring the Jews back to the quarter where they used to live, inside the walls of your city. But, soldiers of the Lord, the Lord will never consent to that. He will thwart their vile endeavours and ruin their sick dreams. He will raise the standing of this great city, through your hands. As long as you are right, soldiers of the Lord, as long as you are right, soldiers of the Truth, our Lord Jesus Christ spoke truly when he spoke with a tongue of fire, saying, "The truth will set you free." So, children of the Lord, free your land from the defilement of the pagans, cut out the tongues of those who speak evil, throw them and their wickedness into the sea and wash away the mortal sins. Follow the words of the Saviour, the words of truth, the words of the Lord. Know that our Lord Jesus Christ spoke to us his children in all times when he said: "Think not that I am come to send peace on earth: I came not to send peace, but a sword.'"

The throngs shook with excitement, reaching fever pitch, and in his roar of enthusiasm, Cyril repeated the words of Jesus Christ: 'Think not I am come to send peace on earth: I came not to send peace, but a sword.' The fervour of the crowd intensified, almost to the point of madness. People began to repeat the phrase after him and they did not stop until another voice rang out, interrupting the chant with a cry like thunder. It was that colossal man who usually brought an end to the fiery Sunday sermons, I mean Peter the gospel reader at the Caesarion church. He sprang from among the crowd, shouting, 'With heaven's help, we shall purge the land of the Lord of the servants of the devil.' The bishop stopped speaking, and the congregation fell quiet except for Peter the reader. Then some of them began to repeat his phrase after him, and one of them added this frightening chant: 'In the name of the living God, we will destroy the house of the idols and build a new house for the Lord. With heaven's help we will purge the land of the Lord of the servants of Satan. In the name of the living God, we will destroy the house of the idols.'

The bishop turned, took up his sceptre, raised it in the air to make the sign of the cross with it. The frenzy of the crowd swept the church and the raucous chants drowned each other out. Reason had no place and a sense of chaos prevailed, heralding some momentous event. Peter the reader was the first to move towards the door, then groups of people followed him out, chanting a new phrase: 'With heaven's help we will cleanse the land of the Lord.'

The nave of the church was almost empty and the voices of those chanting after Peter the reader could be heard from outside the walls. The bishop, followed by priests, came in from his balcony and I did not know where to go. Should I go back to my room and shut the door on myself, as I always did? Or should I stay in the nave of the church, until it was clear what the Lord's will would be? Or should I follow the crowds outside? Without any planning on my part, or any planning of which I was aware, I went out after the crowds timidly and joined them, but of course I did not repeat what they were saying.

Peter, as leader of the throng, headed towards the big Canopian Way, with hundreds of people chanting behind him. The noonday sun was fierce and the high humidity made it hard to breathe. The houses shook from the marching and loud chanting of the believers. Some of them had their windows and doors closed up, while on the roofs of others the residents were standing waving crosses. They stirred up the dust along the street and the merciful angels fled the scene. My heart told me that something terrible was about to happen. I was walking along, pulled by what was happening around me as though I were in one of the visions in the Book of Habakkuk which warn that the world is ephemeral and transient.

After roaming for some time from one district to another, the number of people chanting and cheering diminished as they dispersed into the side streets. Now they were in dozens, spread around between various streets, still chanting the same chants. At one moment I thought the purpose of this clamour was to show that the Christians were the most visible and strongest group in the city, in other words it was an implicit message to the governor, and an open warning to all the inhabitants. But then it changed into something beyond that, something more profound and more horrible.

The rays of the midday sun blazed down, and the air was so stifling it was hard to breathe as I panted after the group of chanters still left behind Peter the reader. I was about to turn back towards the walls of the church, to my impregnable fortress, when I noticed this thin man with a long head, running from the end of the street and shouting to Peter and those with him, 'The infidel woman has mounted her carriage, and she has no guards!'

My heart pounded with sudden panic when I saw Peter shouting and running in the direction indicated by the man with the long head, with the others following him. I ran after them, but wished I had not. At the small church which is halfway along the broad street leading from the Great Theatre to the eastern harbour, Hypatia's two-horse carriage came into view, the same carriage I had seen her mount when she drove away from me three years earlier. The carriage was as it was then, and the horses were the same two horses. Only I was not as I had been. Peter the reader, with his vast frame, rushed off to catch up with the carriage, shouting as he ran. His followers came on behind, shouting incomprehensible words. A few yards before he reached her, he suddenly stopped and turned. One of the group rushed to his side with a ghastly scream and pulled out from under his habit a long knife, a long rusty knife.

✝

I won't write another word, no.

✝

Lord, still my hand. Take me unto You. Have mercy on me.

✝

I'll tear up the parchments. I'll wash them in water, I'll…

'Write, Hypa, write in the name of the truth, the truth preserved in you.'

'Azazeel, I can't.'

'Write and don't be a coward, for what you have seen with your eyes, no one but you will write down, and if you conceal it no one will know of it.'

'I told Nestorius about it, in Jerusalem years ago.'

'Hypa, that day you told a part of it. Today write it down in full, write it all now.'

✝

When Peter took the long rusty knife, the driver of Hypatia's carriage saw him. He leapt like a rat and ran to hide between the walls of the houses. The driver could have driven his horses into the main street and no one would have been able to catch up with the carriage. But he ran away and no one tried to catch him. The two horses walked around confused until Peter stopped them with one arm as he brandished the knife. Hypatia leant her royal head out of the carriage window, her eyes terrified at what she saw around her. She scowled and was about to say something when Peter shouted at her, 'We've come for you, you whore, you enemy of the Lord.'

His hand grabbed at her and other hands grabbed too. It was as if she were floating on a cloud, held up on their hostile arms, and in broad daylight the horror began. The sea of hands attacked like weapons: some opened the carriage door, others pulled at the trail of her silk dress, others grabbed Hypatia by the arm and threw her to the ground. She had her long hair tied up like a crown on her head, but the hair fell loose. Peter dug his fingers into it and twisted the braids around his wrist. When she screamed, he said, 'In the name of the Lord, we will purge the land of the Lord.'

Peter pulled her by the hair to the middle of the street, surrounded by his followers, the jubilant soldiers of the Lord. Hypatia tried to stand up but one of them kicked her in the side and she crumpled. She did not have the strength to scream. Peter pushed her back flat on the ground with a violent tug which pulled out some of her hair. He threw her down and brushed her away from him, stuck the knife in the sash wrapped around his waist, then grabbed her hair with both fists and dragged her behind him. Behind him, too, the soldiers of the Lord started to chant their exultant chant, as he pulled his victim along.

At that moment I was standing transfixed on the pavement. When they came level with me, Peter looked in my direction with the face of an enormous hyena. Beaming with euphoria, he said, 'Yes, holy monk, today we will purge the land of the Lord!' As she writhed on the ground, Hypatia turned over and faced towards where I was standing. She looked at me thunderstruck, her face inflamed with blood. She examined me for that moment and I knew she recognized me, even though I was wearing church clothes. She stretched her arm out towards me and cried out for my help. 'Brother!' she said. I took two paces to the middle of the street until my fingers almost touched her fingertips as she reached towards me. Peter the reader was panting in elation as he walked towards the sea dragging his prize. The others were gathering around their prey like wolves around a baby gazelle. Just as Hypatia's fingers and mine were about to lock, a hand stretched out and grabbed the sleeve of her dress, and her hand was flung away from me. The dress ripped and the man who grabbed it raised a strip of it in the air and waved it around, shouting out Peter's slogan: 'In the name of the Lord, we will purge...', the slogan that became that day the anthem of cheap glory. From the distance a woman approached, her head uncovered, shouting as she rushed towards us in terror. 'Sister! Roman soldiers, save us, Serapis.'

Her dress and her hair streamed behind her. We had moved further towards the sea and the woman started to run towards the crowd and then threw herself on Hypatia, in the belief that she could protect her. Then the unexpected happened. People thrust their hands and arms towards her, pulled her off Hypatia and threw her violently to the side of the street. Her head hit the pavement and her face was grazed, streaked with blood and dust. The woman tried to stand up but one of the crowd struck her on the head with a hefty piece of wood studded with nails. The woman staggered and suddenly fell on her back, right in front of me, with blood bursting from her nose and mouth and spattering her dress. When she fell at my feet, I screamed at the shock of the surprise. I knew her but she did not recognize me. She was shuddering as she breathed her last breaths. And so died Octavia on the day of terror, at my feet, without seeing me.

I stepped back and leant my back against the wall of an old house. I could not take my eyes off Hypatia's body. The attack on her had raised pandemonium and the soldiers of the Lord were raving with that fever that possesses wolves when they bring down a quarry. Their eyes protruded like the eyes of madmen and in their passion they hungered for more blood, more hunting. They gathered around Hypatia as Peter stopped to catch his breath. One of them laid a hand on her again and others joined in, pulling at the front of her silk dress, which was torn and soiled with blood and dirt. They took hold of the embroidered dress at the seams and pulled but it did not give way. Peter pulled so hard so suddenly that he almost fell on top of her, but soon he regained his balance and was back up. He resumed dragging his victim along, while his followers bent down behind him, trying to get hold of Hypatia's dress. Hypatia, the Savante of the Age, the pure and holy, the lady who suffered the torments of martyrdom and in her agony transcended all agonies.

At the corner of the street, running parallel to the sea, stood an old woman with grey hair, waving a cross. 'Skin the whore!' she cried. It was as if the old woman had uttered a divine command. Peter stopped suddenly and his followers stopped a moment too, then they resumed their shrill screams. I left Octavia's body behind me and, aghast, I caught up with the others, hoping that Hypatia might escape them, or that the governor's troops might come and save her from them, or that some miracle from heaven might occur, or... I wasn't far from them but not too close, and I saw the result of the old woman's inspired suggestion. They fell upon Hypatia's dress and ripped it. They fought over the silk dress until they pulled it off her body. Then they pulled off her underclothes, which were tight around her body, and took pleasure in ripping them up as they hollered. The old woman was shouting at them like a hysteric, 'Skin her!' And Hypatia was shouting, 'People of Alexandria!' Those too far away to reach her body were shouting, 'The whore, the witch!' Alone, I was silent.

Hypatia was now completely naked, and completely crumbled in her nakedness. She had abandoned hope of deliverance, completely crushed. They brought a rough rope from I know not where and tied it around her wrist, paid out two or three yards and then started to drag her along by the rope tied to her wrist. Thus I learnt that day what the old woman meant when she inspired Peter the reader and his followers to skin her.

The streets of Alexandria are paved in stone to stop them getting muddy from the rain in winter. The stones are carefully fitted but not without gaps, and the edges are sharp because of the hardness of the stone. They tear to shreds anything dragged across them, and if it has a skin they peel the skin off. If it is a human, they skin him. In this way they skinned Hypatia at the end of their rough rope, shredding her skin off and ulcerating her flesh.

Among the scattered rocks at the edge of the eastern harbour, behind the Caesarion church which was once a temple and then became a house of the Lord where Peter read the gospel every day, there stood a pile of sea-shells. I did not see who picked the first one up and brought it over towards Hypatia. Those I did see were many, all holding shells and pouncing on their victim, and with the shells they scraped the skin off her flesh. Her screams reverberated in the skies above the unhappy city, the city of Almighty God, the capital of salt and cruelty.

The wolves grabbed the rope from Peter's hand and pulled Hypatia off. She was now a piece of red lacerated flesh, or rather many pieces. At the door to the abandoned temple, at the edge of the royal quarter or Brucheum, they threw her on a large pile of wood, and when she was dead they set fire to it. The flames rose and the sparks flew. Hypatia's screams had died away. Her wails of pain had reached the vaults of heaven, where God and his angels and Satan watched what was happening and did nothing.

'Hypa, what's that you are writing?'

'Shut up, Azazeel. Shut up, damn you.'

Wanderings

I remember well how I stood, broken and ashamed, at the gate of the abandoned temple. The crowd was breaking up and the tongues of flame from the wood around Hypatia's dead body were dying down. The rest of her body, like the rest of the wood, was just charred fragments.

I came out of my stupor to realize I had no idea where I should head. Should I go back to the Church of St Mark, which had been my refuge and my shelter for the past three years, and join my brothers there in their ecstatic celebrations of conquest and victory over the last symbol of a dying paganism, and declare with them that we rejoiced that the true faith had been proclaimed and had achieved complete control of the city? Or should I throw myself on the dying embers around the body of Hypatia and embrace it, in the hope of catching a remaining spark of that fire which had burned inside her, and die with her, making amends for my second act of cowardice? The day my father was killed I was cowardly because I was young and powerless. So why did I shy away from coming to Hypatia's aid when she reached out towards me? Octavia tried to protect her, and invoked the help of the god of Alexandria called Serapis, and she ended up a lifeless body cast on the side of the street, with her innocent blood for a shroud. My father did not call for my help, but Hypatia did... The woman caught in adultery did not ask Jesus for help but he saved her from the hard-hearted people who wanted to stone her. And me, I did not save the sister of Jesus from the hands of my brothers in Christ, but they are not my brothers, and I am not one of them, nor am I my old self.

I felt my heart melt like water between my ribs and then turn to air. The sky, the sea, the houses and the embers at the entrance to the burned temple, all turned in my head, and I fainted. When I came to at sunset, terrified, the cold sent a shiver through my body. The front of my cassock was soaked with water, which those around me said they had splashed on me to bring me back to consciousness. There were three of them surrounding me – an adolescent boy, a black woman in middle age and a monk advanced in years. I looked around and found myself lying in front of a small house in the street which runs from the Caesarion church to the burned temple. I did not ask how they had carried me there. I staggered to my feet, and when I stood up my head throbbed with the sound of Hypatia's screams, which still filled the sky for me and mixed with the sounds of the sea nearby, the sea from which I once thought that life began and which I later found out was the end of everything, when I learnt that a time will come when the salty sea will cover the whole world and the colour green will die and life will disappear.

The monk and the boy tried to support me but I pushed their arms away. After stumbling twice I managed to stand upright. In my left hand I grabbed the cross hanging on my chest and yanked it, and the thread around my neck broke. The monk and boy were shocked and the woman broke into tears. I felt a sudden relief when I pulled the cross from around my neck and dropped it to the ground to the amazement of the three. The monk bent down and picked it up and the boy took two steps back towards the wall, and the woman wailed. I moved away, fleeing them, escaping everything.

My steps led me to the Canopian Way, and I followed it eastwards without knowing why I was walking in that direction. I was roaming without forethought, without reflecting on my purpose. I noticed nothing along the way, until I emerged through the Sun Gate after dark. As soon as I went through the gate I ripped my cassock at the front and it hung down at my sides. I walked through the Jewish quarter with its houses stretching along the eastern wall. Their dogs barked behind me and almost grabbed the dangling shreds of cloth, and the night was pitch black.

I met no one along the way, neither Jews nor non-Jews, as though not a living soul remained in the whole world, neither human or jinn, angel or devil. The Lord was not with me, or was resting after a new creation which he had made in another six days. Alone I wandered over mud and sand, along the edges of sea, lakes and salt flats... away from Alexandria.

In the middle of the night I reached the village of Canopus but I did not go in lest someone see me or I see someone. In the early morning I crossed the Canopian branch of the Nile on a decrepit wooden ferry with two oars. Around me were peasants, a goat and sacks full of grain. The owner of the ferry did not ask me for the fare, and I kept walking eastwards. I don't remember the villages and fields I skirted, other than some scenes which now seem like a dream, and images of the lakes I passed, lakes where reeds grew so high they looked like giant thorns stabbing at the sky. The first verses of the Book of Habakkuk kept coming back to me: 'How long, O Lord, must I call for help, but you do not listen? Or cry out to you, "Violence!" but you do not save? Why do you make me look at injustice? Why do you tolerate wrong? Destruction and violence are before me; there is strife, and conflict abounds.'

I wandered like the Jews in the years of their great wandering in the Sinai desert to which I was heading. Why did my steps take me towards Sinai? Was that part of a divine plan which I did not understand? Or was fate playing with me, giving me a taste of every vicissitude, that I should see Christians in this country carry out deeds which I would never have imagined? When I meditate today on the works of fate, I wonder why I left Alexandria through the eastern gate. Was not the western gate closer? Or did I perhaps want to put my years in Alexandria behind me? I went in by one gate and left by the one opposite, as though my stay was just a transient passage which I wished I had not made. Would it have been more appropriate to head west that day and spend the rest of my life in one of the five peaceful cities of the Western Pentapolis dotted along the shore of the sea in the Libyan desert? Are they not distant cities fit for my heavy soul? Or perhaps I turned away from them because those cities are subject to Alexandria. If I had gone there at that time, I would not have met Nestorius in Jerusalem nor seen Martha here, and fate would not have played games with me nor sprinkled salt on my wounds. Even today I find no answer to my questions and have no choice but to say that it was the will of the Lord, the Lord secluded behind the panoplies of His mysterious wisdom or behind our chronic inability to understand who we are and what is happening around us.

'There's no need to talk about that now, Hypa, go back to your story and finish it off, because you are running out of time, for in twenty days you will leave this monastery.'

'Azazeel, don't you ever sleep?'

'How could I sleep when you are awake?'

I kept walking eastwards, inanimate. I was hurrying towards an unknown goal and at some point I realized that I did not even know my own self. My past life no longer existed. Thoughts and images crossed my mind without taking root, just as my feet stepped along the ground without stopping. I felt that everything that had happened to me and everything I had seen in the past days and years were nothing to do with me. I was someone else, not the person that once was and now was no more.

I reached an open area at the end of the Nile Delta, where the land meets the sea in vast marshes, where the water is a mixture of salty and fresh and deep enough only to reach my knees. Dunes of black sand stretched as far as my eyes could see. Here on the surface of the water I threw away my shredded cassock and my head cap. All I had left on was my inner linen gown.

When I threw the clothes away, I felt somewhat relieved of a burden. The late morning breezes rippled the water as I waded in, and with the ripples I felt that I was not walking but flying off to a new world. There was nothing around me as far as I could see in all four directions. Just the shallow water on all sides. I spoke to myself out loud, in Coptic. 'Here the land merges with the water and the sky, and here I shall start anew.' The idea came over me and suddenly captured my imagination. I took off what I was wearing and piled it on top of one of those sandy domes which protruded from the water here and there. Then I waded in until I lost my footing. I headed north and met the wind with my bare chest. I opened my arms wide and started to recite a prayer I had never read in any book, nor heard at any mass.

> In Your name, You who are too sublime to bear
>   a name
> Too holy to be portrayed, confined or labelled
> I devote myself to Your sake, that Your eternal
>   splendour might shine on Your mirror
> And that You might shine with all Your light,
>   Your radiance and beauty.
> In Your name I devote myself to Your sake, to be
>   born again from the womb of Your might,
> Helped by Your mercy.

I began to repeat this prayer with my eyes shut. And with every repetition my voice grew louder, until after dozens of repetitions it became a roar that filled the void around me. The primal void from which things began. When the sun reached its zenith and I no longer cast a shadow in any direction, I bent down and scooped the pure water into my hands. I stood up and threw the water on to my head to wash away everything that had happened. I baptized myself and in that sudden moment of insight I gave myself a new name, the name I am still known by – Hypa – which is just the first half of her name.

✠

After the baptism I picked up my clothes, and when I was dressed I felt like the other person who had been latent inside me. Now I am Hypa the monk, not that boy whose father was betrayed by his mother and killed in front of his eyes. I am not the adolescent who was brought up by his uncle in Naga Hammadi, nor the young man who once studied in Akhmim. I am the other person, aided by the mysterious kingdom. I am the twice-born.

My shadow lengthened in front of me as the sun declined towards sunset, and I walked behind my shadow, which led me to the east. Without expecting an answer, I asked myself, 'Should I walk on to Jerusalem, to seek there the origins of Christianity, or should I keep walking until I reach the place to the east where the world begins, or should I look deep into myself to discover my own east and comprehend the godhead?' I did not wait for an answer because all answers are one. It is the questions that are many.

Shortly before sunset I reached a place where the borders were clear between the land, the sea and the sky and again I saw in front of me trees and people, and realized for the first time that people are like trees and trees are like people, although people have shorter lives. On the edge of a village where fishermen lived, I spent the night leaning my back against an old dilapidated wall that looked about ready to collapse. I slept in a sitting position and in the morning I went into the fishing village. There were not many people in the few houses. I asked a man as thin as me, who was making nets, if he needed my help. He helped me over my hunger with a bowl of fish soup with pieces of white fish meat in it. The fish in those regions are different from the fish I knew in my home country. Fish from the sea is bigger, tastes better and is better suited for human consumption. Before then I used not to eat fish, but that day I took to it as though the person who once did not eat it was someone other than me.

I spent days with the man making his nets, eating with him the food that his old wife brought us twice a day. Then I took leave of him to continue my journey eastwards. A few days later I arrived in a town by the name of Damietta, inhabited by fishermen, boat builders and some merchants. I passed three months in this town, or maybe even a few days more. By day I worked as a carpenter in the shipyards and at night making nets, and I slept only a few hours a night. The boss was the chief fisherman there and had about twenty apprentice workers such as me and about the same number of fishermen and skilled craftsmen. The man was a Christian, if one assumes that a good man must have a religion. He really was good, although he was rich. Why did Jesus the Messiah say it was harder for a rich man to enter the kingdom of God than for a camel to pass through the eye of a needle? I once told that man in Damietta that his job, combining fishing with boat-building, was the best job a Christian man could do, because St Peter the Apostle, the rock on which the church was built, used to work as a fisherman, and Joseph the carpenter had brought up Jesus the Messiah. The man smiled and said, 'I know that, but I did not choose fishing or carpentry. My father and my grandfather before him chose them for me. If I had had the choice, I would have preferred to be a farmer, so that I would not always be frightened that the sea will swallow up one of my men.' He shook his head in anguish and proceeded to inspect the work of the carpenters and fishermen.

After a few weeks staying in Damietta, I started to prescribe medicines for the sick, and they would recover. That made me famous there as a physician. But I was in a hurry to leave them, especially after I turned down an offer from the chief to stay among them forever and take a wife from among them. I bade them farewell and left Damietta. The chief pressed some money into my hand and gave me a bag with a gown of goat's wool, a traveller's blanket and some dry food. It was winter and I left at dawn, and Jerusalem was my goal.

I walked east for days and the green fields became fewer and fewer. The views of the sea and the blue lakes disappeared behind some hills, and the colour yellow prevailed. I was at the gates of Sinai with its unbroken deserts and all the desolation, poverty and sterility they entail. At the edge of the desert there stood a humble monastery, alone in the midst of the sands, and solitary in appearance. I noticed it from afar but I did not approach it, and I did not ask myself what I would eat in the Sinai desert, for there are no green herbs there for me to pick and stuff in my belly, as I used to do earlier on my journey. In fear of the wilderness I had chosen, I spent the night under a friendly tree within sight of the monastery at a distance. At dawn a monk from the monastery saw me when he went out early to graze their sheep and goats. He came up towards me with a loaf of bread in one hand and his shepherd's staff in the other. I had not spoken to another human for two days, but I could not avoid speaking to him once he kindly offered me the loaf.

'Good day, brother. My heart tells me you are hungry.'

'Thank you.'

'Are you planning to cross the desert in that gown and without a mount?'

So began our conversation, which ended in a way I had not expected. In this frail monk I found something I had not found in the monks I had met before – anxiety. He told me he was originally from Damietta and he had fallen in love with a girl there but they forced her to marry another man, and so he chose the monastic life. That happened to him when he was twenty years old and now he had reached thirty, and throughout his ten years as a monk he had asked himself every day if his decision had been wrong or right. His honesty left a good impression on me and I listened to him. I spoke at length to him, and he to me. I told him what drove me out of Alexandria to wander on my way. He made light of it. He did not know of Hypatia and had not heard of her death. He made light of what I told him because he was contemptuous of everything that had happened or would happen in the course of events. His disdain for everything amazed me, and I was yet more amazed at the levity with which he said that if his beloved came back to him he would abandon the monastic life, or become a priest in a church, or go back to carpentry with his father. But, by his own account, he knew she would not come back and so he would spend his life as a monk.

'So you did not say farewell to life when you took your monastic vows?'

'Brother, the monastic way is a permanent attitude towards life, so how could I claim that I have said farewell to life?'

He told me that without emotion, and stood up in front of me to gather his flock, which had taken shelter under the tree around us. He went on to tell me, in his quaint Bohairi dialect, that I should not go into Sinai before dropping in on the abbot at the nearby monastery. I still remember the expression he used. 'He's a man who has to be seen because you will never meet anyone like him.'

I had no objection to passing by the monastery before going into the Sinai desert. In the small church there I met the abbot, who was so advanced in years that I believed it when the people at the monastery told me he was much more than a hundred years old. The wrinkles in his face corroborated that, but the gleam in his eyes belied it. His eyes had a twinkle and a striking brilliance, and his few words showed a serene wisdom. As he spoke to me, he looked towards the cross above the altar. He looked at me just once, after a discussion that lasted two hours, and said, 'If you are looking for the origins of Christianity, as you say, then go to the Dead Sea caves and meet the Essenes, for they are really the Jews, and Judaism is the source. And if you do go there, make sure to meet Chariton the monk, for he is one of the most honest and solitary of men.'

I spent three days in the remote monastery and then left for Sinai. When I left, the monks gave me a gown, chunks of bread baked from fenugreek flour with molasses, and a goatskin water bag. That was my equipment for crossing Sinai, one of the wildest places on earth. At the monastery door I met a water carrier, frail and lame, carrying on his back a water bag no less long than he was tall. When he heard I was going to Sinai, he gave me some advice: 'Don't let the sea out of your sight and don't go deep into Sinai for whatever reason, otherwise you'll never come out again, and look for a donkey to ride, because this desert cannot be crossed on foot.'

I knew the geography of Sinai from passages in the book of Claudius Ptolemaeus, the ancient sage who lived in Alexandria at the time when the world's most distinguished men lived there, and so I knew what the lame waterman meant, and understood his reference. I did not stray far from the northern edge of the desert. Many incidents occurred in the two months I spent crossing Sinai, some of them unforgettable. I passed, for instance, a group of nomadic Bedouin and I treated a young man who had dislocated his shoulder when he fell from an old wall against which they had pitched a tent. The accident happened the day I passed and after he had suffered shoulder pains for two hours I applied to the young man what I knew of the arts of setting broken bones and treating twists and dislocations. His pain abated. Then his family gave him a kind of soporific herb, which he chewed a little, and he then fell sound asleep. The Bedouin treated me with honour the night I stayed with them and the following day they gave me a decrepit donkey, so that in crossing the desert I could have recourse to riding on its bony back, which chafed the insides of my thighs. I bought from them a blanket, some meat jerky and some dry fodder for the donkey. In exchange for what I bought, I paid them the half of what the rich man in Damietta had given me.

Another memorable incident was when I caught up at sunset with a caravan of pilgrims who two months earlier had left Cyrene, one of the five cities of the Western Pentapolis, heading for Jerusalem. I was quite delighted when I saw the caravan, though I had thought myself happy in my solitude. I walked with them a full month until we reached the land of Palestine and they walked on northwards while I went east alone, heading for the Dead Sea in search of the origins of Christianity. At that time I thought there was only one true faith, with a single origin.

The third incident was horrible. In the middle of the desert leading to the Dead Sea, desert wolves attacked me just before dawn. At first they circled around me at a distance, and the donkey's steps faltered and it would no longer respond to me. Why did I go out early that day, instead of waiting for the sun to rise? The wolves howled and drew closer, their barking a sign of how hungry and fierce they were. I had nothing with me to defend myself from them except my stick and my donkey, which threw me from his back and bolted off in terror, with the wolves in pursuit. The heart of the wilderness shuddered at the death rattle of the donkey and the snarling of the wolves as they pulled it to pieces, too engrossed in it to take an interest in me. I went on my way, struck by an idea that suddenly occurred to me: God had sent the donkey here to be a hot delicious meal for animals which He had created as predators. God, secluded behind curtains of glory, does what He wishes with whomsoever He wishes.

✝

And so the parchment is filled, but that does not put an end to the memories which, as I write, seem like a reality experienced twice but seen in a new light as the years go by and as I retrieve them from the remote past. But here my stream of reminiscences unravels and my train of thought almost breaks off, so let me go back in the next parchment to the story of what happened to Nestorius after I first met him at the Church of the Resurrection.

The Rest of What Happened in Jerusalem

I well remember that distant Jerusalem morning, and the heavy air. The memories Nestorius revived when he asked about the death of Hypatia had devastated me throughout the previous night and had taken me back to a time in Alexandria which I always avoid recalling. When the sun rose, I did not feel it and I did not go to morning prayers that day. I stayed sitting on the bench as though stunned. I even forgot my appointment with Nestorius, so he took me by surprise when he knocked on my door, and when I opened it his radiant face appeared, and behind him the light of day.

'Good morning, my son, what happened to you? Your face is pale and your eyes are wandering.'

'Nothing, father, please come in, please come in.'

'Your bed is made and cold. Did you sleep on the floor?'

'Come in, father, come in.'

'I'll open this window. So what happened to you, Hypa?'

We sat opposite each other in silence. He was sitting on my bed looking at me with eyes full of concern and sympathy, while I sat on the bench, bowing my head, the screams of Hypatia still echoing inside me. Ten years had passed since she was killed, but it seemed like yesterday. After minutes of oppressive silence, he invited me to go out and join the prayers in the church, or take a walk around its walls. I looked at him askance and did not answer.

He stood up and said, 'Hypa, walking is good for you.'

'As you wish, holy father.'

I closed the door of my room and Nestorius dismissed the deacons awaiting him outside. I walked next to him in silence, or perhaps unwilling to speak. I was relieved that he did not enter the church, because the mass was long and would be tedious. Nestorius veered away from the wall and took me left towards the slender trees near the city walls behind the church, to the quiet spot which I very much liked and to which I often retreated under the trees. He tried to bring me out of my distracted mood, telling me that the health of Bishop Theodore had improved, and that he thanked me and wanted to see me again. He was even thinking of taking me with him to Mopsuestia to live there. By the time he had finished talking we had reached the site of the slender trees. He asked if I wanted to sit down and I agreed immediately because my legs felt too weak to walk.

He took out what looked like a small bible and offered it to me. 'This is a present for you,' he said. 'From Bishop Theodore, and from me.'

I opened the book and found it was a medical treatise, not a bible. It was Galen's epistle to his pupil Glaucon on therapeutics. I thanked him and he smiled, encouraging me to overcome my distress. He told me that if my memories of Alexandria were so troubling then I should forget them, and that he was sorry if his question about Hypatia had upset me.

Nestorius was sensitive, though his appearance did not reveal it. I feigned a smile and told him that Hypatia was not my only painful memory, and there was no need to apologize. Then to placate him I said, 'I'll tell you the story of the distress that I bear, to share it with someone as eminent as you.'

'Say what you wish, my son.'

I told Nestorius how Peter the reader and those with him dragged Hypatia along the ground, and how then, when her skin had been peeled off her flesh and her organs shredded, they pulled her to the spot where they set fire to her, on the ruins of the abandoned scientific school known as the Museion. At that point I stopped telling the story, because of the signs of anguish I saw on his face.

I did not tell Nestorius the whole story. I did not tell him that I stood gazing at the fire until it died out, after it had devoured Hypatia's body and the remains of the Museion, where I had once dreamed of studying medicine. But I did tell him that I left Alexandria that day in a daze, never to return, and walked stunned and alone along the Canopian Way, through what looked like a city of ghosts.

'Mercy, my God.' Nestorius sighed as he spoke. I looked at him and was alarmed at how the features of his face were flushed with bitterness. I realized I was right to summarize the incident and tell him only the gist of what happened and not the details. I was not surprised when he told me sadly that the magistrates sent by the emperor to investigate what had happened to Hypatia achieved nothing, none of her killers were convicted, and the incident passed as though it had never happened.

'Yes, father, I knew that. I heard it from the pilgrims who come here from Memphis and Alexandria.'

'And did they tell you, Hypa, that Bishop Cyril paid that judicial committee large bribes and showered them with expensive presents to have the matter buried?'

'Yes, father, they said that. They also said that in order to close that bloody chapter Emperor Theodosius II merely sent the monks of Alexandria a warning not to mix with people in public places in the city.'

Nestorius replied with bitter sarcasm, 'A severe punishment. If only they had enforced it.'

The midday sun was blazing above us, and when I saw the beads of sweat on Nestorius's brow I took pity on him and on myself and invited him to my room. 'No, let's go to the church first to pray,' he said. 'After that we'll have a drink of that mountain mint in your room.'

At the church door the chief priest was saying goodbye to some visitors, and when he saw us his face beamed and he approached Nestorius with a welcome and insisted we join him at lunchtime. Nestorius thanked him kindly and declined, saying he would have lunch with Bishop Theodore, but he invited the priest to join the two of them. 'If today you eat with us the lovely food which the monks prepare,' he joked, 'you'll think seriously about joining our church and coming back with us when the pilgrimage days are over.'

'Holy Nestorius, how could I leave my wife and my poor children? Besides, I lost my appetite for food long ago.'

'As for your family, they can live with you in Antioch or Mopsuestia. As for your appetite, Hypa the monk will restore it for you with some of the herbs he has that strengthen the stomach and give you an appetite for good food,' Nestorius said.

The priest laughed and said, 'So you'll look after me the way I looked after you the first time!' When Nestorius asked me what he meant, the priest of the church told him the story of my arrival in Jerusalem, how I collapsed from exhaustion at the door to the Church of the Resurrection, and how they carried me to him. Nestorius looked towards me courteously and said, 'Men are weak, whoever they are, and we are weak, and our only strength is through love.' The priest nodded, then something else caught his attention. With sudden enthusiasm Nestorius said, 'Talking of love, would you like us to hold a council for you today, for you to talk to us about the varieties of love? That would be interesting, because I heard you speak on that subject to your brothers when I visited you in Antioch.'

'The good priest doesn't forget. That was a long time ago. But now I won't hold any councils as long as Bishop Theodore is with us. It's enough to listen to him and drink at the fountain of his learning.'

'God bless you, and him. And now I beg your leave, for the work of the church never ceases,' said the priest.

'In God's protection, reverend. Off we go to prayers, Hypa.'

Prayer has the effect of magic. It calms the soul and comforts the saddened heart. In the same way, masses wash away all our cares, throwing them from our shoulders into the lap of divine mercy so we can rest a while. Then we feel the need to pray again, so long as we believe in the Lord. And if we leave the fold of the Lord, we are alone and become prey to worries and troubling thoughts. We don't need that now! After prayers we came out through the church door and Nestorius's face beamed with love and he was back in his usual spirits. He suggested we go first to have lunch with Bishop Theodore and then go back to my room, and I did not object.

On the way to their guesthouse, the conversation went in every direction.

He told me of the splendour of Antioch, the many fields of learning taught in its schools, the well-stocked library of the bishopric, the simple people who come from the nearby villages, Emperor Theodosius II, the way he hesitated in most matters, and about the bishop of Antioch and his good character. I told him about my days in Akhmim and described to him that lively town on the banks of the Nile, its large temple which had awe-inspiring statues of pharaohs at its gate, some of them ninety feet high. I told him about the statue of the beautiful woman which stood there and who they say was the daughter of the great pharaoh who built the temple.

'I heard that the rest of the Alexandrian professors left the city for Akhmim and have been living there for years,' Nestorius said.

'Yes, father. But Akhmim also has many churches and half the inhabitants are Christian, and good people.'

'Hypa, you're prejudiced in favour of your fellow Egyptians.'

'It's possible, father, it's possible.'

When we saw Bishop Theodore in his room he was delighted we had come. I felt that day the depth of the affection which united them and I hoped to have the same relationship with Nestorius as he had with the bishop. I was at ease in the council room and the food at lunch was really good, with dishes unknown in and around Jerusalem. The bishop tried to please me by identifying the various dishes for me, praising some of them as easy to digest. Galen's book was still in my hand and I thanked him for it and for the invitation to lunch in this holy gathering of priests. He smiled and said, 'I'll send you some more good books after I get back and I'll ask the diocesan scribes to copy for you the works of Hippocrates and other famous physicians.'

'That would be a great honour, your Grace.'

'It would be useful for you, and for the people, God willing,' he said. 'People need medicine and the profession has declined recently. Let's hope that through you the Lord will preserve this useful art.'

Nestorius intervened politely in the conversation and told the bishop that I wrote poetry. The bishop turned to him and told him that his old friend Bishop John Chrysostom used to write poetry early in his life. 'Did I not tell

145

you, dear Nestorius, that they are similar?' he said. Then the bishop started recalling to the gathering many stories about John Chrysostom. He relished telling old stories, as though he were reviving something in the core of his being from the distant past.

Our gathering included an elderly monk who did not speak a word and two priests. As soon as Bishop Theodore had finished telling his stories, one of the priests jumped in with a question: 'How could Alexandria dare to condemn John Chrysostom when he was a saint?' The sudden question dispelled the mood of goodwill which had prevailed in the session. Nestorius looked in disapproval at the priest who asked the question, embarrassing him, and we all took refuge in silence.

Bishop Theodore frowned and spoke irritably. 'There are many foolish things in Alexandria. The current and former bishops committed acts of violence, and I do not like to speak about them or their deeds, which were as remote as possible from the teachings of Christ and the Apostles and most similar to acts committed by those with earthly ambitions. May the Lord encompass all with his mercy, and pardon everyone.'

I expected that Bishop Theodore's remarks would signal the end of the meeting, but all of a sudden the taciturn monk, from whom I had not heard a word since I first saw him, started talking in Greek with an eastern accent. Resting his shoulder on his stick, he spoke intensely,: 'God forgive the Alexandrians what they have done, what they are doing now and what they will do tomorrow. The church of Alexandria will not desist until it collapses and Christianity collapses with it.'

Everyone fell silent and no one looked at anyone else. I glanced around at them all, amazed at the effect of the strange monk's words and how they fell silent after he spoke. He definitely had some status among them, or he would not have spoken so forcefully or disconcerted everyone in this way, although his appearance did not suggest he was at all important. I realized at that moment that in this world the Lord has men who have profound knowledge of the secrets of love, men whose worth is known only to the elect. This monk, it seemed to me, was one of those with a deep knowledge of love. He was very much like St Chariton, whom I saw in the cave near the

Dead Sea. Both of them were elderly, with oriental beards and gaunt frames. Both of them trembled when they spoke, and people trembled when they heard them speak. Was this mysterious monk a brother to St Chariton, or were they perhaps the same person, appearing in different places in different guises, so that these saints could be a sign to people, bearing witness to the Lord's miracles on earth? That is what ran through my mind at the time, along with strange spiritual ideas which I no longer experience in the same way as I did in that faraway time.

Suddenly Nestorius the priest stood up, brushing down his gown with both hands as though he were brushing off the silence which had reigned at the meeting. He told Bishop Theodore that we would leave him to rest, that he was taking his leave to go with me to my room to discuss certain matters, and that he would be back shortly after sunset. That was the end of the meeting at which I saw Bishop Theodore for the last time.

On our way to my room I could not resist asking Nestorius about the taciturn monk who shouted out and whose words had brought an end to the meeting. He told me he was one of the best-known ascetics in the oldest monastery in the land of Cappadocia, which provided Christianity with the three most famous fathers of the Church, known as the Cappadocian Fathers. This taciturn monk, he added, was known for his life of abstinence and asceticism and people told stories of his marvels and miracles, which he insisted on denying. He said the monk was known for staying silent for long periods and rarely speaking, and churchmen greatly revered him. Bishop Theodore considered him one of his spiritual mentors, because at more than eighty years of age he was many years older than the bishop.

'He looks like Chariton the monk,' I said.

'How would you know, Hypa? Have you seen St Chariton?'

'Yes, father, I visited him in his cave some years ago.'

Nestorius wanted to know more about my meeting with Chariton the monk, and I wanted to know more about what the taciturn Cappadocian monk had said, so that day we had much to talk about. We sat together for many hours, our conversation interrupted only by the arrival of a poor man seeking medicine for a severe pain he had in his intestines after eating some rotten food. The only treatment for the man was the general-purpose theriac known as methroditos and I had some of it in my room. I gave it to him and declined any fee with my constant phrase: 'If you want, you can put something in the gift box in the church.' The man went off, and I went back to my conversation with Nestorius, who was pleased to see me treat the sick for charity. 'All that is stored up for you with the Lord, blessed Hypa,' he said.

'Father,' I said. 'I learnt medicine without paying, so how could I charge anything now? As our Saviour Jesus told the disciples, "Freely you have received, freely give."'

We went back to our agreeable conversation and I told Nestorius the rest of the story of my wanderings, what I witnessed around the Dead Sea, and how I met Chariton the monk after sleeping in front of his cave three days running, waiting for him to come out and reluctant to walk in on him and disturb his retreat. Every week a group of visitors would come to Chariton's cell and leave a basket outside, filled with pieces of bread, chunks of dry cheese and a jar of water which would not last an ordinary human more than two days. But he made do with all that till the end of the week. It was the villagers who showed me the cave, and advised me not to go in unless he called me. After two nights of vigil at the mouth of the cave I began to doubt that he was inside it. It occurred to me that maybe he had died years ago and no one had noticed, and the food they left him was taken by wild dogs. But when I fell asleep one day around noon I saw Chariton telling me in a dream that the time had not yet come, and that he would ask for me when the time came. After the third night, my bag had run out of food and I had nothing left but books, scrolls and inks. I was completely resigned as I awaited the signal, not impatient for it and never thinking of leaving the entrance to the cave. That day at noon I heard him calling in a deep and echoing voice from far down inside his retreat. 'If there's anyone out there, come in,' he said.

When I went in, his appearance appalled me. Little was visible but his eyes shining with sainthood, in a face surrounded by tangled hair, above an emaciated body covered in faded black rags. The cave was in the form of a cellar, with many cracks in the walls. The floor was cold and damp, and when I entered it was a relief from the blasts of hot air that had scorched me throughout the three days I had spent alone under the sun, which shines fiercely in these arid regions. I went gently into his retreat, which was full of light and solemnity. He spoke first. 'What do you want from me?'

'Father, I've been alone at your door for days, waiting to see you and receive your blessings, and ask you about things.'

'What makes you think I have the answer?'

'That's what I imagine and hope, father, because my questions torment me.'

'Sit down.'

I sat in front of him politely and talked to him of the doubts which beset me and had led me to investigate the origins of Christianity. I told him of my journey to the Dead Sea caves in the hope of finding answers from the Essenes, and how I found no life in their caves, for all mention of them had ceased, as though they were a fleeting memory. I spoke at length of my horror at the rivers of violence which had swept the land of God and my alarm at the terrible killing which was happening in the name of Christ. I told him candidly of my need for certainty and how I lacked it.

Chariton the monk did not speak until I finished. Then his emaciated body shook and the bones of his chest and shoulders protruded as he spoke to me, saying, 'Certainty comes only through quelling doubts, and doubts are quelled only by putting your trust in the Lord, and that comes about only by recognizing the miracles of His creation, and acknowledging that His miracles come only by affirming the incarnation of God and His manifestation in Christ.' Then he advised me to go on pilgrimage to Jerusalem, and he emphasized that I should not enter the city immediately but should tour the surrounding area and visit the spots where the feet of Jesus the Messiah had trodden, then I should approach little by little the centre, which is the place of His resurrection, and I should not go there until I had received a signal from Jesus the Messiah.

'And from there you came here, Hypa?' Nestorius asked.

'Yes, father, from there.'

Nestorius leant back against the wall and stretched his legs along the bed.

He paused for a moment of deep thought and his face showed signs that he had drifted off into a world of meditation. After a while he shut his eyes a little. Then he looked at me and said something which I memorized and recorded in my papers that evening. 'Chariton is a holy man without a doubt,' he said, 'but his way is different from our way in Antioch. He abandons the world in order to find rest, he probes deep into his own soul in order to save it, and he renounces things only to have them pursue him. But our way, Hypa, is different: we believe with our hearts and affirm the miracles of God, then we harness our reason to help mankind go forward to where God wishes. We believe that miracles are only miracles when they happen rarely. Otherwise, if they happen too often, they no longer count as miracles. The Lord took bodily form once in Jesus Christ to show the path for mankind ever after, and so we do not need to relive the miracle itself but rather to live by the path he showed us, or else the miracle would lose its meaning. Chariton the monk gave your heart relief by clearing your mind of whatever was troubling you. He hoped to dispel the worries of the mind and make the heart illuminate the path to discernment. Because the heart, Hypa, has the light of faith but not the ability to investigate, understand or resolve contradictions.'

Nestorius pointed to the window of my room, towards the dome of the church of St Helena. 'Look with your heart at the magnificence of this church and your heart will be full of faith,' he said. 'Then think about the fact that the saint who built it, Helena, the mother of Emperor Constantine, began life as a barmaid in the brothels of Edessa. How can we understand that transformation in the life of the emperor and his mother, other than by analogy with the miracle of Jesus Christ? And miracles, Hypa, rarely happen. We believe they rarely happen, and then we put reason and analogy to work on the phenomena, until we understand them and resolve their contradictions. That is the case with other things too: we believe, then we use our intellect and our faith is affirmed. This is our way.'

'Some contradictions will remain that the intellect cannot resolve,' I said.

'Maybe your intellect, but after you someone will come who can do it,' said Nestorius.

'Or the contradictions will collapse spontaneously and will be forgotten, and people will not bother with them.'

'True, Hypa, there are many examples of that.'

I felt that the time was right to ask him about the outburst by the Cappadocian monk, whose words had silenced everyone, but I was a little hesitant for fear of annoying him. It seems that with his sharp insight he noticed my hesitation. He looked at me with a smiling eye and a cheerful face and, as he poured himself a cup from the pot of warm mint, he asked me what I was hiding and why I was hesitant. 'You can read my mind and heart, father,' I said. 'I'll tell you frankly that I was most interested in what the Cappadocian monk said. He made me think about the contradictions between Christianity based on sacrifice and love, and those acts committed in Christ's name in Alexandria.'

'Hypa, what's happening in Alexandria has nothing to do with religion,' said Nestorius. 'The first blood shed in that city, after the period of pagan persecution of Christians, was Christian blood shed by Christians. Fifty years ago the Alexandrians killed the bishop of their city, Bishop Georgios, because he agreed with some of the opinions of Arius the Alexandrian. Killing people in the name of religion does not make it religious. It was this earthly world that Theophilus inherited and later bequeathed to his nephew Cyril. Don't confuse matters, my son, for those are people of power, not people of faith, people of profane cruelty, not of divine love.'

'In the church in Alexandria, father, I saw one of the monks who killed Bishop Georgios the Cappadocian.'

Nestorius was surprised at what I said, then he surprised me with his words, because they reminded me of what I had always believed. 'What you saw there was not a monk,' he said sadly. 'Monks do not kill. They walk lightly on earth, following in the footsteps of the apostles, the saints and the martyrs.'

Moving to the Monastery

M y days in Jerusalem varied little until Nestorius came with the pilgrims that year, but after his arrival my time became pleasant and agreeable and I no longer felt like a stranger there. We used to meet mostly in the church, or in my room or at their residence. I always cheered up when he came and my worries abated till I almost forgot them, and they left me alone. But after twenty days were past he told me they were preparing to go back home, now they were sure that the roads to Antioch and Mopsuestia were safe. I was anxious all night and on the day of their departure I woke up early and was at their residence with the first rays of the sun. The square was full of pack animals and the delegation was absorbed in preparing for the journey. Everyone was busy with departure and I worried about how desolate my life would be after they were gone.

From afar Nestorius saw me as he moved among the group briskly and enthusiastically, saying one thing to one person and giving an order to someone else. Everyone obeyed him, and he had great prestige among them. He saw me and approached with a smile. He took me aside at the wall of the big guesthouse, but kept an eye on the people preparing to depart. Then he turned to me and said, 'Why don't you come to Antioch with us? Or join us with the next caravan that comes?'

'Antioch, father, is a big noisy city and I can no longer live in such places. My only remaining aim is to spend the rest of my days in peace.'

'What are you talking about? You're only thirty years old!'

'Is it thirty? It feels like three hundred,' I replied.

Nestorius laughed at my remark and his face beamed all the more. Inquisitively he asked me if I intended to live out my life as a hermit, or as a practising physician. He added in jest, 'Or you could become a priest in our country. If one day you want to give up the monastic life, I'll find you a good Christian wife who will beget a tribe of Egyptians for you in our country.'

'Sir, I tell you I want to live in peace, and then you suggest marriage!'

Nestorius laughed, showing his even white teeth. He adjusted his cap and asked me if I was content to live in Jerusalem. I showed him the palms of my hand as if to say I had no other option. He said that if I wanted to live in peace I should think of living in a monastery. He added politely, 'I won't describe to you how peaceful life is in a monastery, because you Egyptians invented monasticism and monasteries, reviving the traditions you had followed since ancient times.'

Nestorius told me that day that in a green area north of Aleppo there was a monastery affiliated to their church in Antioch and that it was one of the quietest and most beautiful places on earth. He asked me if I would like to settle there and without thinking I said, 'Yes, father, I would like that. I'm tired of living here and nothing will console me in Jerusalem when you're gone.'

Nestorius asked for a pen and some ink, put his hand in his pocket and took out a small piece of washed leather parchment inscribed on both sides, and told me it was a letter to the abbot and that he would give me a warm welcome. He described the site of the monastery to me and told me about the fine climate and how close it was to Antioch, that in fact it was just one day's walk and that I could visit them at the cathedral whenever I wanted. He said he might drop in on me on his travels between the many towns and monasteries in those parts. 'The monastery is more relaxed and safer than Jerusalem, which is surrounded by wilderness on all sides and is far from the capital of the empire,' he said. He paused to think a moment and then continued, 'Soon I might move to Constantinople because the bishop there is ill and they are talking to me about taking on the bishopric after him. As you know, the bishopric of the capital is no less important than the papal see in Rome, and my presence there might be of benefit to Christians.'

'God willing it will be of benefit, father, and fortunate.'

'Let God do with us what he wishes. And now, Hypa, I bid you farewell in the hope that we will meet again, and do not delay in moving to the monastery.'

The caravan moved on, bringing to the surface my underlying anxieties. I walked behind them until they left Jerusalem through the southern gate, which they call the Zion Gate. Then they veered westwards to head to Antioch along the coast road which skirts the great sea. When the caravan disappeared from sight, I had a powerful sense of loneliness and estrangement. I hurried back to my room with a determination to leave for the northern monastery as soon as possible.

I spent two weeks organizing my departure and a third week waiting for the trade caravan which passes close to Aleppo. I thought that travelling with them would be less strenuous than all my previous travels. Most of the merchants in the caravan were Arabs who speak a language the intricacies of which were unfamiliar to me and which I had no intention of learning. Although the language is similar to Syriac, it has no written literature which would encourage me to learn it, and its speakers are people without any special religion. They include Jews, Christians and pagans and in the barren heart of their peninsula they have shrines for idols, and they walk naked in circles around those shrines. They are said to be the descendants of Ishmael and are mentioned in the Torah, but I do not believe that. Those who are Christians have a bishopric in the deserts of the peninsula, which is known as Arabia. They are traders, cunning and warlike.

As I expected, my journey with the caravan was comfortable. On the way we passed by a large town called Damascus, surrounded by orchards and overlooked by a tall mountain. Beyond it the land flattens out and a plain extends northwards as far as Aleppo and the villages around it. After two weeks we reached Aleppo at sunset one day, and I could make out the features of the town only on the morning of the next day. It is a pleasant city inhabited by many Arabs, Syrians and Greeks, as well as some families from Palmyra who took refuge there a century and a half ago when Palmyra was destroyed and abandoned. So it is a city of an Arab character, with Arab inhabitants.

The strange thing about Aleppo is that it does not have a city wall. The houses are scattered around low hills and in the middle stands one enormous hill. On top of that stand the remains of an old castle with ruined gates, though the remaining walls are still high. From the antiquity of the town it seems it was of some importance in previous centuries and then its importance gradually diminished and merchants moved in. I spent the night in the guesthouse attached to the parish of Aleppo and early in the morning a servant who worked in the parish travelled with me to the monastery. He was taking some provisions to deliver to the monks living in the small monasteries dispersed along the roads between Aleppo and Antioch. That's what the servant told me when he saw my surprise at the many things loaded on to the two donkeys that were with him. My many books, which had come from Jerusalem to Aleppo on a camel, now travelled the rest of the way on the backs of two wretched mules.

The distance between Aleppo and the northern monastery is short, no more than half a day's journey, and the plain along the way is open, with green meadows and hills of yellow sand. The parish servant pointed to the first hill that appeared after we left Aleppo and told me that the city cemetery was behind it and that his mother and father were buried there. He said he visited them every week to profit from their example and relive a period that would never return. I asked him if he would like to pass by them, and he answered hesitantly that he did not want to delay or inconvenience me but he would like to visit the graves because after he took me to the monastery he would continue his journey to Antioch to visit his married sister there and he would spend a month with her. I had no choice but to turn aside to visit the graves with him and stay there half an hour while he recited his prayers.

The people there have a strange way of burying their dead. They do not cover them with soil and set up a tombstone for them, as we do in Egypt. Instead they put the dead in openings like long holes, one on top of another, then plug up the openings with a sticky paste made of soil, and trace the sign of the cross on the openings.

While the man was reciting his prayers, I thought about the people I knew who had died. I do not know of any grave for my father, and I do not think he was buried in the first place. Perhaps the temple priests threw his remains in the Nile when they were sure that his killers were gone, and crocodiles ate them. Did the Alexandrians throw Octavia in the sea to be eaten by fish, or did they bury her in that cemetery near the ruins of the royal quarter? Of course Hypatia was not buried: there was nothing left of her to bury. The worms of the underworld ate nothing of her body, because she ended her life like a tree that is burned and changes into charcoal. Coal kindles fire, while a body buried in the ground is ravaged by worms. Was it fitter that Hypatia was burned after her death, so that worms never feasted on her camphorous body? Where do worms come from to eat the dead? The great doctors of antiquity, who dissected bodies dead and alive, never mentioned in their books that they found worms in living creatures, so where did the worms come from after death? Are they latent inside us, such that they appear only after we die? Are they latent also in juicy fruit, old cheese and living bodies, waiting for the creature to die and its flesh to rot, so they can live off death, then die? They say that these worms do not eat the remains of saints and martyrs. Is that a miracle on the part of the saints and martyrs, or on the part of the worms, in that they can distinguish between bodies which are holy and those which are not? But as far as I can tell, the worms do not discriminate and cannot tell the bodies of saints from those of others. They also do not attack the bodies of the mummies preserved in our country in ancient sarcophaguses. And why did the ancient Egyptians preserve the bodies of their dead, using either magic or science to keep the worms away? Or perhaps their bodies were also sacred.

'Come along, father, God bless you.'

The parish servant interrupted my daydreaming, inviting me to resume our journey. On the mule's back I had endless thoughts and questions without answers. Would I be buried one day and would my grave be a hole in a wall, like that at which the servant had said his prayers and asked God to bestow his mercy on his mother and father after they were dust? If I did have one of those graves, who would come to invoke God's mercies by praying at my grave, when I have no family and no descendants? Would these white worms that eat the dead, although they have no teeth, one day feast on me? Or have they already started to eat me without me noticing? I remembered with distress how once in my childhood I saw a dead duck lying between the rocks with worms teeming in its gut. In the bowels of the earth, if we dug it up, we would see worms. Has the earth died and are the worms burrowing into it without us knowing, so that this world fades away into nothingness while we pay no heed?

✝

On the broad dirt road leading north from Aleppo to the monastery we went through open land with reddish fertile soil. They say, the parish servant told me, that the soil on these plains was originally yellow and sandy, and that it turned brown from the blood of the martyrs shed in the days of the persecution, and the soil stayed brown to remind Christians of the time of oppression. That's what the poor man told me and I saw no reason to challenge or contradict his ideas, which he seemed comfortable with. On the way, I picked some herbs to look into their properties and possible uses when I settled down in the monastery. Everything the earth produces has uses and benefits, whether we are aware of them or not.

I was delighted at the scenes along the way and the church servant was pleasant company, quick to help me and look after me. In the afternoon we were walking across those hills which look like big waves, one on top of another, and I was engrossed in my meditations when the servant stretched out his arm and pointed to the top of the highest hill around. 'That's the monastery. We're there,' he said with pleasure. My heart jumped.

The Heavenly Monastery

The day I saw this monastery for the first time it seemed to stand where the earth meets the sky. It was winter at the time and the cool breezes of the day's end were blowing away the weariness of travel and infusing a mysterious splendour into the world. We climbed the hill to the monastery, pushing the mules a little harder. I was hoping that this would be my last stop. I had tired of constantly moving and the time had come for me to find a refuge for the rest of my life and enjoy some peace of mind for a time. Then I would die a quiet death and my soul would slip away from the tumult and commotion of this world to the serenity of the heavens. The monastery looked like the last stopping place on my incessant travels, which had gone on so long that I was no longer at ease anywhere. I thought the will of God had finally brought me here, but later I realized that this was just the imagination of an exhausted man.

The monastery is what is left of an old building which might go back to pre-Roman times, certainly a long time. Some of the monks here think that at first it was probably a castle or the home of a forgotten leader. But because I am familiar with the temples in my native country, those which are still standing and those which are ruins from the centuries which have elapsed, I am sure the monastery building was a temple in former times. In fact it was a magnificent temple. This is what the scattered stones suggest, as well as the fine marble altar around which they built the monastery's big church. The ruins of temples have a special aura which an Egyptian like me cannot mistake.

I have not told anyone here what I believe about the origins of the place, and anyway they are not very interested in history here. They are concerned only with the present and whatever stares them in the eye, and perhaps they are justified in that, or lucky. As for me, when I am in seclusion I have often thought of past times when this place was full of people who believed in the old god. I thought of them and of the god, and the thoughts distressed me – everything is transient, everything on the face of the earth disappears, except the great pyramids of Egypt, which refuse to disappear. Even if the base of the pyramid is invisible under the sands, we can see the rest of the pyramid protruding from the sands and we can be sure that the pyramid is there, however much of it is buried. What happened to the gods for whom they built the pyramids, and to the old god who was worshipped on the site of this monastery for hundreds of years past? Where is that god now, after everything that has come to pass?

After long reflection I realized that the various gods are not to be found in temples or other impressive buildings. They live in the hearts of the people who believe in them, and as long as those people are alive, their gods live through them. If the people die out, the gods are buried with them, just as the god Khnum died after the death of my father, and the last few priests who were besieged in the big temple at the south of Elephantine Island must all have died by now and their temple must have been demolished or been converted into a church for a new god. At the trial of Jesus the Messiah, a man bore false witness against him, saying, 'This fellow said: "I am able to destroy the temple and rebuild it in three days."' But they did not understand that the temple was Jesus the Messiah himself, who really did destroy their temple, then rebuilt it when he rose from the dead after three days. We also did not understand what Jesus meant when he referred to the Apostle Peter, saying, 'On this rock I will build my church', because we did not grasp that every church ever built or yet to be built must be based on the apostolic mission of Peter and his faith, which knew no doubt even if it had times of weakness. For, as it is written, Peter denied Jesus the Messiah three times in one night, and Jesus had foretold what he would do, without rebuking him for the denials he would make or for the fact that Peter would shy away from helping him. Jesus did not want his help, but rather redemption and sacrifice, so what good would Peter's help have been and what harm did his denial do?

I denied Hypatia in the face of her killers and I denied myself for three days with Octavia, because I was afraid. Fear now comes naturally to me, from the day they killed my father in front of me. And today, why should I fear death? I should rather be afraid of life, because it is more painful. And why does not faith falter from time to time, like a summer cloud that scatters and vanishes, delicate and shadowless? I will never build a church and no church will ever be built on me, because I am not a rock like Peter the Apostle and because my faith is tainted by many doubts.

What led me to say all this? What was I saying in the first place? Oh yes, this monastery which aspires to heaven, and the first days I spent here. I was describing the place and I should go back to the story I was telling.

✝

The monastery stands on the top of a high hill, surrounded by other hills and plains. The gate is an opening in an old wall which partially surrounds an open space with old Roman columns, some still standing and others in pieces on the ground. The monastery entrance is on the southern side, with a steep climb up the hill, while on the other three sides there is no slope either up or down, just a steep drop which makes the monastery look like a balcony with vistas to the north, east and west as far as the eye can see. Below the monastery on the southern side there is a small village with houses scattered chaotically, about thirty houses all nestling at the foot of the hill. At the start of the slope leading up to the gate on the right-hand side there are rooms of the kind that soldiers live in, and on the day after I arrived I found out it was the base for a contingent of ten Roman soldiers who have been living below the monastery for years to protect it, after it was the target of many attacks by thieves and highwaymen. Imagine how wicked they must be, to attack a monastery and rob monks who had already renounced all the possessions of this world!

At the foot of the slope on the left-hand side, where the hill is less steep, there are green expanses of land in the form of broad terraces, with an abandoned cottage in the middle. The dry trees surrounding the cottage and the withered bushes around it and above it show that this land was cultivated in the past in the ancient Babylonian manner, as with the Hanging Gardens. But where did they get the water needed to irrigate the plants, or did they perhaps rely solely on the rains? I wondered about this as I climbed the slope, and I found out the answer later.

Nobody stopped me as I climbed towards the monastery or when I walked in. The open space at the entrance was bounded on the western side by an old rectangular building of white stone, which appeared at first sight to be separate from the monastery. That is the building which I would convert into a library once I had settled in. On the left of the entrance, on the western side, several buildings stood together: the main church, then a large storeroom, then a two-storey building which, judging by its appearance, provided rooms for the monks and underneath, on the ground floor, a guestroom, a small kitchen and a large dining hall. On the side opposite these buildings there was a chicken run and next to it a stable roofed with palm fronds, with three donkeys and many goats and sheep. On the left as one crossed the square there was an empty area strewn with old stones and the capitals of broken columns, where the prickly boxthorn grows. On this northern side of the monastery stands the little church, next to a large detached room which I knew at first sight was the abbot's room.

At the end of the square on the eastern side stood a building like a closed box, large and mysterious, which they called the citadel. The building is about three storeys high but it has absolutely no windows or doors, just a smooth wall with only a small hole at the top, hardly big enough for a person to pass through bending down, if he were to climb the steps of the ladder which hangs down from the hole. The ladder is made of plaited rope, with wooden runners so that it can be rolled up when necessary. The roof of the building is in the form of a large dome steep on all sides and so smooth it would be impossible to stand still on it. I may have more to say about this building later.

After we went through the monastery gateway, which had no gate, the servant unloaded my luggage in the middle of the square and asked me to wait while he informed the monastery people of my arrival. While I was gazing out at the plain which stretches away from the western edge of the monastery, where the paved road to Antioch can be seen, one of the monks came up and greeted me, and told me that the abbot would meet me in a while in the refectory. The refectory was an old dilapidated building roofed with palm trunks and fronds. The stones of the walls are carefully laid but there are cracks in the edges. An earthquake must have struck in this region long ago, bringing down the building which was standing here, and these parts that remained became a monastery.

The abbot came into the hall with two monks of kindly Antiochian appearance. The faces of the monks here are friendly, unlike those of Egyptian monks, which are hard and sickly from excessive fasting and from the predominant colour of the silt which the Nile flood brings every summer. The abbot is a venerable man not yet so elderly, with a quiet voice and a calm manner, and dignified. His face beamed when he read the letter from Nestorius the priest and at once he welcomed me to join them.

After dinner a young monk rose and took me to the room which I described when I started writing. He sat with me for an hour, quietly explaining to me the way of life in the monastery. The way of life is not very different from the way of life practised in most monasteries – a little work during the day, and many prayers and hymns for most of the time. I wanted to ask the monk about the mysterious building at the far end of the monastery compound, but I preferred to bide my time.

My first days in the monastery were quiet and pleasant. I spent my time reading and worshipping, and my soul was at peace. The reverend Nestorius was right: this monastery suited me in mysterious ways which I could sense but not rationalize. The only thing that troubled me was that massive and silent building with the domed roof and the mysterious aura, standing alone at the far eastern edge of the monastery. With the passage of days I learnt some things about it, but even more things were impossible to discover. They said they called it the citadel because in the past the monks took refuge there from constant raids by robbers. They would spend the night inside and preserve their goods and their lives within its walls. They would go in and out of this safe womb using the ladder hanging from the opening high up. It was not in fact solid but contained rooms linked by corridors, and in the base were buried the monks who had passed away over the last hundred years, which was the age of the monastery. I was also told that they built this protective building on top of the cemetery seventy years ago to share in the spiritual power of those buried. The building has four secret floors rather than three, with a stone stairway that snakes up through the middle, linking the ground to the ceiling by way of the four floors. The stairway has one opening at the top which can be closed from inside with a thick block of copper.

They said in whispers that about fifty years ago the monks stayed inside the dark building a whole month while the robbers besieged them and camped out in the big church, but the robbers found no way to storm the monks' refuge. Many astonishing miracles took place during that month. The first and most amazing was that the face of Christ appeared three nights in succession in the full moon, and the last of them was that the robbers woke up in alarm during their last night, drew their swords and started to fight each other, driven by a terrifying frenzy. They did battle until they killed one another, and in the morning their bodies were strewn across the open space in front of the big church. All of them died within one hour and there were more than twenty of them. Everyone here confirms this story and swears that the abbot witnessed it himself when he was a young boy.

The building and the stories about it puzzled me. I imagined the interior in the form of corridors coiled around each other as in an ant colony, but built above ground and overlooking on the southern, western and northern sides a deep chasm which no one could climb from the plains below the high hill of the monastery. I had a notion to enter the building but I did not tell anyone, and I never saw anyone else go in throughout the time I was there. They say here that after the contingent of Roman troops came twenty years ago the raids stopped and the troops spared the monks the trouble of constant fear and hiding all the time. No one goes into the building any longer, except when one of the monks dies, when they bury him in the cemetery at the base. No one has died here in the past five years so I have not had the chance to go in with them or even to see them go in. I have been told, secretly and indirectly, that in a secret room in the building the abbot keeps the nails which were hammered into the hands and feet of Jesus the Messiah when he was crucified in Jerusalem, and that these nails glow at night, and that when they hid in the building the monks used that light to see in the dark. This is what they whispered to me two years after I settled in the monastery.

Weeks after I arrived the abbot asked me to spend part of each day in the building on the left as one comes in through the dilapidated gate. The building consists of a single large hall on the western side of the monastery. He said he would set the building aside as a clinic for any sick people who might come from the nearby houses and villages. He said I could also turn it into a library where I could arrange my books and some of the other books which were piled up in boxes in the room next to the refectory. I liked the idea and at first I spent long days there without any patients coming. I took the opportunity to have a look at my books again and browse through the books which I took out of the boxes. Most of them were New Testaments and prayer books. I arranged the books on wooden shelves which the village carpenter skilfully made, just as I had commissioned, all along the western wall opposite the side with the window overlooking the level inner courtyard of the monastery. I organized the books by subject: medicine and pharmacy first, then history and literature, and before all else books on Christianity. In the middle of the hall the carpenter successfully repaired the table and chairs, and so I ended up with the library of which I had long dreamed. I was at ease there because it was as far as possible from the mysterious and frightening building which lay right on the other side.

Two days before the carpenter finished his work we were at the door of the big church after the end of Sunday mass and a plump boy of about fifteen was sitting on a stone in the corner of the open space which stretches from the monastery buildings to my own building on the western side. The abbot called him and he came running up, happy for no particular reason.

The abbot told me I could use the boy's help in the work of the library and treating the sick, and he suggested that he hoped the boy would learn useful things from me. I nodded my head in consent and after invoking a blessing for us he added, 'He'll be helpful to you, because he's a good boy and his name is Deacon.'

I smiled when I heard the boy's name, Deacon. His appearance and age did not suggest he was a deacon. Was he given that name in the hope that one day he would become one? At the goat pen I asked the boy and he told me the abbot gave him that name when he was still a baby. I was surprised and the boy seemed to have no objection to telling me more. I sat on the wall overlooking the plain to the west and the boy told me how they found him as a baby at the door of the big church one Sunday morning. He was two days old and so weak that he did not have the strength to cry. The abbot offered him to the local Christian women, for one of them to take him but none of them was willing. But a poor woman, one of the initiates, volunteered to breastfeed him twice a day, and the wife of the village priest volunteered to give him shelter in her house. So they joined forces to help him and the abbot gave him the name Deacon.

'The mother I never knew abandoned me because she was afraid,' said the boy.

I was amazed at the simplicity with which the boy told his story, without any regret or shame, as though he were telling an ordinary tale which could happen to anyone. That was the first lesson I learnt in this monastery and it was very useful in a mysterious way. We have no need to be ashamed of things imposed upon us, whatever they be, as long as we were not responsible for them. To a great extent that helped me forget what my mother had done to me in my childhood, and what I had done and had not done because of my fear and my weakness.

Deacon the plump boy became my assistant in all my work, and as the days passed I discovered that he really was a good boy, with a pure heart. Together with the monk we called Pharisee, he worked hard to help me organize and clean up the books until the place became worthy of the name library.

Several months after moving here I settled down and began to feel that this monastery was my final resting place. At that time I was about thirty-five years old. I was still a young man with high ambitions. In those days I was in the habit of saying my prayers in the dead of night, then joining the other monks at mass. When they all made their way to their work, I made my way to the library and would leave it only to go to prayers.

At the beginning of my stay here the monks would insist that I join them for lunch and I would decline, saying that I made do with one meal a day. The ascetic life I lived had taught me to survive on very little food. The abbot too ate only one meal a day. He is a man pure in spirit, cheerful and energetic, and spends most of his time in prayer and preaching. He sleeps little and he talks to the villagers who visit the monastery in a friendly tone full of love. The people in the village below the monastery and in the neighbouring villages know his worth and are well disposed towards him.

The first patient to visit me for treatment was a relative of the abbot and a childhood companion of his, several years his junior. He had chosen the life of a farmer and in his youth he and his father had improved a swathe of land on the plains which stretched north of the monastery. Then he and his family lived deep in the countryside. The man was more than sixty years old and suffered from such constant nausea and vomiting that he had lost much weight and his strength had declined. I took his pulse and it was weak. I examined his urine and stool and determined that he was suffering from gastric debility and indigestion. I treated him with mild restoratives for the intestines and stomach and forbade him foods that are hard to digest, without forcing him to make too many changes to his usual diet. After his digestion had recovered, I gave him a powder made of bitter berries which grow in Egypt, mixed with seeds which have an astringent effect on the stomach and strengthen it by removing the moisture. In treating him I did not observe the medical principle which people often propound these days and attribute to Galen, I mean the principle that every patient must be treated only with plants that grow locally. I do not believe it is correct and I have never seen it confirmed in any book. After four weeks the man had completely recovered and was back in good health. After his recovery the man came to the monastery bringing many presents from the bounty of his land. My prestige rose among the monks and the abbot was happy.

After I had been here four months there arrived at the monastery three large trunks containing the books which Bishop Theodore of Mopsuestia had promised me in Jerusalem that he would have copied. I was quite delighted by the books and began with pleasure to arrange them in the empty spaces on the shelves. I had an enjoyable time reading them. I would spend a long time among the books and when night came I would fall asleep seated in the library. In my room I kept the books which were banned and those which were not permitted to the general public: in all about a hundred books and scrolls. Those in the library amounted to more than a thousand. The books donated by Bishop Theodore included his own commentary on the Gospels and the Acts of the Apostles, a complete set of the twelve books of Hippocrates, and fourteen of the sixteen books known as *The Compendium of the Alexandrians* because the ancient doctors of Alexandria extracted it from Galen's epistles and scattered fragments.

As the days and months passed people came to know me, and patients began to trickle into the monastery from the surrounding regions seeking medical treatment from me. Most of them recovered through the mercy of the Lord and good medicine, and I became famous in the nearby villages and towns. Sometimes their doctors would ask my advice, I mean their novice doctors. When the abbot visited me he would often tease me, saying, 'Blessed Hypa, you came to this monastery as a physician monk, and now you are a monk physician.' He told me that many times in jest and with a broad smile. One day I answered that I was also a poet, and he laughed and said, 'Be a good physician and after that be what you want to be.' He seemed to sense my distress at what he said, and he tried to placate me by insisting that I read him some of my poetry. He surprised me when he told me that he loved literature, that he read Cicero's speeches and had memorized long passages of them. Without thinking, I said, 'Cicero was a pagan, father!'

'Yes, but he was very eloquent and gifted by the Lord. St Clement, one of the revered early fathers, loved to read his works.'

'But father, he used to reproach himself for that, and it is said that in a dream he heard a voice rebuke him, saying, "Clement, you are a Ciceronian, not a Christian."'

'These things, Hypa, reflect one's inner struggles and the spirit's constant agitation, which flares up and then dies down. Enough of that for now. Won't you read me your poems?'

'Tomorrow, reverend father, I will read you some.'

'So until tomorrow, if the Lord so wills.'

The abbot usually speaks in Greek, but he also speaks Syriac perfectly and sometimes he speaks in that language. Most of the people in these parts know the two languages but the abbot has a profound knowledge of them both. He simplifies his language when he speaks with the ordinary believers, though his sermons and speeches are eloquent and elegantly phrased. What he does not express in words he usually expresses with his eyes and hand movements, and he always deals with his monks, who revere him, using looks and gestures. I went into his room several times when I first settled in the monastery and I never saw any books there. When I had discussions with him I discovered that he recalled quotations from memory without consulting or looking at books. I do not mean the Gospels and the Acts of the Apostles because of course he knew them by heart. But the strange thing was that he remembered many pages of the diaries of the early fathers and could recite from memory the resolutions passed by the holy synods. He even remembered Cicero's speeches! He is a truly holy man, and puzzling. When did he read all these works? And why doesn't he read now? Was he really one of the monks who holed up for a full month in that building, fifty years ago? Why not, because he is about seventy years old, and if the date of the event is correct it would have happened when he was in his twenties. Tomorrow I will ask him, after I have read him my poems. That is what I intended to do that day but destiny had something else in mind for us. The next morning, while I was sitting in the library, sorting out my poems and choosing the ones to read to him, I heard the sound of approaching footsteps from behind the door. The sound on the gravel suggested there were four or five people coming and I thought they were monks come to hear my poems with the abbot, but it was not the abbot.

It was an unexpected delight when the door opened and, beaming with pleasure, in came the good father, the pure Christian spirit, the reverend priest Nestorius.

'Good morning, Hypa, I've come specially to see you,' he said.

'Welcome, reverend father, what a blessed occasion, by the Virgin Mother.'

A group of people came in behind him, trailing their solemn ecclesiastical garments. Judging by their clothes they were all from Antioch. The abbot came in with them, and behind him three of the most senior monks in the monastery. We all sat down on the twelve chairs surrounding the table. They were a holy gathering and I was delighted when the abbot said, 'The reverend Nestorius is on his way to Aleppo to renovate the parish church and offices and he asked me about you as soon as he came through the monastery gate, and he would not sit down until he saw you.'

'This is a great honour on his part, and on your part, reverend father,' I said.

At noon two monks came in carrying plates. It was the first time anyone other than I had eaten in this large hall since I turned it into a library. The conversation ranged far and wide and the priests and monks joined in until Nestorius sent them off to rest from the day's journey and prepare for the next day's trip. When the three of us were alone – Nestorius, the abbot and I – he said he was delighted to hear that my reputation as a physician had spread among the people of the region. 'Some of those in Antioch mention you with goodwill, affection and admiration for your skill, although you have not yet spent a year here,' he said, 'and the brothers there have asked me to suggest you move to Antioch, if you want, and I told them I would repeat the offer to you, although you rejected it that day when we were in the house of the Lord in Jerusalem.'

'I thank you for your kindness, your Grace the reverend bishop, but I am content here,' I said.

'So be it, but why haven't you planted your medicinal seeds and herbs, if you intend to stay? Or does the good abbot prevent you?'

'No, father, not at all. I haven't discussed the matter with him yet.'

Nestorius gave the abbot a friendly look, paused, and then, adjusting his cap as he spoke, said we should set about cultivating the land without delay, because growing medicinal plants would bring much benefit to my Christian patients. Then he reminded the abbot of the old disused well in the middle of the open space between the monastery buildings and the library, suggesting we use the well water to irrigate the plants in summer. Nestorius looked towards me and said, 'This holy monastery is on high ground and on both sides of the path leading up to it there are terraced pieces of land that are good for farming. At the bottom one could grow plants indigenous to hot countries and at the top plants from cold countries.'

The abbot smiled and said, 'Well, holy Nestorius, so you're also an expert in agriculture.'

'This, reverend father, is basic information, but I'm thinking of something big, as though we were building a hospital and a big church in this monastery,' Nestorius said.

The abbot approved and endorsed the idea, but I was wary of it. I was still frightened of having people clamour around me and I felt like a stranger among them. Here I had found rest from the commotion of the world but if what Nestorius wanted was to happen I would help bring it about, out of respect for him, and then I would move on to live in any nearby monastery and I would be happy to stay away from other people. That's what I thought at the time, but then events unfolded.

After sunset, the monastery servant came in with a large table set with pieces of cheese, grilled eggs, bread, sugarloaf, a jug of milk and some fruit. It was not a fasting day. The abbot took a slice of peach and chewed it slowly as usual, then bade us farewell, saying: 'That will do me till tomorrow. Enjoy your food, for you are still young, and carry on your conversation. Blessed Nestorius, I'd be delighted to see you early in the morning before you leave. Hypa knows the guestrooms and will take you there whenever you want. I leave you in the Lord's care.'

We ate only a few mouthfuls, washed down with some milk, then we left the library and went into the monastery courtyard. It was autumn time and the night was very still. The air had a pleasant chill and a rare clarity. I told

Nestorius that here I felt close to heaven, that I no longer felt nostalgia for my home country and that my doubts no longer recurred. 'Ever since I came here,' I added, 'I've felt that the world is safe.'

He smiled, tipped his hands in the air in resignation and said sadly: 'The world is still in turmoil but I have kept away from it.' He added, 'The raids by the barbarians and the northern tribes have weakened the frontiers of the empire, the Kurds in the east are restless and the Goths are also turbulent. As for the big Christian cities, they are full of intrigues and mysterious conflicts and gloomy speculation.' He told me of many other things which were making a stir in the world from which I had withdrawn, including that Bishop Theodore's health had deteriorated, his seventy-nine years were taking their toll and he would feel lonely after the bishop was gone. He said Emperor Theodosius II had written to him about the diocese of Constantinople and he would go there soon to be installed as bishop of the capital. He was not overjoyed. He said he had many things to finish off in the diocese of Antioch and the parishes around it, and that he had to complete projects that he had begun because he did not know what would become of them after he moved to Constantinople. He was worried and he wanted me to raise his spirits.

'Father,' I said cheerfully, 'to be the bishop of the imperial capital at the age of forty-seven is something significant and a great blessing, so do not despair.'

'Stop that, Hypa. My heart is not at ease in Constantinople. I am not comfortable among the leaders of this age, because of the way they are,' said Nestorius.

'The Lord will take care of you, master, and protect you.'

Nestorius turned the conversation in another direction, admiring the clear night air and its pleasant refreshing coolness. He told me he had brought me some books and medicinal herbs from Antioch and I said I would be eternally grateful for his interest in the monastery. We spent the first half of the night talking of many things until I almost plucked up the courage to ask about the mysterious building on the far eastern side of the monastery, in the hope that he could tell me something about it, but the moment I mentioned the building, as a prelude to asking, he yawned and I had no choice but to invite him to rest in his room. I accompanied him to the door of the guest quarters and went upstairs to spend the night in this room of mine. I was in a sociable mood, overcome by a heavenly exhilaration, marred only by the feeling that I had missed an opportunity to ask him the truth about the mysterious building.

Early in the morning I was waiting for Nestorius at the door to the guest quarters, with two or three other monks. He came out, beaming as usual, and we all prayed in the church. Then I took him to the breakfast table and after that I went down to the bottom of the hill with him. He and his companions went on to Aleppo and I climbed back to the monastery. I stopped at the gate and watched the small convoy as it disappeared out of sight between the rolling hills which rise above the plains.

✝

Then began the year 428 of the birth of Christ, in which many events took place. Bishop Theodore passed on to the kingdom above and in spring Nestorius moved to Constantinople, where he was installed as bishop of the imperial capital. I was settled in the monastery and more patients came to me seeking treatment. The year passed, and the next year too, quietly and happily. Then the year 430 came along, with events that shook up everything in my life that had been stable, especially the events that took place towards the end of the year, at the beginning of winter. For in those days the dispute between the church leaders intensified and Martha appeared in my life, like a sun burning in the sky.

The Inner Suns

Before the recent violent upheavals began and disasters struck, I used to divide my time between sleeping in my room or in the library, praying with the monks in the morning, meeting patients in the early afternoon and reading and writing poetry until I fell asleep. I slept little and my dreams were tranquil. I would often hear poems in my dreams and I would wake up to write them down. Because of that I started to put my scrolls and inkwell next to my pillow. At the time I delved into the secrets of the Syriac language and fell in love with its written literature, especially the story of Ahiqar the wise man, which I first studied under a teacher in Akhmim called Wissa. He taught us ancient languages, including Aramaic, or Syriac as Nestorius likes to call it. Here I had seen other copies of the story of Ahiqar with variants, and I had intended to compare these many copies to extract a precise edited text of this instructive story.[9] I had such a wonderful time in those days, which now seem remote. At sunrise I would sit on the rocks which lay at the edge of the monastery wall. The wall was in ruins at the northwestern corner and looked over the vast plains which stretched as far as the sea coast far away and the city of Antioch. At the time I wished I had supernatural eyesight and from my position on the monastery

9. This is an Aramaic (old Syriac) story which tells the tale of the wise man Ahiqar, chancellor to King Sennacherib, how destiny betrayed him and how he emerged serene, as well as his advice to his nephew. It is strikingly similar to the story of the wise man Luqman, and his advice to his son. (Translator's Note)

wall I could see distant cities: Antioch, Constantinople and Mopsuestia. It would be a miracle of which I would tell no one, if it happened, I mean if the Lord granted me that gift. Only rarely does the Lord like to reveal the miracles which he performs through his saints. But I am not a saint: I am a physician and a poet who dresses as a monk, whose heart is filled with love for the universe and who expects to pass the remaining years of his life without sin, so that his unblemished soul can ascend to the heavens where the light of divine glory shines. Those were the limits of my life at that time – just one year ago.

The abbot had become close to me, in fact at that time I was the person in the monastery closest to him and the one who spent most time sitting with him, especially after the monks Laugher and Pharisee left. The abbot would often call me to his large three-windowed room, or he would come to me in the library shortly before noon and stay until lunchtime. Lunch was his only meal, but he tried to be present in the dining room at breakfast and dinner to read psalms to the monks and speak a few words to them. He would always ask me about my patients and whether I had written any poetry. He would be happy when I read him something new, in fact he started to memorize some of my poems. When I read them to him he would look at me with the same benevolence that I remembered from my father when he looked at me in the old days. Fatherhood is a divine spirit that flows through the universe, bringing heavenly grace to the young through their fathers.

I will never be a father and I will never have a wife and children. I will never give this world children to torment in the same way I was tormented, because I cannot bear to see a child suffer. When I heard the crying of a sick baby that his mother was bringing to me for treatment, I would run to meet them at the library door, take the baby from her and rush it inside, where among the medicines I keep many remedies for childhood ailments. The infants often suffer, either from wind in their bellies or because their mothers do not look after them properly or do not produce good milk. For the mothers I prescribe foods that improve the breast milk and I loosen the nappy and anoint the baby with an aromatic oil I have invented, tested many times and found to be beneficial. The babies would often urinate towards me when I undid their nappies. I would laugh and take pleasure in the joy of the mothers who brought their children crying in pain and suffering and left me with their children calm and sleeping on their shoulders. There is nothing in the world more sublime than easing the pain of a human being who cannot express his pain. Did not Jesus the Messiah come only to save lost souls who are heedless of their many sins? Jesus endured pain to spare us from sin. That idea was the starting point of one of my Syriac poems which the abbot liked and learnt by heart. Shall I record it here? Why not? The poem runs:

> By enduring pain He saved us from sin,
> By His sacrifice He redeemed us.
> With love He descended, with love He ascended
>   and with love He traced the way,
> And guided people to peace, and gave joy to the
>   faithful.
> He suffered the fire of Earth to bring down on us
>   the cool breezes of Heaven.
> He offered His soul as a sacrifice on the Cross,
> To atone for our lack of faith, that we might
>   obtain salvation.

The poem is long and it is one of the poems of mine that Martha was later to sing, breathing her spirit into the words and dispelling the sorrows of the audience. Her singing brought tears to my eyes several times, when she sang and looked towards me in one of the recitals that brought us together. My encounters with Martha are another story, which I will not tell now because I am recalling the days of serenity when I felt at ease within the walls of this monastery and when my inner suns rose over the horizon of mercy until I forgot my torments, my doubts and my constant uncertainty. I came to feel that I was living in the clouds and could almost sense around me the rustling of the wings of the angels that fill the sky. It was then that I discovered for the first time the secret of the monastic life, the virtues of seclusion and the serenity of escaping the tumult of this world. I was certain that the world had no value and that when I left it behind me I would exchange the cheap pleasures of the body for the precious prospect of the spirit.

In those days I had nothing to disturb my peace of mind, other than those dreams which sometimes took me by surprise without warning, to remind me of my burdensome legacy and the secrets I harboured. Some nights I would wake up weeping and trembling when I saw my mother in a dream looking with contempt at my father. My father was humble even in my dreams, never speaking a word to me. He would just look at me with great anguish as he rowed his boat or drew in his nets with no fish. It was my mother who often spoke to me in those dreams and often she would roar with laughter and wake me up in alarm. Although these dreams would come to me infrequently, they might come twice or more in the same night.

One night I saw Hypatia in her white silk dress with the hems decorated with golden thread. She was radiant and friendly. In my dream I was a young man of no more than twenty and she was the same age as she was when I knew her. I dreamt she was reading a chemistry book to me, although she never in her life studied that science. I was memorizing what she was reading from the book as she read the lines and ran her finger along them. Her finger was elegant, her fingernail bright white, as it passed lightly across the words. She would turn towards me with a smile as she read, and when I wanted her to embrace me, she embraced me. When I took her in my arms I found she had changed into Octavia covered in her own blood and I woke up terrified.

Several times I had strange dreams: the salty sea roiled by many eddies and my mother trying to escape them while I watched her in fear, standing naked on the beach. She was calling me by the name which Octavia had chosen for me and which no one knew but us: Theodhoros Poseidonios. Then her call turned into a cry for help and that quickly became a scream which echoed across the firmament and woke me exhausted from my sleep and left me sleepless for the rest of the night.

Last year I spoke to the abbot twice about the mysterious building. The first time he took refuge in silence and did not answer me. The second time we were sitting one morning and the sun was about to rise from behind the building. I told him I would not ask him again if he did not want to tell me. The morning was clear and it was summer. The abbot bowed his head for a moment, then told me that in ancient times this monastery was a temple to the god of fertility and pastures and the goddess of the fields. In the old days people believed that they met on top of this hill and made love. For hundreds of years worshippers would come here from far and wide, so they built a temple and over time set up tall columns until it became one of the largest temples of the ancient world.

In the time of King Solomon, the son of David, the Jews wanted to convert the temple into a house of the Lord and they secretly sent a squadron of soldiers to demolish it, but that proved impossible for them to achieve because of the solidity of the structure and the large number of priests living there and of people visiting. They say that the Jewish squadron was completely wiped out in mysterious circumstances and Solomon in anger sent more of his soldiers to demolish it, but they could not do it either because of the powerful amulets buried beneath it and the spells of the ancient priests. No one could decipher the spells or thwart their magical power.

So the temple remained standing until the time of Jesus the Messiah but it fell into ruin as the years took their toll. When people abandoned it Azazeel and his cohorts – devils and fiends – moved in and lived inside the temple with their human followers, who at that time worshipped the devil. But when Azazeel failed to tempt Christ, as is written in the Gospels, and the word of the Lord triumphed, a mighty earthquake took place and the temple was destroyed. All that remained was these stones here and there and the broken columns. Then it happened that some of the early fathers were preaching in the region, and the Romans killed them. Their disciples buried them in this eastern part of the temple and when Christianity spread in this parts the spot became a place of pilgrimage. This building was built over the tombs of the martyred fathers for fear they might be disinterred by the pagans, who resented the followers of Christ and hoped to restore their old temple to its former state. The Christians erected this structure to surround the resting place of the early fathers and at the wall on the side of the square there were three contiguous walls, which could not be breached because of the hardness of the rock and the thickness of the three walls. As for the other three sides, they were fortified by nature because they were on high ground overlooking the precipice. Eventually the building became a refuge and stronghold for monks.

The abbot paused a while, then continued: 'When I was fifteen I was here when bandits surrounded us and we spent five full days in the building, not a month as is said. We almost perished of hunger and thirst. When the bandits failed to breach the walls they gave up and left. They didn't know there was nothing in the building to steal anyway.' The abbot paused again a moment, then added, 'There's no truth to the story about the nails which were hammered into the body of Jesus and which glow by night. That, Hypa, is all I can tell you about this building, so after today do not ask me about it again.'

The abbot had finished speaking, but I was still puzzled and my thoughts were confused. I did not understand much of what he said. He had been speaking to me as though he were reading from a text he had memorized. Even his face showed no expression as he spoke.

I hesitated a moment, then without thinking I pursued the subject. 'But father, I've heard subdued sounds coming from inside the building when I put my ear to the wall. That's happened to me several times.'

'Hypa, those are sounds that come from inside you, not from inside the building. There may be big rats or snakes or insects in the building, because it hasn't been opened for many years.'

'But father, you'll open it if one of the monks dies.'

'No, we no longer bury anyone in it, and it will never be opened,' he said.

The Hypostasis Pharisee

The monks in this monastery and in the surrounding areas differ from their brothers in Egypt and Alexandria. Both groups are pious, love the Lord and have a deep interest in divinity, but the approach of us Egyptian monks is tougher and more inclined towards arduous forms of worship. That is no surprise because we Egyptians invented monasticism and gave it to those parts of the world where Christians live.

The monks here are amazed at my asceticism and my spiritual exertions. They admire my patience as a reader and my constant application as a writer. They were, and still are, surprised at how I sleep in a chair most nights and how I stay secluded in the library most days, so much so that several months after I arrived they started to call me Hypa the Strange. Little by little their surprise diminished as they grew accustomed to me and came to know me better. But they continued to call me 'the Strange', and sometimes 'the Physician'. Here they are less interested in news about Alexandria than the monks in Jerusalem, and so they pestered me less. In fact, the truth be told, they did not pester me at all, though in the beginning they were keen to find out what was behind the connection between me and Bishop Nestorius. When I told them the truth about how we met in Jerusalem they relaxed, and when they found out about my skill in medicine and the arts of healing they became more friendly. When they had observed me for months and had not noticed anything troubling in my behaviour they were reassured. They used to visit me in the library and sit with me in the upper courtyard after the long masses.

At the start I was not very talkative or sociable, and they respected my silence and my solitude. Then day by day I became more like them. I started to enjoy sitting with them and delighted in their constant cheerfulness. My closest friends were two of the most honest monks. One I called Laugher or, in full, the Dignified Laugher because he combined the two qualities, which rarely occur together. After two years with me here, he recently moved to Antioch, where he settled in the suburbs in a monastery they call Eupropius.[10] While he was here he filled everyone around him with joy, love and serenity. The features of his face, especially his upper lip which arched to reveal his teeth, gave the impression that he was always smiling. He did in fact smile often, as if the Lord had favoured him with good news to dispel any cares he might have. He had a glint in his eye and would laugh on the slightest pretext, and when he laughed he would cover his mouth with his hand like a girl. But he was also quick to tears. He was present once when I was treating a poor child who had an inflammation in his neck of the type we call Persian fire, and he burst into tears and left because he could not bear to hear the child crying. After that he would leave the library as soon as any patient came in. I could not hold back my tears when I said goodbye to him at the monastery gate on the day he suddenly left, and I never saw him again after that, although I often longed to see him and I missed his company.

The other monk is now the one closest to my heart. He has spent twenty years of his life here and he is the monk most like the abbot, though twenty years younger, fatter and with a thicker beard. He is strikingly short with a large belly, so when he walks quickly, as he always does, he looks like a rolling ball. His hands and feet are as tiny as those of a small boy and he also has the smile of a boy or an adolescent. But what makes him look like a man is his baldness, his thick black beard, his puffy cheeks and the black rings around his eyes from staying up late or indigestion. His eyes are wide, full of intelligence and curiosity, and he is goodhearted in a way which strangers would miss but which is obvious to those who grow close to him.

10. Historical sources indicate that Nestorius became a monk in this monastery and it is strange that Hypa the monk did not refer to that here. (Translator's Note)

At first I saw him several times in church, then with time we became as brothers, especially after he helped me with great enthusiasm to prepare the library, which had been an abandoned building. As he helped me arrange the books on the shelves he would look at them like someone fascinated with texts, but I rarely saw him reading. The monks here call him by a strange name: the Hypostasis Pharisee. I started calling him by the same name, which neither irritates nor pleases him.

At the beginning of our acquaintanceship, when we were sitting at the monastery gate one day, he told me he was of Arab origin and spoke the languages of both the Arabs of the north and those in Yemen. At the time I did not know there were two Arabic languages, northern and southern. He told me his father was a wealthy man who worked in trade and lived in a large house in the middle of Aleppo. But he died young and when his uncle married his mother to preserve his father's wealth, Pharisee left their world and joined the parish there as a servant and then as a deacon. He became a monk at the age of twenty-five and lived in seclusion for three years, then came here and settled in the monastery.

When I came to know him better, he told me some of his secrets, such as the fact that in his early youth he disobeyed the Lord with women several times and wrongly saw them as fair game for erotic adventures. Then he suffered for his sins, repented and confessed to the abbot everything he had committed. He found out the secret of how to tap into the mercy of the Lord through confession and he gave up the debauchery which had both troubled and delighted him. But after he joined the church he hated women, in fact he could not abide any female, even if she were a dumb animal. One day I said to him, after he had talked at length in denigration of females: 'Take it easy, Pharisee, the Earth is female and the Lord came from the Virgin.'

'No, Hypa,' he replied. 'Femininity and women are the cause of every misfortune. Earth, sky, water, air and plants are neither female nor male, but the Lord's gifts to Adam who was led astray by his wife Eve, and what happened happened. The Virgin Mary is a solitary exception and the Lord made her faultless so that our Lord Jesus Christ could stem from her and to show us that the most sublime things can come from the least of things, just as pearls take shape in sea shells. Or else what would the Virgin be, had she not given birth to Christ?'

I was surprised at him saying 'stem from her' but I did not want to argue with him, because he had not studied theology in Egypt to know that 'stem from' is a philosophical term that should not be used to express incarnation and that Christ took from the body of the Virgin his humanity, and hence he was half human, judging by what they used to say there.

At the time, he stopped for a moment and gazed into the distance, then suddenly, as though he had discovered something important, he said, 'Look at this monastery, and all the monasteries and churches, why does peace prevail in them? Because they do not have women in them, and are spared all the calamities and betrayals that women cause.'

'Are all women unfaithful?' I asked him.

'Yes, definitely. The only man who could be sure that his wife was faithful was our ancestor Adam because his wife had no other man with whom to betray him, either in her bed or in her imagination. Yet she still betrayed him with Azazeel the accursed and allied herself with Azazeel against Adam.'

Pharisee loved to talk at length. He would shake his head when he was engrossed in telling a story, wave his arms in the air and illustrate the words with his hands and fingers as though he were talking to someone who was deaf. He did not like to be interrupted and he never looked at the face of the person he was arguing with. When he was carried away, it was as if he were addressing another group of people. Once, to provoke him gently, I said, 'And what about convents?' He gushed like a waterfall in full flood. 'Argh, they're an innovation that has no basis. Monasticism means chastity, serenity and abandonment of the ephemeral world and one of the most important features of it is avoidance of women, so how can women practise it? Have you not seen what Matthew the Apostle wrote in his Gospel, quoting Jesus as saying that anyone who can bear to renounce marriage should do so and what Paul the Apostle says in his first Epistle to the Corinthians: "It is good for a man not to marry."'

'But Paul the Apostle said in the same epistle that since there is so much

182

immorality in the world, each man should have his own wife and each woman her own husband.'

'But after that he said that those who are unmarried should stay unmarried.'

Pharisee was very argumentative that day but he is no longer like that. He has memorized all the legal books, the four Gospels and the epistles of the Fathers. He cannot stand heresies and banned writings, and is suspicious of the non-canonical books which we recently started to call the Apocrypha. He is always rebuking me for keeping copies of the banned gospels in my room, but he has never told anyone else of this secret, which I revealed to him one year after I settled here. Philosophy enrages him greatly, although he is in fact inclined to philosophizing, which is by nature close to theology. He is interested in the resolutions of the local synods and the great synod held a hundred years ago in Nicaea, attended by the bishops who drafted for us the famous creed. He is curious about the interpretations of this creed and the commentaries on the interpretations. Naturally he is interested in biblical exegesis and he has a great passion for everything related to the hypostasis or nature of the elements in the Trinity. He never stops talking about it, thinking about it and taking a dogmatic position on it. That is how he acquired his nickname Pharisee,[11] which those close to him have expanded into the Hypostasis Pharisee.

The monks loved to rile him by asking him about the nature, essence and intrinsic reality of Jesus Christ, and about some of the many other expressions which are synonymous with the puzzling word hypostasis, especially in those regions which speak Greek, Syriac, Arabic and other less important languages. Pharisee knew all the variants of the word in these languages, and as soon as he met me he asked what the Egyptians and Alexandrians mean by the word hypostasis. I told him that it means the person or intrinsic entity and that we rarely use the word in speech, and he said 'Well done!' If he responded to the

11. Pharisee: an epithet applied to those who are dogmatic in religious matters, derived from the name of the Jewish group who adhered to the externals of Jewish law and argued against Jesus Christ. In Christian times and to this day the term has come to mean 'dogmatic'. (Translator's Note)

monks' provocation, and he generally did, he would embark on an explanation of the three holy hypostases: the Father, the Son and the Holy Spirit, and he would go over in intricate detail all the citations, the schools of thought and the heresies, finally coming down on the side of the view that God and Christ, the Father and the Son, are one hypostasis or one nature. The monks would often drift away from the group, while he remained deep in his explanation, until the last listener also left or prayer time came and at the church door he was forced to break off his interminable presentation. He was always saying that he would write a thesis on the three hypostases. Then a few months ago the abbot categorically forbade him from broaching these hypostatic matters again and reprimanded the other monks for bringing the subject up with him. None the less the nickname the Hypostasis Pharisee stuck, even after it was forbidden to talk about the subject.

During a pleasant conversation one day I asked the abbot why he prevented the monks from discussing the question of the hypostasis. He answered firmly and decisively that it was a sterile debate and likely to provide opportunities for strife and heresies, even if it was discussed calmly for the purpose of theological study and as conversation to pass the time of day. 'The monastic life is more important than that,' said the abbot, who was visibly displeased. Like everyone else I agreed with him and none of us ever discussed the matter again.

Four months ago they summoned Pharisee to Antioch at short notice. He went there and stayed away a month, and I missed him greatly. Then suddenly he came back, as he had gone, but he was a little changed, without the calm smile which had adorned his face most of the time. When I asked him what had happened during his month in Antioch, he held his tongue.

✝

At the end of the year 429 of the Nativity storm clouds gathered and we received from Constantinople reports that were disturbing and sometimes incomprehensible to me. Bishop Nestorius, for example, had convened a local synod there, at which he stripped some priests of their ecclesiastical rank and sentenced them to expulsion because they disagreed with his opinion that the Virgin Mary was the mother of Christ, or Christotokos. The priests collectively insisted on what they and most people believe – that the Virgin was Theotokos, or the mother of God. We also heard that Bishop Nestorius had destroyed a church belonging to the Arians in Constantinople, obtained a decree from the emperor to hunt down the followers of Arius, declared war on members of the Church of the Martyrs[12] and declared them guilty of heresy and deviation from the true faith.

I did not understand what was happening in the capital of the empire and I was not interested in checking the veracity of these jumbled reports. Naturally I did not suspect Bishop Nestorius of any wrongdoing and the monks here did not accuse him of anything in front of me, because they knew that I liked him. And I do truly like him and to this day I persist in my affection for him, preserving it in spite of the vicissitudes of time.

In the course of those dark days I caught sight of Martha for the first time, and the day I saw her it did not occur to me that her flame would burn me.

✝

In the last week of that year, meaning the year 429, a caravan of monks passed by on the night we were celebrating Christmas, trying to kindle some festive cheer to warm ourselves against the bitter cold of that winter, which almost froze the tips of our fingers off. Unusually heavy rain had been falling without cease, and the caravan, with a priest, three monks and two servants, climbed the hill to the monastery on its way from Antioch to the land of the Kurds beyond the eastern desert. They said that they were going to preach

12. These were followers of the Roman Bishop Novatius, and since the end of the fourth century AD they had agreed with the Donatists in North Africa and the Melitians in Egypt in rejecting penitents who had once abandoned Christianity but then reconverted after the age of persecution. At that time they were known as the Church of the Martyrs.

the gospel there in a country called Pars and that they intended to build a big church there in the hope that it would one day become a bishopric. Because the rain was so persistent and the road was cut the travellers spent two nights with us, then left on the morning of the third day to continue their journey. I accompanied them to the foot of the hill with some of the monks from the monastery and then said goodbye to them. On the way back I was thinking of the eastern desert, which one has to cross to reach the land of the Kurds. They told me it was extremely arid, with salty soil, and that in summer when the heat is fierce it has flies and other insects which cling to the traveller's face to try to extract the moisture of his body, and that some people may have died from all the flies clinging to their face.

Later that day I wanted to drop in on the abbot in his room to see if he could confirm the reports I had heard of this eastern desert, but his door was closed. At the door I found two women waiting, the trails of their dresses fluttering in the winter wind. When I approached, one of them gave me a dreamy look. I was startled and left immediately for my room. The cold air had frozen my limbs but inside I was excited by the woman's glance, which came to me from behind her diaphanous silk veil, so at the time I could not see her features. From the balcony of the upper floor of the monks' building, I noticed the priest of the church walking towards the two women. At the time I did not care to find out what was happening. I just closed my room door behind me and sought warmth in the protection of the Lord.

In those days the walls of the library were turned into wooden cupboards because when we had the downpours I was worried that water might seep into the wooden shelves on which the books, parchments and scrolls were put. Although the library was well roofed I was afraid that water might come in through the cracks in the walls, and there is nothing more dangerous to books than water: it rots pieces of leather parchment and papyrus scrolls, and makes them stick together forever. Besides, the ink runs when it gets wet and the lines are completely wiped out. I spoke to the abbot on the subject and he quickly summoned the village carpenter. We helped him cover the shelves with wooden doors and the books were then held in what looked like cupboards, but after that I missed something I had always enjoyed –

looking at the rows of books on the shelves. Whenever I went into the room, I would go straight to open all the cupboard doors, and I would not close them until I was going out.

After weeks of lengthening nights and the onset of winter diseases, the cold eased a little and the sky cleared up. One night, when the clouds lifted from the dome of the firmament, which was pure black and studded with stars, we were preparing to go out to the large church to say the last prayers of the day after gathering in the dining room for dinner and some hushed conversation. The abbot held me back with a touch of his hand, and I slowed down until the other monks had moved away. Jubilant and proud, in a voice weakened by age and many ordeals and destroyed by many spiritual exercises and prayers, he whispered to me, 'Bishop Nestorius wants you for an important mission. He will meet you in Antioch tomorrow, after sunset.'

Tomorrow after sunset! So I would have to set out with the first rays of the sun, because the journey to Antioch could take the whole day and might be prolonged by the effects of the rain which had poured down over the past weeks. I was anxious to see Nestorius and talk to him, so much so that I had thought of visiting Constantinople to see him. And now he was remembering me, and asking to meet me hurriedly in Antioch. Hurriedly? What had happened? And what motive made him rush the meeting? Perhaps he was not going to stay long in Antioch, perhaps he was there for a few days to visit his brothers and would then sail back to Constantinople to attend the Easter festivities there, and he wanted to see me before he left. Or did he perhaps want me for some other reason? So be it, because anything that required that Nestorius see me must definitely be something benign and only good could come of it. Or perhaps he wanted me to go with him to the seat of his new bishopric, or was he going to invite me again to stay in Antioch? Or did he want to start expanding this monastery and build the hospital we had talked about in the past?

'So what do you think, my son? Why are you so distracted?' said the abbot.

The abbot's question brought me back from the labyrinth of possibilities which had swept me far away. I listened to him and took heed of his advice, which that night took the form of 'Don't leave too late in the morning, my son. Take some food for the day and some fodder for the donkey. Don't uncover your head on the road, for the air is cold. Don't stop at the villages you come across, or else night might fall while you are still on the road. I'll give you a letter for Bishop Nestorius. Put it in his hands and don't let anyone read it before him. If he offers you anything, accept it, for he is a man blessed of heaven. Leave your ego outside his gate and act in front of him like a corpse in the hands of the washer. Meeting him will bathe you in light and spiritual power, so prepare to rejoice. Obey his instructions and be as he wants you to be. And submit your being to the will of the Lord.'

The Leap of the Past

After the mass I hardly slept all night, just some fleeting snatches, for some reason I was not aware of. Half an hour before the sun rose I joined the monks in the small church to say the first prayers of the day, waiting for the sunlight to bring some colour to the sky. When the colour on the horizon was more blue than black, I prepared to set off for Antioch. The monastery courtyard was quiet and the air was still. The donkey, tied to a peg close to the gate to the animal pen, looked as though he were waiting for me at his tether and knew that we had a long journey ahead of us, or perhaps he knew that because he saw me approaching with the bag of fodder. I rode the donkey out of the monastery gate as the first rays of the sun lit up the world in splendour.

At the gate I saw one of the soldiers from the Roman troop contingent, wrapped up in his heavy camel-wool cloak. He was lying on the floor next to the broken-down wall, snoring loudly in his sleep. I said to myself, 'Here's the monastery guard, asleep under the protection of the guard of the universe, who never slumbers. Why don't the priests, the bishops and the monks take a lesson from him and leave the matters of the world to God and refrain from their internecine strife? Today, when the chance arises, I shall ask Bishop Nestorius whether there is any truth to the reports, current among the monks, that he has oppressed those he views as heretics. I shall also ask him about what he said in the sermon he gave at his installation as bishop, when he addressed the emperor saying, 'Help me in my war on unbelievers and I will help you in your war with Persia. Give me an Earth free of heresy and I will give you the keys to Heaven.' If it is true that he said such strange things, then he must have changed since I knew him, and must now be seeking earthly things, not heaven, and I would not like to see him do that.

The guard did not notice us leaving. Even his dog, lying beside him, took little interest in my passing. The dog raised its head and saw me, twice beat its tail lightly on the ground and then lay down again. On the slope leading from the monastery hill down to the plains which stretch to the horizon, I leant back to keep my balance on the donkey's back. In spite of the abbot's admonitions my head was bare. The last of the night breezes ruffled through my hair and the cool air was delightful. The donkey's pace suggested that he was cheerful too. He loved to go down the hill: all creatures like to go down and take pleasure in that, except mankind, who is deceived by delusions and driven by dreams. Mankind takes pleasure in rising and climbing. Perhaps that is instinctive in man, since he is an extension of God on High and so he likes ascents, which take him up to his elevated origins, towards the Father who is in the heavens, the Father occluded beyond the folds of the heavens.

As light spread across the land, the donkey and I walked across the flat land, the monastery behind us and the world stretching westwards before us. After a while we came to the long road which leads in the direction of Antioch, a road so long that it looks as if it never ends. The Romans paved this road with stone centuries ago. Why didn't they pave roads in the Nile valley? The Romans never took any interest in Egypt, only inasmuch as they could plunder wheat and wine from it. Or perhaps the annual flooding of the Nile was the reason why they did not pave the roads in Egypt, since it tends to displace stones, except the stones in the old temples, because they are too massive and too stable to be affected by the Nile flood. But being massive and stable did not protect them from the Christians. In the town of Esna in southern Egypt I saw ordinary Christians destroying the pictures drawn on the great temple by scratching the surface of the walls. They tried to erase the pictures at the top of the columns and on the high ceilings by throwing mud at them. When it proved difficult to cover them, because the ceiling was too high, they came up with an extraordinary idea. They would bring green reeds, grasses and old rags and set fire to them in the main hall of the temple and the other big rooms. The thick black smoke was enough to coat the reliefs with a layer of soot. They did this for so long that they were able to cover the ceilings with black and the reliefs were effaced. After that, they turned the temple into a huge monastery, including five churches.

The road to Antioch is long. When the sun grew fierce above us and the donkey found its stride, I nodded off into brief dozes full of visions. I love these moments halfway between waking alertness and snatches of sleep. I imagine that God decided to create the world in such a moment. God does not sleep, He only tires and rests. His rest is like the sleep of us his human children. Sleep is rest full of dreams and visions. I wonder if the Lord dreams. Who knows? For maybe this universe with everything in it is just one of His dreams.

When the sun was high in the sky and the road unwound under the tapping of the donkey's hoofs, I had more brief naps and dreams. That day I saw many visions – the soft egg-shaped rocks moving from their usual spots and floating on the water of the Nile, drawn by the current towards the great sea; the hills to the east of the valley in my native country, its arid stones adorned in greenery, grasses and trees, beautiful where once they were dreary; many faces laughing; Octavia asleep in her diaphanous silk dress; seagulls on the wing above the waves of the sea; the walls of Jerusalem turned sparkling white. Whenever I dozed off, I saw a new sight.

The sun was directly overhead and the donkey tired, so we rested under some shady bushes on the edge of a small and sleepy town called Sarmada just off the road. I preferred that we rest at some distance from the houses and the people of the town. I could see the houses from afar, still beneath the midday sun. The donkey was happy as he chewed the fodder, which was enriched with corn. I was not so happy with the bites I took slowly from my loaf of bread. At the time I had an unusual desire for boiled eggs, but it was a fasting period and there was no question of yielding to my cravings. Will my desires continue to torment me all my life? Why haven't I lost my craving for things, after all these prayers, masses, ascetic practices and varieties of abstinence? Is it not time that I transcended childish ways and refrained from the illusion of taking pleasure in trivial things? I must be resolute and determined with myself or else I will become like this donkey, enjoying his fodder. Does this donkey know that the universe has a Lord?

I dozed off and when I awoke the shadow of the trees had swung a little towards the east. I mounted the donkey and rode past the town without giving the scattered houses a single glance. At the time Sarmada meant nothing to me, and how would I have known then that these humble houses once held Martha, who was to shake me through and through. I learnt that from her weeks later, after I had passed unawares through the town.

I reached Antioch before sunset. The city has a large gate and much tumult, like all great cities. I had no trouble reaching the main church, next to where Bishop Nestorius was staying in the adjoining guesthouse, as the abbot had told me the night before. A cheerful young man volunteered to take me from the city gate to the door of the guesthouse. Antioch is bigger than Jerusalem but smaller than Alexandria. Judging by their features, the people are pleasant, their faces more cheerful and friendly than those of the Alexandrians, and less sad and hard than those of the Egyptians. When I drew close to the big church, I saw more clerics in their decorative ecclesiastical garments moving around the church, a splendid building with high walls like all strongholds of religion.

At the small garden at the entrance to the guesthouse I told the guard I had come in response to a summons from Bishop Nestorius. He showered me with welcomes and took me in at once. As he took the donkey's halter he told me that Bishop Nestorius was attending a service in the big church. 'If you want to join them, I'll take you there,' he added. 'I recommend you do that, because at this holy service there are three senior bishops, so do not miss this rare opportunity, goodly monk.'

The hymns and the night prayers lasted until the dawn mass and the church was full. The mass was impressive, with hundreds of monks, priests and believers, and innumerable candles and lamps with flickering flames. The lights rippled like waves and angels hovered in the church air. I was overwhelmed by the anthems and the melodies as the young deacons chanted: 'Blessed are thou, mankind, with the grace of heaven.' The sanctity of the place bathed my heart in light, dispelled my fatigue from the day's journey and inspired me to seek heaven. I went up to the altar to take communion and when the priest put the wafer in my mouth and I sipped the diluted wine, I felt for a moment that they were indeed the body and blood of Jesus permeating my body and my whole being. Taking communion is an extraordinary ritual if the symbolism of it complements our faith. When I turned from the altar, I felt that delightful dizziness which convulses the soul during mass. When I noticed Nestorius in his bishop's garments my heart leapt and I was flooded with that joy that sometimes comes to us from beyond the universe.

The mass lasted two hours, until the sun rose and its light came in through the church windows. I left the church with hundreds of others, all of us filled with grace. I hurried to the courtyard of the guesthouse to be ready to receive the reverend Nestorius. He arrived within minutes, surrounded by a group of priests and flanked by two bishops whom I soon discovered to be John, the bishop of Antioch, and Rabbula, the bishop of Edessa. When the reverend Nestorius saw me, he came forward to welcome me and I noticed that those around him looked at me with respect. None of them knew me but they knew that if Nestorius took an interest in a monk then he must be significant. I am insignificant, but the Lord works in mysterious ways.

At the door to the guesthouse Nestorius whispered to me that he would now leave me to rest and would see me after the noon prayer. A young servant took me to a room on an upper floor for me to rest a while. The room was square, tidy and clean. In the right-hand corner was a small bed, under a window in the shape of a large cross, and on the opposite wall hung a wooden cross and a brightly coloured icon of the Virgin Mary carrying her infant at her breast. I sat on the edge of the bed, drawn to the picture of the Virgin, whom they portray here with features different from those we know in Egypt, though her spirit is one and the same in all the pictures, and her head is covered in the same way in all the icons.

The Virgin… I looked at her at length that day until I fancied I could really see her in front of me. What peace you pour into our souls, Immaculate Virgin! What beauty radiates from your calm face and your lidded eyes!

Ah, if only I had lived in your time and bathed in the light of your presence, Mother of Light! Are you aware of me? Can I rest my head on your holy and immaculate breast?

I stood up and pressed my face against the image of the Virgin, shut my eyes as warm tears ran down into my beard. I stayed a moment clutching the icon, and sensed that she was carrying me up to a distant heaven. I felt two tears descend from the Virgin's eye, wetting my cheek, and I broke into sobs. I embraced the icon, clung to it in fact, and from it emanated a coolness, a tranquillity and peace of mind. Celestial light filled my head and chest...

'Hypa.'

'What is it, Azazeel? What do you want now?'

'Tell me about Antioch, meeting Nestorius and the rest of what happened.'

I went back to the bed and threw myself down on it, as though I had returned from a whirl around the distant heavens. Unexpectedly I fell into a deep sleep which lasted till around noon. That day I did not sleep seated, as I usually do. I woke up cheerful, my heart full of love. I decided that when I went back to the monastery I would compose a hymn to the Virgin Mary, starting with the words: 'Wellspring of compassion, source of light.' I went down the stairs, lit by daylight which streamed through many windows of unusual shape. Many priests, deacons and servants were walking up and down the long corridor which links the rooms and the lobbies. I asked after Pharisee the monk but could learn nothing about him. I asked where Bishop Nestorius might be and they took me to a large hall at the entrance to the big guesthouse. The high windows of the hall overlooked a little garden and on all four sides benches were arranged, covered with antique cushions of coloured wool.

Nestorius was sitting in the right-hand corner of the room, holding in his hand a large book. Five old men surrounded him, including the two bishops who were with him at the mass. When he saw me he put the book aside and stood up to greet me. I hurried up to him and kissed his hand. He kissed my head and blessed me. Then he had me sit nearby among them. I still remember the conversation word for word.

'Your Grace, I've been longing to see you,' I said.

'You should have let us know, even if only by sending a letter to Constantinople.'

'I'm sorry, father, but I'm not accustomed to writing letters.'

'But you are in the habit of writing marvellous poems. Did you know, Rabbula, that Hypa is a poet no less talented than you, and like you he writes poetry in Syriac and Greek, although he is of Egyptian origin and Coptic is his first language?'

Bishop Rabbula smiled sullenly out of courtesy. Then he said that he would not judge the quality of my poems until he heard them from me. 'Only his poems show if a poet has the gift of poetry,' he said, 'and the testimony of his admirers does him no good, even if they have the prestige of Bishop Nestorius.' Everyone laughed solemnly at his subtle wit, though it did not amuse me. Bishop Nestorius picked up the book that was in his hand when I entered and proffered it to Bishop Rabbula. I took it from him and passed it on to Rabbula, who put it carefully on his knees.

'This, Hypa, is the translation of the Gospels which Bishop Rabbula did from Greek to Syriac. Have you seen it before?' Nestorius said.

'No, reverend father, but I've heard of it. It is without doubt a splendid work.'

Bishop Rabbula ran his hand over the cover of his book and his face glowed with pride. He shook his head boastfully and said, 'This is a modest effort. I wanted it to divert people in our church from the Diatessaron and the infidel who translated it.'[13]

I would have liked to take the translation and look at it, but I dropped the idea because of the arrogance I detected in Bishop Rabbula. After a while the two priests took leave of us, while the two bishops and a man from Antioch wearing priest's vestments remained. I knew the two bishops because of their reputation and Nestorius had introduced me to the priest with the words: 'This is the priest of our church, Anastasios. He comes from Antioch but

13. The Diatessaron was a summary of the four Gospels in Syriac, written by a Greek intellectual by the name of Tatian. The book was widely available but the clergy did not like it because Tatian was a pagan.

he's with me in Constantinople now. He is a brother with a distinguished intellect and a heart full of faith.'

I nodded to the priest in friendly greeting and he nodded coldly in response. His face had a certain severity, and a vigilance for which at first I could see no reason, but in our conversation what he said brought to light what was hidden in his heart. When Bishop Nestorius began to speak, everyone stopped smiling and it seemed we were about to take up some weighty matter.

'Hypa, I sent for you to consult you about something,' Nestorius said.

'I beg your pardon, father, but who am I to advise His Grace the reverend Nestorius?'

'It's a matter than concerns Alexandria.'

My heart thumped and I shivered. Again Alexandria! So it was a weighty and grave matter, fit to wipe away the smiles which shortly before had graced the faces of those present. Nestorius reached out towards me, offering a papyrus scroll, inscribed with many words in two parallel columns, the first in Coptic and the other in Greek. At the top of the scroll a headline in the two languages made my heart stop. 'The epistles of Pope Cyril, Archbishop of Alexandria, the Western Pentapolis, Egypt and Abyssinia, Successor to St Mark the Apostle and Pastor of his Mission, followed by the twelve anathemas which Pope Cyril placed on the person of the heretic Nestorius.'

When I saw the headline, and when I later read the epistle, a slight shudder shook my body, as though hot sand rather than blood were coursing through my veins. I had a sudden foreboding that terror was inevitably on its way. The past was leaping ahead of us from its hiding place, and the claws of hatred were about to dig into our bare backs.

Pregnant with God

My eyes ran quickly over the lines of the scroll and I scowled at what I saw. Nestorius asked me to read Cyril's three epistles and see whether the Coptic translation was any different from the Greek version. He leant back against the wall, while I bent my head forward slightly. I read the first lines of the first epistle meticulously and in a raised voice, but my voice soon began to falter and drop as I delved deeper into the text of the epistles, which were as bellicose as daggers drawn. I had known the first epistle for some time already, and the second too, because I had seen copies of them in the monastery in Greek. They had been in the possession of the monk Pharisee and he had lent them to me. I gave them back to him the next day without comment on my part, ignoring the sarcastic smile on his face when he took them from me. At the time I thought that the matter would go no further. The first and second epistles contained hostile and censorious inquiries, written by Cyril, about reports that Nestorius rejected the beliefs of both ordinary and leading Christians, especially their belief that Mary was the mother of God.

I read the first epistle quickly, looked at the Coptic translation and found it faithful to the original Greek text. I told the three bishops that, and Bishop Rabbula nodded in agreement. Bishops Nestorius and John did not move. Anastasios the priest pursed his lips and shows signs of aggravation and irritation. The Coptic translation of the second epistle had expressions which were insulting and harsher than in the Greek text, which in turn was harsher than the text of the first epistle. I read them the letters in the two languages and pointed out the slight differences in the Coptic translation, I mean the words which were harsher.

The third epistle, which was followed by the twelve anathemas, was the strongest in tone and contained the most severe threats, in both languages. It began thus: 'Cyril and the ecclesiastical synod held in Alexandria in Egypt send the greetings of the Lord to the most venerable Nestorius, our partner in service...' When I read that to them and told them there was no difference between the Greek and Coptic versions of the preamble, Bishop John of Antioch commented sarcastically to the effect that Bishop Cyril always started off polite.

In response Nestorius said, 'It's a ruse, Your Grace. He starts by addressing me with honorifics in order to arouse people's rancour. After that he incites them to hold me in contempt, so they will curse me as a heretic and praise him for his politeness.'

Bishop Rabbula pointed the tips of his fingers at me to indicate I should carry on reading. His gesture was ridiculous, with a trace of disdain for which I knew no reason. I looked at him in a way that meant his gesture was inappropriate, but he was not looking in my direction. He was looking down, dejected.

I resumed reading the epistle, the language of which soon turned fiery in both languages. It contained violent passages, hostile towards Bishop Nestorius, starting when Cyril told him, 'You have greatly scandalized the whole church, and have cast among the people the leaven of a strange and new heresy. How can we any longer, under these circumstances, make a defence for our silence, or how shall we not be forced to remember that Christ said, "Do not think that I came to bring peace on the earth; I did not come to bring peace, but a sword. For I came to set a man against his father, and a daughter against her mother."'

Other incendiary passages followed, including the one where the bishop of Alexandria tells Nestorius: 'It would not be sufficient for your Reverence to confess with us only the symbol of the faith set out some time ago by the Holy Ghost at the great and holy synod convened in Nicaea: for you have not held and interpreted it rightly, but rather perversely; even though you confess with your voice the form of words. But in addition, in writing and by oath, you must confess that you also anathematize those polluted and unholy dogmas of yours.'

At this place in the epistle my voice dropped so low that it was almost inaudible and I was so uncomfortable that I stammered and stumbled on the words. I stopped for a moment, and they fell silent. Then Nestorius signed to me to continue and I resumed reading the impassioned epistle. 'We confess the Word to have been made one with the flesh hypostatically, and we adore one Son and Lord, Jesus Christ. We do not divide him into parts and separate man and God in him... He is God of all and Lord of the universe, but is neither his own slave nor his own master.'

The words of the letter and its message exhausted me, as did jumping between the Greek original and the Coptic translation, so much so that I was about to ask their leave to rest a little, and spare me the task completely. But I found I had almost completed the papyrus scroll, leaving only those lines entitled 'The Twelve Anathemas'. The first of them read: 'If anyone does not confess that Christ (Emmanuel) is God in truth, and therefore that the holy virgin is the mother of God (for she bore in a fleshly way the Word of God become flesh), let him be anathema.'

At this point, Bishop John of Antioch asked me what was the Coptic equivalent of the Greek word 'anathema', meaning 'curse', and I told him that the Coptic word has the meaning 'excommunication' and there was no great difference in meaning between the two words, for in the two languages they both meant the penalty inflicted on apostates, infidels and heretics.

I went back to reading Cyril's anathemas, which were brief and definitive, leaving no room for interpretation or alleviation of their devastating impact. In the end they all meant that whoever stood in the way of what he decided was orthodox dogma – 'let him be anathema, let him be anathema, anathema'. In this way the last twelve paragraphs of Cyril's letter laid out these anathemas, with which the church of Alexandria struck a spark, lighting a flame which flared up and blazed until the fire engulfed the whole world.

✝

When I finished reading, a heavy silence fell upon the gathering. I found it hard to breathe, as though a mountain were weighing on my chest. Among the three bishops and Anastasios the priest a sense of anguish prevailed. Nestorius opened his right hand in a gesture of puzzlement, his lower lip taut in derision and amazement at Cyril's words, which he definitely was not hearing for the first time.

Bishop Rabbula broke the spell which had silenced us. 'Do you really think Cyril has written to the emperor about this?' he asked Nestorius.

'Yes, holy Rabbula,' Nestorius replied. 'First he wrote two letters to Pulcheria, the emperor's elder sister, and to Empress Eudocia, because he knows they are influential. Then he wrote the emperor a long letter, signed on the back by dozens of priests and bishops. The palace courtiers told me that, but the emperor has not replied yet and I doubt he will reply.'

Bishop Rabbula bowed his head, deeply worried and vexed to the utmost. Suddenly Anastasios the priest burst into speech, spewing out the words like flames of fire. 'Let us resist this assault immediately, let us stand in the face of all those heretics who say that the Virgin is the mother of God, because the Virgin was a woman among women, just a woman among women, and it's impossible that God should be born of woman.'

Anastasios the priest was shouting in fury, almost wrenching his throat from his stiff neck, where the veins were bulging fit to burst. It looked as if he wanted to keep shouting, but he stopped when a young deacon knocked on the door and came in bringing us cups of a warm drink, which we drank in silence. I don't remember now what we drank. The deacon whispered something in the ear of Bishop John of Antioch, then went out straight away. Immediately the silence again descended on us.

Bishop Rabbula broke the silence by clearing his throat, and then he spoke: 'Don't you think, Nestorius, that we should make a truce with the Alexandrians?'

'No, Rabbula. I will never make a truce in this matter. Let Cyril abandon his sick delusion that he is the defender of the faith on earth.'

Bishop John intervened, trying gently to calm Nestorius down, but his attempt was in vain. He was addressing him by the Greek form of his name, Nestoriios, and speaking to him with affection and respect. John of Antioch seemed to me sincere in his affection for the reverend Nestorius as he tried to placate him with phrases such as 'Don't be angry, my reverend brother Nestorios, lest the devil find his way into your reason and disturb your peace of mind.' But Nestorius's anger did not subside, and he was arguing back, saying, 'If we are not angry for the sake of our belief, reverend father, the devil will find his way into the heart and spirit of this religion.'

I had never seen Bishop Nestorius flare up in this way. At the time I felt most uncomfortable at how the bishops were talking about this sensitive subject in front of me, and I wanted to take my leave of them, but Nestorius suddenly asked me what I thought about what I had read them.

'As you are well aware, your Grace, I am out of touch with what is happening between the major churches, and I have no knowledge of the details of this matter, even if I have heard the broad outlines. But I was apprehensive some months ago when we received the letter in which you forbade the laity and church leaders from repeating the word "theotokos". I was yet more anxious when I heard of the friendly correspondence between the bishops of Alexandria and Rome, and that they had agreed to reject Your Grace's views.'

Bishop Rabbula nodded his head, impressed by what I said, as though he found it persuasive. Then he turned to address me for the first time, saying that the rapprochement between Alexandria and Rome was temporary and its only purpose was to weaken the diocese of Constantinople in the person of Bishop Nestorius. As for Nestorius's letter banning the word 'theotokos', it was sent only to the eastern churches and was unlikely to have reached the Egyptian churches and monasteries and had not been translated into Coptic. He added that he thought that what had angered Bishop Cyril was reports of the sermon which the reverend Nestorius had made the day he was installed as bishop, when he said, 'Jesus is human, and his incarnation is a compromise between the Eternal Logos and Christ the human. Mary is the mother of Jesus the human being, and should not be called the mother of God. It is not right that she be called theotokos.'

I was surprised that Bishop Rabbula was able to recall Nestorius's phrase word for word and that he dared repeat it so forcefully in front of the author, at a time when we were in the midst of these upheavals. I was inclined to go along with Rabbula and discuss with him the views of Nestorius, which we knew were in origin the opinions of the late Bishop Theodore of Mopsuestia. But I held my tongue and confined myself to nodding my head. When I did not interrupt him, Bishop Rabbula continued, still looking towards me without seeing me. 'Bishop John of Antioch wrote a lengthy answer to the three letters of Bishop Cyril, discussing the matter with him in detail, as the reverend Bishop Nestorius had done before him,' he said, 'but they could not come to agreement. Now Bishop Nestorius wants to respond to the anathemas from the bishop of Alexandria with counter-anathemas. I believe that would stir up more conflict and many forms of enmity, and would inflame contention and strife between the big churches.'

Bishop Rabbula was eloquent, and what he said was severe and persuasive. That was no surprise, as he was a renowned ecclesiastical poet. It was he who, through his famous poems, had prevailed against the ideas propagated in the poems of the Syrian gnostic Bardaisan, who was described as an apostate. The poetry of Rabbula was now more famous than Bardaisan's poems, especially after Rabbula took up the post of bishop of Edessa, gained prestige among the people there and became the chief Christian in those eastern regions, so much so that his poems and hymns are sung today in most masses and on holy days. None the less there was something in Bishop Rabbula that I found troubling.

I sat in silence out of politeness, uncertain how to escape this meeting, to which I was paying little attention. My mind wandered, but then the reverend Nestorius looked towards me, his face red with anger, and asked me, 'Do you believe, Hypa, that the monks in the many monasteries in Wadi Natroun and in the deserts of Egypt agree with Cyril in what he says?'

'They'll agree with him in anything, for they are the army of the church of St Mark, and the loyal soldiers of the Pope of Alexandria,' I replied.

'Pope, hmm, then so be it.'

John of Antioch looked at Nestorius with paternal affection. He was about to speak but Rabbula of Edessa stood up grumpily and asked their leave, saying he wanted to drop in on the Roman governor of Antioch in his residence, then come back to attend the prayers. He asked Bishop John if he would come along with him. John hesitated a moment, but Nestorius decided the matter, saying, 'Go together in the protection of the Lord, for I want to be alone a little with Hypa the monk.' They departed side by side, leaving us secluded in the corner of the room. Nestorius whispered something in the ear of Anastasios the priest, who stood up at once, and we were alone.

After a moment's silence, I said in a friendly manner, 'Father, I am anxious for you. I do not advise you to challenge the church of Alexandria.'

'Hypa, I'm not challenging anyone, but Cyril wants to proclaim his authority over all the churches in the world.'

Nestorius began to repeat what I already knew, how he believed it was wrong to call the Virgin Mary theotokos, because she was a saintly woman but not the mother of God, and it was wrong for us to believe that God was a child who was born from the womb of a woman in labour, who urinated in his cradle and needed a nappy, who felt hungry and cried for his mother's breast. 'Does it make sense,' he asked, 'to believe that God suckled at the breast of the Virgin, and grew day by day until he was two months old, then three months, then four. The Lord is perfect, as it is written, so how could he take the form of a child, when the Virgin Mary was a human who gave birth from her immaculate womb by a divine miracle, and after that her son became a manifestation of God and a saviour for mankind. He was like a hole through which we have been able to see the light of God, or like a signet ring on which a divine message appeared. The fact that the sun shines through a hole does not make the hole a sun, just as the appearance of the message on the signet ring does not make the ring a message. Hypa, these people have gone quite mad, and have made God one of three.'

I kept my silence out of respect for Nestorius's anger and pity for him. He soon calmed down and spoke in a gentler tone. He told me, and I summarize, that the temporary manifestation of Almighty God in the Messiah Jesus was a grace that God gave us and we should not throw to waste this divine gift by extrapolating and getting carried away with our superstitions about how Christ was divine from the time He was in his mother's womb or since He was a child. He said it was wrong to believe the Virgin Mary gave birth to God, because God endures in His eternal everlasting perfection. He is the only One, neither is He born nor does He die, but He is manifested at times and in occlusion at other times, in accordance with His will.

The reverend Nestorius looked into my eyes with eyes full of sorrow, and said, 'Is there anything strange in what I assert? Or is the strangeness rather in what Cyril and his followers say? Hypa, the danger goes further and is graver than the word "theotokos", which both the public and the learned bandy about. It's a question of true faith, and whether Christianity is able to address the heart and mind of man in every time and place. The pagans scoff at our superstitious excesses, and after them, other scoffers will arise from amongst us to ridicule these delusions and try to bring them down and so bring down the whole religion. The gospel and divine miracles, Hypa, are a rare mystery, and if they are done to excess they lose their meaning, and we lose our faith and defy reason.'

I knew this view of his by heart, but I let Nestorius elaborate, out of politeness and out of respect for his righteous anger. When he had finished and was quite calm again, I asked him politely, 'Why don't you leave ordinary Christians and the ignorant to their own beliefs, mixed with delusions which they find comforting and which are appropriate to their understanding, while we explain the facts to theologians, the clergy and the priests of the churches, because they are capable of understanding these subtle theological matters? Then we could leave the laity to learn from them, generation after generation, without confronting them.'

'Why should we resort to this trick?' said Nestorius.

'Out of necessity, your Grace, out of necessity, to escape the fangs and claws of the lion of St Mark!'

Nestorius smiled at my pun, because with his sharp mind he realized I was referring to the belief, common in Alexandria, that St Mark the Apostle of Alexandria adopted the lion as a mascot, or rather the Alexandrians gave him, and gave themselves, the symbol of the lion, in that they depicted St Mark the Apostle in their books and on the walls of their houses writing his gospel with a lion crouched next to him, looking at what he was writing. The brief smile had restored to Nestorius's face some of the serenity which I had known in earlier times and which I had missed since the start of this unexpected meeting of ours in Antioch.

I wanted to ask him if there was any truth in the reports we had been receiving for the past year, the reports that he had oppressed his opponents, demolished churches run by the Arians and expelled them from Constantinople and so on. But I felt that the moment for this had not yet come, so I bided my time.

After several minutes of calm, Nestorius sat up straight, adjusted his cap and turned towards me. He looked anxious and his smile could not disguise what he was going through. Visibly disturbed, he told me he had sent a forceful response to Cyril's first letter and was now planning to respond to this latest letter, and was also thinking of sending me to Alexandria to debate with him on the subject.

'I beg your pardon, reverend father, but do you think that Bishop Cyril will listen to me, or even respect my visit in the first place?' I said.

'Why not?' he said. 'You have been a monk since your early youth. You are a scholar of dogma, you speak eloquent Greek, and you studied in Alexandria.'

'And I fled the city on a memorable day.'

'Do you think he was aware of that at the time? His elation at the killing of Hypatia must have distracted him from the fact that you were gone. By the way, Hypa, did you ever meet him at a private gathering while you were in Alexandria, the great city?'

Nestorius uttered the famous sobriquet with a sarcasm that did not conceal his distaste at describing the city as great, and at the city's enthusiasm for promoting itself at the expense of the papal see in Rome and of the imperial capital Constantinople. Because he expected me to answer his question, and because I loved Nestorius like a father and did not want him to meet the same wretched fate, I told him something I had always tried to keep secret. It was for his sake that I told my story.

'I met Bishop Cyril on a single occasion. At the time I had been in Alexandria for two tedious years during which I submitted to the will of the Lord and set aside my dream of excelling in medicine. I spent my time there either praying with the monks, attending mass on most days, dozing off in most of the masses, and taking regular classes at the theological school, to learn again what children learn in primary schools in Upper Egypt. At the time I was studying the kind of medicine practised by people who sell perfumes and medicinal herbs and by farmers in my home country. I persevered in this course, passively and without enthusiasm, and I realized that since I had come to Alexandria the dreams which had tied me to the city had turned into nightmares which weighed upon me and from which there was no escape. Then the day came when the senior priest at the church of St Mark told me I would have an audience with Bishop Cyril the next morning after mass. At the time I was about twenty-five years old and naturally I spent the night lost in labyrinths of anxiety and insomnia. The next day I went in to see Bishop Cyril after waiting two hours at his door. As soon as he saw me he asked me how old I was. I told him, and then I said that I originally came to Alexandria to immerse myself in studying medicine, and he responded with a question the meaning of which at first I did not grasp.

'Who is the greatest of those who have immersed themselves in medicine?' he asked.

'Your Holiness, it is said to be an ancient Egyptian by the name of Imhotep or the famous Greek, Hippocrates. Or perhaps, father, you mean the Alexandrian doctors who came after them, such as Herophilos, or those who studied in Alexandria, such as Galen.'

'Wrong, all your answers are wrong. All those you mentioned are pagans and not a single one of them could cure a leper, or with a touch of his hand bring the dead back to life,' he said.

'I'm sorry, your Grace, but I did not understand what you meant.'

'Our Lord Jesus Christ, monk, is the polymath of medicine, so learn from him, and from the lives of the saints and the martyrs. Tap into their spiritual power through your piety and faith.'

Cyril spoke severely to me and what he said did not reveal what he really and surely thought. At the time I preferred to stay silent, while he said something to the effect that I was about to end my period of training in the city and he intended to send me, starting the next summer, to one of the monasteries in arid Wadi Natroun in the heart of the desert, south of Alexandria, where, as he put it, there would descend upon me the blessings of the pure earth, which is rich with the remains of the saints who gave their souls for Jesus and for His sake abandoned the world. Cyril sat up straight and, without looking in my direction, continued. 'And I might send you to one of our monasteries in Upper Egypt or in Abyssinia. The children of the Lord there need our support.'

Cyril stopped a while as though in deep thought, then he looked towards one of his priests and said, 'Perhaps it would be appropriate for us to send him to Akhmim, because the people there face tests of faith. In recent years many people from here have fled there and many people there are studying sciences which are of no benefit.'

I was at a loss to answer him. Then, in a moment of courage or stupidity, lowering my voice, I asked him in all politeness, 'And what, your Holiness, are the sciences which are of no benefit, that I might know them and make sure I avoid them?'

'Good monk, they are the absurdities of the heretics and the delusions of those who devote themselves to astronomy, mathematics and magic. Understand that and stay away from such things, that you may follow in the ways of the Lord and the paths of salvation. If you seek history, then you have the Pentateuch and the Book of Kings. If you seek rhetoric, you have the books of the prophets. If you seek poetry, then you have the psalms. If you seek astronomy, law and ethics, you have the glorious law of the Lord. Arise now, monk, and join the prayers, and perhaps our Lord the living Christ will grace you with a kindly glance.'

✝

Nestorius listened with such interest and concern that I felt he could discern behind what I said the hidden meaning which lies deeper than the superficial sense of the words. After a moment of portentous silence, he turned towards me with the old paternal sympathy which I had always found in him. 'I'll excuse you, Hypa, from the mission of going to see this man. I'll answer his stupidities myself and meet his anathemas with counter-anathemas that I shall enshrine in a letter like his own. But let's leave that aside for now. Tell me how you are coming on in the monastery.'

I remembered the letter from the abbot and I quickly took it out from inside the folds of my cassock and passed it to him. He opened it carefully, looked at it, then said with an interested smile, 'Samuel the monk wants to enlarge the church and build a wall for the monastery. Assure him, Hypa, that I'll talk to Bishop John on the subject today, and with the help of God the bishop will fulfil his request.'

Nestorius called for an inkwell and pen and took from his pocket a small piece of parchment on which he wrote a letter to the abbot, then sealed it with his seal and gave it to me. I asked him if I could go back to the monastery the next morning and he told me he would sail at dawn for Constantinople. Then he stood up, embraced me goodbye and sat down again, alone. At the door I remembered a question I had been repressing, so I went back and asked him. 'Father, if the dispute between you and Bishop Cyril grows worse than this, will the other bishops support you?'

'Hypa, there are many bishops in the world, east and west, and their inclinations vary. You go in the protection of the Lord and do not worry, for God is our helper and our aid.'

I wanted him to be clearer, so I said, 'Father, I mean Bishops John and Rabbula.'

'John of Antioch is a righteous man and we have been friends for many years. As for Rabbula, I do not know what he intends to do. Don't worry, Hypa. Don't worry, my child, because this world, with everything and everyone in it, is not worth believers worrying about.'

On the Outskirts of Sarmada

O n my way back from Antioch I had planned to drop in at the Eupropius monastery to visit Dignified Laugher the monk, because I missed him. But for some mysterious reason the idea escaped me and I decided to go straight back to the monastery. As I left the eastern gate I noticed something strange: the donkey, which I had always considered a stupid animal, began to hurry along the way as though it knew the way back. It walked along without the least guidance from me. The tapping of its hoofs showed its elation and delight at heading back to its home and its tether in the pen at the monastery. Donkeys long for their roots and take pleasure in returning home, while I am terrified of the idea of going back to my country, even on a short mission.

But in fact I was terrified specifically of going back to Alexandria, because for someone like me it would be fraught with dangers. Anyone who leaves Alexandria, either in anger or as the target of someone else's anger, should not go back. The test of time has proven that. Origen went back to the city after leaving in anger and the bishop at the time, Demetrius known as the vine-tender, made him suffer grievously. That was two hundred years ago and the bishop of the city at the time was not as powerful as the bishop today, and Alexandria at the time was not known as the Great City. The façades of the houses and walls of the churches were not yet full of images of Mark the Apostle, with the lion crouched beside him, and Origen was not a wretch like me! None the less at their hands he tasted bitterness and woe. Eighty years later the Alexandrians lured Arius the monk to Constantinople from his exile in the land of the Goths, also known as Spain, where he had settled quietly and comfortably at the end of the earth, after excommunicating him, deposing him and blackening his reputation. They were not content to let him die in peace, and when he was tricked into going and meeting Bishop Alexander in the court of Emperor Constantine, in the hope of a reconciliation and an end to the theological dispute which had angered Alexandria, Arius met his horrible fate and died of poisoning. The bishop of Alexandria at the time was not as powerful as the bishop today, and Arius was not a poor man like me.

As the donkey clip-clopped steadily along the gravel road, these thoughts made my head spin. Neither the verdure of the gardens around Antioch nor their beauty could help me escape the eddies and currents of Alexandria. Much violence surrounded the history of the city, which for years I had dreamed of visiting and which, once I arrived, I longed to escape – the city where I was trapped until that calamitous day. I would have liked to fulfil Nestorius's request and help him in what he was about to do, but how could I return to Alexandria? And would Cyril expect a monk like me to argue with him and explain to him Nestorius's theological concepts? He would not meet me in the first place, but would annihilate me. If I escaped him, would I escape the public and the Lovers of the Passion if they knew I had come as a representative of Bishop Nestorius, whom they see as a heretic? The people of Alexandria have no mercy and do not fear punishment for their deeds. They killed Hypatia in front of all the inhabitants and they were not punished. Before that they killed the bishop of their own city, George of Cappadocia, and pulled his body apart on the main street. Emperor Julian, who renounced Christianity, was too cowardly to punish them and confined himself to saying, in an outrageous imperial decree, that he would pardon them in honour of Serapis, the god of Alexandria.

How could I return to Alexandria after what I saw there and found out about the city? Who knows what they said about me when they found out that I had run away on that fateful day. Perhaps one of the pilgrims return-ing from Jerusalem had spoken to them about me. Would the fact that I adopted the ecclesiastical name Hypa conceal me from the gaze of the church of St Mark and the claws of the lion? Did I let down the reverend Nestorius by declining to carry out his request? Or did the Lord reveal something to him, something to make him abandon the idea of throwing me into the furnace that is Alexandria? Or did he notice my fear when I told him the story of my meeting with Bishop Cyril and then he relieved me of this frightful mission, which would have been pointless anyway?

The questions spun around in my head, but then something strange the donkey was doing caught my attention. We had gone about halfway and it was midday. I found the donkey heading for the bushes under which we had stopped at noon two days earlier when we were going to Antioch. Under the bushes the donkey's legs stopped stock still and he began to twitch his ears as though to tell me it was his lunchtime. Donkeys surely cannot be stupid. They are stoical by nature and stoicism may sometimes look like stupidity, and sometimes like cowardice. It seems I have been a donkey all my life.

I dismounted and took the wooden saddle off the donkey's back. He sighed with relief. I tied his front legs together with the rope attached to one of them and hung the nosebag around his neck. He started to chew the fodder with pleasure, slowly. I had no desire to eat, nor to sleep, not even to think. I leant back against the trunk of a bush and shut my eyes, overwhelmed by a mysterious sense of relief that I was almost back at the monastery.

After a period of noontime calm, a young man of close to twenty years of age passed by. He came from afar, walking along the paved road, holding the lead of a nanny goat, followed by three of her kids. He came towards me on the other side of the road and asked me kindly if I needed anything. I thanked him, sat up and asked him if he could possibly find us some water to drink, for the donkey and me. With great enthusiasm he said there was a well nearby, tied his goat under the bushes and rushed off towards the houses in the town. He came back in a while carrying a large earthenware vessel gurgling with clean fresh water. I drank from it until my thirst was quenched, then the man took the vessel from my hands, put it in front of the donkey and took the nosebag off his neck. The donkey bent down to drink.

The young man came back to me and sat politely in front of me at the edge of the shade from the bushes. He seemed shy and I wanted to engage him in conversation as a way of expressing my gratitude towards him. I asked him which town he was from.

'From this town, father,' he said, 'Sarmada.'

I looked towards the town as it slept peacefully under God's sun, which shines on good and evil alike. The town was small with humble houses, no more than a hundred of them. On the edges there were a few orchards and groves of olive trees. I could not see anyone at the houses. Could it be that they were sleeping at this middle time of the day, although the days are short at this winter season? The young man was sitting in silence and I asked him if he was a shepherd, as he appeared to be.

'No, father,' he said. 'Sometimes I work at the olive press on the western end of town and this is my aunt's nanny goat. I took her yesterday to stay the night at our neighbour's, who has a strong billy, and now I'm taking her back to my aunt after she spent the night with the billy.'

'I understand, my child, I understand.'

The look in the young man's eyes was no surprise when he mentioned the goat and described it as strong. My donkey was still gulping down the water, enjoying the coolness of it, and the little kids were nuzzling their mother's stomach. The young man remained seated at the edge of the shade, facing me. The sunlight lit up his left side, while the shade of the bushes fell on his right. The man had tucked up his cloak and was sitting cross-legged. I could see his knees and the whiteness of his legs, which were hairless, unlike a man's. I examined his features and they seemed more like those of a woman, especially as he had no beard. His hair had a golden streak and his eyes were greenish. His face and his neck had traces of the sun and his hands were unusually soft for those of a poor man.

The young man was unsettling. I took from my bag a copy of the Psalms written in a fine Greek hand and began to look at it. The man was fidgety as though he wanted to tell me something, but I pretended to be busy, reciting the psalms in a low voice, and he calmed down. When I stopped murmuring, the man crept towards me, still seated, and said that he would like to confess to me. I explained to him that confession should take place in church and that a priest should hear it, not a monk like me.

'But father, the priest in our church knows me and I'm too embarrassed to confess in front of him,' he answered.

'Overcome your embarrassment, my child, to show that your faith is strong and to prove that you repent and acknowledge the sin you have committed.'

The young man bowed his head and his face showed a mixture of embarrassment, uncertainty and distress. I looked at him again, scrutinizing his features, and I had a strange feeling about him. He had a humility and an innocence, with his long white face slightly gaunt. The sparse hairs on his chin made him seem more like an adolescent than a man, and his gentle demeanour made him look more like a woman. The submissive way he was sitting struck a chord of sympathy in me and led me to wonder what sins this poor, strange young man might have committed. I thought he was just a boy who was making too much of his mistakes, and I doubted his sins would go beyond the minor and trivial things that people do and which then trouble their consciences until they find someone into whose hands they can offload the burden of guilt. Confession comforts them by making forgiveness possible and by affirming the compassion of the Lord.

I said to myself, 'He's only a young child and it would do no harm if I took pity on him. He needs someone to listen to him and guide him to the true faith.'

'Listen, my child,' I said. 'You can go to Antioch and confess in one of the big churches there,' I told him.

'It's a long way, father, and the priest there might recognize me. I don't think I'll meet you again, so hear my confession.'

'But, my child...'

'Please, good father, I beg you.'

'Tell me what you have to confess,' I said.

I closed the Psalm book, pulled my cap down towards my forehead and bowed my head, preparing to take confession for the first time in my life, and the last. That day I heard from the man things which I cannot now write down in full, although I did intend to write here everything that happened.

But what the man told me was extremely obscene and strange, and it had never before occurred to me that such things happened. Among the abominations which he confessed was that since the age of puberty he was in the habit of copulating with goats. He would wait until he was alone with a nanny goat that wanted a male, then in the depths of night he would hold her between his thighs and have his way with her. When he told me this, I did not want to show my discomfort in front of him, so I stayed calm and stared at the ground where I was sitting, as I tried to put together the words with which to respond, embellishing my answer with verses from the Gospels. But he did not give me time. After that he confessed that his widowed mother, who was forty, saw him one night as he was in the act with a goat and was greatly distressed for him. She rebuked him soundly as she washed between his thighs. Then she sat and wept at length, lamenting the poverty that prevented them from finding him a wife.

'My child, all the poor get married,' I said.

'Their poverty, father, is not as extreme as ours.'

I choked in distress and I did not want to hear any more from the young man. But he insisted, broke into tears and started sobbing. When he had calmed down a little he told me that his mother had committed with him the worst of all sins. One moonlit night in summer, as she was sleeping beside him in their hovel under the broken roof, their bodies met and it happened.

I was so embarrassed by what the young man was telling me that I could not listen to more. The man was going into the details of what he and his mother did together, and I was most distressed. He told me they did it together most nights and for the first few nights they sinned two or three times. I noticed that he had gone beyond the stage of embarrassment and was now enjoying telling the story.

I interrupted him. 'Enough of this, my child, enough. You must keep away from her immediately, look for a good wife and think about your sin through constant prayer and attending mass.'

'But she cannot do without me, father!' he said.

I was amazed at the young man's brazenness and at the smile of relief that spread across his face. He looked even stranger than before and his eyes seemed suspiciously cold. Were the signs of remorse which he showed a while ago just an illusion I had imagined? Or was it that he was relieved to have confessed and no longer felt how serious it was to commit this heinous sin? I looked at the sky far away. A thick cloud was passing over us and I felt it was a long way to the monastery. The shadows had inclined towards the east and it threatened rain. I wanted to set off to finish the journey back. When I gathered my cloak about me in readiness to stand, the young man asked me to stop.

'Will you not hear the rest of my confession, my father?' he asked.

His expression 'my father' rang strangely in my ears. His voice no longer had the diffidence of someone distressed, as was the case before he confessed, and I could no longer stay with him. In fact I regretted listening to him in the first place. I told him the hour was late and I must resume my long journey. He said he had not yet finished his confession and he had even more serious things he wanted to confess to me.

'No, my child, there's nothing more serious than what I've heard from you,' I said.

'Oh yes there is, good monk.'

'I cannot listen to any more.'

I stood up hurriedly, stuffed the Psalms into the pocket of my jellaba and put the nosebag under the donkey's saddle. The man left me to untie the fetter from around the donkey's legs without offering to help. Although previously he had followed me like my shadow, I did not expect him to say anything in farewell. But he walked close behind me, almost touching me, and in a voice that smacked of shameless bragging he told me he now enjoyed what he was doing. I ignored him. He said he did the same thing with his sister when her husband was travelling with a caravan and she stayed the night with them. I ignored him. He said he enjoyed what he did with her and she enjoyed it too but now she was pregnant by him.

Without looking towards him I mounted my donkey and pulled the reins towards the road.

As I moved away, the young man shouted after me in great anger and suppressed spite.

'Why are you running away, monk? Stop and hear about the pleasures and delights which you have denied yourself. I have lots and lots of them,' he said.

I dug my heels into the donkey's belly and it headed east with all the resolve it could muster. The donkey shot off as though in flight, or perhaps the donkey realized, as I did, that this was no young man but rather the devil, appearing to us in human form to make a fool of me.

The Lady

I reached the monastery before sunset, my clothes sticking to my body with sweat, although the air was cold. My head was ringing with apprehensions and churning with thoughts. Halfway up the hill leading to the gateway I noticed the abbot sitting on the large square stone with a bible in his hand. He was reading it, which was unusual given that he knew the four Gospels and the books of the Old Testament by heart. When he saw me, he closed the bible and stood up. His expression betrayed the anxiety hidden within him. I came up to him and dismounted. I kissed his hand as usual and I could tell from the trembling of his fingers that his mind was troubled, or rather that his heart was perturbed. On our way to his room he asked me about my journey and what happened in the meeting with Bishop Nestorius. Then in his room he asked me what I had seen in Antioch and he offered me a bowl with a handful of dried fruit.

I started by telling him that I had delivered his letter to Bishop Nestorius and that he promised to carry out the request it contained. I gave him the letter Nestorius had sent him and he opened it. He looked at it quickly, then folded it up and stuffed it under his pillow. I was surprised that he took so little interest in the letter. I told him that in Antioch I had met the three bishops and the priest of the church in the capital, all of them in one place. He was not surprised at that, as if he already knew of it. Then I thought I had to tell him about the mission that Nestorius had intended to send me on and how something had happened and Nestorius had changed his mind.

When I had told the story, the abbot waited a moment, then spoke. 'My child, there's no point in you going to Alexandria.'

His words came as a relief, easing the burden of guilt I felt at abandoning Nestorius in his ordeal. Because I was still bewildered by what had happened to me on the way back from Antioch, I told the abbot about the devil who appeared in the form of the young man on the outskirts of Sarmada. He smiled weakly, shook his head and said, 'Go and rest, Hypa. As for that young man, he was just one of those jokers who like to amuse themselves by making fun of monks.'

I prepared to take my leave, without discovering the secret of the abbot's evident anxiety and without asking him. Before I left his room, as though speaking to himself the abbot said, 'Azazeel has tricks and disguises that are more subtle and cunning than that. May the Lord bestow His universal grace on all of us.'

✝

The next few days and months passed tediously, then summer came upon us and the heavy hours of daytime stretched out, while the fleeting nights grew shorter – the nights that mark our lives as passing patches of cloud mark out daylight hours. I often used to, and still do, gaze into the horizon in the afternoon and at sunset and feel that the clouds in the sky are in the form of divine scriptures, or messages from God in a language which is not spoken and can be read only by those who realize that it is based on shapes rather than letters. This realization was one of my secrets, though I did one day divulge this secret to the abbot, who bowed his head for a long time and then said, 'Perhaps they are a manifestation of that which is deep inside us, of the word of God which is latent within us.'

Among the strange events which took place at the end of last summer, that is the summer of the year 430 of the Nativity, was that doves landed around the monastery. One morning a large flock of mountain doves came down, doves which we usually see alone or occasionally in pairs. This time, many dozens of them suddenly covered the monastery hill and circled the air above. The monks were delighted, except for Pharisee, and they saw it as a miracle foretelling that the site of the monastery would receive many blessings from heaven. The mountain doves are different from the domestic kind that people breed at home in Egypt and which they eat when young. They are smaller in size and harder to digest when eaten, and their feathers have a subtle sheen. They have only one colour, namely grey, unlike the domestic pigeon, which comes in white, brown and mixes of colours, so it is easy to tell the individual pigeons apart. But mountain doves are uniform, like many clones from one dove. Their wing feathers are light grey and the tips of their wings have two dark bands. The grey has a slight sheen, especially on the head and the neck.

One strange thing about these doves is that they do not take fright when people move, so when people came very close they would just fly a short distance and land nearby. Only Pharisee was keen to frighten the doves and drive them as far away as possible, while the other monks were surprised at his behaviour and could not understand what was behind it.

The second day after the doves landed, the monks came up with all kinds of explanations for why they had landed and why they were staying around the monastery. Some said they had moved here to enjoy the verdure of the hill, while others said they sensed the spirituality of the place and liked the company. Yet others said the doves were obeying a divine command to live here, a command given so that the monastery would be graced with the presence of God and the spirit of peace. Doves really do have an aura of peace. I enjoyed watching them in the early morning and before sunset. I would spend ages contemplating their behaviour, marvelling at how they would spend the night in cracks in the walls and in places where the stones had broken loose, without nests to nestle in and hatch their young, as we know from the habits of domestic doves and in fact of birds in general.

On the third day after the doves landed I was sitting at the wall overlooking the northern plains. We had finished the morning prayer and I had no desire to go to the library. I stayed a good time watching a group of doves flying between the columns and the walls, sometimes landing on the ground and picking up with their beaks whatever they found fit to eat. I was sitting still and the doves grew accustomed to my presence and were coming close, just as the birds grew accustomed to the flute of King David and landed around him. After a time I could tell the male doves from the females, and I noticed that they all showed constant goodwill towards each other and did not lay special claim to one mate rather than any other. All doves like each other. The male ruffles up his feathers and walks around a nearby female nodding his head, and if she stays still he mounts her, and otherwise he flies off to another in the hope that she will stay still. Meanwhile the first female waits for another male to come hovering around her and if he pleases her she acts willing by moving close to him and not flying off, which amounts to permission for him to mount her. Doves copulate often and all day long never cease from courting and coupling, especially in the afternoon and shortly before sunset. I was sitting happily at the wall with the doves around when Pharisee appeared from afar, with his usual rolling gait. He sat down near me and started to pick up pieces of stone to throw at the doves and drive them away from us. I asked him what he was doing and he said angrily that the doves covered the monastery with excrement and the constant cooing of the males disturbed people asleep at dawn. I gave him a sceptical look, unsure if he was telling the truth, and he added, as though he were announcing a secret, that the doves aroused the passions and induced people to commit sins, so people should not look at them if they wanted to be godly. Pharisee's ideas are as strange as he is.

The fourth day after the doves landed they left as suddenly as they had come. The monks lamented their departure, as I did after listening to them for the past three days. I spent the night in the library and in the first part of the night I had dreams full of doves. In the second half of the night I lit a candle, as though I was going to look at the books, but my mind was wandering far away, assailed by questions without answers. Where did the doves go when they left us? Were they really a sign to us and a portent from heaven, or was it just a coincidence? Will the doves come back after a time, or was this an event which will not recur? Why don't people learn from doves how to live in peace? The dove is a simple bird and pure in spirit. Jesus the Messiah once said, 'Be as innocent as doves.' The dove is peaceful because it has no claws, and people should renounce the weapons and military equipment which they hold. The dove does not eat more than it needs and does not save food, so people too should give up hoarding supplies and stashing away resources. Doves live a life of perfect love: the males do not distinguish between a beautiful female and an ugly female, as people do. As soon as a dove reaches the age to fly it no longer recognizes any father or mother but joins the other doves in a perfect community where selfishness and individualism are unknown. Why don't people live in this way, reproducing in peaceful groups, as was the case with humans in the beginning? All would live as one, living a wholesome life, then die without drama, as other creatures die. Men and women would choose partners to suit them, to live together lovingly for a time, then part if they wished and join up with someone else if they wanted. Everyone would treat the young as the offspring of all, and women would be like doves, asking the males only for courtship and brief encounters, because women…

'Hypa, what you are writing is incompatible with your monastic status.'

'Leave me alone, Azazeel. You invited me to write, so let me write what I please.'

'But you are going too deep. You still have much you were going to tell, and time is short.'

'You're right, you wretch.'

✝

One hot afternoon in the months of autumn in the year 430 of the Nativity I was watching the clouds as usual, trying to decipher the symbols or bring to light the hidden message within me, based on what I could see in the shapes. I heard voices coming from the direction of the monastery gate, so I rose from my usual sitting place on the dilapidated wall which overlooks the broad northern prospect, and crossed the open space to see what the hubbub was about. Halfway up the slope which climbs to the gate from the plains below, near where there is a ramshackle cottage which has been abandoned for years, there were two men, two mules and two women, one of them old and the other in colourful clothes but whose features I could not make out well.

When they had unloaded the mules, the men went off with the animals and the women stayed behind, struggling to get the luggage into the cottage. Were they going to live there, I wondered. As I thought the question over the priest came by on his way out of the monastery. He lives at the bottom of the hill in one of those small houses built around the hill and he was bound to know some of the story. When I asked him, he told me that two women had come to live in the cottage, after the abbot gave them permission out of sympathy for their circumstances. He added, 'The old woman is ill, so I expect she will come to see you for treatment.'

At the dinner table the abbot was in his usual place reading psalms to us. He ate only a piece of dry bread with us and then thanked the Lord. He gestured to me and when I came up next to him he leant towards me and said in a whisper that a small lyre would arrive on Saturday from Aleppo, and that he would assemble some deacons and a girl with a good voice for me to teach them some hymns they could sing at mass on Sundays, as they do in big churches. 'You could arrange some psalms for them, or some short verses from your poems, or some of Bishop Rabbula's poetry, because people love to hear music during mass,' he added.

I nodded in agreement and I liked the idea, because I am by nature inclined towards music and chanting. I almost told the abbot that he was right when he decided to go ahead with his plan. Then I had second thoughts and said, 'Reverend father, as for musical instruments, didn't John Chrysostom forbid the use of them in churches?'

'That was forty years ago, or more, my child,' he said, 'and he did not say they should be banned, but that the Lord held them in contempt and liked to be glorified by human voices. Our brothers in Edessa and Nusaybin studied the matter at several synods and came to the conclusion that it is permissible to use musical instruments in churches.'

'Yes, sir, but what about the girl singing in church?'

'She will come in from the outer door and she will chant standing outside the chancel, behind the deacons.'

I have always believed that music is a holy and heavenly art, which we can use either to chasten the soul or to arouse the passions. In my childhood I was fascinated by the pictures of musicians on the walls of the temples in my home country. I would say to myself, 'If they hadn't dedicated music to worship they would not have depicted the musicians on the temple walls.' But I did not talk about the subject at all with any fellow Christians. And now the days turn and the gifts of the Lord fall in our hands without any effort on our part, so we take pleasure in music. I asked the abbot for permission to go to the library but first I told him, 'Tonight I shall set about composing a chant, an amalgam between the psalms of David and some refined monastic ideas.'

'Under the protection of the Lord. Wait, my child. The chant will be in Syriac, because it's the majority language here,' he said.

'Of course, holy father, of course.'

I crossed the courtyard from the refectory to the library, full of enthusiasm and pleasure. The light of the autumn moon carpeted the ground and reflected off the white pebbles, which looked like jewels strewn among the sand in the courtyard. The night breeze was refreshing and my spirit leapt, soaring in exultation. My heart pounded as in my childhood when my father pulled up his nets from the water of the Nile, or when my sick uncle's wife called me to dinner, or when I left Naga Hammadi and headed for Akhmim. In fact our life is nothing but such rare moments of pleasure.

When I went into the library an idea occurred to me. I would dispense with the music of the lyre or give it a limited role in the chant by arranging the music to be sung by the boys and the girl with the melodious voice. In that way I would avoid as far as possible the objections of those who disapproved of musical instruments, and I would combine the lines of my poetry, which the girl would sing, with the psalm which the boys would chant. I would compose my chants in the fifth metre under the Syriac system, which includes the pentameters and hexameters which I favour more than any other. That night I said to myself, 'I shall fill the big monastery church and all the churches around with spiritual chants that soar to the kingdom of heaven.'

I sat at the long table and lit the lantern, then scanned the shelves of books around me, wrapped up in my enthusiasm. I went to the shelves on the right and took out the Syriac translation of the psalms. When I opened it, my eyes fell by chance on Psalm 16, and I wrote the first line of it on the parchment, then added to it, until I had this:

> *Preserve me, O God: for in Thee do I put my trust.*
> *Bless the people of the church, for they have no*
>   *refuge but Thee,*
> *Fill their hearts with a joy which Thou alone can*
>   *grant,*
> *Preserve me, O God: for in Thee do I put my trust.*
> *On the straight path which Thou hast traced I walk.*
> *In the lives of the saints and martyrs I seek*
>   *guidance,*
> *And return to the soil from whence I came,*
> *Then live the life that knows no death.*
> *Preserve me, O God: for in Thee do I put my trust.*

✝

I spent the whole night composing and amending the words, driven by unbounded enthusiasm. Shortly before dawn I was inspired to write other lines, with words that were elegant, refined and precise in meaning, words that had never occurred to me before. I intended to compose music for the seven prayers and for the holy days, to make up a book of daily prayer, and write for the monks a wonderful hymn of a profound nature to be chanted by monks who pray constantly in their rooms. I told myself that in this special hymn I would put in words the most subtle secrets in the finest possible language. I would compose it in three movements – the first soft with few words, the second repetitive and full of phrases glorifying God, the third fast and joyful with melodies that take flight on the tiny wings of angels. I would divide my time between medicine and poetry, treating bodies with the former and souls with the latter, because the word can have an effect on man that powerful medicines do not have, since it has an eternal life which does not end with the death of the speaker.

I did not go back to my room that night, but slept in the library, filled with a mysterious joy. The next day I missed the morning prayers in church and I had no appetite for breakfast, so I stayed in the library until midday. Pharisee came to check up on me. I reassured him and told him what I was doing, but he was not as delighted as I was. I asked him why and he said he did not like singing, especially from a girl. I felt sorry for him and I was about to say, 'On the contrary, you like singing, you like doves, and you like women, but you are frightened of all that and you cannot bear liking these things, so you dismiss them to have an easy life.'

I did not want to upset Pharisee by telling him what I really thought about his attitude, especially as he had complained to me that he suffered from constant insomnia. I took his pulse and it was irregular. I asked him about his bowel movements and he said he had constipation. I gave him a tiny amount of scammony powder, mixed with plenty of aniseed to loosen his bowels with one dose, and sedative and somniferous herbs to be drunk for one week after midnight prayers. This was the prescription I thought best for him.

I went out with him to the big church and said the noon prayers with the monks. After that the abbot told me that the singing boys and the girl would come to the library the next day. He, too, had started calling it the library.

The next day in the afternoon the clamour of the children put an end to the calm around me. They came with Deacon, who knocked lightly on the door, and when I opened it I found six boys and two girls with him, aged between seven and nine. That day they came with their families and they filled the place. Some of them played around, and some of them stared at me. They had bright faces with innocent expressions, for time had not yet diminished their capacity for innocent wonder. I sent off their parents with Deacon to the churchyard, and had the children stay behind. One of the mothers stayed standing and, without looking at her, I told her gently that she should wait for her son or daughter at the gate or in front of the church.

She said that she was not mother to any of the children, nor to anyone else. 'I'm the singer,' she added tersely.

I was shaken by what she said, or perhaps I was pleased, but at the time I did not want to show my pleasure nor that I was shaken. I called the boys. 'Come inside, stand in a line, starting with the tallest.' Then, without turning towards her, I said, 'And you, my girl, stand on the side opposite them.' The children lined up and organized themselves by height with a slight adjustment on my part. I asked each one to sing individually the first line of Psalm 16. Their voices were of varying quality, but overall they were acceptable. Children's voices are by nature pleasant and clear. After I had finished with them I turned to the one who described herself as the singer. She was about twenty years old, as far as I could tell. I could not make out her face clearly because I do not look at women's faces and take no interest in their appearance. It was her dress that drew my eyes to her, for it was an unusual style for these parts, but in any case modest and dignified.

I looked down when I spoke to her, asking her to sing in a certain way the first and second lines of the hymn which I had composed. I read the lines to her with a melody which I made up, and she asked me if she could sing it with another church melody which she remembered, and I agreed. At the moment I raised my eyes to her face, she removed the headdress which hung down on her forehead, took two steps back, shut her eyes with matchless grace and lifted her face towards heaven. After a moment of silence and shyness, she sang. What a radiant voice I heard, descending serenely from the folds in the clouds! Her voice evoked the fragrance of rose bushes and the spirit of pure green meadows. She sang 'And take pity on my weakness' as though she were about to weep. Then she sang, 'And I have no help other than Thee!' I trembled inside as her lips quivered, as she strung out the words until they reached the highest heavens. Her singing was of a rare beauty.

The children who were with us fell completely silent when she sang, absorbed in her singing, as though they had flown on the wings of the melody to some distant place, and I felt as though I were alone in the far-thest corner of the vast universe. When I recall that moment now, I can feel her magical voice take me out of myself to a place beyond all things. The heavenly echo of it reverberates between the distant mountain tops and melts the heart between my ribs. My God!

When she finished singing a deep silence reigned. I wanted to signal to her to sing again, in fact I wanted her to sing until the world ended and the Day of Judgement came, but the situation did not allow for that. While she was adjusting her head covering so that it again fell down over her forehead, it dawned on her that her voice was extraordinary and that the melody she had sung was finer than the one I had suggested. She also realized that I was taken by her singing, and entranced, and many other things. As for me, at that point I no longer knew anything.

My eyes were fixed on her face until it struck me that this was most improper for me. Her face was small, rounded like a pear, and her fine features showed through her veil of thin black silk hanging down from her headdress. The headdress looked like a crown, only prettier, with delicate embroidery and at the start of its many pleats little coloured stitching. Her black velvet dress, full at the breast and tight at the waist, suggested a perfect figure. At the time I deceived myself, telling myself that her figure was no business of mine, perfect or not. What mattered was her rich voice which went so well with the hymns, for she had been trained to sing. Perhaps she had grown up close to a church or a monastery and had taken part in a choir since her early childhood.

When the abbot sent them some sweets, the children reverted to their boisterousness. I shared the sweets out among them, including the singing girl. I did not want to keep them too long on our first day, so I sent them all off after asking the Lord to bless them. I told them their singing was beautiful and that we would meet again the next afternoon, because the next day was Sunday and the monastery would be crowded with visitors in the morning. They gambolled out through the door and the girl walked after them with a striking dignity.

As she passed by me, without looking towards her, I asked her, 'Will you not tell me your name, good maid?'

'I am no maid, father, and my name is Martha, an old word which means lady.'

The Anxiety Nearby

The night after I first saw Martha I had terrible insomnia and stayed awake till dawn. In the beginning I did not think much about her being the girl who was not a maid. It was her rich voice, and its resonance inside me, that caught my attention. I spent the night rephrasing some of the words to match the register of her voice and I tried to compose some new hymns especially compatible with its warmth and richness. In the depths of the night I was buffeted by many thoughts, hopes and anxieties. Would people come to mass to hear Martha? Would the monastery church be thronged with ordinary believers, and might her fame as a singer reach as far as Antioch and Constantinople? Was she perhaps married? What sort of man could bear to approach such beauty? What does she have to do with me? I have enough to keep me busy and fill my time with worries. How is the reverend Nestorius and what is he up to? Has Bishop Cyril gone easy on him, or is he planning something else to attack him with? I'll write him a letter tomorrow and send it with the first traveller going to Constantinople. I'll ask the abbot if he wants anything from Bishop Nestorius so that I can mention it in the letter. He'll be delighted with the letter, because he knows that I am no longer in the habit of writing letters. I'll write a wonderful hymn and dedicate it to him, and write it on the back of the letter. He'll be pleased with it and one day he will come to visit the monastery and I will have it sung for him with Martha's angelic voice. Martha – how old is that girl? And why did she tell me so firmly that she was not a virgin?

On Saturday the lyre which the abbot had ordered did not arrive, and he was upset. I assured him we would not need it because I could make do with the voices of the singers, and he was relieved. I told him I would devote the time between the nine o'clock prayers and the noon prayers to seeing patients, and the time between the noon prayers and the three o'clock prayers to training the singing group, and the night to prayer and reading. He prayed to the Lord to bless me at all hours of the day, and added, 'If you have finished the Lent fast, my child, then take care of your health a little, because tonight your face looks very pale and drawn.'

We finished the sunset prayer, which here they call the 'eyelash' prayer and I went back to the library delighted. I was not aware of the paleness which the abbot had noticed. I thought he meant that I seemed distracted and preoccupied. Taking precautions, I went and took my pulse with my other hand and found it regular. I shut the door behind me, took off my clothes and began to press my finger at the points where the blood flows on the surface of the body and the flow at those points was excellent. I looked at my face in the sheet of silver that covers the Bible, and the effects of time were evident. Age had suddenly caught up with me: the whites of my eyes had turned yellow, my beard had grown wild and grey, like the beards of hermits who live in caves and grottoes. Why had I so neglected my appearance that I was now a pitiful sight? Had I forgotten that I was a physician and that I must preserve my appearance or else none of my patients would have confidence in me? A physician has to look after his appearance, as the eminent Hippocrates wrote hundreds of years ago and as physicians ever since have pledged. But never mind, every disease has a cure, and every problem has a solution. I mean to say, most diseases have a cure and most problems have a solution.

I left the library with resolve and rushed across the courtyard to my room. Out of the trunk I took the gown which a priest in Antioch had given me a year earlier after I gave him some simple treatment for colic and he recovered quickly. Why did I fold up this habit and keep it packed away for so long I am lucky the moths did not destroy it? I'll wear it tomorrow. At the bottom of the chest there's an old pair of scissors, rusty but sharp enough to trim the wilder parts of my beard. From under the table I took some simples, including dried herbs which are soaked in water for an hour, then put on the eyes as a poultice to remove the yellowness, some of which are mixed with oil and applied to the face to improve its colour by attracting the blood, and some aromatics which are made into an infusion to lave the body with, giving it a sweet scent and making it smoother to the touch. Tomorrow morning I will be a new person, fit to be called a good monk and poet.

I did everything that needed to be done, then slept like a log in my room. Weeks had passed since I last slept there, because in the summer months of last year I spent the nights in the library, preferring the cool air there, or rather too lazy to go from there to this stifling room of mine. Just before dawn I woke up briskly, filled the bucket with water from the big trough near the refectory, and warmed it up a little on the kitchen stove. Then I went up to the room, closed the door and set about rubbing my skin with rough palm fibre to remove what was left of the herbs. As I bathed I massaged my limbs with pumice, and finally I put on the elegant ecclesiastical garment which I had forgotten in the trunk.

When the abbot saw me at the church door on Sunday morning he smiled broadly and said, 'Hypa the monk has found the elixir of life. Last night he was two steps away from death, and here he is this morning, reverted to a young man in his twenties.' Embarrassed at his teasing, I replied, 'This, my Lord, is how physicians and poets should look. What you said yesterday reminded me of the pitiful state I was in.'

As he went into the church, surrounded by monks, for the morning prayers, he said, 'May the Lord bless you, Hypa, and through you serve your brothers and your patients.'

When Deacon saw me as we left the big church, he gave me a sly and childish smile which I did not understand. I paid little attention because that day I was busy thinking about something more important that the significance of his smile. At midday three of the monks helped me arrange the library. We put the books which were scattered about the room back in their place on the shelves and brought in a long bench for the singing boys to sit on. We put it on the right as you come in through the door, with two wooden chairs facing it, one for the singing girl and the other for me. We moved the long table to the corner facing the door and in the other corner we put a small table for me to write on when I wanted or at which I could sleep in a chair. This made the place roomier, cleaner and more spacious.

In the early afternoon one of the monastery servants knocked on my door and told me that two women had come seeking treatment. I closed the music book and rose to meet them at the door. It was a pleasant shock: Martha in her distinctive dress, with an old woman of about sixty. I concealed my surprise and my delight and invited them in. The servant stayed standing at the door a while and then left.

Martha began the conversation: 'Father, this is my aunt, who's been coughing at night for months and none of the usual remedies have done her any good.'

'Don't worry, aunt. When do you get the coughing fits?'

'All night long and at the start of the day,' she said. 'I feel my chest rasping with the attacks.'

I took the old woman's pulse and it was irregular. I noticed that her body was very thin. I asked her if I could put my ear against her back to hear her breathing. She stepped forward, resting on Martha's arm, until she was standing in front of me, and then she turned around. I bent my face down towards her back and put my ear against it. Martha was looking at me with a smile. I heard a grating which suggested that the old woman's chest was full of phlegm and other fluids. The treatment was easy: an infusion of antiphlegmatic seeds to be drunk warm, good covering in bed and drinking camomile in the usual manner.

'Don't sit in front of the oven for the next two weeks,' I advised the old woman, 'so that the smoke doesn't agitate the fluids in your chest.'

'We haven't renovated the oven yet, father, because we've only been your neighbours for a couple of days, and we found the oven in the cottage in ruins,' she said.

'So you're the new neighbours,' I said. 'I can see your cottage from this window. Are you living there alone?'

'Yes, father.'

The two women answered simultaneously. Martha's voice was louder and more pleasant, and when she raised the silk veil hanging over her face I looked towards her warily to find a radiant smile, standing out modestly like a clear sun on a cold winter's day, or like a fresh breeze on a stifling summer's night. Her smile was...

Confused, I stood up and scooped some of the seeds from under the table. I brought them back to put them in the old woman's hands. Martha put her hand out first and I had no choice. I avoided touching her hand, but when she closed her fists around the seeds she touched the back of my right hand, whether intentionally or not. I felt a shiver running up my arm and I could still feel it days later. I asked them if they had any camomile and Martha said 'Yes'.

Then she turned to her aunt. 'Stand up and I'll take you home, then I'll come back to study the chant.'

The old woman leant on Martha's arm and they began to leave. My eyes followed them. I was sitting on the chair opposite the bench for the singers and I did not move from my spot. At the door Martha turned towards me as she lowered the veil, hiding her sweet smile and her light brown eyes.

Martha was not gone long. When she came back she found me sitting on the square stone which the earthquake had moved in ancient times, in front of the library door. Her gait as she approached suggested a mysterious elation. She sat opposite me on a nearby stone, and asked me, 'Haven't the boys come yet?'

'I sent Deacon to fetch them, to spare their mothers the trouble of climbing the hill. They'll come in a while,' I said.

I tried to distract myself by looking at the parchments I was holding but it did not work. I took a small bible from my pocket and was about to start reading, but she unexpectedly spoke out.

'Father, there's something different about you, compared with the day before yesterday.'

'Yes, this gown is new,' I said.

'Just the gown?'

I ignored her remark, but it pleased me – though I did not show my pleasure. I started to think about how it might go with this new neighbour, who did not seem content to be just a neighbour. She had broken through the barriers of my privacy and seclusion in this monastery since the day I first saw her and heard her sing. I was anxious. I asked her to wait while I fetched some papers, and I deliberately shut the library door behind me so that she would not think of joining me. I felt that she was smiling behind me but I did not look in her direction. I stood still, inside the library behind the closed door, while she sat in the open courtyard. When I heard the clamour of the boys coming from afar I opened my door and invited them all in, and Deacon too. So began the first of many singing lessons. I don't remember how many there were but I do remember well what happened in them and much of it I will narrate.

The Caravan

The lyre reached the monastery a full week after we had started training without it. The group was now used to singing without accompaniment, and I made do with little use of the lyre. The training lasted several weeks, as the boys' singing improved day by day, while Martha's singing was excellent from the first day. Sometimes she would sing verses which were not from my poems and which she was not going to sing with the boys in church. She would arrive shortly before them, and then they would join her for the usual practice. The other days of practice would take place in the big church, between the noon and the afternoon prayers. The abbot attended the first days of practice in the church and when Martha sang he rested his brow on his stick. When she was in full song, there were tears in his eyes. His head remained bowed until we were all gone and when he saw me in the refectory in the evening he gave me two grateful pats on the shoulder and said nothing.

On the second day of the final days of practice in the church, Martha came early to me in the library as usual, before the boys arrived. She knocked on the door and came in, striding across the carpet with a pretence of bashfulness. She lifted the veil from her face, gave a broad smile and told me that her aunt's nocturnal coughing had started to diminish and the croaking in her throat was almost gone. She also told me that her aunt planned to weave for me a waistcoat of black wool for me to wear at night in the approaching winter. The two of them were skilled at weaving on the loom and made their living from this work, or so she said.

I asked her, 'The day I saw you why did you tell me so firmly that you were not a maid?'

'Because I am not a maid!' she said.

'Does the abbot know that?' I asked.

'How would I know whether he knows or not?'

I felt that she was hedging so I kept quiet. She realized I was annoyed so she moderated her tone and told me that the church priest, a distant relative of her mother's, knew she had once been married, but when they came to live here, he had introduced her to the abbot with the words: 'This girl and her aunt are Christian folk and poor. The old woman is sick and if you would let them live in the ruined cottage it would be a great favour on your part, because they don't have any relatives or any patron.' She added, 'That's what the priest said that day, so I was a girl as far as the abbot was concerned. I told him that I sang church chants and the songs which the potters sing from my early childhood, so in his eyes I became a singer. That's how he introduced me to you, good kindly father.'

Martha pronounced the word 'kindly' with such great affection and such extreme graciousness that I could not help but raise my face and look straight into her eyes. I saw how limpid the irises were, the colour of honey mixed with green, and how the beauty of her thick eyelashes framed the beauty of the roundness of her eyes. I saw how full were her eyebrows, created by God with perfection. Glossy black, they highlighted the pure whiteness of her face. Her hair, judging by the strands that hung down from under her head-dress, was the same jet black as her eyebrows, glossy and lustrous. Martha was a miracle of divine beauty, her face childlike and impetuous, beautiful as an image of the Virgin, but she also had a bold expression most disconcerting to someone like me.

I looked up at her headdress, with its pleats of silk folded with such precision, and studied it at length. How long, I asked her, did it take her to arrange it so carefully?

'No, father, it takes no time at all,' she replied. 'It's sewn like that in the first place, and after that you just put it on your head to hold the silk veil which hangs from it.' With a sudden movement I had not expected, she lifted her headdress off and a cascade of thick and soft black hair tumbled down. Her hair was imprisoned under her headdress, longing to be free, and when it framed her face she was evidence of the divine genius in creating mankind. What beauty was hidden under her head covering! What a look I saw in her eyes! Her look stung me and her beauty so awed me that I was about to faint.

Quickly I said, 'Cover your hair, my girl, Lord preserve you.'

Slowly and deliberately Martha wrapped around her head the hair which she had unleashed on the whole of creation. She lifted it with one hand and with the other closed over it the silken crown with the pleats and the delicate coloured stitching. She did not turn away from me, but I pretended to be busy looking at the bookshelves. I picked up a book lying at hand and started to turn the pages without reading a word, nor even seeing a single line.

She broke the silence, saying, 'This dress is all Damascene. It was my mother's and I took it after she died.'

'So you're from an Arab family?' I asked.

'I've been told that in the olden days my family were rich people in Palmyra, but they fled the city when Aurelian destroyed it, may the Lord curse him.'

'My child, do not let your tongue acquire the habit of making curses. Palmyra was destroyed a long time ago.'

'Yes, father, a long time ago. And after that my people dispersed across the world. My family first settled in the city of Aleppo, then they moved to Damascus and they became poor. There they produced my mother, who married a Damascus man, and brought me into this world,' she said.

'So you know Arabic and Syriac?'

'And I sing in the two languages.'

We heard the clamour of the boys arriving, so Martha lowered her Damascene veil and sat up straight. We moved to the church and when the chanting began my mind was wandering far away.

The next day Martha came early with her aunt, who bent down to kiss my hand, showing gratitude that I had treated her. But it is the Lord who heals. The old woman sat with us until the boys came and we did not speak of anything that day. They all went off, and the day passed without me seeing any more of Martha's face than was visible through her thin silk veil.

The next day was memorable because as we were coming out of church after the three o'clock prayers we heard a great uproar and a jumble of voices coming from the direction of the monastery gate. We rushed to the gate and the abbot, the priest and all the monks hurried after us. At the foot of the hill we saw a large caravan, with pack animals resting at the slope to the monastery. There were more than fifty camels and the same number of mules, along with some donkeys, and many merchants of various ages. Three of them, with colossal frames, came up towards us, supporting a man who was even vaster than them and hardly able to walk. Two soldiers from the contingent accompanied them, smiling like idiots. The man they were supporting was about fifty years old, wearing Kurdish clothes spattered with blood. Because he was so heavy and had lost his strength, his helpers brought him up the hill with great effort. Two of them were holding him up under his armpits, and one man, shorter than them, was supporting him from behind his back. The other merchants stood around watching with great interest from their place at the foot of the hill. When the group came close to us, I saw a trickle of blood running from the mouth of the man they were carrying, and I noticed Martha and her aunt standing outside their cottage, watching in amazement at the commotion that suddenly surrounded us.

The abbot took two steps towards them and the men approaching told him that the caravan leader, the man they were holding, needed urgent attention from the monastery doctors – as though the monastery had any doctor other than me! They said the man was about to expire and would die unless we urgently did something to save him. The abbot cleared the way for them and they brought the man into the courtyard and sat him on the platform near the goat pen opposite the gate. The abbot took me by the hand, advanced towards them and asked them what had happened to the man.

'The poor man drank from the devil's well,' they said.

The abbot told the monks to go back to their work and the two soldiers sat at the monastery gate. I took one of the merchants aside to try to find out what had really happened, and the two others joined us. I learnt from them that the caravan was heading to Antioch from the land of the Kurds, which lies beyond the eastern desert, in the marches between Persia and the Roman Empire, and that three nights ago the boss had drunk from a disused well in the desert – a well the caravan men call the devil's well – because he wanted to prove there were no devils in it. He drank the well water at night, and the next day he began to vomit blood, and he continued to do so for two days, without eating, until he was on the verge of death. Then the villagers advised them to come to the monastery because he would surely perish before they reached Antioch. So they had brought him in the hope he could be saved, whether by medicine or by some charm or anything that might cure him. The short man added, 'He'll be a good Christian if you cure him. He and his family will be important initiates who will soon join your religion.'

The Lord imparted to me the cause of the man's suffering and the treatment that would save him. I took the boss's helpers over to where he was sitting in a heap and whispered to the three of them that the treatment would be difficult and he would have to endure what I was going to do and not be impatient. The man was resigned, breathing rapidly and his eyes were wandering, as though the devil they imagined truly possessed him. In a croaking voice the caravan leader kept repeating: 'Do what you see fit, with the help of the Lord, do what you see fit, with the help of the Lord...'

The abbot was standing close to us, watching anxiously what was happening, and Martha was standing next to her aunt at the gate, looking at us warily. The Roman soldiers were looking at Martha from behind and whispering to each other. I brought a rope from the goat pen and asked the helpers to tie their leader to the platform by his hands and feet. Then I whispered to Martha to fetch a bucket of muddy water and dissolve plenty of salt in it, then bring a jug of cold fresh water, scented with essence of mint. Martha hurried off to do what I asked and I went to the monastery kitchen and took plenty of scraps of bread and food leftovers.

To the astonishment of all I leant down towards the sick man's ear and whispered to him that he must eat everything I put in his mouth and try to swallow it, or else he would never recover. He nodded in agreement and I started to stuff the rotten food in his mouth after mixing it up and soaking it in some of the water. The poor man began to swallow it with great difficulty. When he stopped swallowing I shouted at him and he opened his mouth and I started to stuff in more of the food. He was swallowing it reluctantly and gasping. When his insides were full I shouted at him to bear with me for a moment in what I was going to do. I took some straw mixed with goat dung from the floor of the pen, and tried to push it into his mouth. He moved his face to the left and right to avoid it and tried to break free from the ropes. Everyone around me was terrified and Martha was holding the bucket trembling. I took the bucket from her hand. I pinned the man's thigh down with my right knee and tried to push the straw in with one hand while I made him drink the salty water. The man kept resisting me and I kept shouting at him, 'This is the only cure. Be patient.'

When I felt that his strength was ebbing and that his insides were full, I stood up straight, forced his lips apart and poured more salty water in his mouth. When the man was about to expire completely and his vigour was quite spent, I asked his assistants to untie him. I moved away to where Martha was standing, watching the scene with her beautiful, bewildered eyes. The abbot was sitting on a large rock, anxiously resting his head on his stick.

When the ropes were untied, the man sprang up and rushed towards me like a bull. He raised his arms in the air as though he were about to wring my neck. I did not move. He stood in front of me a moment, panting, his hands outstretched in the air and sweat dripping from his brow. At that moment he looked like a giant who had escaped from some ancient fairy tale. Suddenly, what I expected and what I intended finally happened. The man turned and ran towards the wall of the goat pen, crouched on his knees and began to vomit in the most ghastly manner. I went over to him and began to shake his shoulders from behind, urging him to vomit more, and he did so. Everyone was appalled and astounded.

When the man had finished vomiting I washed his face in the salty water left in the bucket and had him drink some of the water scented with mint. He soon recovered his strength and was elated. He stood up laughing, came over to me, took my hand and started to kiss it, saying, 'The devil is out of my belly.' His companions cheered, as did the rest of the caravan men who had lined up at the monastery gate.

'Allow me, father,' I said, addressing the abbot. He stood up and I took him, the caravan leader and his three assistants to the place where the man had vomited. Martha joined us. I pointed to the man's vomit for them to look and explained to them what the man was really suffering from. 'Those tiny worms you see are a kind of leech that lives in brackish water. When the man drank from the disused well that night, he swallowed some with the water without seeing them. The worms that went deep into his intestines were killed by the stomach's digestive powers, but those that stayed in the upper part of his stomach began to suck his blood and make his stomach bleed. His stomach expelled the blood, which he vomited.' Then I said, 'So now you know the devil that's in the well.'

They all laughed like children whose father had come home from a journey and I advised them to give the man goats' milk to drink, and to give him only a little soft food to eat until he had completely recovered his strength on the third day. One of the monastery servants brought him a jug full of milk and the man glugged it down with relish. Then, unexpectedly, he asked me, 'Can I sleep here a while?'

The abbot took him to one of the rooms next to the small church and left him to lie down there. The crowd moved away towards the caravan resting beneath the monastery but first many of them came and greeted me and kissed my hand. Shortly before sunset the abbot came to me in the library, along with the man who had been sick and who had now put on a sumptuous gown. The two men who had held him came in too, full of joy, and behind them four of the monks. The abbot said the man wanted to reward me for my medical services, but I told him that I took no fee for treatment and that it was God who had cured him.

The caravan leader came forward, sat on the chair nearby and said, 'Holy monk, God chose you as the instrument of my recovery and I will carry out with pleasure whatever you ask of me. I have plenty of money, goods and clothes, so do not hesitate to ask.'

'Thank you, good man,' I said, 'but I ask nothing of no man, and I take no fee for treating people.'

I said that and I bowed my head as if to end the conversation. The man stood up and kissed my head, begging me to accept whatever he would send by way of a gift. I told him, 'Don't send anything. Believe me, I need nothing, but ask the abbot if he needs anything for this place. If you want, you could give the girl who helped me a dress for her to wear when she sings in church on Sundays.'

The Storm Brews

The caravan left at dawn, and at noon Martha opened the library door without knocking. I was engrossed in reading Galen's book on the human pulse and the sound of the door creaking took me by surprise. I looked towards the door and saw her standing on the raised threshold, surrounded by the light shining in behind her, like a houri who had come down to earth wrapped in heavenly light to bring us peace and fill with kindness a universe which had previously been full of oppression and injustice. The sunlight framed her on all sides, so that she seemed enveloped in light. I shall not forget that moment as long as I live. Before I realized it, my hand had taken off my head cap with the crosses on it, in a gesture of welcome to the light which suddenly shone from the doorway, and at that moment I was sure that Martha was the most beautiful woman the Lord had ever created.

Her dress hugged her chest and waist gently, then fell in many folds, like a circle centred on her small feet on which she wore shoes of the same colour. On her head she had a scarf of glossy silk, holding her hair in place without hiding any of her face. On each side of the scarf plaits hung down to her breasts. Her dress was of purple velvet, rucked at the shoulders, then falling and opening, but tight around the arms. The sleeves were long and wide enough at the cuffs for the gilt embroidery to show on the back of her hand. The same embroidery decorated the hem of the dress and the border of her headscarf. Martha left me to contemplate her for a moment, tilting her head gently to the right and resting her fists on her hips. With a haughty gait and a smile she came towards me, holding the flowing dress at her thighs with the tips of her fingers and lifting it a little. The velvet folds and the train of the dress with the gilt stitching rippled with each graceful step that brought her floating towards me.

'I see you like description, but that's enough. Carry on with your account of what happened. Your description of Martha excites me.'

'Get thee hence, Azazeel.'

When Martha approached me, I looked up to the bodice of the dress. I gazed at the many buttons, arranged in two lines running up the bodice from the navel to the base of the neck, crossing on their way the fullness of her breasts. When she came closer to me, I looked up to where her neck met her fine chin, but my head was too low for me to look deep into her eyes. I think it was then she understood my torments, but she added to them with a serene smile which drew my gaze to the dimples in her cheeks. When at last I looked into her eyes, I plunged deep into a sea of honey.

'What do you think, father,' she said, 'this is one of the three dresses the caravan leader gave me yesterday evening.'

'Beautiful, Martha, very beautiful, my child.'

'It's slightly tight at the chest, but with time it will stretch to fit me.'

'Yes, yes, come, let's sit at the door.'

'Father, it's still too early for the boys to come. Let's sit here.'

'No, Martha, that wouldn't be right. Our place is over there.'

It was not appropriate for us to sit in the far corner of the library, since the nearby window cast light only on the table where I read. It was better to sit at the door, to avert any suspicions. There was more light there too and I would be able to see the dress better. Martha followed me over and sat in front of me on her chair. She put her hands under her thighs and started to swing her legs back and forth. The dress shimmered as she moved and made me feel even dizzier. She was looking straight into my eyes while I avoided looking towards her. Without me asking she sang a song I was not familiar with, and then I looked at her, no longer able to resist.

When Martha sang, she was yet more beautiful. When she was absorbed in singing, she raised her fine chin and shut her eyes, as though she were confiding in heaven. Her singing that day acted on me like a drug, first numbing the surface of my body, then seeping deep inside me. Her voice transported me to a distant and infinite horizon, then it began to convulse me, filling me with sadness upon sadness until I lost all sense of who I was. When she finished singing, I was finished too.

'Won't you put your cap on, father?' she asked.

Her question bewildered me, then reminded me I was not even aware that my head was still uncovered. In truth I felt only her overwhelming presence as it took possession of me and drew me out of myself towards her. I stood up reluctantly and fetched my cap. On my way back I had no qualms about looking at her. She, too, was looking at me with a mysterious smile which enhanced the magic of her face. I had to say something but the words on the tip of my tongue just vanished. I was telling myself that her beauty was cruel to those who knew her, cruel because it was too deep to be endured, too distant to be reached.

'Why are you looking at me like that, father, and saying nothing?'

'Nothing, Martha, nothing. I'm thinking. Tell me, how old are you? When did you get married? And where is your husband, and your family? Why did you come to live here with your aunt?'

'Those are many questions, father. I'm twenty, and the other questions I will answer in the days to come, every day one question.'

'All right, Martha, all right. Tell me when you want and however you like.' But would the days to come play out in the way I would like? I have grown accustomed to seeing you over the past few weeks and after a time the singing practice will come to an end. So on what pretext will I see you after that? Monks don't welcome women coming into their monasteries, but I am resigned to the fact that you have found a way into my heart. Will I be content to see you only on Sunday mornings, singing in church with the choir? No, I will find another pretext. I shall plant medicinal plants on the land around your cottage and commission you to look after them, and every day I will pass by to check up on the crop, and see you without arousing suspicion. That could go on for years and years! And perhaps the day will come when they tell me that Martha is going to marry one of the farmers and will go off to live in his house. That day you will leave behind your elderly aunt and leave me to suffer.

'You've gone back to thinking and not saying anything!' Martha said.

'Yes, Martha, I'm thinking about you.'

'I know. I can sense you, Hypa.'

The way she pronounced the 'p' in my name frightened me, because I never thought she would dare to call me simply by my name. At that moment I was looking at her lips and saying to myself: is this girl deliberately arousing me, is she fooling with me? Perhaps she's fallen in love with me after coming to know me and seeing my skill at healing her aunt and my sensational treatment of the caravan leader yesterday, to the amazement of all.

At the time I saw the admiration in her eyes and felt her pride in me. But would proof of my medical skill induce her to fall in love with me, me who trails around in holy garb and lives in a monastery? And then she's just a girl of twenty who does not know what love is in the first place. What is love? You don't know what it is either, you wretched monk. What happened with Octavia twenty years ago was not love; it was sin. No, it was pure love on her part, and sin on mine. My few days with her were extraordinary, but at the time I did not know what they were worth. It ended with me losing her, and I lost myself in that dreadful way because I was afraid of her love and chose to run away from her. Then, when she was killed in front of my eyes, I inherited a wound that has never healed. Do you think I'll lose Martha too, she who sits in front of me swinging her feet like a playful child? And will I ruin myself for the sake of an obscure and passing fancy? No, that would not do. All you have to do is pull yourself together. Bear with the turmoil you are going through. Understand that love is a storm that lurks in a distant corner in the depths of the heart, always eager to sweep away everything that stands in its path. You are a reverend monk and an eminent physician, so do not give love a chance to sweep you away, or else it will hurl you into the desert as an outcast. But on the other hand you are also a poet, and you have these feelings of desire towards this beautiful girl who is sitting in front of you, taking pleasure in teasing you and causing you trouble. And then you are forty and she is like a daughter to you, and tomorrow you might find she has thrown herself into the arms of another man, and you can go back to your usual gloom and bleak existence.

What other man could deserve Martha and know her value? No one but I understands the depth of the magic in her eyes and the wonder of the secret hidden within her. A man other than I would turn her into a peasant woman of the kind that fills the villages. Careful, she was married before. What kind of man was it that she married? I wonder, did she submit to him in the long winter nights? Did he taste the delights of her nubile body? Did she have her fill of him? Have mercy on me, my God.

'Do you want me to go, and come back when the boys come?' she said.

'No, you can stay a while. They will come presently.'

'But you are silent and you no longer look at me.'

'Martha, you…'

I had intended to divulge my feelings for her and explain what I was going through, and she had prepared herself to hear something important. She folded her arms across her breast and stopped swinging her feet. She was just as beautiful when she paid attention and listened. Her eyes opened wide, making them yet more beautiful. But that time I did not say anything, because just as I was about to speak my mind, after looking long and deep in her eyes, we heard the clamour of the boisterous boys coming from the monastery gate.

I stood up straight away, fetched my papers and gave Martha a copy so we could start the singing and bring an end to this dreamlike interlude between us. The boys started reciting the psalm, then Martha sang the verses of poetry, overwhelming all my senses and sweeping me away, out of this world. I came back to earth to the boys singing the psalm again, then when she sang again I floated away to another universe.

When they left, Martha lingered a moment to ask me if these were fasting days, and I told her they were not. She whispered, 'I'll bring you something.' She quickly disappeared, and came back a while later carrying a plate of those sweets for which Aleppo and the surrounding villages are famous. One of the monks was sitting with me when she came. She put the plate on the table and left without a word. The monk resumed his description of the contractions which gave him pain in the intestines whenever he ate anything other than boiled food.

That evening I took the sweets with me to the refectory and the monks who ate them said how good they were. When I thanked Martha the next morning she told me that these fancy sweets were a present to her from the caravan leader. It looked like the man was very generous, because the previous night the abbot had told me at the dinner table that the man had given him a sum of money to build the monastery wall and a wooden gate in the shape of a large cross.

I did not tell Martha that I did not eat any of the sweets, and I did not tell her anything else either because that day she came very late after the boys had taken their places in line. She said that she and her aunt had been busy building a new oven and that day her singing was unsettled. She was wearing the Damascene dress she had worn when I first saw her. Martha left with the boys as soon as the practice was over and I spent the rest of the day in great misery.

That day I looked often towards the cottage from the library window, and I saw plenty of activity: Martha in her house clothes coming and going, her aunt in her dark black clothes, sometimes sitting at the loom and sometimes standing, three boys singing as they repaired the walls of the animal pen in front of the cottage, the carpenter banging nails into the door. They must have many repairs to do, other than the oven. Shortly before sunset, much smoke rose from the new oven and the activity died down.

That night I thought of sleeping in my room, so that the smoke rising from the new oven would not trouble me, then I decided instead to close the window and stay in the library, because it was closer to her. I shut my door, lit the wick of my lamp and went back to reading my only copy of Galen's book on the human pulse, hoping to find solutions to the confusing aspects of this text, which was full of copyist's errors. That night I missed dinnertime and I did not attend the night prayers with the other monks. After prayers, two of the monks from the monastery visited me, one an old and dignified monk, the other younger and stouter. With them came a visiting monk who had stopped at the monastery on his way from Rome to Jerusalem.

The visiting monk did not say a word throughout our conversation and I hardly noticed him. In fact I do not remember now what he looked like. I just remember him looking down at length in silence and that, according to the other two monks, he was carrying a letter from the pope of Rome to the bishop of Jerusalem about an important meeting. I was surprised at what I heard and did not understand the mystery of why this monk was travelling alone by land rather than by sea, the usual route. Why was he avoiding the big cities and why had he not passed through Antioch on his way? But I did not want to burden him with my questions, especially as I felt that night that he preferred to stay silent. The mystery came to light later and I realized that behind our backs they were arranging the ecumenical council which created such an uproar in Ephesus.

While the two monks sat with me a while, I prepared for the visiting monk some medicine for a burning feeling he had in his chest. We spoke about the big churches in Rome, the many monasteries spread across the seven hills of the city, when the time would come to start building the wall which would surround the monastery, and many other things. They left me at midnight, and at the door the younger, stouter monk told me with a smile that the girl who had recently moved into the cottage sang at the party which the merchants held two days earlier to celebrate the recovery of their leader. Highly suggestively, in a manner inappropriate for a monk, he added that the caravan leader and the girl seemed very friendly and that after the banquet she accompanied him to his tent.

I was devastated.

The Storm Blows

I did not shut my eyes all that night, and when the sun rose at daybreak my body and soul were fevered. I stayed tied to the window overlooking the cottage until I saw Martha come out languidly to hang a sheet on the clothes line behind the oven, which they had lit the day before and from which the smoke was still rising. I threw on my clothes and rushed off towards her. It was her aunt who saw me first and she came towards me full of cheer. I asked after Martha and she called her. She took her leave, saying she had to revive the fire in the new oven because the fire had to be lit three days in succession. I nodded and stayed standing where I was, close to the cottage.

Martha came out in her house clothes, swaying as she walked as though she were deliberately taking her time. She was barefoot and on her head she wore a scruffy scarf which had once been blue. Although her clothes were shabby she was cruelly beautiful in the early morning light. When she stood before me, jealousy tied my tongue and I could not say a word.

She spoke first, saying, 'What is it, father? Are you travelling somewhere today?'

'No, but I want you to tell me something. Did you really go with the caravan leader to his tent the night they stayed here, and did you sing to them?'

'Why do you ask?'

'Because I...' I did not finish. I had nothing further to say. I felt a burning in my throat, I found it hard to breathe and my soul was pained. Suddenly

I turned to go back to the monastery and left her behind me without looking at her, not even once.

I went straight up to my room, shut the door behind me and curled up in the farthest corner, my head between my knees and my arms wrapped around. Inside me I heard a babble of discordant voices, tormenting me, tearing me to pieces and mocking me. After a period of self-absorption, I started to groan, as though I had hooks or scalpels tearing at my liver. I felt sorry for myself, despised myself. Is this what you wanted, what you were working for, good monk and poet? To be the laughing-stock of people because of an ignorant girl about whom you know nothing? How could you let yourself become the plaything of a flirtatious woman, simply because you think her beautiful? You kept wondering if she was a virgin, but the caravan leader whom you cured understood that she was a wanton woman who would go with strangers to their tents at night. What misery have you brought upon yourself? I wanted to give her a dress through the caravan leader but he found his way to her and showered her with gifts – three dresses and fancy sweets… There may be other gifts which she did not mention. You introduced her to him so you have only yourself to blame, and you so proud that you can heal the sick. My God, I know You will punish me for my sin, so have mercy on me. I confess all the lust I have committed in my heart, all the rules and enduring commandments I have broken. I ignored what is written in the Gospel according to Matthew: 'Anyone who looks at a woman lustfully has already committed adultery with her in his heart. If your right eye causes you to sin, gouge it out and throw it away. It is better for you to lose one part of your body than for your whole body to be thrown into hell.'

My God, I know that I have sinned, so bestow Your pardon upon me and do not throw me into hell right away. Fire burns inside me, burns me up. Turn me into ashes or dust strewn along the road. Have mercy on me, because I can bear no longer the constant torment. My God, I am wretched, broken, meek. I am grieved and You are merciful. Jesus the Saviour, in his first public sermon, said, 'Blessed are the poor in spirit, for theirs is the kingdom of heaven. Blessed are those who mourn, for they will be comforted.

Blessed are the meek, for they will inherit the earth.' And I, my God, I do not aspire to the kingdom of heaven, nor to inherit the earth, nor even to be comforted. All I beg of You is that You put out the flame burning inside me and bring an end to the pain which has driven me to this corner, outcast and despised.

'Father, are you inside?'

I heard Deacon's voice, along with his frantic knocking on the door of my room, and it wrenched me away from the misery in which I was drowning. Perhaps it was a sign from heaven, to save me from the pitiful state to which I had brought myself.

'Father, are you asleep?' Deacon called again and kept knocking. I stood up unsteadily from the dark corner, and leant against the wall as I raised the latch of the door. The light coming in from behind Deacon hurt my eyes and his voice distressed me.

'Father, you're here!' he said, 'I've been knocking on your door for an hour. I didn't know you slept so soundly.'

'What do you want, my son?'

'They want you in the library.'

Deacon went off and I almost collapsed on the floor, as though I had pulled myself together for his sake, or needed his sudden, unwelcome presence as a prop. They want me in the library! Who is it that wants me now? I do not want to see anyone, and I do not want anyone to want to see me.

With heavy steps I went down the stairs, as if descending from the summit of desolate Mount Qusqam towards the desert which stretches away to the west. The courtyard of the monastery was empty and the midday sun dazzled my sad eyes. I walked towards the library like a traveller fighting to stay awake, my mind hard at work wondering who might be awaiting me in the library. With difficulty I reached the half-open door, and pushed it gently.

'Martha!'

'Yes, father, I've been waiting for you for ages.'

'What do you want now?'

'Sit down, father, I beg you.'

I sat down, without looking towards her. I was almost in tears, but I fought them back and overcame them. Martha stood speechless, and after a long silence I looked at her, and saw that she too was on the point of tears. She was looking down at her left knee. Her thin silk scarf, black like her loose dress, hung down around her face. The blackness of her dress enhanced the radiant whiteness of her childlike, innocent face. After contemplating her for some moments, I felt she was so perfect that she could never have done the wanton deed that I had imagined, and that if she were truly a wanton woman, the Lord would have deprived her of this angelic countenance and given her instead the countenance of a whore. If she were truly a frivolous woman, she would not have bothered to come to me and sat in front of me so silent and so innocent, so suggestive of chastity.

Martha raised her face towards me and, her eyes filled with a sad beauty, she looked deep into my eyes and spoke. 'I beg you, Hypa, do not misjudge me. Injustice is cruel and I have suffered much from its cruelty in my life.'

'Did you go to that man's tent, Martha, the night you sang for him?'

'I'll tell you everything,' she said.

In words full of candour, before finally bursting into tears, Martha told me that the caravan leader sent to her that day towards sunset, with one of his retainers, three dresses, a sack of wheat and another sack of dried fruit. The man told her it was a gift from the caravan leader for the people of the house next to the holy monastery. So he said. And after sunset the same retainer came back to tell her that they had learnt from the neighbours that she sang well the songs of the potters, known by the name Ququye. He said they were holding a banquet for the monks and the people of the area to celebrate the recovery of their master.

Martha stopped a moment, then she continued. 'The man told me that if I went to sing, the caravan boss would pay me, so I went to them with my aunt and sang. The songs of the Ququye, as you know, Hypa, are respectable songs, with nothing shameful about them, and many of the monastery monks and deacons were present, as well as most of the people who live around the monastery. I expected to see you there and I kept looking out for you throughout the evening, but you did not come. When we had finished, the caravan leader took us towards his tent, my aunt and me. He went in and came out with a dress for her and some money for me. We took what he gave us and went back to our cottage and did not go out again till the next day.'

Martha said all this with a tone of complete sincerity. When she had finished she bowed her head and broke into tears.

I had to speak, to comfort her. 'They told me you went with him, and I thought. . .'

'Do not think ill of me, Hypa.'

'Ah, now you're calling me by my name!'

'I'm sorry, I was confused, and happy because you have wronged me with your crazy ideas.'

'Happy, Martha!'

'Yes, because your crazy ideas prove to me that you love me, as I love you.' She stood up straight away and fled away to her cottage. She left me in a state that merciful God alone can know, the God who is occluded beyond his farthest heavens.

The Prospect of Love

Love can have dramatic effects, wielding awesome powers which I cannot withstand or endure. How can a human being tolerate the emotional swing between the burning valleys of hell and the balmy meadows of heaven. Whose heart will not melt when subjected to the sweet breezes of love, the searing winds of desire, the fragrance of flowers, fiery blasts, then sleeplessness at night and anxiety by day? What should I do with my love when the storm of it has raged and blown me away to somewhere I did not expect? Should I rejoice in Martha's love, or should I fear it? They will say that I beguiled her, or rather they will say that she beguiled me. I shall never escape from this love which Martha has kindled with a single word, which turned it into passion, and I have no experience of frequenting the world of passion.

That day the Lord had mercy on me and no one intruded on my solitude except Deacon, who dropped in on me after noon to tell me he was on his way to pick up the boys. I told him that today they would have a rest from singing practice. He must have told Martha that, because she did not come at the usual time that day. In the afternoon I was longing for her and I told the abbot after the three o'clock prayers that we must go ahead with the plan to grow medicinal herbs on the slope because it was the season to plant them. He welcomed the idea and called two of the monastery servants to help me prepare the ground. Deacon and another boy joined us, and when Martha saw us coming towards her cottage her face shone with the light of love and my heart went out to her. From afar she called out 'Welcome, father,' and when we were alone together she whispered to me, 'I was longing to see you, Hypa.'

Deacon stood on a piece of land, flat as a platform and overlooking the cottage, and shouted out that it was ready and good for planting. I explained to him that we needed five spots of the same area, terraced like the gardens of Babylon. He laughed idiotically and said, 'What are those gardens of Babylon? They must be a long way from here.'

The next morning the owner of the big farm, the first patient I treated here, sent two professional farmers who lived on the land and three workmen. Over three days they put in order the land surrounding the cottage, turning it into five large terraces as I wanted. In the middle of each terrace they dug a channel for water and at the end a place where the water would fall down to the channel on the terrace below. We would bring the water from the rock tanks on the western side of the monastery where the rainwater collects every winter and stands stagnant until the next winter. The herbs I intended to plant would not need much water anyway.

On the afternoon of the third day they planted saplings on the edge of the five terraces so that the thick roots would prevent the edges from eroding when the winter rains fell. When they finished their work at sunset the sight was magnificent, and Martha was delighted. When the workmen and the farmers had gone she came up to me, so close that her shoulder almost touched me, and said, 'Among all the plants our cottage will look like a palace in paradise.' I didn't know how to answer but she knew what to tell me. With her honey-green eyes she looked into my eyes and said something which took my breath away. 'I love you very much, Hypa.' Then she hurried off to her aunt.

I walked up to the monastery gate, buoyed by my love, in fact I was borne on the wings of angels. I hurried across the courtyard, avoiding meeting anyone so that I would not hear a word from anybody, after what I had heard her say. I went up to my room with her words 'I love you very much' ringing around me. I shut my eyes to the echo of her words, trying to retain them within me. A wonderful daze led the way to sleep and my night was full of delightful dreams, all of them featuring Martha. In the morning I was another person, not the one I had known through all the past years of my life.

✝

Two days had passed without any singing practice and on the Wednesday morning the abbot asked me when to expect the hymns to start in church. I did not hesitate to answer. 'We'll be ready next Sunday, father.' His face beamed with a smile of satisfaction.

Deacon dropped in on Martha when he went down to pick up the boys. She came slightly before them and I saw no objection to her waiting for them with me in a far corner of the library, because I was sitting there before she came. She was wearing a black velvet dress, decorated at the sleeves with a band of shiny red silk which ran from the base of the neck to the back of her hands. The same band ran around the hem of the dress and covered the top of the bodice. She looked like the princesses I had seen in my dreams in my childhood, or the angels which hover in my imagination when my mind is clear.

Before she sat down she told me that on her way she had seen the abbot and had asked him if her dress was proper for singing hymns, and he had given her his blessing. She added, 'So now you can't object to my dress, though it does accentuate my bosom and make me a beautiful woman.'

'With or without this dress, you are the most beautiful woman to walk the earth,' I said.

'Sweet words. Where do you find such heady words? But wait, why didn't you tell me you instructed the caravan leader to give me those dresses? The abbot told me yesterday what took place between you two.'

'I didn't order him to do anything. I said he should give you a dress and he gave you three.'

'He gave more because he wanted to thank you more, my love.'

'What did you say, Martha?'

'To thank you more.'

'I don't mean that.'

'Ah, you mean "my love". My love, my love.'

Our eyes made contact and I lost all sense of my surroundings. I think she felt the same way. Lost in each other's gaze, we were not aware of the passage of time. We stayed silent, immersed in what we shared, until the clamour of the boys and Deacon arriving dragged us apart. We went straight into the singing practice, in the library that day, not the church.

The singing went better than ever, and every now and then we would look at each other in such a way that the boys would not notice, nor Deacon who was sitting at the table nodding to the rhythm. But I did notice an unevenness in the way Martha sang the words on the long notes. When the boys were gone I asked why her heart and her voice were perturbed, just to tease her, and she said in seriousness that she had some pain in her chest and had been coughing badly the last few nights. What she said worried me. I stood up at once and fetched some seeds which have the effect of soothing a cough and making it easier to breathe. I realized that the smoke from the oven was the reason why her chest was inflamed. When I came back with the seeds, I passed them to her and she stretched out her hand to take them, and she closed her hands on mine. It was the first time we had touched, and at her touch I lost a part of myself to her. I was standing in front of her and she was sitting where her aunt had sat the first day they came to see me.

'Aren't you going to listen to my chest, Hypa?' she said.

I understood what she meant. She wanted me to put my ear on her back, as I had done with her aunt. I hesitated a moment, then I sat next to her and she stood in front of me. She turned and took two steps back until my knees almost touched the back of her knees. At the time I did not worry that any of the monks or any patient might come in on us through the open door or that the abbot might come to visit me, as was his habit. I thought of nothing but her and I was emboldened by the fact that I had heard no footsteps on the gravel in the courtyard.

The silence was complete, and my desire for her was overpowering. I pressed my ear against her back to hear her pulse and find out the cause of the rasping in her chest. But there was nothing wrong with her chest and all

I heard was the steady beats of her heart, loud. I felt that the beats were calling me. I lingered, listening, enjoying the feel of the velvet dress pressed between her body and the side of my face. Without thinking I put my hands on her hips and pulled her gently towards me. She leant back until her bottom touched my chest. Then she put her hands on my hands and brought them round to meet in front. She squeezed my hands and I squeezed her stomach. I raised my hands, with her hands on top, until I touched her breasts with my palms. She pressed my hands with hers and I pressed her breasts beneath. At that moment I ejaculated in great spurts, like a flood pent up since time long past, watering land that had cracked from twenty years of drought. Martha trembled, the same tremble I had witnessed twenty years earlier in the wine cellar, but Martha's trembling was more gratifying and more receptive.

She turned her face towards me, with my arms still wrapped around her. She gave me a soft kiss on the cheek and hurriedly slipped away towards the door. I stayed sitting for a long while, bewildered, then stretched out on the big bench and fell into a deep sleep, sweeter than normal sleep.

Longing

I woke up at dawn the next day and found myself hugging one of the coarse pillows which were on the bench. I got up like a man brought back to life after aeons. I shut my eyes and imagined myself embracing Martha and recalled the ecstasy of the previous day. As the light of the lazy sun spread, the farmer who planted seeds arrived with three workmen who knew about farming. I accompanied them to the hanging gardens around Martha's cottage and caught sight of her twice as we planted and prepared the soil. In the afternoon when we had finished, I sent Deacon to fetch the boys and I dropped in on Martha to invite her to the last practice, because we had two days before we would start to sing at mass, just two days.

Martha joined me without delay and sat in her usual place in the library, with me facing her and her facing the door. I felt she was close to me. If she stretched out her arm, and I stretched out mine, then our fingertips could touch, even interlock, and a single force would flow through us, enclosing us until we left every other world behind us. Then my heart would surge and my mind would go blank, and were it not for a remnant of fear I would steal a march on my own death and my soul would escape my body, to soar through worlds of eternity and never return to this ephemeral body and its agonizing desires.

Martha turned to me, showing the full sun of her face. She took off her black diaphanous cap, and her hair fell down around her face, making her look yet more beautiful. I was looking at her in silence when she surprised me with a question. 'Hypa, don't you feel homesick for your country, the place you were born?'

'Why do you ask?'

She turned towards me with just a twist of her right shoulder, but that was enough for my mournful eyes to see how her neck rose to her queenly cheeks. She must have descended from some bygone royal line which had lost its kingdom in the vicissitudes of time but whose features showed up in their distant progeny. Smiling angelically, she said, 'Will you answer my question with a question?'

'It's not one question, Martha. I have many questions for you.'

'Ask me anything and I will answer you, my lord.'

I could not help but smile, and she smiled too and there was a twinkle in her eye. She turned full towards me and my eyes fixed on her breast. I was unable to avert my gaze from the spot where I would have liked to lay my head. She was not bothered that I was gazing so intently at this forbidden spot. Perhaps she wanted to offer her breast to me to soothe away the sorrows which had afflicted my soul for so many years, and put an end to the age of abstinence. Ah, if I had rested my head on her breast that day, I would have knelt in front of her, put my head between her breasts, held her to me, melted into her and died.

'Aren't you going to ask me?' she said.

Her question brought me to my senses. I looked up to her neck, her cheeks, her nose, delicate as a flower bud, to the sea of liquid mountain honey in her eyes. Adrift, I held fast to words. 'Martha, tell me about your family.'

'That's a long story.' Her smile was almost a laugh now. She leant her shoulders back a little, then began to tell me stories. She recounted many unconnected happenings, about her grandmother who never tired of talking about the city of Palmyra, which was destroyed when her grandmother was still a child; about her father who was a blacksmith in Damascus, well known there for his skill at making fine swords out of Damascus steel, famous for its quality. For some reason which she did not reveal, or which perhaps she did not know, her father moved to Aleppo but the people of Aleppo would not accept him and he spent years there trying to join the Christian community and serve the parish, but they refused because his wife, Martha's mother, was a pious pagan and had once been seen lighting candles secretly on the remains of the abandoned temple which used to stand on the road to Aleppo. Her father had to spend five years under the scrutiny of the deacons and priests until the bishop agreed to let him enter the fold of the Lord. Her father did not stay long before moving his family to that small village which nestles beside the road between Aleppo and Antioch, Sarmada, and there she was born nineteen or twenty years ago.

'So your father lived as a pagan?'

'We didn't know what religion he was until his death. He died early, in his early forties, but in any case he wanted to be Christian.'

'Did he die a Christian?'

'He was killed.'

She shed two tears, and my heart went out to her. I was about to stand up and hug her to my chest, as I had imagined, or hold her face in my hands as I used to do with my uncle's white doves. Was Martha just a white dove which had alighted in this world from beyond the clouds? Why did I not hug her that day? She was mourning for her father, mourning for herself, mourning for the desolation of this world.

The next day I asked her about her husband, and she wept many tears as she told me that she was nine when her father met his end after a dispute with a group of highwaymen for whom he made swords. Two months after his death her mother told her she was going to marry her off. By the word 'marry', all she understood was that a man would come to live with them. The husband was more than fifty years old, a wanderer who dealt in swords and other weapons. He collected them from the makers in the big cities and travelled to countries far to the east, selling them to a group of warriors called the Shankara, or so she said.

'Do you mean Shabankareh?' I asked.

'I don't know exactly, I was very young.'

'They're a group of Kurds who live on the borders of the land of Persia, and their name is derived from the word for shepherds in the Kurdish language,' I told her.

'How do you know all these things?'

'Because I once treated one of them and because I'm an old man, twenty years older than you.'

'No, my love, you are my little child, my beloved.'

She stood up, kissed me and moved away. I would have wrapped my arms around her but she went straight back to her place, looking warily towards the door. I sat up straight and asked her to tell me what happened to her husband who was forty years older than her. She said that he wasn't a husband in the usual sense and she stayed two years with him without knowing what married life meant, until one scorching summer's day. It was midday and she was playing with the neighbourhood children behind the house when an old woman who lived nearby called her and took her by the hand to her husband. Her mother wasn't at home. The husband was alone, sitting on the ground with his back to the wall. All he had on his colossal body was a short jellaba rolled up to show his legs, which were covered, as she said in disgust, with thick hair.

She spoke with a trace of lingering pain as she continued. 'The old woman stood with me at the door to the room, happy for some reason I could not see. Then she dipped an old copper cup into the water jar near the door, poured some of it into her cupped hand and wiped my face. Then she undid my plaits and wet my hair with water. He was smiling at the old woman, who began to drag me towards him, then threw me in his lap. I was like a little bird who had fallen on a giant's thigh. When the old woman left, he pulled me towards him so hard that I felt my ribs breaking between his arms. Then he began to explore my body with his rough hands. I wasn't very curvy at the time, but he started to squeeze under my arms, then moved on to my breasts, which had hardly developed. I was submissive and frightened, anxious because my mother was not at home. He stripped me completely naked, laid me on his bare thighs without taking off his jellaba and began to run the palm of his right hand over my stomach and legs. I had a strange unfamiliar feeling, shut my eyes and submitted to him. Suddenly he slipped his finger inside me and I started to bleed. I screamed, jumped out and ran towards the door. He stood up behind me and grabbed me by my hair with his hand, which was stained with my blood. I kept screaming as he held me, then he threw me violently into the corner of the room, where I curled up with my head between my knees. I fell asleep like that, or completely lost consciousness, until my mother came and took me in her arms.'

'That's enough, Martha, that's enough,' I said.

'No, I'm going to tell you everything, so that you know how life has abused me.'

Martha's story shook me to the core, especially when I learnt that her husband, in spite of his large body, did not sleep with other women, and that when he came back from his travels he would amuse himself with her whenever the opportunity arose. When she reached fifteen, her mother died and her husband forbade her to leave the house. He would go away on business for weeks and came back to find his plaything awaiting him.

Her floods of tears soaked the bodice of her dress but she insisted on telling me more, perhaps to unburden herself of the memories or because she wanted to make me aware of what she had suffered, or perhaps because she wanted to share with someone else what she had been hiding behind her angelic face.

She wiped the tears from her cheeks and continued. 'His rough lips would open in a stupid smile when I hurried to fetch a bowl of water to wash his chapped feet. That was on my mother's advice and I made it a habit whenever he came home and threw himself down, pretending to be exhausted, on the mud platform at the entrance to our two-room house. After some weeks, when he had grown used to having me massage his feet in the water, he started ordering me to keep massaging them until he fell asleep. He used to sleep seated and snore loudly. After weeks of going to sleep that way, he started ordering me to shut the outer door and sit down again, then he would play with my breasts with the toes of his right foot, until he fell asleep. After weeks playing constantly with my breasts, the day came when he ordered me to take off all my clothes and come and sit at his feet. With one foot he would ravage my naked body while I massaged the other foot. One scorching hot day I was drying his feet when he stuck his right foot in my mouth and ordered me to suck his toes. I refused and he pushed me in anger with his left foot. The powerful shove threw me on my back and I was sprawled on the ground. He guffawed, delirious at my subdued scream and my arrant nakedness spread beneath him. He stood up, like a rock about to fall on me from a mountain top. That day I wished he had thrown his clothes off, pounced on me and taken me by force so that I could die beneath him and be rid of him. But he did not do what I wanted. He just put the bottom of his left foot on my lower belly, rubbed it and laughed. I can feel his heel crushing me now.'

'Take it easy, Martha, and thank the Lord for saving you from this unrighteous man.'

She stopped a while and looked down at her knees, recalling distant memories. I gazed with sympathy at her cheeks and her long eyelashes. When two new streams of tears began to flow and her cheeks took on a slight flush, her face had a serene virginal quality which was both disconcerting and heart-wrenching. I wanted to hug her but I hesitated, then I yielded to my hesitation. If only I had stood up, I would have wiped her cheeks with my hands, clasped her to my chest, stroked her hair, shut my eyes and inhaled her inner fragrance. She would have rested her head on my chest and I would have wrapped my arms around her until we merged into one, as still and immutable as a white marble statue full of symbolic power.

Why didn't I embrace her? I stayed still, did nothing, until she continued, her voice a whisper now, or as good as a whisper.

She said, 'I was lying on the floor beneath him, screaming, and when he raised his foot I escaped from under him towards the door. I opened it and ran through the village streets, terrified and naked. My screams filled the lanes and people were looking. A woman took me inside her house and covered my nakedness with an old jellaba. In the evening, people gathered and he came home drunk, his vast frame reeling. He then divorced me because

I had not produced any children! And he threw me out of our house. I had nowhere left to live, so I went to this aunt of mine in her old house in Aleppo and spent the last three years there. I learnt to sing there, and because we found it hard to make a living, and I was constantly harassed, we left my aunt's ramshackle house, and I came with her to live here, next to you.'

'Dry your tears, Martha, and go off home before the boys come, because they are about to arrive.'

'Will you come to me when you're finished with them?' she asked.

'Yes, I'll come before sunset to see you in the cottage, and I'll come again tomorrow after daybreak. After today no day will pass without me seeing you.'

I don't know how I summoned up the courage to say those last words, but she was pleased with what I said, and I was pleased with her smile and her dreamy look. She stood up to adjust her headscarf quickly, and hurried away.

At the door she turned towards me, and I sat there paralysed. 'I'll be waiting for you. Don't be long, Hypa,' she said.

She spoke my name as though she were the angel who would bring me back from the dead on the Day of Judgement, for me to wake up and dissolve in divine light. At the door she tightened her scarf, dropped the thin silk veil over her face, then threw one end of it over her shoulder. She took two steps towards me, and whispered her reproach. 'I asked you questions and you gave me no answers. You asked me, and I told you everything.'

'I'll tell you today, everything you want to know,' I said.

When she was out of sight, I stood up and watched her from the jagged crack in the wall, then from the hole between the wooden cupboards, then from my only window. I saw her reach the monastery gate and veer to the right to go down the hill. She disappeared from view little by little – her feet, her waist, her head. When she was completely gone, I was quite beside myself. I wished impossible wishes and when I came to my senses, my head leaning back against the wall, I spoke to myself at length to distract myself from what I longed for, to dig out the roots of desire from my heart. I wanted to die instantly, to save myself from my uncertainty.

The sun was sinking and I heard the sound of the boys coming, so I prepared to receive them. I did not take long over practice and when I had finished with them I told them it was the last day of practice and we would meet in the church on Sunday mornings, starting in two days' time. I went out with them to the foot of the hill and asked Deacon to come back to meet me in the field near the cottage after he had dropped them off.

Martha was waiting at the door in attractive house clothes. All her clothes are jellabas of the kind women wear in these parts – but she was enchanting. She met me at the cottage entrance and invited me in. Her aunt repeated the invitation, and I went in, and the aunt brought us something cold to drink. I don't remember now what it was but I do recall that it tasted good and that as I drank my eyes were feasting on the sea of honey in Martha's eyes as she sat in front of me on the floor. The opening in the bodice of her jellaba revealed the firmness of her breasts. I could not help but look at them, until Martha noticed and closed the opening with both hands. She smiled, looked at me with affection and bit her lower lip.

I looked around the cottage – a single room with wooden sides of flimsy construction, with a smaller room attached without a door, I think a toilet. In front of the door there was a small piece of level ground and on one side the oven which they had recently restored and which was still giving off a little smoke. Next to the oven there was a small room with walls of old brick, also without a door. Martha was looking at me, smiling and content, and her aunt was taking a small pot out of the oven, in which the fire had almost died. It smelt of delicious cooking.

'I'm going to take some food to the soldiers,' the old aunt said.

Martha stood up at once, took a palm-frond basket from the corner of the cottage and put the pot of cooked food in it with the help of an old rag. It smelt delicious. Her aunt took her leave and went on her way with the pot. Without me asking, Martha answered the question that was puzzling me. The men of the Roman guard contingent, whom the aunt called the soldiers, had agreed with her the day before that she would cook them a hot meal every other day. Either they would come and take it or she would take it to them shortly before sunset. They would send the meat, vegetables and the cooking money in the morning, and enjoy their meal in the evening.

That was because, according to Martha, they did not like the food which came to them every day from the monastery kitchen.

When the aunt went off with the basket I was sitting on the short and wobbly bed, listening to Martha as she told me the story of the cooking, which did not greatly interest me. She asked me if I was hungry and I shook my head as I gazed at her. Martha understood that I desired her and she came towards me with a smile. She approached without saying a word, until her breast almost touched my face. When she put her hands around my head to rest it on her breast I was in raptures. Still seated, I clasped her firmly and she sighed in my ear. I lifted her dress up her legs with both hands and she slipped it off her shoulders. Martha stood before me completely naked and I tousled her hair with my fingertips. I was overcome by the power of her beauty. I threw off my gown, and we did what men and women do when they throw off the cloak of modesty.

✝

We sat next to each other without speaking, and after a while her aunt came, calling for her from outside the cottage, as though she wanted to warn us that she was coming. Martha did not jump as much as I did. I quickly dressed and moved closer to the door, panting constantly. Martha joined me after throwing on her dress and she hugged me from behind affectionately. We went through the door together and found her aunt putting a small seat in front of the loom.

Martha asked her, 'Were they all there?'

'Yes, and they asked after you.'

When her aunt sat down at the loom, we went out in front of the cottage to sit at the edge of the cultivated land and look out over the western horizon which stretched out in front of us, a place where no one could see us. Evening had started to fall and Martha was singing in a whisper, the song of someone wooing a loved one. The dusk breeze was gentle. When we sat down on the stones at the edge of the slope, Martha sat close and asked me about my native country. I told her some of what had happened there. After a moment of silence she sighed and asked about the house I lived in there. I said that it must be in the same old place on the hill overlooking the Nile, and it must now be closed up and in ruins, because houses fall apart when the inhabitants move on. Martha looked at me with sympathy and love. She put her hand on my shoulder and asked me, 'Is it a long way to Egypt? How long does it take to get there?'

'If we went by sea and then sailed up the Nile, we would get there in a month,' I said.

'Hypa, let's go and do up the house and live there together for the rest of our lives. We can take my aunt with us and she can look after our children, and I'll be free to look after you.'

'How would that be possible?' I asked.

'We would get married and if you like you could be the priest at the church there. In any case, you're a skilled physician and you can earn well from your work. We would live our best days together, and we would have children and a beautiful house.'

Martha could be excused, because she knew nothing. She did not know that I could not live among the people of my home country. The children who insulted me in the old days for what my mother had done had now become men. They would look on me with contempt. Neither did she know that I could not go back to Naga Hammadi because my sick uncle would have died by now and perhaps his Nubian wife would also have died, and I would have no place there, and they would have no need of my medical knowledge.

'This is something that requires deep thought, Martha,' I said.

'Don't think alone. Let's think together about our future life. I will be faithful to you as long as I live, and a mother to your children, and...'

We heard the voice of Deacon talking to her aunt as he hurried towards us, and we broke off the conversation. Martha stood up from next to me and sat on the ground instead. When Deacon reached us, we both stood up. We walked through the herb seedlings as we climbed the hill towards the monastery gate. Martha left us there and went back down to her cottage. No chance arose for me to look back at her.

Deacon was hungry and I went to the dining hall with him. We helped the kitchen servants lay the table, and they mumbled their thanks. I was hungry too. Deacon ate quickly, then stood up and headed to his room to sleep. At least that's what he told us. Obviously I had to wait for everyone to arrive. The monks trickled in like tortoises that hardly knew their way, and after a while the abbot came in with three monks. Unusually for him, he seemed to be visibly distressed when he entered and shouted, 'Good evening, children of Jesus. Come close so we can start our prayers.'

The abbot recited the evening prayers, and I paid little attention because I was busy thinking about what had happened with Martha. Then everyone said 'Amen' in unison behind the abbot, and I asked myself, 'In all our prayers could we possibly be repeating the name of the ancient Egyptian god Amon, confusing an "e" for the "o" in his name.' I wondered, 'Why do all things, not just religion, always have their origins in Egypt?' and I asked myself why I should not go back to my home country to live there, given that I was no longer fit for the monastic life.

I felt a sudden longing for the Nile, which runs across the land like the arm of God, with the Delta its hand and fingers. I remembered the sailing boat which carried me down the river, the hamlets and villages slumbering along its banks, the way the tree branches hung over the water's edge, how green were the fields that stretched as far as the eye could see, how the birds would burst into song at dawn and at sunset. Ah, distant Egypt. I almost shed a tear of nostalgia. After a dinner noisy with the mutterings of the monks everyone prepared to leave the refectory. As we were leaving, the abbot beckoned me over and the others understood that he wanted to be alone with me. They hurried off towards the church, leaving enough space for the abbot and me to be alone.

'You looked distracted tonight, Hypa,' he said.

'I am anxious, father, I feel homesick.'

'This is anxiety of the spirit, my child. It flares up and then dies down.'

'But father, I can no longer bear this constant anxiety. I can never find a place to live in peace and a way to settle down,' I said.

'Are you worried about what's happening in Constantinople?'

'What is happening in Constantinople, father? Has something dreadful happened to Bishop Nestorius?'

'No, my child, not yet. With the will of the Lord, things will quieten down and no harm will come to him, with the will of the Lord,' the abbot said.

'You have made me more anxious, father. What is going on?'

'The emperor has accepted Cyril's request to hold a meeting of the heads of all the churches in the world, to examine Bishop Nestorius's doctrine, and the meeting will take place soon in the city of Ephesus.' The abbot bowed his head and started to mutter a prayer, the side of his face resting on the top of his stick. I saw how worried he was, and he did not want to say more.

Lost in thought, I walked away from him, then I remembered something and went back. Hesitantly and absentmindedly, I said, 'Father, should we start the singing in the mass on Sunday, the day after tomorrow, or should we ...'

'No, Hypa. We'll have to postpone it. The time is not yet right.'

The abbot spoke without looking up towards me, and I walked away, deeply desolate.

The Prohibition Violated

I did not see Martha all of Saturday because I was busy with the kitchen servant, on whose underarm I performed a surgical operation, lancing a large abscess which I had been treating with the well-known black ointment over the previous few days. The time for opening it had come. At first I thought it would be a simple operation which would not take long but I found that the man's constitution was weak and the pus had reached his chest. He bled so profusely that he almost perished in front of me, had it not been for the mercy of the Lord. I spent the rest of the day treating the wound, removing all the pus from it and dressing it with anti-ulcerants. When I came down from my room after washing, the sun had set and it would have been inappropriate to drop in on Martha in her cottage after nightfall.

At prayers I alternated between feelings of rapture, anticipation and other forms of emotional turmoil. When we came out of the church, Pharisee the monk was walking next to me with heavy steps. In the middle of the small courtyard I asked him if he would like to come with me to the library, and he agreed without enthusiasm. While I was opening the door for him, I asked him if he had any more news of the ecumenical council which was expected to take place. He told me in brief that Bishop Cyril had arrived in the city of Ephesus with Shenouda, the famous monk from Akhmim and the leader of the solitaries, at the head of a large Egyptian delegation including priests, Alexandrian monks and many laymen. They were now awaiting the arrival of the bishop of Rome and the emperor, for the council to begin.

Hesitantly he added that many bishops had arrived from all over Christendom, but Bishop John of Antioch had gone off to Aleppo two days earlier to wait for the Roman contingent to accompany him there, because the roads to Ephesus were not safe these days.

'The roads? Or is it Ephesus that isn't safe?' I asked. As I spoke I offered him a drink of carob, sweetened with taffy.

He took it from my hand without looking up at me. After a pause he continued, 'I don't know, Hypa, I don't know. Don't make me say things I don't like to say.'

Unusually for this time of year, the night air was cold. I asked Pharisee if he would like me to make a fire with some wood and dry twigs in the brazier, meaning the large brass bowl around which we would gather in winter to keep ourselves warm. He nodded in agreement. By the time the wood was alight and sputtering in the bowl I was deep in thought about what the abbot had told me after supper the previous day and what Martha had told me on the edge of the slope at sundown.

Pharisee interrupted my thoughts, sighing and saying, 'The council will be stormy and it will oust Bishop Nestorius.'

His words troubled me and drove away the image of Martha which I had imagined among the dancing tongues of flame. I decided to stay silent to give him a chance to elaborate, as he liked to do whenever he found a willing listener, and I wanted him to distract me from my thoughts. I was right to stay silent, and he did speak at length, just as I expected. He began to trace his words in the air, as he usually did when he was caught up in telling a story. It was as if he were addressing other people, rather than me. He did not even look at me. With bitterness, he said: 'You didn't believe me when I told you that our dispute over the nature of Christ is the essence of our religion, and that this essence is subtle and problematic, and portends schism and discord. The monks here made light of the subject, the abbot forbade any discussion of it, the priests in Antioch reprimanded me and warned me of excommunication and expulsion if I wrote the treatise which I was planning to write. They let me back here only when I gave them a sacred oath that I would never again bring up the question of the hypostasis. But everyone disagrees about this. The Egyptians insist that God was incarnated fully in Christ from the time He was in His mother's womb, that in Christ the divine and the human are inseparable, that He is wholly and completely God and the Lord and that He has no human nature distinct from His divinity. What Bishop Cyril said in his last letter is definitive: the body of Christ was not transformed to become divine, and God never assumed corporeal form, even when Christ was an infant in swaddling clothes.'

Pharisee looked towards me as though he had just discovered I was there. He looked at me as though he could see someone else hidden within me. Pharisee had a strange way of looking which confused those who did not know him. He raised his eyebrows, opened his eyes wide and took off his cap to show his shiny bald pate. He wiped his brow with the palm of his hand, and said, 'Look at Bishop Cyril's power of expression when he says "God is made one with the flesh hypostatically, for He is the God of all and He is neither His own slave nor His own master. Like us, He came to be under the law, while at the same time Himself speaking the law and being a lawgiver like God. He is one hypostasis, one person, one nature, son and Lord, and since the holy Virgin brought forth corporeally God made one with flesh according to nature, for this reason we call her Mother of God." Bishop Cyril is very eloquent, Hypa, and he knows what he is saying, and he will never go back on what he has said, and Bishop Nestorius will never retract his belief that God adopted Jesus as a manifestation of Himself, and for the sake of God the unseen we worship the visible Jesus, aware that they are two persons, that is, according to Nestorius, Christ the Assumer, or the Logos of God, and Christ the Assumed Man who is called by the name which he adopted.'

Involuntarily Pharisee stretched out his hands towards the flames to warm himself, rubbed his hands together and said, 'Bishop Nestorius believes what he heard from Bishop Theodore the Interpreter and others, and asserts that God manifested Himself in Christ the Man. So how can the two sides agree, when each of them has taken a position contrary to that of the other? The further they go in their doctrines, the deeper they go in their differences and the wider the gap between them grows. Even if they agree on the nature of

Christ they will still disagree on the hypostasis of the Holy Spirit, which is mysterious and confusing. Neither of them will ever accept what they did not previously believe, so all that remains is confrontation, then conflict and then war. War, Hypa, is a force that finds its way into people and overwhelms them. It flares up and rages inside them, and does not abate until it destroys them. It stirs up strife between them and they lose heart. Their vigour fails and their spirit is broken. War. Did Jesus Christ mean it when He said He came to earth to bring a sword?'

Pharisee stared into the blazing fire and, like a Zoroastrian seer, started to conjure the unknown from the shape of the flames. He paused for a while, and tears began to form, then trickle down his puffy cheeks into his beard. I thought he had finished but he wiped his face with the palm of his hand and continued, this time in a voice which was uncharacteristically shaky. 'Religion is a heavy debt which no one can repay. Our religion condemns us, condemns all who profess it, more than it condemns those who do not believe, but it also condemns unbelievers. Everyone is condemned, everyone is lost, and the heavenly Father is a distinct hypostasis hidden behind all these doctrines. He does not reveal Himself to us in full because we cannot grasp His full presence. He transcends the word hypostasis, transcends the word nature, beyond our comprehension. He is remote from us and we are remote from each other, because we are all indebted to our delusions. The hypostasis itself is a mysterious delusion which we have invented and asserted, and then we have argued about it and we will fight each other over it forever. The day may come when everyone has his own private doctrine, different from those of others, and the basis of Christianity will be undermined and the holy law will be forgotten. That day... will be... I will go up to my room!'[14]

Pharisee suddenly left me, as though I had not been with him in the first place, and he did not bother to shut the door after him. The crunch of the

14. On the edge of the parchment there is a long commentary, written in Arabic in tiny writing, including the following paragraph: 'It seems to me that this monk by the name of Pharisee was truly inspired, for a thousand years of war between the churches have passed and that war was the sole reason why I left my home in the east. It is well known that rivers of blood flowed in Alexandria after the death of Bishop Cyril and

gravel under his feet grew fainter as he walked away and disappeared into the depths of the night. Stillness prevailed around me and I felt very alone, and lonely. I shut the door, took off my cap and stretched out close to the warm embers, my back on the floor and my arms akimbo. I fell into a sleep like a coma.

✝

The dawn chorus of the birds woke me up but I remained stretched out on the floor. I felt like someone who had returned from a long journey and was about to embark on a journey that would last even longer. I tried to summon up the strength to stand but I could not do so. I dozed intermittently without dreaming until someone knocked on the door. At first I thought it was one of the monastery servants but when I opened the door I realized it was one of the guards from the Roman contingent.

'The old woman wants you at the gate!' he said.

Which old woman could that be at this early hour? I went out anxiously and saw Martha's aunt in the twilight, sitting on the square rock next to the gate. She had an old piece of wool over her shoulders. When I approached her, she stood up politely and tried to kiss my hand. The guard left us and went down the hill, as though he were going down to the contingent's base. I sat on the square rock and the old woman sat on the ground. The air was so cold that my shoulders began to shiver.

'What brings you here so early, aunt?' I asked.

'I want you for something important,' she said.

Her 'something important' was strange. The old woman wanted me to persuade Martha to go back to Aleppo to sing there, because living here was too hard, she said, and they had to resort to living on what she could earn

the Christians persisted in destroying the city and killing the non-Christians – the Jews and the pagans. In fact the Christians rose up against the bishop of their city, Bishop Proterius, tore him limb from limb and set fire to his body. They also fought against Bishop Timotheus of Alexandria and much slaughter took place in the great city. Today the city is largely forgotten, since it fell into the hands of the Muslims.'

from singing. The old woman took me by surprise when she said, 'As long as Martha isn't going to sing in church, then let her go and sing in Aleppo.'

How did the old woman know that we had postponed the singing? The abbot had just told me, so how did the news reach her so quickly? Someone who lives in the monastery must be visiting them or perhaps the abbot told their relative the priest, and he told them. I did not worry too much who told them, because the most important thing for me at the time was that Martha might go to Aleppo to sing in the evenings to vile Arab and Kurdish merchants, and I was being asked to push my only bird into a cage of wild cats.

'But Martha told me you were working on the loom and cooking for the soldiers.'

'All that does not make a profit, sir. No one buys what we weave and the soldiers are miserly.'

It took me aback that she called me 'sir'. She did not say 'father', and she no longer addressed me with deference, as she used to do. Had Martha told her what happened between us? Why was the old woman complaining now about the hardships of life and their dire circumstances? How dare she come to see me before sunrise to ask me about something like this?

'Go back home, aunt, and I'll speak to Martha about this in the afternoon.'

I wanted some time to think and I did not want to give the old woman the impression that I was upset. I went straight to the big church to join the other monks in preparing for Sunday prayers. Before entering the church I looked over towards the ruined gateway and saw the old woman sitting in her spot and the guard who came and knocked on my door climbing the hill again. I stood there a moment, watching from afar. I saw the guard come up to where the old woman was and sit on a rock, where I had just been sitting.

From over the stone wall of the monastery wall I saw them talking, but I could not hear what they were saying because of the distance. The way the guard was sitting was striking. He was speaking as though he were resuming a conversation which had been interrupted, leaning forward with his elbows resting on his knees, waving his hands in a way that suggested he

thought that what he was saying was important. The old woman was nodding as though she agreed with what he was saying. I was about to go out
and find out what it was all about but I heard footsteps on the gravel, coming
towards me.

'Good morning, Hypa.'

It was Pharisee with his podgy face, which was now even podgier, and
with red eyes that suggested that he had not slept. I rebuked him gently for
his sudden departure the previous night, and he said he was sorry but he
had been upset. I asked him whether he was ill and, grumbling, he replied,
'On the contrary, I have all the symptoms of the diseases of the spirit!' We
went on with heavy steps and entered the big church by the inner door. A
sense of apprehension hung over the place and was evident on the faces of
all the monks.

After the prayers were over and the visitors had gone, I went down to
Martha's cottage and called out for her. She joined me at the edge of the cultivated land. It was quieter there and a better place for us to sit because no
one could see us. I looked into her face at length, trying to discover what her
innocent features were concealing, but I could see nothing. I asked her about
the guard who had been talking to her aunt in the morning and I begged
her to speak honestly and tell me what was really happening.

'He wants to marry me,' she said.

'How?'

'Just as people get married, Hypa. He says that he came only two months
ago and will stay here for years, and there's nothing to stop him marrying.
He wants to live with us in the cottage or rent a house for us in the village.'

'But...'

'I don't want him, Hypa. I want you. And if you abandon me I shall go
back to Aleppo, because living there, though hard, is easier than here.'

'And who told your aunt that the hymns in the monastery church had
been postponed?' I asked.

'The Roman guard who asked me to marry him. He's of Greek origin, in
his thirties and his name is...'

'I don't want to know.'

I felt great anguish, and Martha was looking absentmindedly towards the distant plains. After a long moment of silence, Martha suddenly stood up to sit down beside me. When she put her hand on my shoulder, I looked around for fear there might be someone to see us. There was no one around us, just a mountain dove pecking at the ground with its beak.

From inside came a whisper, pressing me to put my hand on her thigh and lose myself with her in erotic passion, then keep her by my side for the rest of my life. It was the same whispering voice that I came to know several weeks later. It was the voice of Azazeel, alluring me with a call from deep within me: 'Don't lose Martha the way you lost Octavia twenty years ago.'

'That was not my voice, Hypa. That was the call of your own soul.'

'Azazeel. Don't try to confuse me. Let me finish what I'm writing. I don't have much time and I am sick at heart, because I shall leave in a few days.'

'Good, I'll shut up, and shut up completely. But it wasn't my voice.'

✝

Close to two months have now passed since I last sat with Martha, at the edge of the land planted with seeds. It was afternoon and at the time I did not succumb to the call that came from inside me, tempting me to lay my hand on her and taste the pleasure of love. Instead I was thinking what that would lead to. I would become more attached to her, and she to me, whereas I was supposed to have severed relations with the superficialities of this world, let alone relations with a woman.

But Martha was not like other women, she was more like a child or an angel. How could I leave her to the embraces of this Roman guard of Greek origin, whose name I did not know? How could he understand her as I understood her, how could he love her as I loved her? Would she warm to him one day and whisper her songs to him in bed? Martha was not like other women, but if she went to sing in the inns of Aleppo, amidst the villainous and drunken Arab and Kurdish merchants, she would soon become a fallen woman, embraced and passed around from one itinerant man to another.

Martha had spent years singing there and she had told me nothing of what happened to her in those times, and I had not asked her. Or perhaps her aunt tricked me all along, to make me run off with her and marry her. How could I marry her, when I had spent my whole life as a monk? The twenty years I had spent in monasteries I would offer as a dowry to a woman in her twenties, and then in ten years' time I would be an old man in his fifties and she would be a beautiful woman in her thirties. She would be interested in men, covetous eyes would gaze at her and maybe men would reach out to touch her. Would I spend the last years of my life protecting and restraining her? Would I end up guarding a woman, after a life of so many changes that I no longer know how exactly to describe myself? Am I a physician or a monk, consecrated or impenitent, Christian or pagan?

Martha was sitting next to me that day, but all these thoughts made me forget that I was beside her. After a long silence, she touched the back of my hand with the tips of her fingers and broke my train of thought. Speaking with a charming twang, she said, 'Hypa, take me with you to your home country. Let's get married and stay there for the rest of our lives.'

'Is it true what your aunt said, that you plan to sing in Aleppo?' I asked.

'She wants that, but I want only you. So let's leave this place.'

'How, Martha, how? The people in my country are mostly Christian.'

'What does that matter to us? We're also Christian,' she said.

'In the religion of Christ we are forbidden to marry.'

'Forbidden!'

'Yes, Martha, forbidden. In the Gospel according to Matthew, it says: "Anyone who marries a divorced woman commits adultery."'

'Commits adultery? So what did we do in the cottage yesterday? Did we not commit adultery there?'

Martha slipped away from my side, as the soul slips out of an emaciated body weakened by chronic ailments. I did not look towards her as she walked away to the cottage and I did not move from the spot until Deacon came and summoned me to the abbot's room. He said the abbot wanted me urgently. My legs were numb and I almost collapsed to the ground when I tried to stand, but I held on to Deacon's arm. We walked up to the monastery from the path that passes uphill of the cottage, so that I would not meet Martha's old aunt. I was exhausted. When I went in to see the abbot, beads of sweat were streaming from my forehead, running into the folds of my clothing like trickles of rain.

SCROLL TWENTY-SEVEN

The Iron Rod

I went into the abbot's room through the half-open door and found him deep in prayer. When he had finished he told me he had been praying for Nestorius. He also said he was going to call on the monastery people and all the Christians living in the area to fast for a week, with constant masses and prayers, starting from that night, to solicit divine grace on behalf of Christians and to relieve the distress of the great churches. I was surprised at what he said, but then he told me he had heard that Bishop Cyril, the bishop of Jerusalem and a group of other bishops and priests had decided to convene an ecumenical council the next day, chaired by Cyril, and Nestorius did not plan to attend.

My head spun for a moment and my breathing faltered. The abbot said that Bishop John of Antioch, Nestorius's ally in his ordeal, had sent a message to the bishops and priests gathered in Ephesus, telling them he would be a few days' late because the journey was dangerous. 'The trip is really perilous these days, because the sea is rough and the land route is not safe. Bandits are active and unrest prevails everywhere,' he said.

I began to sweat more profusely, had mysterious tremors and felt dizzy. I did not ask the abbot to elaborate but he stressed that everyone was apprehensive about what might happen in Ephesus, and that he personally was frightened. I was so shocked by what he said that I could not answer, and I was fully convinced that the horror of the storm was on its way, because I had lived in Alexandria for two years and in those days long ago I learnt how storms can blow up. I did not ask the abbot how the news had reached him but I did ask him if these reports of his had been confirmed. He nodded sadly and said he wanted me to deliver to the bishop of the parish in Aleppo a letter about what was happening in Ephesus.

When the abbot uttered the word Aleppo, my mind began to wander and my head spun with questions: why was Aleppo suddenly closing in on me on all sides? The city was lying in ambush for me, ravaging me and sweeping me away, along with everything around me. Aleppo, the city of taverns, which called out to Martha, the city that obsessed her, and obsessed me. Aleppo, the parish in turmoil the more the fires raged in Ephesus. Or was it a message to Bishop John of Antioch? What was happening around me?

Suddenly the abbot stood up and said he would write his letter that evening and I could go off with it the next morning after mass. I asked leave to go to my room and join him an hour later in the church. When I went out into the courtyard the monks were busy preparing for something I could not make out. I did not speak to anyone on my way to my room and my legs would hardly carry me up the stairs. I shut the door to my room but I did not light the lamp. I sat in the darkness for a while, then lay on my back without spreading my arms along the floor. I closed my eyes and saw Martha, not smiling. I covered my face with my arms and I saw Octavia dying. Then I saw Nestorius walking along, his head bowed, surrounded by sullen soldiers. Then I saw him alone, on top of Mount Qusqam.

I sat up, filled with a fear the source of which I did not know. I asked myself: should I go to church now, to feel a little peace of mind? The night prayers must have started. Being in a group would relieve the anxiety, since nothing is more conducive to fear than being alone. Or should I go to Martha's cottage nearby and mend what was broken in our relationship, then sleep on the floor under her bed? Does Martha sleep in the bed where we made love two days ago? Or does she lie on the floor like me? I don't know much about her. I've never seen her from the inside. In fact I've never seen anything from the inside. I always skirt around the surface of things and never go deep. In fact I think I'm afraid of looking deep inside myself, yet I know the truth about my ambiguous self. Everything about me is ambiguous – my baptism, my being a monk, my faith, my poems, my medical knowledge, my love for Martha. I am one ambiguity after another, and ambiguity is the opposite of faith, just as Satan is the opposite of God.

✝

I had a bad night and in the pitch dark I was tormented by strange impulsive thoughts. I would have liked to go to Martha's cottage and slip into her arms, or climb up to the pulpit where the abbot gives his sermons to the people, spread my arms in the air, summon up my strength and fly off to Nestorius. He would be praying alone now and he would no doubt be pleased to see me. I would have liked to go back to being a child in the old days, with a mother other than the one I had, and another father like the one that was, a large family to be proud of me whenever I recited a new poem, two wives who loved me, one like Octavia and the other like Martha, or to be like the male mountain doves, simple and innocent, snatching a moment with whichever dove came close, then flying off with her.

These impulsive thoughts began to pull me towards the dark core that lies within the self, leaving me at the bottom of a deep chasm from which there was no return. I felt a chill deep in my bones. I tugged at the coarse tablecloth folded on the table and put it over my shoulders. I left my room and headed for the church, but I walked past it and did not go in. I went on with heavy steps towards the monastery gate. The stars in the sky showed that dawn was approaching, but the darkness enveloped the universe and enveloped me. None of the Roman guards were at the gate, not even their dog. I looked towards Martha's cottage, haunted by impossible hopes and exaggerated fears.

✝

I sat at the monastery gate a long while, plagued by thoughts, most of which I was too weak to resist so I let them sweep me along. I set sail to distant worlds, beyond this world. I went back deep into past times when human suffering was unknown, times before the beginning of creation as told in the Book of Genesis. Who existed before mankind existed on earth? God, the angels, Satan? What did they all do before we existed and they had us to worry about?

The first thread of the light of dawn appeared and at that moment I felt for the first time that I was not alone. I felt that someone could see me, from where I did not know. I don't mean God, but someone else close to where I was, hidden somewhere near at hand. I looked around and pricked up my ears in the hope of finding something to confirm my feeling or belie it. I told myself it was just one of those delusions that insomniacs have after long sleepless nights. There might be a fox or a wild rabbit nearby, or a thief who had discovered that the monastery guards were asleep most of the time.

I picked up a stone from the ground and threw it to the right, then threw other small stones in all directions. Nothing moved and all I heard was the sound of the stones as they fell on the gravel. So it was my mind playing tricks, the effect of sleeplessness and fear of the hidden unknown. I stood up and I felt the same thing following me. I stopped in the middle of the empty courtyard, and it stopped. I walked on in trepidation, and it walked on too. I shuddered inside.

The interior door of the church was closed, so I walked until the mysterious building stood in front of me, with the monks' rooms on my right. I hurried to the right and climbed the stairs to this room of mine. I closed the door firmly behind me and stayed in the darkness. I told myself: the sun will soon rise so there's no need to light the lamp, it would be best to rest a little because it will be a long day. Between snatches of sleep and moments of wakefulness, I felt that whatever had been with me was still there, but I was no longer afraid of sensing it, as I had been. I was sure I had closed the door and that I was alone in the room, but sure also that there was something close by me.

'Hypa.'

I heard the deep call and a sudden fear swept over me. Goosebumps appeared on my arms and a shudder shook me, centred in my head. The voice that called me was audible but where did it come from? It did not come from anywhere in particular, but rather from every direction.

'Hypa, can't you see me?'

I looked around and could not see anything. I looked inside myself and through the filters of fear and worry I saw a pale face. Was it the young man I met on the outskirts of Sarmada? Or was it that elegantly dressed and wily man I met on the road back to Assiut from Mount Qusqam? He had the same eyes as the man in Sarmada and the same ironic smile as the man on the road. So I was right to be wary of them. The abbot did not believe me when I told him I had met Satan in broad daylight. Satan. Let it be, what could he do with me?

My last question to myself relieved some of my fears and brought along behind it many other questions: 'Where could you take me, Satan, you wretch? Do you want to undermine my faith in Christ? Or haven't you realized that I no longer believe in the same way as I did? Will you tempt me with seductive women? Don't you know what happened long ago with Octavia and what is happening now with Martha? Or do you want to lure me on to the paths of heresy? What in the first place is the true faith, to which heresies might be the opposite? There could be no heresies if there were no orthodoxy. And what is orthodoxy? Is it what they decree in Alexandria, or what they believe in Antioch? Is it the faith of the early fathers, the pious and the venerated, or is it the pagan beliefs whose followers persecuted the early fathers, who then with time became pious and venerated?'

Questions without answers swirled inside me. 'Is the true faith the faith of Cyril, or is it the faith of poor Nestorius, who will soon join those excommunicated before him – Paul of Samosata, Arius the exile, Bishop Theodore of Mopsuestia. All the heretics here were revered there. All the patriarchs are discredited, except among their followers. Satan plays with everyone, so do you think he's now trying to play with me? Is it not enough for him to play with those preparing for war in Ephesus? And that fire he is stoking in all the churches. He is never satisfied, can never make do with a single request. Why else would he be calling me now? Why is he always harassing me? Why did he pick a fight with me openly in Sarmada?'

His face was sharper in the darkness. I examined the features which had first appeared and found they had changed. It was no longer the elegantly dressed man with the leprous pock-marked face or the young man I had encountered. The face had become more delicate and smaller, and now looked more like Martha's face than anything else. I stared and then it was completely Martha, with her sweet smile and her fine head leaning to the right as she spoke. I called her softly but the face clouded over and vanished, just as trails of smoke break up. The features lost their shape and the image of Martha was gone. I was confused and after wandering around blindly a long while a deep sleep came over me and I no longer noticed my surroundings.

✝

In mid-morning the abbot sent a monk to my room to find out why I had not appeared. I told him I was unwell because of the cold at dawn. In the afternoon Deacon came to check up on me. My throat was dry and my head was ringing. I asked him for news of the ecumenical council and his brief answers aggravated my sickness.

'They began today and the emperor hasn't arrived yet. The carrier pigeons brought the news,' he said.

I closed the door behind me and lay on my back in the darkness, then I curled up on the ground, bent towards the wall with my arms around my head. I was tempted to sleep but I had a recurrent feeling that the same invisible being was with me in the room. My mind wandered and I saw Martha again, now in the form of trails of smoke which formed inside my head. I spoke to her and she did not answer. I moved closer and she moved away. I examined her face and it changed into a face similar to my mother's face. She moved so close to me that I could feel her breath. She did not smell of my mother, nor of the aromatic oil which Martha wears. Everything has a smell, even stones, but what I saw had no smell. It was a face whose features slowly changed and at every moment took on a new guise.

At sunset I stood up, overcome with the feeling that I was rising from the dead on the Day of Judgement. I went out of the room trembling and found the monastery wrapped in complete silence. The sun was low in the western sky and the mysterious building had taken on a reddish tinge. As I went down the stairs, the large church nearby seemed distant. I found the descent too tiring so I went back to my room and slept again.

In the dead of the night the wild ideas came back to haunt me: why don't I get up now and take Martha far away from here? Or leave everything behind and travel to Ephesus? The Alexandrian monks and bishops there will not know me. I'll be close to Nestorius in his ordeal and the situation might change in his favour when the emperor and the bishops who support him arrive. The emperor will protect him because he's the bishop of his capital city, and I'll go back to Constantinople with him when the ordeal is over.

'Hypa, this ordeal will not end until Nestorius is eliminated.'

'Who are you?'

'Don't you recognize me, really?'

The mysterious presence had started to speak and when it spoke its face faded and lost its features, which before had vacillated between one face and another. I did not know what to say in response, but I was no longer afraid of having it around me.

'I'm not around you, Hypa. I'm inside you.'

I assumed that madness had snatched me away from my troubled world and that I was now delirious. I said that perhaps I was asleep and this was just a passing dream. Yes, it's a passing dream and I will wake up from it and it will be a memory I will soon forget. I've started to worry about everything around me and the worry gives rise to fears. I must relieve my anxiety a little.

'You're worried by what's inside you, Hypa, because you know what's going to happen in Ephesus and you know you're going to lose Martha, just as you lost what was yours before: the dream of excelling in medicine, your hope of deciphering the mystery of religion, love for Octavia, infatuation with Hypatia, peace of mind through ignorance, belief in superstitions.'

This time the voice was a clearly articulated whisper, then the features of the face appeared again, clearer and more distinct. It looked like me and the voice was my voice. This is another me, other than me, trapped inside me. No harm if I talk to myself a while and say frankly things one should not normally mention: my longing for Martha, my fear for her and my fear of her. I am lost in the wastelands of the self and I am not optimistic about the coup Bishop Cyril is expected to pull off in Ephesus. It will be horrific. Cyril is the head of the church of St Mark in Alexandria and the word of Mark means, among other things, the heavy hammer which in our country we call the mirzabba, the iron rod.

The Alexandrian hammer will inevitably fall on Nestorius's head and the walls of this monastery will shake, and of all the monasteries and churches under the diocese of Antioch. Glory will be the destiny of Alexandria alone. Even ancient Rome will decline and die, like every ancient city. I have to escape this world full of the dead.

'Let the dead enjoy their death. Take Martha and go back to your home country.'

'Shut up and go back where you came from, you mysterious and alluring presence!'

'You take me back. It's you who created me.'

'I didn't create anyone. I'm dreaming now.'

'In that case your dream will last a long time, Hypa!'

'You're calling me by my common name, so what's your name?'

'Azazeel.'

The Presence

My mind wandered and I saw trees filling the universe. I saw myself walking through forests with tangled branches and trees. I woke up and found Deacon sitting beside my bed. When I touched the front of my jellaba, I found it soaked in warm water. My mind wandered again and Azazeel came to me with a distinct face, which seemed to shine in the darkness. Then I woke up properly. The door to my room was open and the daylight shone in on me between the cassocks of the monks standing at the door. They were saying words I did not understand. The ceiling of the room seemed to be high, far away from me.

I heard bells clanging constantly, rattling my bones. Then the bells stopped suddenly and Azazeel came with a smile. He sat down quietly in front of me, then crept towards me. I felt his face with the tips of my fingers and it was moist and slippery. I was afraid to touch it. After a while he stretched out his cold hand to my forehead, and I felt a chill which seeped into my head and relieved my fear. In my dream I slept, and I saw in my dream that I was dreaming.

'Hypa.'

'What do you want, Azazeel?'

'I want you to be strong, to recover from the state you're in.'

To recover would be disastrous. To be oblivious is more pleasant, an oblivion illuminated by the many suns and moons that fill the red twilight sky within me. I saw myself wandering around the monastery, alone. I went into the mysterious building from the opening at the top, and roamed from room to room until I reached the bottom. There were no rusty nails shining in the dark and all I found there was darkness piled on darkness. I sat on the spiral staircase and summoned Azazeel to keep me company in my solitude. He came and sat next to me. Together we left the mysterious building, which was no longer mysterious, and we found the monastery hill completely empty. Not a person, not a stone, not even those buildings which had been standing there. Just small pebbles, cypress trees and blue grasses covered the place. Azazeel whispered to me that this was the monastery hill as it was in the distant past, before mankind existed, before God created man.

Then he asked me, 'Did God create man, or was it the other way round?'

'What do you mean?'

'Hypa, in every age man creates a god to his liking, and his god is always his visions, his impossible dreams and his wishes.'

'Stop that talk,' I said. 'You know where you stand with God, so don't mention Him.'

'My name comes up, Hypa, whenever His name comes up.'

My mind wandered so I let Azazeel say what he wanted and I left. After a while I went back to him and he was talking to himself. I listened, and I heard him say in some strange language something to the effect that God is hidden inside us and mankind is unable to delve deep enough to find Him. In ancient times, when some people thought they had drawn an image of the perfect god, they found out that evil is intrinsic to the world and has always existed. They created me to justify it. So he said...

I no longer argue with what Azazeel says. I couldn't argue with him anyway. Several times I felt I was shivering and hungry and he would put in my mouth a spoonful of soup which had neither smell nor flavour. I would swallow the soup, which would hurt my throat. Then I would fall asleep. Sometimes I would see Deacon, not Azazeel, and he would give me the soup and water to drink. The water tasted better.

There are various opinions and accounts of the origins of Azazeel, some of which appear in ancient books, and some of which are borrowed from eastern religions. Not all religions believe he exists and the ancient Egyptian experts did not know of him. It is said that he was born in the delusive imagination of man in the time of Sumer or in the days of the Persians, who worshipped light and darkness together, and that the Babylonians learnt of him from them. The most famous reference to him is in the books of the Old Testament which the scribes wrote after the Jews returned from the Babylonian captivity.

In Christianity, all denominations assert that he exists and do not allow for any doubt in the matter. He always has the status of enemy of God and enemy of Christ, though his status towards the Holy Spirit is not clear. The ancients say of him that he created the peacock, and it says in an ancient inscription that they accused Azazeel of committing and inciting only abominations. He wanted to prove to them that he was capable of creating beauty, so he created this bird. Once I said that to Azazeel and he smiled and shrugged his right shoulder in surprise.

I heard the sound of little birds all around me and found the door to my room open, with Azazeel sitting silent at the door. I wanted to hear my voice come from him so I asked him which of his names was his favourite. He replied, 'They're all the same to me – Iblis, Satan, Ahriman, Azazeel, Beelzebub, Beelzaboul.' I told him that in Hebrew Beelzaboul meant the Lord of the Rubbish, and Beelzebub meant the Lord of the Flies, so how could he take no interest in the differences between his various names and see them as all the same? 'They're all the same. The differences are in the words, not in the meaning, which is one,' he said.

I came to and saw Deacon wringing between my lips a piece of white cloth soaked in cold water. He then opened it out and put it on my forehead. I touched my face and it was covered in beads of sweat, as was the pillow. I asked Azazeel what was the common meaning of his many names and he said: 'The Antithesis.'

Azazeel is the antithesis of the deified God. That's what he told me in a whisper in another language, not the previous language which I did not know. But I understood what he said and I was fascinated with the concept. So he is the antithesis of the God we know and whom we have defined as absolute good, and because everything has its opposite we have assigned as absolute evil an entity that is the antithesis of the one we had initially postulated. We have called it Azazeel and many other names.

I whispered to him, 'But Azazeel, you are the cause of evil in the world.'

'Hypa, be sensible. I'm the one who justifies evil. So evil causes me.'

'Have you not sown strife between the bishops? Confess!'

'I perpetrate, I don't confess, which is what they want from me.'

'And you, don't you want anything?' I asked.

'I am you, Hypa, and I am them. You see me at hand whenever you want or whenever they want. I'm always available to bear burdens, ward off sins and exonerate every convict. I am the will, the willer and the willed. I am the servant of mankind, the one who incites believers to pursue the threads of their fancies.'

I felt dizzy and could not see clearly what was around me. I was in a place like my room and this face staring at me was like the abbot's face, and the hymns I heard sounded like his voice. The air was stifling and the humidity made it hard to breathe.

I let myself fall into a faint, just to rest a while, and a shiver shook me inside. I saw the sea at Alexandria and I saw myself circling deep in the water. Then an endless maelstrom swept me away.

✟

For a time I stayed trapped in the heart of the maelstrom which had taken me, examining the consistency of the water around me.

✟

'He's woken up and he's asking for food.' Deacon's voice came from behind the open door of the room. I didn't pay attention to the meaning of what he said until he came in on me, full of cheer, and said, 'The food will come shortly, father. We thank the Lord you have recovered. It's a miracle from heaven. Everyone said you would die but I knew you would survive the fever.'

'What fever, Deacon? I don't understand anything.'

'Don't exert yourself, father. Relax, and the food will come.'

I was very hungry and I longed to go outside into the daylight, but I was too weak even to sit up. My strength had completely dwindled. I could hardly say what I wanted and I asked Deacon to help me sit up straight. He lifted me under the arms and leant my back against the wall. I almost fainted but I heard footsteps approaching.

Pharisee was the first into the room and his eyes were sparkling with delight. After him came a monk with a cup of soup. I took some sips but it hurt my stomach at first. Then the hunger got the better of the pain and I drank the whole cup. The monk went out and Deacon followed. Pharisee stayed at the door. I smiled at him with all the strength I could muster, and he came closer. I could see the tears in his eyes.

'Take me to the library,' I said.

'Not now, Hypa. The sun is hot. We can go late in the afternoon.'

Was the midday sun now stronger than I could bear, I whose bare head withstood its fierce rays for years? I wanted to speak to Pharisee but fits of drowsiness made me dizzy, then swept me away into unconsciousness. I hardly felt it when he put a blanket on me, went out and closed the door. When I came round again I had no idea of the time, and I was hungry and thirsty once more. There was no one in the room for me to ask for water. Leaning against the wall, I struggled to my feet, then staggered towards the water jar, which was covered with a round piece of wood. I lifted the lid, filled the copper cup and started to gulp down the water with unusual voracity. Water is the origin of life and my body was dried out, like a piece of land cracked through long drought.

I leant my head against the wall and tried to gather up my strength. But I was too weak and I sat where I was for a while, until I was finally able to stand up again. When I opened the door, the light of the sun hurt my eyes. I shielded my eyes with my sleeve so that I could stand the light. I walked along, supporting myself against the wall of the corridor which links the monks' rooms. I breathed deeply, then suddenly remembered Martha and shivered.

I saw the monks coming out of church after the three o'clock prayers, wearing their holy day cassocks. They saw me and cheered, and most of them came up to me. I met them at the bottom of the stairway, after walking down with great care and with trembling legs. On our way to the library I found out from them that the fever had lasted a full twenty days. I wondered what kind of fever it could be that went on so long, and with such a short gap between successive bouts. Was it the diurnal fever, which brings bouts at night? Or was it the tertian fever, in which the bouts come every other day? It was certainly a severe fever rather than a chronic one, or else it would not have hit me in this violent manner. Twenty days. Acute fevers tend to kill the patient in less time than that. How did I survive? What course of treatment did they follow with me? Where's Deacon for me to ask him? What happened in Ephesus? What were those visions that came to me during the bouts of fever? Was I really speaking to Azazeel, or was it just my fevered imagination?

We reached the library with difficulty. One of the monks went ahead and opened the door for us. I found everything covered in dust. Places degenerate if people abandon them. One of the monks quickly found a piece of cloth and wiped the dust from where we were going to sit. About ten monks were hovering around me. I asked them for news about the ecumenical council and they all answered at once. Bishop Cyril had taken the initiative and, cheered on by the Egyptian monks and the general public, convened the council before the emperor arrived. Cyril chaired the meeting and collected signatures from a group of bishops and priests to an ecclesiastical decree deposing and excommunicating Bishop Nestorius. Bishop John of Antioch and Nestorius held another council a few days later in the same town, and also gathered signatures from a group of bishops and priests, to a resolution deposing and excommunicating Bishop Cyril. When the emperor arrived from Constantinople with the bishop of Rome, they were angry at what had happened and, along with a group of bishops and priests, passed a resolution deposing and excommunicating the two main bishops. So Nestorius and Cyril were both excommunicated and expelled from the ranks of bishops and dismissed from the church.

What utter madness was this? I looked at Pharisee, who had remained silent throughout the conversation. After a while he shook his head and pursed his lips, without saying anything. The abbot came in and the monks stood up out of respect for him. He indicated that he wanted to be alone with me so they left one by one, delighted that I had recovered from the fever but worried about the news from Ephesus.

The abbot was about to speak when a servant came in with a square wooden board and on it an old copper cup full of soup and small pieces of chicken meat. He also brought a plate with some fresh fruit. The abbot waited till the servant had gone, then he offered me the soup and I took it with both hands. He urged me to drink it and I did so. He passed me the plate of fruit and insisted that I eat some. I took a piece and put the plate aside. We did not speak for a while, and the abbot was busy reciting prayers under his breath. I could not make out the words. When he had finished his muttering, I asked him, 'So father, what is it that's been happening in Ephesus?'

'It was the turmoil and ambitions of the world which won the day.'

'How will it end?'

'Today they are holding the council officially, chaired by the emperor and the pope of Rome, although it's Easter.'

'Happy Easter, father. But do you think the crisis will pass?'

'I don't think so, Hypa. Satan is on the rampage in Ephesus.'

I was perturbed that the abbot mentioned Satan – Azazeel – and I was so distressed at the sorrow which lined his face that I shuddered. The abbot noticed, stood up and advised me to rest until my days of convalescence had ended peacefully. He urged me to go back to my room to rest but I asked his permission to lie in the library, because I felt claustrophobic in my room and thought I could relax more among the bookshelves. He nodded in agreement and prepared to leave, while I prepared to sleep on the bench near the door.

Before leaving, he took me by surprise, saying, 'After the eyelash prayer, my child, you should say the sotoro[15] prayer, because it fends off the accursed Azazeel and destroys the powers of his assistant devils.'

15. There are seven prayers a day in the Syriac and Coptic systems. The rimsh (eyelash) prayer is performed at sunset. The Syriac word *sotoro* means 'protection' or 'protector'.

Loss

After preparing to sleep I heard Deacon's voice coming softly from behind the door. 'Are you asleep, sir?' he asked. I invited him in and he came in with a piece of black cloth in his hand. He offered it to me and I opened it out with my hands. It was a black waistcoat, decorated at the edges with crosses in the same thread but grey. I understood immediately and Deacon made it yet clearer and more certain: Martha and her aunt had moved out a week earlier and the old woman had left me this present with Deacon. Martha had left with him the briefest of messages for me: 'Against my will'.

Martha had gone to Aleppo against her will. What compulsion had driven her to leave while I was in the throes of my fever? Could she not have waited a few more days? She must have given up hope that I would recover and concluded I was bound to perish. She left me to my death and went to look for a life for herself. That's the way of women. All of them, as Pharisee said, are faithless and immoral, and he knows more about them than I. Now I am convinced I had deceived myself with delusions of my own making and had committed unforgivable sins with Martha. She took me out of my world, then abandoned me when she thought I would die. I wish I had died and gone to rest.

'They took all their belongings with them, father, so I don't think they are going to come back and live here again,' Deacon said.

'Yes, Deacon, that's obvious.'

'Do you think, father, I could ask the abbot permission to live in the cottage?'

'Deacon, you're still too young to live alone. You'd do best to stay in the priest's house. Now let me go to sleep.'

'Call me if you need anything, father. I'll be nearby.'

Deacon invoked a blessing upon me and left. I prayed to God to take me out of myself and let me rest. My head was ringing and I managed to sleep only for a few short snatches. My moments of sleep gave me pain, and pain in sleep is a bad sign, as is well known among doctors, from the words of Hippocrates: 'If in chronic diseases sleeping causes pain, then that is a sign of death.' Let it be. My death and my life are now the same to me, and maybe death would be preferable. But I have recovered from my fever, whether it was chronic or acute, and my sleeping pains are pains of the spirit, not the effects of the fever.

I got up off the bench and busied myself with prayer. I performed the sotoro prayer before the set time and repeated it again and again until night had fallen. As though to prove that the prayer was ineffective, I felt Azazeel close by me, more than at any time before. So he was not a dream or a phantasm that came to me when my mind was confused in the bouts of fever. Now he was close. I felt him looking at me and not speaking. Or perhaps I had thrown myself into the bottom of the pit of madness.

Before dawn I woke up to the sound of footsteps crunching across the gravel at speed and coming towards the library. It was Pharisee's gait and I thought he must be coming to see how I was. I finished my prayers and opened the door for him. He came in carrying a cloth full of fruit, and we sat down opposite each other at the big table.

'How are you now, Hypa?' he asked.

'Better, and I think I'll improve. Why do you look so worried?'

'The news just came. The holy council, chaired by the emperor, has restored Cyril to his status as bishop and has confirmed that Nestorius is deposed and exiled.'

'What are you saying? How did that happen?' I asked.

'The bishops abandoned Nestorius, except for Bishop John of Antioch, and for well-known reasons the emperor and the pope of Rome did not want to anger Alexandria. When Bishop Rabbula and his people saw that the balance was in favour of Cyril they turned on Nestorius and denounced him. Then the council drafted a new creed, with additions to the creed endorsed a hundred years ago in Nicaea.'

My eyes clouded over. I closed them and wrapped my head in my arms resting on the table. In the midst of my despair a subtle point occurred to me. The council of Nicaea was not a hundred years ago, but 106 years ago. What happened exactly a hundred years ago was that Emperor Constantine set up the terrible committee of fanatical priests in an attempt to placate the bishops. That was in the year 331 of the Christian era. The committee set about inspecting libraries and breaking into people's houses to collect books by philosophers and heretics, copies of the apocryphal gospels, and religious books at variance with the doctrines established by the bishops, as well as gnostic epistles. They gathered all those books in public squares in cities and villages and burnt them openly, with threats of woe for anyone who hid these forbidden books. Woe! I raised my head and asked Pharisee, 'What are they going to do with the reverend Nestorius?'

'He's no longer reverend. They will banish him to some remote place under Alexandria's control, the Libyan Pentapolis or Akhmim. I don't know exactly. The council also condemned Bishop Theodore of Mopsuestia and denounced his views.'

I was shocked and depressed at the news Pharisee had brought. I stood up to open the window overlooking the monastery courtyard. My head was spinning and I was so unsteady on my feet that I almost fell to the floor. Pharisee caught me and helped me sit down again. He opened the window and we sat in silence for a moment. Then he started murmuring and I could tell from his eyes that he wanted to tell me something else. But I couldn't listen to more. In spite of myself I started crying and could not hold back my tears. I quickly wiped the tears from my face.

Pharisee opened up his cloth and offered me some of the fruit, saying it was fresh from Aleppo and he had brought it for me to regain my strength. I was perturbed at the mention of Aleppo. I looked into his eyes and saw in them a trace of sympathy. He urged me to eat but I declined. I pushed the cloth aside with the back of my hand. I asked him if anyone had come from Aleppo. He said no, and told me that this summer fruit had been sent by a Christian merchant as a gift to the monastery. Again he pressed me to eat some. When he offered me a large apricot, I took it from his hand and put it aside. He looked around the library, then said that the air was stifling. He asked me if I would like to go out and sit at the gate, and I agreed. I leant on his arm and we went out, dragging our feet like women in mourning.

As we were leaving, we found Deacon asleep on the ground near the door and I urged him to go home, assuring him that I would no longer need him for anything. Dawn was on its way as we proceeded to the gate. The moon was not shining in the sky because it was on the wane. We sat in the darkness, on the stone where I was sitting the day Martha's aunt came at dawn to tell me about their plan to go to Aleppo, the stone where the Roman guard who asked to marry her later sat. Did she say goodbye to him when she left? What encouraged him in the first place to propose marriage? I wonder if he won any favours from her in the twenty days when I had the fever.

I was looking towards the cottage, which was sunk in darkness, and Pharisee was sitting cross-legged on the ground, silently tracing criss-cross shapes in the dust with a dry stick. A cool breeze blew up. I closed my eyes and filled my lungs with it, then gave a sigh of pain. Pharisee pointed his stick towards the cottage and said that the women had gone. I did not answer. He said he had not been enthusiastic about our project to sing in church. I did not answer. He said he had not felt comfortable about the woman called Martha, and my heart pounded. Dawn gave the sky a reddish tinge and the air felt cold. I asked Pharisee if we could go back to the library for me to sleep a little, and he stood up with me. I did not lean on his arm on our way back, and before he left me at the door I asked him if he was hiding anything from me.

He said, 'It's you who's been trying to hide your thoughts, but we all knew!'

'What do you mean?' I asked.

'Nothing, Hypa. But when you had your fever attacks, you often called out a woman's name – Martha. The fact that she is gone is a blessing from the Lord, for you and for us, because we, as you know, want only the best for you and that woman was something quite inappropriate.'

I shut the door of the library behind me and threw myself down on the bench nearby. I don't know how I fell asleep but I woke up in alarm at dawn, went straight to the table and devoured all the fruit in the cloth. I was eating like someone sick with canine hunger and I was crying. I put my head in my hands, with my elbows on the table, and burst into tears and sobs. I recovered after a while, and one idea had swept all other ideas from my head: everything was over, Nestorius was defeated, Martha had disappeared, Azazeel was gone and the people in the monastery knew the truth about me. My whole life was over and ahead of me only death remained.

'You have a long life ahead of you, Hypa, so don't think about death now.'

'Azazeel, where have you been?'

He explained to me that he had been, and would always be, around me, and that the real world was what was inside me, not in events which flare up and die down, which end only to start again, or for something else to begin. I was surprised that he was not hiding and that when he appeared he was not morose. I was still bent down, my head on the table, with my eyes closed, gazing into the void.

I asked him, 'Should I take some poison to escape my predicament, so that my soul can return to its origin?'

'Have you gone mad? Death has no meaning. All the meaning is in life. I am always alive, and I will die only when you die and when those who believe in me die, and those who discover that I exist inside them. You have no right to kill me off by dying before your time is due.'

'How can I go on living after everything that has happened?'

'Live to write, Hypa. That way you will remain alive even when your time to die has come, and I will remain alive through your writings. Write, Hypa, because he who writes will never die.'

Azazeel loves life because it is fertile ground for him. That's why he hates those who advocate banning merriment and festivities. He cannot bear ascetics and those who cut themselves off from life. He calls them idiots! I stood up and shut the window which opens on to the monastery courtyard. The morning light had begun to shine and I wanted to keep talking with Azazeel.

I leant my forehead against the wall and asked him, 'Was it you I met on the outskirts of the town of Sarmada, and when I came down from Mount Qusqam in Egypt?'

'What are you saying? I don't exist independently of you. I am you, Hypa, and I can only be in you.'

'Don't you appear in the form of particular people, Azazeel?'

'Incarnation is a myth.'

I heard the sound of footsteps and I opened the window again. It was a group of monks coming to visit me, as well as two servants carrying a big table with breakfast on it. They told me that the abbot would join them and we would all have breakfast together here. It was very kind of them.

The abbot recited some psalms and then spoke to us, but as though he were addressing me in particular: 'Children of the Lord, let us pray to God this blessed morning, thanking Him for his blessings and soliciting His mercy. Know that God is always present in our hearts, even if His Throne is in heaven. I have seen that many of you were distressed by what happened in Ephesus, that your faith was shaken and your hearts perturbed. What happened is saddening to us, so may the Lord bestow his pardon on all of us. But our way, we monks, has nothing to do with problems of theology and the arguments between the heads of the churches. Those flare up from time to time and then die down, so let them be. In the meantime we have our way, which we have chosen with the help of the Lord. One thing brings us together – the love of the Lord, the Gospel of Jesus and reverence for the Holy Virgin, whether she be the mother of God or the mother of Christ. We have renounced the clamour of the world, and we know the Virgin in our hearts, not through the words of the theologians or their sects. Here we will adhere to the creed they drafted in Ephesus and we will rally people around it in the fold of the Lord, or else Satan will play tricks with the common people if they are disunited. We have a way to God which is not defined in any written creed or by any special words. The monastic life has a mystery which transcends words, rises above language and is too subtle to articulate. Monasticism, the communal and monastic life, will remain a beacon to guide the faithful, a path for those who have dedicated themselves sincerely to their love for the Lord, and who have deep faith in Jesus Christ and reverence for the Virgin.'

I liked what the abbot said and I had a little to eat with the monks, but I was aware of Azazeel sitting in the far corner of the library, smiling mischievously and scornfully. The monks said goodbye and the abbot reminded me that I needed to rest. He asked me if I wanted anything from the monastery kitchen and I thanked him.

In the afternoon I felt dissatisfied and uneasy. I was alone in the library and I summoned Azazeel in the hope that his strange opinions might distract me from my pain. I asked him what he thought about what the abbot had said in the morning. He answered with a smile, deliberately trying to irritate me, 'What could the abbot say, other than what he said? Otherwise he would have to find somewhere else to manage, rather than this monastery.' I thought he was unfair to the venerable father and when I shouted at him to be polite, he disappeared.

In the early evening I sat down at the table and made up my mind to write a new hymn. My head was ringing with poetry. I performed the night prayer alone and prepared pieces of parchment, then wrote this poem:

> My God, cast a ray of Your eternal light,
> Light up my dark heart and dispel my loneliness.
> Our Father which art in heaven, bestow on earth
>   glad tidings of solace,
> For all of us are saddened and our sorrows are
>   painful.
> Christ the Saviour, You are our beginning and
>   our end,
> You are our survival after our world perishes.

I wrote the verses after many laborious attempts, as though I were digging the words out from deep inside myself and drawing blood. My body was still fragile and I was on the point of falling into a deep sleep which would have taken me far away, but suddenly Azazeel's voice rose up from the deepest and darkest spot in the emptiness inside me. His voice melted my heart and made me feel that the sky had collapsed to the ground and I was trapped between the two. He was saying, 'When will you write the real story, Hypa, and stop being evasive and singing about the pain you feel? Don't be like a dead man who speaks for the dead to please the dead! Tell the truth in your heart. For example: "Martha, revive within me for a moment the harmony we shared, to bring light to my darkened heart and dispel my loneliness."'

'Shut up, you wretch. I will sing only of the living Christ, because poetry is like a string of pearls and the Christ Jesus said: "Do not cast pearls before swine."'

'Now you're comparing Martha to swine! Wake up, Hypa, and come to your senses. Your desire for her is crushing you and breaking your heart. Go to her, take her and leave this country. Delight in her and make her happy, then heap curses on me because I tempted you. Then all three of us will thrive, having fulfilled ourselves.'

I said to myself, 'I'm not going to listen to Azazeel's attempts to shake my faith. He's a cynic and a troublemaker by nature. I'll wash my heart with the water of certitude and hold fast to my faith against his temptations, his heresy and his predilection for transient pleasures. However attached I was to Martha, it was temporary, like everything in this world, and I will not sell the eternal for the sake of the transient, or what is precious for the sake of what is cheap. I will live my life in the living Christ.'

'Is he alive? How so when the Romans killed him?'

'He died for some days, then He was resurrected in glory from the dead.'

'And how did he die in the first place? How could you believe that the Roman governor, Pontius Pilate, a mere man, could kill Christ, who is God?'

'That was the only way to save mankind.'

'No, that was the only way to save Christianity from Judaism!'

I did not want to hear more from Azazeel but he kept whispering strange ideas in my ear as I slept. He said many things, such as that the Jews be-littled the idea of the divine, which mankind had long struggled to articulate. The ancient human civilizations elevated God, but in their Torah the Jews had Him preoccupied with mankind, and then He had to be restored to heaven again. So Christianity came to assert that God existed on earth along-side mankind in the person of Christ and then, borrowing from ancient Egyptian myths, to raise Him to His original place in heaven, after God sacrificed Himself, as they claim, to save mankind from the sin of their ances-tor Adam. Were all sins erased after Christ? Would it have been difficult for God to forgive mankind with a simple order, without imaginary suffering, a humiliating crucifixion, an inglorious death and a glorious resurrection?

✝

Azazeel disappeared inside me and kept quiet. A sudden peace filled me, and then I felt a void enclosing me. After a while I rested my head on the void and slipped into sleep.

The Creed

W
e magnify you, O Mother of the True Light and we glorify you, O saint and Mother of God, for you have borne unto us the Saviour of the world. Glory to you, O our Master and King: Christ, the pride of the Apostles, the crown of the martyrs, the rejoicing of the righteous, firmness of the churches and the forgiveness of sins. We proclaim the Holy Trinity in One Godhead: we worship Him, we glorify Him, Lord have mercy, Lord have mercy, Lord bless us, Amen.'

That is the introduction to the creed which has come to us from Ephesus, with strict injunctions to circulate the creed among all people and recite it in all churches with the appropriate reverence. I mean reverence for the text, I mean the text of the creed, I mean the creed of belief, I mean belief in God, the God whom Christianity restored to heaven.

I spent two days in the library arguing with Azazeel until I convinced him of some things, while he convinced me of some other things about which I had been indecisive. One thing he persuaded me to do, which coincided with a whim of my own, was to retire to my room these forty days to write down what I have seen in my life, from the time I fled my father's village up to my departure from this place, tomorrow, to do what we have agreed I would do.

Now the forty days have passed and my writing ends today. I have recorded only what I have remembered or experienced deep inside myself. This is the last piece of parchment and most of it is still free of writing. I shall leave that space blank in case someone comes after me to fill it. I will sleep a little now, then wake up before dawn, put the pieces of parchment in this box and cover it with soil under the big rock at the monastery gate. With it I will bury the fear I inherited and all my old delusions. Then I will depart, as the sun rises, free…

A Note on the Text

Youssef Ziedan's novel *Azazeel* took the Egyptian and Arabic literary scene by surprise when it first appeared in 2008. Egyptian writers had previously played with the history of ancient Egypt – most notably Nobel laureate Naguib Mahfouz with his three novels set in the Pharaonic period. But, as Professor Ziedan is acutely aware after the controversy he has aroused, the brief Christian era of Egyptian history, which lasted for a few hundred years up to the Muslim invasion of 639 CE, is a gap that Egyptian authors had avoided, either out of deference to the Coptic Orthodox Church or because the period appeared to offer little that would resonate with a modern Arab readership. Most of the extant histories of the period were in the hagiographic tradition, written by Copts for Copts to celebrate the sufferings and achievements of their martyrs and founding fathers.

Within months, piles of the novel appeared on the pavements of Cairo, alongside the self-help manuals, political memoirs and teach yourself English books that are the staples of the Egyptian popular book market. Many casual readers of *Azazeel*, at least initially, took at face value the literary device that is the framework for the novel; the notion that the story, written in Syriac and recently discovered in northern Syria by a European antiquarian, was the work of an Egyptian monk born in Aswan, southern Egypt, late in the 4th century CE. If that were indeed the case we would, of course, need to rewrite the whole literary history of the world, for there is no autobiographical work of comparable intimacy from such an early date in any language.

The response of the contemporary Coptic establishment to the novel was immediate and vitriolic. Some Coptic commentators seemed unaware of the distinction between historical fact and historical fiction, arguing that there was no historical record that a monk by the name of Hypa ever existed and denying that the events narrated in the book ever took place. However, the main thrust of the Coptic critique was that the novel misrepresented Bishop Cyril of Alexandria – a revered figure in the Coptic tradition – and was an unwarranted intrusion into theological controversies that the Christian Church had resolved internally many centuries ago.

In his subsequent non-fiction work *Arab Theology*, Professor Ziedan argued that the cultural traditions of the peoples of the Arabian Peninsula and the Fertile Crescent were unsympathetic to the idea that gods and humans could exchange roles – an idea central to the Orthodox Christian belief in Jesus Christ's divinity at birth. Taken in conjunction with some of the conversations related in *Azazeel*, Ziedan's theory could be interpreted as being sympathetic to the Nestorian 'heresy' (Nestorius believed that no union between the human and the divine was possible) or as advocacy of the Qur'anic position that God is not born and does not give birth.

Professor Ziedan has responded to say that one of his main aims was to argue against violence in any religious dispute and that the history of the period is part of his own heritage as an Egyptian, not the exclusive purview of the Coptic hierarchy. The English-language reader, however, can safely ignore these controversies and enjoy the work for its narrative power, for its evocation of a neglected period that was formative in the evolution of Christianity, and for its sympathetic portrayal of the humble monk Hypa's struggles with doubt and with the temptations of the world.

As a translator, *Azazeel* offered the unusual experience of handling an Arabic text almost wholly detached from the cultural context of Arabic literature, which hardly existed at the time of Nestorius and Bishop Cyril. Hypa is presented as a man whose mother tongue was the south Egyptian dialect of Coptic, the last form of ancient Egyptian language, and who wrote in Syriac, a Semitic language related to Arabic, quite distinct but now almost extinct. Although this was in many ways liberating, it could have posed a different challenge – that of trying to finding a voice for a narrator who has no parallel in existing literature from the same cultural milieu. But I soon came to see Hypa as a kind of Everyman; commonsensical but slightly naïve; pious with a healthy dose of scepticism; inquisitive about the affairs of the world while simultaneously reluctant to be fully engaged. Above all, he is honest with himself, and his honesty shines through in any language. Furthermore, Professor Ziedan's writing style is widely attested for its clarity and eloquence, qualities that greatly simplify the translator's task.

Inevitably, in tracking down the historical events, personalities, place names and ideas that appear in the novel, I learned more about the period than I ever expected. I was particularly struck by Professor Ziedan's meticulous commitment to the original sources. His accounts of the death of Hypatia in 415 or of the proceedings of the First Council of Ephesus in 431, for example, contain nothing incompatible with the historical records that have survived. That in itself is an eloquent riposte to many of his critics.

I must thank Professor Ziedan for the hours he spent clarifying aspects of the text, and to Jane Robertson, who handled the copyediting with sensitivity, made valuable suggestions and asked all the right questions.

Jonathan Wright
London, August 2011

Youssef Ziedan is an Egyptian scholar who specializes in Arabic and Islamic studies. He is a university professor, a public lecturer, columnist and the author of more than fifty books. In 2009 he was the recipient the International Prize for Arabic Fiction.

Jonathan Wright studied Arabic and Turkish at Oxford University and has worked in the Middle East for most of the past thirty five years, mostly as a correspondent for the international news agency Reuters. Since he turned to literary translation in 2007, his translations have included Khaled al-Khamissi's *Taxi*, Rasha al-Ameer's *Judgment Day*, Hassan Blasim's *The Madman of Freedom Square* and Alaa el-Aswany's *On the State of Egypt*.